The Highlander
Next Door

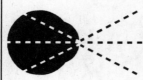

THE HIGHLANDER NEXT DOOR

JANET CHAPMAN

THORNDIKE PRESS

A part of Gale, Cengage Learning

GALE
CENGAGE Learning·

Farmington Hills, Mich • San Francisco • New York • Waterville, Maine
Meriden, Conn • Mason, Ohio • Chicago

GALE
CENGAGE Learning®

Thorndike Press® Large Print Romance.
The text of this Large Print edition is unabridged.
Other aspects of the book may vary from the original edition.
Set in 16 pt. Plantin.

LIBRARY OF CONGRESS CATALOGING-IN-PUBLICATION DATA

Chapman, Janet.
  The highlander next door / by Janet Chapman. — Large print edition.
    pages ; cm. — (Thorndike Press large print romance)
    ISBN 978-1-4104-7535-0 (hardcover) — ISBN 1-4104-7535-2 (hardcover)
    1. Large type books. I. Title.
PS3603.H372H54 2015
813'.6—dc23   2014036954

Published in 2015 by arrangement with The Berkley Publishing Group,
a member of Penguin (USA) LLC, a Penguin Random House Company

Printed in the United States of America
1 2 3 4 5 6 7 19 18 17 16 15

*This one is for you, Lucy,
for having the sense of humor
to laugh* with *us and not* at *us.
Thank you for loving my brother.*

WELCOME TO SPELLBOUND FALLS

A magical place in Maine

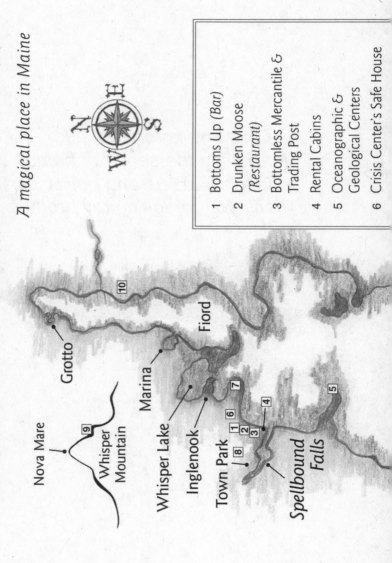

1 Bottoms Up (*Bar*)
2 Drunken Moose (*Restaurant*)
3 Bottomless Mercantile & Trading Post
4 Rental Cabins
5 Oceanographic & Geological Centers
6 Crisis Center's Safe House

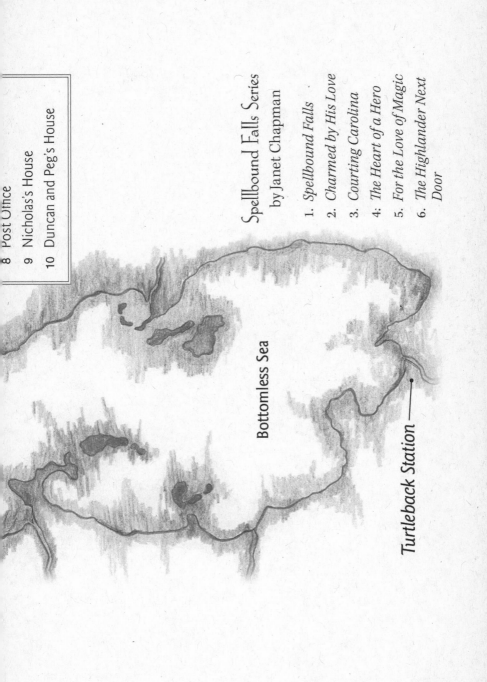

8   Post Office

9   Nicholas's House

10 Duncan and Peg's House

Spellbound Falls Series
by Janet Chapman

Bottomless Sea

Turtleback Station ———

CHAPTER ONE

Despite knowing the orcas and sharks inhabiting the inland sea were under strict orders not to harm humans, Niall put more power to his strokes when he felt something brush against his leg — because, hell, he wasn't completely suicidal. An idiot, maybe, for taking a moonlight swim, but he figured he'd rather face a killer whale than go chest-to-nose with a pint-sized spitfire determined to drive him crazy.

Birch Callahan hadn't been on the job a week before she'd started telling him how to do *his* job; the only problem being that as chief of police, Niall was fairly certain that didn't include stirring the good people of Spellbound Falls into more of an uproar. He really couldn't arrest a man for being a penny-pinching grouch, and even if he could, it wasn't like he had a jail into which he could throw the poor bastard. But if he caught wind of *Mrs. Grouch* poisoning her husband again . . . well, maybe sitting in some sturdy wooden stocks in the town park would cool off the couple.

He'd have to check if public punishment was legal in this century.

Not that there was anything private about the Kents' domestic little war.

Niall stopped swimming and listened to the steady breathing off to his right, then silently sank below the surface when he spotted the broad head coming toward him. But remembering he wasn't suicidal, he resurfaced well behind the dark mass of solid muscle and fangs to see his pet swimming in circles, its head craned out of the water as it searched the moon-bathed swells with obvious alarm.

"Hey, pooch," he whispered, causing the huge Chesapeake to whip around with a startled snarl. "Ye worried a shark might mistake you for a tasty harbor seal?" he added with a laugh, heading for shore when the dog started paddling toward him. But not about to bite the hand that fed it, Shep merely powered past with a grumbling growl as Niall settled into an easy pace and let his mind return to his pint-sized problem.

For a woman who supposedly had enough university degrees in human behavior to be running Spellbound Falls' new Crisis Center, Birch Callahan didn't seem to know when she was being played. If Noreen Kent was being abused by her husband of forty-six years, Niall would place *himself* in those stocks.

He still wasn't sure how wanting a new cookstove had turned into a full-blown war between the couple, much less how it had escalated into the townspeople taking sides. But hell, Logan was still unsteady on his feet from his bout of food poisoning, even though Noreen swears she hadn't deliberately undercooked the now-infamous dinner. As for showing up at the women's shelter and claiming she feared for her life after Logan shot the offending stove point-blank with both shotgun barrels . . . well, Niall couldn't arrest a man for destroying his own property, considering his wife hadn't even been home at the time.

Noreen was a drama queen, and Birch was only feeding the drama by publicly siding with the seventy-year-old woman. That Birch had personally escorted Noreen back to the scene of the crime to gather some belongings only further proved Niall's point that the spitfire had more passion for her job than common sense. All of which was why, upon finding himself a bachelor, Logan was now eating three meals a day at the Drunken Moose — ironically spending more money than the cost of a new stove — although the poor bastard was dining alone as of late, since he apparently couldn't operate a clothes washer any more than he could work a toaster.

Niall stopped swimming again when he heard Shep's excited barks mixed with the shouts of their neighbor, then powered toward shore with a groan of defeat at the realization he was going chest-to-nose tonight after all. He waded onto the beach and ran up the lawn, but broke into a grin when he saw the tug-of-war taking place in the driveway he shared with the shelter. Aye, Birch might be driving him crazy, but it was more from lusting after the beautiful woman than wanting to throttle her.

Shep finally ended the tug-of-war by simply snapping the broom handle in half, only to quickly grab up the bristled end and tear around the dooryard with his prize.

Niall reached Birch just as she straightened from picking up what remained of the handle and plucked it out of her hand when she headed after Shep. "For the love of God, woman, do ye truly have no sense of self-preservation?"

Birch rounded on him, even as she pointed

at the small white dog peeking out from under the car parked next to the main house. "He was terrorizing Mimi again." She then pointed at Shep. "Next time I'm going to take a shovel to the amorous idiot."

Niall speared the broken handle clean over the roof of his tiny cottage. "You don't go after a powerful dog with nothing more than a broom."

"I'm not afraid of a mutt that's too dumb to even realize Mimi's been *spayed.*"

Niall closed his eyes and tried counting to ten, but only made it to five. "Then I suggest you become afraid," he said softly so he wouldn't shout. "Because a less understanding dog would have latched on to *you* rather than the broom."

Birch reached in her pocket as she turned toward Shep, who had stopped running victory laps in favor of dropping his prize in front of Mimi. "Maybe a mouthful of bear spray will knock some sense into him."

Niall plucked the small canister out of her hand and threw it past his pickup in the direction of the camp road.

"Hey!" she yelped, rounding on him again.

"I ever catch wind of you spraying Shep," he said, not even trying to disguise his anger, "and I will arrest you for cruelty."

Her eyes widened in surprise, even as she

took a step back. "I see. You refuse to do anything about an abusive husband, but you won't think twice about arresting a woman for defending herself. Is that how the law works for you, Chief MacKeage?" She then muttered what Niall assumed was a French curse before he could respond, and spun on her heel. "I can see why this town needed a women's shelter, if you and your stupid dog are examples of the male population." She suddenly stopped and turned to him again. "And I want you to start wearing a robe when you go swimming."

"Excuse me?"

"This place is a *sanctuary,*" she whispered tightly. "And the last thing my residents need is to be traumatized by an all-but-naked man strutting down to the beach every evening and reminding them of the hulking brutes they've run away from."

For the love of God, Logan Kent barely came up to his wife's nose, Macie Atwater's man was a pacifist, and the new girl, Cassandra, had run away from her slap-happy *aunt.* "Those traumatized residents?" Niall asked, gesturing at the four women lined up along the shelter's porch rail, two of whom were smiling, one who was scowling, and — good Lord, Birch's mother just winked at him. Niall smoothed a hand over his naked chest. "Are ye sure my size and lack of clothes is bothering *them,* Birch?"

Obviously realizing she was the only one being bothered, Birch crossed her arms under her lovely bosom. "I told you I prefer you call me Miss Callahan."

Niall made it all the way to the count of six and calmly said, "We're on the same side, lass. I care about your residents as much as you do."

"Then go arrest Logan Kent."

"It's not against the law to shoot a cookstove. Nor is it a crime," he added softly, in deference to their audience, "to call your wife an old windbag during an argument."

The poor woman gasped so hard that she took another step back. "Verbal abuse is just as victimizing as physical."

"What about relentless nagging?" he shot back, still keeping his voice low. "Is harping on a person until he explodes also considered abuse?"

"It's not the . . . That doesn't mean . . . *Mon Dieu,* you are such a *man.*"

"Why, thank you for noticing," he said, smoothing down his drying chest hair.

"You're impossible!" she hissed as she turned and stormed off.

"Then we're even," he whispered. "Come on, Shep," he said when Birch kicked the

15

broom out of her way and crouched on her hands and knees to retrieve Mimi.

"I want you to start chaining that mutt," she called out as Niall headed to his cottage. "Or do you also have a double standard when it comes to leash laws?"

Only able to guess what a leash law was, Niall turned to see Birch clutching the small dog to her bosom, her chin lifted in challenge. "A chained dog isn't much help against an intruder looking to cause trouble for one of your residents. Why don't ye try seeing Shep as your first line of defense instead of as the enemy?"

She dropped her chin into her pet's head of curly white fur. "Then make him stop terrorizing Mimi."

"You don't think terrorizing is a bit extreme to call a good-natured dog trying to get to know his pretty new neighbor?" *Like his owner is trying to do,* Niall refrained from adding. "If you'd give them some time together instead of always rushing to the rescue, you'd realize Shep is only wanting to play."

Her chin lifted again. "Mimi was mauled by a large male dog when she was a puppy and nearly died. She's perfectly fine with females and only gets snappy and defensive around huge males."

16

Just like her owner, Niall decided. "I will keep better track of Shep," he said with a nod, heading for his cottage and breaking into a grin at her muttered thank-you — even as he tried to imagine all that spitfire passion in bed.

"Niall's right, you know. If you would just spend some time with Shep, you'd realize he's nothing but an overgrown puppy."

Birch stopped searching for her can of bear spray and aimed the flashlight beam at her mother's chest. "That monster is no puppy."

"Shep's barely three. Niall rescued him from an abusive owner a year ago."

"He told you that?"

"No. Peg told me."

Birch went back to working her way up the driveway. Peg was married to Duncan MacKeage, who was Niall's cousin. Besides being a town councilman, Duncan owned a construction company and worked almost exclusively for the ultraexpensive Nova Mare and Inglenook resorts in town, which were owned by Maximilian and Olivia Oceanus.

Olivia was the one who had hired Birch as director of the Spellbound Falls Crisis Center a little over a month ago, although the shelter and equally new Birthing Clinic in the basement of the town's only church were really the pet projects of five local women. Olivia's mother-in-law, Rana Oceanus — whose husband, Titus, was reputed to be richer than God — seemed to be the head benefactress, while Olivia, Peg, and Julia Salohcin did most of the hands-on work. Director of special events for Nova Mare, Julia was married to a veritable giant named Nicholas, who also worked for the Oceanuses as head of security for both of the resorts. Rounding out the close-knit, civic-minded group was Vanetta Thurber, owner of a restaurant named the Drunken Moose and a bar aptly named the Bottoms Up.

Near as Birch could tell, with the exception of Vanetta, all the women were spending their husbands' money as fast as the men could earn it. Come to think of it, all the women were married to giants — again, except for Vanetta. Everest Thurber managed the Bottoms Up for his wife and seemed to be the only normal-sized male in the lot, as well as the only one of the men who was from Maine. Well, Niall and Duncan were supposedly from a town south of here, but their accents didn't really fit, as Mainers living this close to the border usually sounded more Canadian than American, much less Scottish.

Not that Birch cared who was bankrolling the Crisis Center, as long as everyone left her alone to do her job. Even though she'd been hoping to get a position at a prestigious university close to Montreal, she'd snatched up the first job she could find, even if it was in the middle of nowhere in a foreign country, to protect her mother from the last parasite she'd married — husband freaking *four.*

Honest to God, most twelve-year-olds were less naive than her mother.

Hazel Callahan (Birch had once again insisted her mom take back her maiden name after divorcing The Leech two months ago) had never met a person she didn't like. And if that person happened to have a Y chromosome and buckets of charm, Hazel usually fell in love with him — usually within days. In fact, she'd married parasite number two, His Highness the King of Nowhere, not three months after Birch had left for college. Her mother had then shown up at her graduation four years later with The Loser, and married The Leech when Birch had made the mistake of leaving Hazel alone to go after her doctorate. Husband number one had managed to hang on through most of Birch's teenage years, but The Bastard had hit a tree and died — and hopefully was rotting in hell — while celebrating his wife's thirty-fifth birthday by using her money to take his mistress skiing in Europe.

Ironically, Hazel had never married her prom-night sperm donor, although that hadn't prevented Birch from having to deal with his family.

Basically, calling the men her mother seemed to attract like magnets *likeable* was about the same as calling a hundred-pound Chesapeake Bay retriever a puppy.

"Word is Niall caught the guy beating Shep," Hazel continued. "Only no one knows for sure, because he refuses to talk about it. Peg said Niall was living in Pine Creek with his cousin at the time when he just showed up one day with the thin, badly limping dog."

Well, that would explain his reaction when she'd threatened to spray Shep. Birch went back to searching for the bear spray her next-door nemesis had thrown into the night — likely wishing he could throw *her* instead. The conceited jerk — thinking she even noticed his hulking size and broad chest and sculpted muscles.

She sure as heck never noticed his piercing green eyes.

"You wouldn't really have sprayed Shep, would you?" Hazel asked, awkwardly bending to move a fern out of the way.

"Of course not. I was just trying to make a point."

"And what point would that be? That Niall better not mess with you any more than Shep better mess with Mimi?"

"I was letting him know I'm not afraid of him or his stupid dog. And who does the guy think he is, anyway, lecturing me about going after *any* dog with a broom? Does he think I'm just going to stand back and watch Mimi get mauled again?"

"I believe Niall was pointing out that *you* could have been mauled. It's his nature to be protective."

"Why? Because he's a cop?" Birch muttered, thinking the man's nature ran more along the lines of being bossy. He was condescending, too, dismissing her concern for Noreen and apparently only enforcing the laws *he* wanted to.

"No. Because he's a highlander."

Birch stopped searching again. "A what?"

"If you would get your nose out of those emotionally draining women's fiction books long enough to read a good steamy romance, you'd recognize an authentic Scottish highlander when you saw one."

Birch kicked an ankle-twisting rock off the driveway into the woods. "*Mon Dieu,* Mama, you have to stop downloading those stupid novels off the Internet. And you need to stop flirting with Chief MacKeage."

"My word of honor," Hazel said, obviously fighting a smile as she held up her hand in a Girl Guides of Canada salute. "I will not marry Niall."

"You couldn't even if you wanted to, because they limit people in the States to four marriages," Birch said, figuring she already was going to hell for all the lies she'd told her mother in the last two months, so what was one more?

"Honestly?" Hazel said in surprise. She shrugged and resumed searching. "Then I guess that means there's nothing to stop *you* from marrying Niall."

Birch silently groaned, knowing exactly where this conversation was going — again. "I'm really not in the mood to discuss my love life."

"What love life? Oh, here it is." Her mom straightened and handed Birch the canister of bear spray, the flashlight once again revealing her smile. "Come on, admit it. You're attracted to Niall."

"What on earth makes you say that?"

"Oh, I don't know. Maybe because you haven't said one civil word to the man since you discovered him living next door? So I can't help but find myself agreeing with Queen Gertrude: 'The lady doth protest too much, methinks.' "

"You're actually quoting Shakespeare to me?"

"William was the bard of love," Hazel said with all the conviction of a dedicated theater junkie.

"Gertrude wasn't talking about love in that scene," Birch countered. "She thought the woman in the play Hamlet had staged for his murderous stepfather was *promising too much* by saying she would never remarry if her husband died. So instead of taking shots at my love life, you might try quoting your beloved William to yourself."

That got Birch a laugh. "I should have known taking you to the Stratford Festival in Ontario every summer would come back and bite me on the butt."

"What *I'm* protesting is that Chief Mac-Keage refuses to take Noreen seriously."

Hazel rolled her eyes. "You know as well as I do that Noreen is not a battered woman. Personally, I think Logan is the one who should be seeking shelter here."

"He discharged a gun inside their *house.*"

"I would have shot that stove, too, if I knew how to load a shotgun. I'm just surprised Logan had the strength, considering he still looks like a soft breeze could knock him over. Noreen nearly killed him trying to make her point."

"She did not undercook that chicken on purpose. The oven had a faulty thermostat and two of the burners had quit working. Logan wouldn't have gotten sick if he simply would have bought a new stove in the first place."

Hazel blinked at her, clearly nonplussed. "Will you please tell me why you insist on believing Noreen?"

"Because I have to believe *every* woman who comes to me saying she's being abused. Don't you understand, Mama?" Birch said gently. "It's not my place to judge these women or decide if they are or are not in danger. My job is to give them a *voice*. I can only make sure they're safe and empower them until they grow confident enough to empower themselves."

Birch squeaked in surprise when her mother suddenly threw her arms around her in a fierce hug. "Oh, *bébé,* you are so wise!" She leaned away to clasp Birch's face, squishing her cheeks. "And I am so proud of you for championing women."

Birch gently wiggled free and bent to pick up the flashlight she'd dropped. "I'm just doing the job I was trained to do." She straightened and shot her mother a crooked smile. "And that includes championing abused men."

The flashlight revealed a twinkle in Hazel's eyes. "Including Niall MacKeage?"

It was Birch's turn to roll her eyes. "If someone's going to be stupid enough to threaten a hulking brute who runs around with a gun strapped to his chest," she said, shoving the spray in her pocket and heading down the driveway, "then I would take Chief MacKeage's side."

Hazel fell into step beside her, grasped Birch's hand, and playfully swung it between them. "Can you explain something to me? If you know Noreen is exaggerating this fight with her husband, why do you keep insisting Niall arrest Logan?"

"Because I need *him* to take Noreen's claim seriously, too. This time it might only be a lonely woman caught up in all the attention she's getting, but next time it could be a life-and-death situation. I need to know I can count on the police."

Her mother pulled them to a stop. "At the risk of sticking my nose in your business, has it occurred to you to simply tell Niall that you know what's going on, but that it's important the two of you work as a team on these matters?"

"He's a cop, Mama. At best he would laugh in my face, and at worst he would arrest Noreen for making false charges against her husband."

"Oh, *bébé*," Hazel said sadly. "Not all police chiefs are like your *grand-père* St. Germaine. In fact, very few are as cold-hearted as Fredrick." She nudged Birch's shoulder. "However, I believe highlanders are attentive husbands and good lovers."

"Who told you that?"

"I've gathered as much from Peg. And I don't know if you've noticed, but the twins she's carrying will make her *sixth* and *seventh* children."

Birch headed down the driveway again. "Duncan has them living halfway up the fiord where their home can only be reached by boat, and word is his cousin, Alec Mac-Keage, is building a house all the way at the north end of Bottomless. So what I've *noticed* is that highlanders apparently like to keep their wives isolated and pregnant." She turned and walked backward, shining the flashlight at her mother's feet to illuminate the uneven driveway. "I've also noticed that except for Vanetta and Rana, all the women on the Center's committee are pregnant. And so is Macie, and now maybe Cassandra as well. Hasn't anyone in Spellbound Falls heard of birth control?"

Hazel stopped walking and clasped her chest. "Oh, wouldn't it be wonderful if there's something in the water around here and you also become pregnant?"

Birch stumbled to a halt. "Are you nuts?"

"Well, at the rate you're going, I'll be *dead* before you give me grandbabies."

"You only just turned *fifty.*"

"There really could be something in the water if you believe the legend written on a plaque in the park," Hazel went on excitedly. "It claims that any couple who kiss while standing in the mist rising from Spellbound Falls will fall deeply in love."

"When were you in the park?" Birch asked, trying not to sound alarmed that her mother had gone into town without her.

"You remember. I took little Charlie and Ella for a walk there while you were talking to Peg and Olivia outside the Trading Post last week."

"Oh. Yes. That's right."

Damn if her mother didn't get that twinkle in her eyes again. "Maybe you and Niall could go sit in the park for your little talk about solving Noreen's problem."

Having absolutely no idea how to respond, Birch silently turned and walked up the path to the back porch of the main house, making a mental note to drink only bottled water from now on.

And never, ever, be in that park at the same time as Chief MacKeage.

CHAPTER TWO

Niall sat in the moon-cast shadows of the Bottomless Mercantile and Trading Post with his ears tuned for any sound other than the muted roar of the falls several hundred yards away and wondered what made him think he had any business being the police chief of Spellbound Falls and Turtleback Station. Hell, forget he was a lawman; he didn't have any business even being *alive.*

But when Titus Oceanus shows up in twelfth-century Scotland looking for a husband for his daughter, only a suicidal idiot would refuse the powerful magic-maker's personal invitation to come compete for her hand. Niall was just thankful his twenty-first-century cousin, Alec, had decided to eliminate the other five time-traveling suitors before helping Niall find sanctuary with two of their magical clansmen in Pine Creek. Not that he wouldn't have manned up and married the beautiful and intelligent Princess Carolina if Alec hadn't finally come to his senses. But in all honesty, Niall was more attracted to pint-sized spitfires than he was to leggy princesses who looked him nearly level in the eyes.

Since about three weeks ago, however, he was finding himself attracted to one tiny redhead in particular — even if she did seem to have a chip on her shoulder when it came to males. But when he looked past her prickly behavior, Birch's eyes reminded Niall of the heather growing wild all over his long-lost highlands. And though she might appear as delicate as a kitten, there was no mistaking the woman had a lion-sized attitude when it came to protecting her residents.

Birch's choice of professions did baffle him, though, making Niall wonder if she might have had some personal experience with abusive men. Why else, according to Duncan, would a woman spend eight years in university to get advanced degrees in social work, only to move to a small town in a whole different country? Birch had even dragged her mother into the wilderness with her, although both women's wardrobes suggested they were city people.

Niall released a silent sigh, just as baffled

as to what *he* was doing here. Despite the responsibilities that came with having been laird of the MacKeages, he often found himself missing the simplicity of twelfth-century Scotland, when a man knew which side of right and wrong he stood on, how to serve his clan, and how to treat women and children. Nine hundred years ago, life was at worst an everyday struggle for survival and at best a testament to a person's willingness to embrace that struggle.

And if they were lucky, to actually find joy in it.

Basically, he'd been born in a time when men were men and women loved them for it. But for the twenty months he'd been living in modern-day Maine, his everyday struggles had been those of displacement, frustration, and too often bewilderment — decidedly foreign notions for a warrior who had once owned his destiny.

In his original time, for instance, if a woman found herself dealing with an abusive husband or father, she merely brought her complaint to her laird, and he would go pay the bastard a visit. Few men were foolish enough to anger their laird a second time, but if the abuse did happen again, punishment was swift, painful, and publicly humiliating. Despite having little say in matters back then, women were recognized as the very heart of a clan. Whether young or old or married or widowed, they were respected for their contributions, protected by all, and revered for their amazing strength of spirit.

Which was why, when Birch had first come to him with Noreen's claim two weeks ago, Niall had immediately paid Logan Kent a visit. What he'd found was a once-strong, wiry woodsman with joints stiffened from years of laboring in harsh weather, who now found himself with only a modest savings, a small monthly government check, and a powerful fear that he hadn't planned well for old age. So as all once-strong, self-reliant men were prone to do when they felt an uncertain future pressing on their shoulders, Logan had turned tightfisted and grouchy. And like any roost-ruling woman who suddenly found herself with a husband constantly underfoot and sticking his nose in her business, Noreen had panicked.

Nay, he couldn't arrest a man for being scared.

Niall looked at his watch and grinned in satisfaction. None of the buildings in town would be decorated with crudely spray-painted cartoons again anytime soon, he decided. But then, he didn't suppose the small gang of vandals was in any hurry to continue their crime spree, since he was fairly certain one of the little hellions had pissed his pants two nights ago when he'd found himself being chased by a *hulking brute* with a badge and gun and a growling dog with equally lethal fangs.

But upon realizing the culprits couldn't be more than twelve years old, Niall hadn't put much effort into the chase, figuring a good scare, as well as learning the new police chief wasn't a nine-to-five lawman, would make them see the error of their young ways.

Not that he had a jail to toss them into if he had decided to catch the little idiots, which was why the idea of public punishment was growing on him. That is, assuming the local grange ladies would let him erect something in their precious town park. But again according to Duncan — who had been reluctant to give his twelfth-century ancestor a gun and badge in the first place — the newly remodeled park highlighted by the sixty-foot waterfall that roared through the center of town was nothing short of sacred ground.

In fact, Niall had been warned to keep an eye on the grange ladies in particular, several of whom were well into their eighties, as they had a tendency to drive as if they owned the road. And with the summer tourists starting to trickle into town, it was his job to stop vehicle-pedestrian collisions *before* they happened. He'd also been charged with keeping a small mob of zealots from clogging the road as they protested what they considered to be an evil, devil-worshipping cult that had a settlement halfway down the west side of Bottomless. He was also supposed to enforce the newly implemented speed limit in town, write up people who didn't cross the road on the newly painted crosswalks, break up bar fights when they became too rowdy for Everest Thurber to handle, and in general keep the peace.

Oh, and keep an eye on the shelter residents in exchange for living in the newly renovated bunkhouse rent-free.

Aye, life may have taken its toll on a man nine hundred years ago, but there had been a hell of a lot fewer laws to deal with. Who in their right mind considered it a crime for a man to ask a bonnie young lass out to dinner? Something Niall had discovered last fall when Jack Stone had threatened to throw him in jail — which Pine Creek actually *had* — for stalking a minor. For the love of God; in his old time, lasses usually had a babe and another one on the way by the age of sixteen. And they preferred marrying a warrior in his prime who had already proven his cunning, rather than an untried youth who could leave them widowed the first time he went to battle. Marriage was about survival for women, and near as Niall could tell it still took two people and a village to raise children.

A concept that when voiced aloud in the presence of twenty-first-century women, he'd discovered quite by accident, wasn't well received. That was why Laird Greylen MacKeage — who, ironically, had also been displaced from the twelfth century — had taken Niall on a camping trip last fall and quietly explained modern courtship. Grey had not, however, been able to explain modern women. Even being married to one for over forty years and having *seven* daughters, Grey had remarked with a shake of his head, had done nothing to help him understand what went on inside a modern woman's mind.

Not that either of them had understood women in their original century, they'd both admitted halfway through a bottle of Scotch, only that they had desired them.

Niall took one last look around and stood up, then gave a single sharp whistle as he stepped onto the sidewalk and headed toward home, his mind wandering to the many things he *did* like about this century.

He certainly liked modern forms of transportation. If it had an engine, he wanted to drive it — although he'd learned the hard way that the faster a vehicle went the more violent the crash. And he absolutely loved flying. His first experience soaring higher than birds had been at the mercy of Matt Gregor, his cousin Winter's husband, in a tiny jet that actually traveled faster than the speed of sound.

Matt also happened to be a powerful tenth-century drùidh who had come here hoping to trick Greylen's youngest daughter into helping him kill his brother. But upon discovering she was a powerful drùidh herself, Winter had found a way to save Kenzie *and* mankind from the upset Matt had caused to the Continuum. The deeply-in-love wizards were expecting their third child in a couple of weeks, and the new Tree of Life species their combined powers had created would ensure mankind's continuance for many more millennia.

All with Titus Oceanus's blessing, of course, since all the drùidhs scattered throughout the world answered to him. Or they did up until a month ago when Titus had turned his authority over to his son, Maximilian, thus making Nova Mare the new reigning seat of power. And now everyone was waiting to see what would happen to Atlantis, since the mystical island Titus had created to cultivate his Trees of Life — which kept mankind's knowledge safe from the constantly warring gods — was no longer needed.

Whatever the elder magic-maker had planned, Niall expected it would be . . . epic.

"Hey, pooch," he said when Shep came tearing across the road from the park — ignoring the newly painted crosswalk — and fell into step beside him. Niall noticed his first officer was wet. "Looks to me like you've been worrying the fish at the bottom of the falls instead of watching for our vandals," he said with a chuckle. "The least ye could have done was caught us a couple for breakfast."

With a grumbling snarl Niall took as an apology, they continued past the church and turned onto the camp road, making the mile walk in companionable silence as Niall found himself recalling the fantastical tale his father, Ian MacKeage, had told him nine centuries ago.

Ian had vanished several years earlier, along with Laird Greylen, Grey's brother

Morgan, and their cousin Callum. Since the MacKeages had been at war with the Mac-Bains at the time, Niall had been elected laird not a month after the four men had gone missing and were presumed dead. The story Ian had given everyone upon suddenly reappearing several years later — despite looking a good twenty years older — had been plausible, though highly unlikely.

But about a month after Ian's return, his age-bent father had asked Niall to take him on a hunting trip. Only rather than looking for game, Ian had spent the next four days and nights explaining where he'd been living for the last *thirty-five* years. It seemed an old drùidh named Pendaär — whom they'd know as their clan priest, Father Daar — had needed Greylen to sire his heir. The only problem was the woman destined to be the highlander's match lived in twenty-first-century America. And being somewhat inept, the old drùidh's spell had sent Ian and Morgan and Callum, as well as the six MacBain warriors they'd been fighting at the time, forward with Grey. Hell, even their warhorses had gotten sucked into the magical storm.

Of the four MacKeages, Ian had been the only one who'd left behind a wife and children, and of the six MacBains . . . well, all but Michael had died over the next three years chasing lightning storms trying to get back to their original time. So upon finding himself alone in the modern world, Michael had moved to Pine Creek and purchased a Christmas tree farm right next door to his old enemies.

In fact, it had been Michael's twenty-first-century son, Robbie MacBain, who had brought Niall's father back when Ian had asked to go home to die. Having discovered he was a Guardian with magical powers of his own, Robbie had granted Ian's request, along with the assurance that the old man would have many years with his wife and grandchildren before he got planted.

Probably the most fantastical part of Ian's tale was that upon arriving in Maine, the four MacKeage warriors had purchased a mountain and built a ski resort. Niall gave a silent chuckle, remembering his father saying how he'd thought the notion of riding people up a mountain on tiny benches hanging from a puny cable, just so they could ski down on two thin pieces of wood, was nothing short of crazy. And, Ian had said as he'd spat on the ground, noble warriors had no call to be in such a useless business. But that very nobleness had compelled them to embrace their laird's decision, and today TarStone Mountain Ski Resort drew people to Maine from all over the world.

Much like the Bottomless Sea was doing in Spellbound Falls.

Except unlike in Pine Creek, Spellbound Falls' and Turtleback Station's appeal was the work of magic. A little over four years ago, in what was arguably an outrageous attempt to impress a woman, Maximilian Oceanus had conjured up an earthquake to open a huge subterranean fissure beginning in the Gulf of Maine and continuing all the way to the Gulf of St. Lawrence. Mac had made the underground river surface in six lakes in Maine and one in Canada, moved several nearby mountains, and cut a deep fiord at the north end of Bottomless Lake — thus changing the forty-mile-long, freshwater lake to an inland sea just so he would have saltwater to *swim* in.

And the bastard had done it without cracking a single window.

The new Bottomless Sea had actual tides, was home to all manner of marine life, and had inevitably put two sleepy wilderness towns on the worldwide map. Towns which now needed a police force to make sure the small horde of tourists flocking to this ninth *natural* wonder of the world didn't piss off the locals.

All of which made his father's time-traveling tale not so fantastical. But then, twenty months ago Niall had also had the pleasure of riding a lightning storm. And, by God, he had decided he never wanted to ride one again. So he'd hightailed it to Pine Creek before Titus Oceanus — or his enforcer, Nicholas — could send him back.

Except no one had even tried going after him. And upon learning it was Titus who had suggested Duncan offer him the position of police chief, Niall was beginning to suspect that instead of bringing him here to marry Carolina, the elder magic-maker may have had something else in mind for him all along.

And here he thought the two theurgists — divine agents of human affairs — were supposed to protect man's free will, whereas Titus and Mac seemed to have developed a habit for quietly directing it. Mac had practically hit Duncan over the head with the magic to get him to marry the widow Peg Thompson and her four little heathens, and Titus had all but dared Alec to walk into Nova Mare and steal Carolina. Hell, even their man Nicholas hadn't been safe from the meddling Oceanuses, with the mythical warrior now happily married to Julia and expecting their first child. A boy,

Nicholas had assured everyone; the first of *six*. But maybe the man did know about such things, since it was rumored he was actually the son of the Norse god Odin.

Niall turned into the shelter's driveway with a heavy sigh, tired of trying to guess why Titus had brought him here. He stopped and looked at the darkened downstairs window he knew was Birch's bedroom and hoped whatever the old bastard had in store for him didn't involve returning to the twelfth century. Because for as much as he loved his homeland, he didn't miss his clansmen's constant looks of sympathy. Nor did he miss the daily reminder of his own ineptness whenever he'd stood at his keep's window and gazed down on Simone's grave.

Nay, Titus had no business setting him up to protect the good people of two small Maine towns when a mere slip of a seventeen-year-old girl could outfox him with nothing more than a smile just to go get herself killed not three hours before they were supposed to meet at the altar.

CHAPTER THREE

As drinking establishments went, Niall supposed the Bottoms Up might be considered typical for a tourist boomtown situated in the middle of the wilderness. The two powerful wizards, mythical warrior, modern highlander, and twelfth-century laird sitting at the back corner table, however, were not exactly typical patrons — Duncan coming the closest as the only native-born Mainer, although the contrary bastard did have the questionable good fortune of being able to command the magic.

Even though the tables were filled mostly with local men enjoying libations and hearty food on this unusually mild weeknight in early June, Niall knew the bar would soon refill with tourists. The happy hour crowd catching up on town news usually headed home fairly early, since most of them had to be back at work by sunrise. But even before the barmaids could wipe down the tables, a new wave of men and women would come tromping in, hungry and thirsty from spending the day hiking and fishing and cruising Bottomless on tour boats, as well as browsing the steadily growing number of craft shops all vying for their tourist dollars.

Though slightly larger in population and sitting at the southernmost end of the new Bottomless Sea, Turtleback Station was actively — even aggressively — competing for those very same dollars. That is, except when the two towns had called a ceasefire in their little tourist tug-of-war long enough to vote on sharing a police force. There'd been a bit of an uproar, though, when the Turtleback councilmen had learned Niall had been given free housing in Spellbound, and had argued that since they were larger and therefore more vulnerable to crime, the police chief should be stationed in Turtleback.

Not that either town had a station yet. Hell, Niall had had to rig his own pickup with a siren and lights and radio, and even supply his own gun.

The Spellbound councilmen had in turn argued that Turtleback was thirty miles closer to the county sheriff's office (which was still over sixty miles away) and already had a deputy living in town — conveniently forgetting that Jason Biggs was responsible for patrolling nearly four hundred miles of county roads. And then the councilmen, backed up by a second citizen vote, had offered to contribute *sixty* percent of the combined law enforcement budget — assuming anyone could call covering salaries and gas an actual budget. And so because the good people of Turtleback were apparently more frugal with their dollars than worried about getting robbed, Niall was living in the Crisis Center's dooryard and using his truck as a mobile office until he had a stationary . . . station in each town, into which he would eventually post three more full-time officers.

Niall waited until Jasmine finished handing out everyone's drinks, then softly tugged on her apron before she could leave. "Wait up, lass. Does Macie not usually work Thursday evenings?"

"Usually," Jasmine said with a snap of her gum. "But she called me an hour ago and asked if I'd come in and cover the rest of her shift."

"Is she ill?"

The questionably legal-aged waitress shrugged. "She looked fine to me."

The only reason Niall wasn't questioning the girl's age was because he knew Vanetta was too sharp of a businesswoman to risk losing her liquor license by hiring a barmaid who wasn't even old enough to drink.

Jasmine stopped chewing and leaned closer. "I got the feeling Macie left to meet someone," she whispered loudly to be heard over the din of many conversations. "My guess is she snuck off to see her baby's daddy, since Everest said the guy was in here earlier."

"Why do you say she's sneaking off?" Mac asked, his grin implying he wasn't the least bit apologetic to be eavesdropping. "Macie is a grown woman."

Jasmine looked at him in surprise. "You're kidding, right? Have you *met* Warden Callahan? The woman would have a cow if she knew Macie was seeing the guy she ran away from and would probably go after him with that bear spray she carries." The girl shot Niall a smile. "Wouldn't it be ironic if you had to arrest the new crisis counselor for assaulting a man? Bet you wouldn't mind tossing *her* in jail, if you had one."

Okay, then; apparently his neighborly little war was becoming as public as the Kents'. "It's Miss Callahan's job to protect her residents," Niall said, not unkindly. "Sometimes even from themselves." He held up his hand when Jasmine started to protest. "I

46

know Johnny wasn't abusive, but Birch might be worried he'll try to talk Macie into going back to the colony. And I'm sure she wouldn't have a problem with the two of them meeting at the shelter, since it's also her job to help couples reconcile."

"Yeah, okay," Jasmine said, striding off with another snap of her gum.

"*Warden* Callahan?" Mac drawled.

"The woman's heart is in the right place."

"You're defending her?" Duncan said in surprise. "Didn't you tell me a few days ago that ye wanted to take the little termagant on a one-way boat ride up the fiord?"

Titus set down his glass, his sharp green eyes lighting with interest. "Are we about to witness another infamous wife-stealing?" The old theurgist arched a regal brow. "You don't believe three weeks is rather quick to decide a woman is *the one,* even for a MacKeage?"

"The idea was to *leave* her there," Niall said, taking a drink to hide his scowl.

"So, Chief," Titus continued with a chuckle, "is there a reason you're still the sum total of our police force nearly two months after its inception?"

"Aye," Niall said with a grimace, even though he was glad for the change of subject. "To date my choice of applicants have been four boys barely weaned off their mamas, three men whose bellies are so big they likely haven't seen their peckers in years, two gentlemen old enough to be my grandfather — one of whom told me he has a device planted inside him to remind his heart to beat — and one character I suspect only wanted the job because of our proximity to the border."

"What is so alluring about working near the border?" Titus asked.

Niall shrugged. "If I had plans to move contraband between countries, I might feel that few people will question a man roaming the woods all hours of the night if he's wearing a badge and gun."

Titus's eyes lit up again. "That was an astute observation." He looked at Duncan. "And you were astute as well, for seeing what a fine chief your ancestor would make."

Duncan dismissed the compliment with a tight grin and looked at Niall. "Didn't any women apply for the positions?"

"Three," Niall snapped, not liking this subject any better.

"And?"

"And none of them appeared to be a good fit."

Duncan shook his head. "We explained

that you have to seriously consider women applicants so they can't sue us for discrimination."

"And I told you that I'm not putting a woman in harm's way." Niall took another drink to keep from growling, then lowered his glass with a glare. "I'd be spending more time watching her back than my own."

"You've met Trace Huntsman, haven't you?" Mac interjected. "Married to Matt Gregor's sister, Fiona."

"Aye," Niall said with a nod. "Trace and Fiona and the twins often visited when I was living with Matt and Winter. I've even been down to Midnight Bay a couple of times and had the pleasure of hauling lobster traps on Trace's boat."

"Then maybe you should ask him about putting females in harm's way," Mac went on. "Since Trace told me he preferred having women soldiers watching his back when he was fighting his war." Mac's grin widened when Niall started glaring at *him*. "Trace feels that because of their physical disadvantage, women are better at reading the subtle clues people — men in particular — give off, and can often disarm a situation before it turns deadly."

Niall looked at Nicholas, who, he noticed, appeared more interested in his ale than the conversation. "How many women are on *your* security force?"

"Three at Nova Mare and four at Inglenook," Nicholas said with a shrug. "I've found our women and younger guests seem to prefer dealing with female guards."

Niall decided it was time to change the subject again and turned his attention back to Duncan. "I still contend that thirty miles is too far apart for towns to be sharing a police force. Even at sixty miles an hour, which is pushing the limit of safety on that road, it can still take me thirty minutes to get on-scene."

"It beats waiting two or three hours for a county sheriff to show up," Duncan countered. "That's why the plan is to station a couple of officers in each town while pooling our resources to save on administrative costs."

"What resources?" Niall countered back. "I don't even have *one* station."

"We're working on that."

"And while you're working on it," Niall went on, "see if ye can't get your fellow councilmen to pony up enough money for me to hire a secretary. When I trained with Jack Stone, it was obvious that Ethel is the heart of Pine Creek's force for keeping everything organized, answering the phone, and dealing with walk-ins."

"I'll try, but don't hold your breath." Duncan suddenly sighed. "It's hard for people who've lived paycheck to paycheck all their lives to wrap their minds around a budget that now involves millions of dollars instead of a few hundred thousand."

"But are the towns not collecting millions in taxes?" Titus asked. "What with all the new businesses springing up and the grand year-round homes being built to replace the old seasonal camps, the town coffers should be flush with dollars."

"Aye," Duncan admitted. "But the older folks are stubbornly tightfisted, and they don't like the idea of building an infrastructure that's turning their wilderness into small cities — especially if they can sneak by with what they have."

Such as not purchasing a new cookstove if two burners were still working, Niall thought as he grinned into his ale.

Apparently not liking *this* subject, since he was directly responsible for turning Spellbound and Turtleback into small cities, Mac lifted his glass in salute. "To progress," he offered, "and the wisdom and courage to embrace it." He looked at Titus. "Speaking of which, how is your mass exodus coming along?"

Titus let out a resigned sigh of his own. "Folks becoming set in their ways is a timeless affliction, I'm afraid."

"How many are left?" Mac asked with a chuckle.

"Eight families for a total of two dozen stubborn souls. And don't think the irony is lost on me that it's the younger islanders who are reluctant to leave. I finally gave them the choice of being gone in two weeks or becoming instant celebrities when an army of twenty-first-century scientists descend on their long-lost mythical home."

"Wouldn't it simply be wiser to leave Atlantis lost?" Duncan asked. "Are ye not worried that any number of nations will go to war over it? Hell, at least seven countries have laid claim to Antarctica."

Apparently deciding that was a rhetorical question, Titus turned his attention across the table. "Is there a reason you're quieter than usual this evening, Nicholas? You appear ready to fall asleep in your cups."

"Julia is *nesting*," Nicholas said as he glanced at Mac. "Has Olivia shaken you awake in the middle of the night yet and informed you the nursery needs to be finished by *yesterday*?"

Mac crossed his arms over his chest, his expression equally beleaguered. "By the time Julia is pregnant with your sixth *son,* you'll be lucky if he's not sleeping in a bureau drawer, since the more children you have the less nesting is needed, apparently. Olivia has put Sophie and Ella in charge of decorating their new sister's room, and to date I've ordered and canceled *three* different furniture sets, now know more about *themes* than any man should, and have painted the walls *five* times."

Aye, Niall thought with a silent chuckle; having been told last week that Olivia was expecting another girl, the wizard obviously didn't like that Nicholas was having only sons, since it was looking as if young Henry would be Mac's only male heir.

"Why don't ye just have the resort facility crew do the painting?" Duncan asked, obviously fighting a grin.

"Because Sophie informed me that modern dads *participate,*" Mac explained — Sophie being his twelve-year-old stepdaughter.

"Oh, come on," Niall said. "What does a wee babe care what color its room is? I'm not even sure they can see past their noses for several months."

Three sets of incredulous eyes turned on him, and Titus merely sighed again.

"The babes don't care," Duncan said.

"Their *mothers* do."

"Women nest," Nicholas muttered, "and the nest has to be lined with *perfect* feathers."

"At least for the first one or two babes," Mac added. "Then they turn everything over to the older siblings and us husbands."

"Aye," Duncan agreed, "while constantly threatening to kill us in our sleep if we get them pregnant again."

"Until their friends get pregnant," Mac countered, shooting a pointed glare at Duncan and then at Nicholas, "and they suddenly announce they want 'just one more.' " Mac then turned his glare on Niall, as did the other two expectant fathers. "You want to be part of this conversation, MacKeage, go steal yourself a wife and get her pregnant."

Knowing he didn't have a hope in hell of changing *this* subject, Niall stood up with a laugh. "Thank you for the advice, gentlemen, but I believe I'll wait for a brave lass to come along and steal *me*."

"You might want to be careful what you wish for," Titus said quietly, "lest you find yourself being taken on a one-way boat ride up the fiord by a pint-sized spitfire."

On that note, Niall hightailed it for the door as he tried to recall if he had ever referred to Miss Callahan quite that way around the scheming old magic-maker.

Niall exited the Bottoms Up to find Shep licking an ice-cream cone being held by what appeared to be a three- or four-year-old tourist; the only problem being he wasn't sure if the little girl was wanting to share her treat with a dog that looked her level in the eyes, or if she hadn't dared say no. As for the girl's parents . . . Well, the mother looked poised to whisk her child to safety and the father appeared ready to use his camera bag as a weapon even as he kept snapping pictures of his daughter feeding a stray dog in Maine. Niall cleared his throat, causing Shep to whip his head around in surprise, only to sigh when the dog turned back and gave the girl's *face* a lick before trotting over — too happily licking his own snout to be feeling guilty, apparently.

Niall sent the parents a sheepish nod and stepped into the brightly painted crosswalk glistening under the newly installed street-lamps, which were already on even though it was nearing the longest day of the year. But the town proper sat in the looming shadow of Bent Mountain, which was responsible for the waterfall that thundered into a deep pool of frothing water before

Spellbound Stream continued under the foot- and road bridges and shot into Bottomless.

"Am I going to have to take ye back to Kenzie Gregor for another little talk?" Niall asked when they reached the old railroad bed the grange ladies had converted to a footpath. Besides being Matt's brother, Kenzie was an eleventh-century highland warrior who lived down on the coast near Trace Huntsman, along with their good friend William Killkenny, an Irish nobleman who'd come to this century seeking Kenzie's help when an old hag's curse had turned him into a dragon twelve hundred years ago.

Maine, it would appear, was growing rife with time-travelers.

When Niall had first gotten Shep, he'd barely been able to get close enough to tend his wounds, and coaxing the snarling, defensive dog to eat out of his hand had been an exercise in patience. Shep's distrust of people — males in particular — had at first forced Niall to camp out in the woods for fear of putting Winter and her children at risk. That is, until Matt had suggested the dog might benefit from a visit to his brother in Midnight Bay, since Kenzie was able to . . . talk to animals.

Not that Niall thought the highlander's

gift strange, considering Kenzie had spent several centuries living as various animals — most recently a black panther — before Winter had helped Matt turn him into a man again.

Niall stopped on the trestle bridge and crouched down to grab hold of Shep's snout, forcing the dog to look at him. "The deal is you're supposed to be an *invisible* first officer," he explained, talking only loud enough to be heard over the thundering falls. "The whole point of ye not wearing the K-9 police vest Jack Stone gave ye as a going away present was to make you appear unassuming."

But when Shep merely took another swipe of his sticky nose, Niall stood up with a chuckle. "Aye, maybe there is nothing more invisible than a street beggar." He scanned the length of town in the deepening dusk. "Now if I were Macie, where would I plan on meeting a man I wasn't even supposed to talk to?"

Not in a public park, he didn't think.

Niall looked up to see several daring tourists standing on the viewing platform perched at the top of the falls, thinking the forested trail leading up to it had many resting benches where two young lovers could meet. But he just as quickly decided that a woman growing cumbersome with child probably wouldn't risk the steep climb.

Niall headed toward the park at a leisurely stroll, nodding to fellow strollers as he decided he would drive down to Turtleback tomorrow. Trying to split his time evenly, he'd made a point of visiting all the businesses in both towns like Jack had suggested — not that he'd needed to be told the value of building a good rapport with the people he'd sworn to protect, since that in essence had been his job as laird. He turned down the path leading to the park that surrounded the deep pool at the bottom of the falls, giving a chuckle when he passed the bronze marker telling the legend of a mystical spell being cast over any couple brave — or foolish — enough to kiss while standing in the mist.

Niall wondered if he were brave enough to kiss Miss Callahan in the mist.

Nay, that probably would be foolish, as the woman would likely spray him with bear repellent, then push him in the pool.

Apparently needing a drink to wash down the ice cream, Shep bolted for the water, and Niall chuckled again when he heard a loud splash not a heartbeat after the dog disappeared into the mist. He continued following the path, which wound through plantings of young fir and white birch trees surrounded by carefully tended flower beds, then stopped at a signpost. Deciding the less-traveled, thickly wooded trail that followed the base of the mountain offered plenty of places for a private meeting, Niall headed into the forest as he kept his ears tuned for the sound of conversation.

Not really worried he might be overstepping his duty to serve and protect, since he only intended to make sure Johnny truly was a pacifist, Niall grinned at having guessed correctly when ten minutes later he heard two people talking against the backdrop of the distant falls. He left the trail and quietly made his way through the forest that was nearly pitch-black now that the sun had set completely, then crouched several feet away from the couple sitting on a fallen log — his grin widening at the realization that, if anything, Johnny better hope Macie was also a pacifist, judging by her tone. But not five minutes after Niall had settled comfortably against a tree, Johnny suddenly stood up.

"Come on, Mace," the young man said as he stood facing her. "How many times are you going to make me apologize for something I had no control over?"

"Dan didn't let the lack of control bother him."

"Because he was *new*. He didn't have anything invested in the settlement, so what did he care if Sebastian kicked him out?"

Dan, Niall happened to know, was actually Dante — an Atlantean warrior Nicholas had brought to Nova Mare as a security guard. It had been at Titus's request that Dante go undercover at the colony, hoping to learn what sort of magic they were practicing.

"I swear to God," Macie said tightly, "you'd better not tell anyone it was Dan who helped me escape. I told you that in confidence."

Johnny gave a humorless laugh. "Exactly which god are you swearing to, Mace? Certainly not the one we've been trying to call forth, because he's *still* not here."

Aye, but he was, Niall thought with a scowl, only nobody knew what the bastard looked like or where he was hiding.

"That's because he's supposed to be a *goddess*," Macie shot back. "And why would *she* be in a hurry to show up if it means having to deal with Sebastian?"

There was a long silence, then a heavy sigh. "Are you ever going to forgive me?"

"Are you ever going to leave the settlement?"

Another silence, and then, "Getting close to the kind of magic that can move mountains was your dream, too, Mace."

"It was, until Sebastian showed up and started bossing everyone around," she muttered, standing up and starting back toward the park.

"But the baby's gonna be here in a couple of months," Johnny said as he ran to catch up with her. "And I really want to be part of its life. And yours."

Unable to hear Macie's answer because they were too far away, Niall got to his feet and followed. He watched Johnny catch hold of Macie's hand when they reached the park and give her a hug that lasted until a group of people walked past. The young man stepped away, hesitated, and made a helpless gesture, then turned and walked up the path to the trestle.

Macie continued staring after him until he disappeared down the road in the direction of Turtleback, then sat on one of the benches along the outer edge of the park. Niall walked over and stood in front of her, breaking into a grin when she gasped and nervously glanced at the trail she'd just exited before looking up at him in horror.

"Would ye care for some company, Miss Atwater?" Niall asked. He gestured at the woods behind her. "And maybe allow me to meddle in your business a little?"

She dropped her gaze, her cheeks clearly flushed in the lamplight, and scooted over to make room for him on the bench.

Niall sat down beside her and stared at the mist rising from the pool. "I don't have Miss Callahan's schooling," he began, keeping his voice only strong enough to be heard over the noise of the falls. "But I do seem to have a knack for taking a man's measure." He shot her a grin. "As well as an occasional woman's. And from what little I overheard of your conversation, it appears to me that your child's father is a good man. He might have his priorities confused, but his heart seems to be in the right place."

"Johnny didn't do anything when Sebastian realized I was pregnant and dragged me out of the bathhouse wearing only a towel and then locked me in a room for *two days,*" she returned, a touch of anger in her voice. "There's no telling what would have happened if one of the other men, a guy named Dan, hadn't helped me escape."

"I've had the pleasure of meeting Sebastian," Niall said, nodding when she looked over in surprise. "I made a point of introducing myself the day after I became chief of police to let him know I was dealing with the people protesting the colony."

"I'm never going back there."

"What I'm trying to say is that I can see how your young man got caught up in Sebastian's vision. Charisma is a powerful force, and when someone like Sebastian shows up with an agenda similar to your own . . . well, few men are immune to that sort of passion."

"Then how come none of the women fell for his charisma?"

"Because history has taught women to distrust power. Tell me, did ye not find it odd that Sebastian made Johnny one of the five priests, when there were older men to choose from?"

She looked toward the pool and frowned. "Most of the older men left with their wives and children a couple of weeks after Sebastian showed up and started talking about creating a new god. Most everyone that stayed is in their twenties."

Niall nodded. "Which likely suited him, since younger minds are easier to bend."

"How do you know so much about men like Sebastian?"

"Ye may not have noticed, but I happen to be a man." Niall set his hands on his knees and pushed himself to his feet, then turned and extended his hand. "On second thought, I think it's time I get ye home before you're missed."

Macie slipped her hand in his and let him help her stand. "You're not at all like Sebastian," she said with all the conviction of an innocent lamb.

Niall tucked her arm through his and started up the path toward the road. "Don't let my good looks and sunny nature fool ye, lass. All men have agendas."

"If that's true, then what's yours?"

"To see you happy," he said, patting her hand clutching his arm. "Which I suspect for you would be a home of your own and a husband you can count on to help raise your babe in a loving and secure environment."

"You think I should marry Johnny?"

"I'm thinking ye might consider letting the man prove he loves you more than he loves the power Sebastian has given him. What I heard tonight was Johnny asking if he had any chance of winning back your trust."

"But how can I ever trust him again?"

"You could start by letting him court you proper," Niall suggested. "If Johnny were to move into town and get a job, would that not show how much ye mean to him?"

"And if he starts talking about us returning to the settlement together?"

"It's a simple matter of saying no." He patted her hand again. "And ye have a mighty powerful ally to help keep him on the right path."

"You?" she said, the lamplight exposing her smile.

"Nay," he said with a chuckle. "Your babe. I noticed Johnny's gaze kept going to your belly when he wasn't soaking in the sight of you."

Macie stopped when they reached the old railroad bed and turned to him. "You think Johnny would take me on a real date?"

"I guess that's something you'd have to ask him."

She stared up at him for several seconds then suddenly started walking again. "Maybe I will." But then she sighed. "Birch will probably go ballistic if Johnny comes to the house to take me out."

"Or she might help ye get ready for your date. She's on your side, too, Macie. We're all hoping to see you settled into the life you want."

"Um . . . you don't think Birch wants to see me settled *without* a husband?" Macie flashed him another smile. "I wouldn't say she actually hates men, but I think she finds you guys are more trouble than you're worth."

Niall merely chuckled, figuring the lass may be right.

"Hazel told me Birch sold their house in Montreal," Macie continued, "then made Hazel move here with her. Apparently Birch thinks her mother is too trusting, especially when it comes to men. And she treats everyone as if they're twelve; Hazel *and* the shelter residents."

"Because she *cares.* If this were just a job for her, I doubt the shelter would have gotten so many residents in the three short weeks it's been open."

"She's actually going out and *finding* them. I think it was Ezra who told her that he saw a bruise on Cassandra's face when the girl came in the Trading Post with her aunt last week. Birch got directions to their house, drove out to the Binghams', and came back with Cassandra that same afternoon. And she talked Noreen into leaving her husband, and even took her home to pack up some of her stuff." Macie shrugged. "I just wish she would care a little less . . . intensely."

Seeing the lass hug herself when a breeze sent the mist swirling toward them, Niall took off his jacket and settled it on her shoulders. He then pulled out his shirttail so it hung over the back of his belt, gave a single sharp whistle to call Shep, and started toward his truck parked in front of the post office. "I'll give ye a ride home," he said as Macie pulled the edges of his jacket around her with a murmured thank-you. "What?" he asked when he saw her glance over at him — specifically at his chest.

"Have you ever shot anyone in the line of duty?"

Niall touched the butt of his pistol sticking out of the shoulder holster he was wearing. "Nay, just seeing the gun usually makes a man settle down."

"How come you don't wear it on your belt like most policemen?"

"Because I prefer to keep it hidden under my jacket." He flashed her a grin. "My size alone seems to make women and children nervous."

"You're going to look funny wearing a jacket when the weather finally warms up."

"Aye," he agreed, walking to the passenger's side of his truck. "Shep, no," he rushed on when the dog came racing up just as Niall opened the passenger door.

"Ewww, he's soaking wet," Macie said with a laugh, stepping back when Shep gave a good shake and covered them both with cold water.

"We're still working on our manners," Niall said dryly as he helped Macie up into the seat. He handed her the seat belt, then closed the door, headed around the front of the truck, and got in behind the wheel.

"Wait, what about Shep?" Macie asked when he slid the key in the ignition.

"He'll run home."

She grabbed his arm when he started the engine. "But it's a good mile. Why can't he ride in the back?"

Niall nodded over his shoulder. "Because the backseat is full of paperwork and riding in the truck bed is dangerous. If I have to stop suddenly, he could be thrown out."

"You're really going to make him run all the way home?"

"You walk to and from town nearly every day, and last time I looked, Shep had two more legs than you do." Niall checked for traffic and crossed the main road at a diagonal. "And the run will dry him off," he added, the headlights illuminating Shep racing down the camp road ahead of them.

The cab filled with a companionable silence, Macie not speaking again until they were nearly three quarters of the way there. "Were you serious about my asking Johnny to take me on a date?"

68

"Didn't the two of you go on dates before you came to Maine?" he asked, remembering Macie telling him she was from California.

"I'd only met Johnny a couple of weeks before we got here. We just . . . um, we hooked up in Colorado at a rally protesting a new mineral mine. And when I told him I was making my way to a settlement in Maine that had been started by people who thought there was magic in this area, Johnny decided to come with me."

"Ye weren't worried that messing with something powerful enough to actually move mountains and turn freshwater lakes into inland seas might be dangerous?"

"Naw," she scoffed, giving a negligent wave at Bottomless. "If magic caused that earthquake, it's long gone. Other than occasional sharp claps of thunder when there isn't even a cloud in the sky, nothing strange has happened around here in four years. And when some of the scientists came into the Bottoms Up and I asked them about the thunder, they assured me it was just aftershocks shifting the mountains."

Nay, lass, Niall thought with a silent chuckle, it's the energy being manipulated by several powerful magic-makers causing those sonic booms.

"So about Johnny," she continued as he turned down the shelter's driveway behind Shep. "Do you really think I can persuade him to leave the settlement?"

"Maybe the question should be, have ye thought about what happens if he does."

"What do you mean? Then we can get married and be a real family."

"Simply having a child together doesn't make a family, lass. Not if the parents aren't first and foremost committed to *each other.*"

She opened her door when he shut off the engine, then slid out before he could get around to help, the porch light revealing her smile as she handed back his jacket. "Everyone in the settlement always teased that Johnny and I already acted like an old married couple. Or they did until Sebastian showed up." Her smile turned sad. "I want the man back that I fell in love with a year ago, and I want us to get married and live here in Spellbound Falls. I don't care what the scientists say; this *is* a magical place, and I want to raise my baby here with Johnny."

"Then go after him with everything ye got, lass, and don't stop until he's on his knees begging you to marry him."

"Oh, I will definitely make him get on his knees," she said with a laugh, grabbing the shoulder strap of his holster and pulling him down, then giving him a kiss on his cheek. "Thank you," she said softly, "for caring enough to spy on me, and then for not treating me like I'm twelve."

Niall wrapped her up in a careful embrace, only to have her suddenly pull away when the screen door on the main house screeched open then slammed shut and he looked over to see Birch running down the stairs.

Macie rushed to meet her. "Hey, Birch, what's the hurry?"

"What are you doing home early?" Birch asked, making a point of looking past her at Niall. "Are you sick and Chief MacKeage gave you a ride home?"

"I, ah, I did leave work early because I was a little woozy, but I thought a walk in the park might make me feel better." Macie nodded in his direction. "That's where Niall found me, so we just sat and talked for a while."

"In the park?" Birch said on an indrawn breath. "You were in the park *together*? I mean . . . um, that was nice of him to give you a ride home. Wait," she rushed on when Macie started toward the house. "Did you happen to see Cassandra in town?"

"No," Macie said with a frown. "She told

me this afternoon that she was locking herself in her room all evening to study for a math final. She's not there?"

"She wasn't when I just checked," Birch said, waving her away, then striding up to Niall — he assumed to make sure he could see her scowl. She glanced back just as Macie disappeared inside, then rounded on him again. "You stay away from Miss Atwater, you understand? You especially have no business sitting with her in that stupid park. She's confused and emotionally vulnerable right now."

"Excuse me?" Niall said, apparently more confused than Macie.

"The girl's barely *twenty-one.* And in my book, that makes her off-limits."

"Wait. Ye think I'm —"

"In fact, all my residents are off-limits, no matter their age. They're here because they're *all* vulnerable. Now, come on," she added before he could respond, grabbing his arm and trying to drag him around the front of his truck. "We need to go find Cassandra before she really does get pregnant. I'll drive the camp road then look around town, and you go check out the town docks and park trails. *Come on,"* she repeated, giving his arm a tug when he stopped at his front bumper. "I swear there's a baby epidemic going on around here. Aren't they teaching sex education in school?" When tugging didn't work, she tried pushing. "Cassandra's pregnancy test might have been negative today, but we need to find her before the little twerp she's seeing convinces her that he must be shooting blanks. Chief MacKeage!" she cried when she still couldn't budge him. "Your job is to protect the citizens of Spellbound Falls, and that includes clueless girls."

"And maybe that girl in particular?" he asked, gesturing at the large tree growing beside the house — the one Shep was standing under, his tail wagging as he looked up.

Birch spun around, her gasp letting him know she was just in time to see the pair of flailing feet disappear in through the window. *"Les maudit tannant!"* she hissed, spinning back to him — her expression making Niall decide that whatever she'd said wasn't nice. She pointed at the house. "I'm having that stupid tree cut down." She then pointed at him, even as she started backing up. "And I better not ever hear about you sitting with one of my residents in that stupid park again, you got that?"

"Yes ma'am," he said with a nod, turning away and striding toward home before she caught his grin — only to suddenly stop and look back at Birch storming in the house as he finally realized what had her hackles up about that park.

Aye, he thought with a chuckle as he headed toward home again; it would appear Miss Callahan believed in legends.

CHAPTER FOUR

Surprised to find Hazel sitting next to the unlit woodstove in the Bottomless Mercantile and Trading Post, since it was the first time Niall had ever seen the woman in town alone, he was even more surprised that Sam Waters was sitting next to her, the two of them engaged in a lively conversation. It wasn't that the man wasn't sociable, but rather that Sam's father and co-owner of the store, Ezra, was usually the one making the ladies laugh and carry on like schoolgirls.

But Niall lost his own grin when he noticed Hazel's right pant leg had a small tear at the knee and that the jacket lying across her lap was muddy. "Do I need to go find my ticket pad and write ye up for disorderly conduct?" Niall asked as he stopped in front of them and bent down to make a point of examining Hazel's surprised eyes. "A little early in the day to be falling down drunk, isn't it, Hazel?"

Those deep brown eyes crinkled with laughter and she swatted his arm as he straightened. "Oh, Niall, you big tease." She held up her wet jacket, her expression turning fierce. "You want to ticket someone, you chase after that crazy woman who *sped up* the moment I stepped into the crosswalk."

"From the description Hazel gave me of the car," Sam said, getting to his feet, "it appears to have been Christina Richie."

"Are ye hurt, Hazel?" Niall asked.

She lifted her other hand, which was holding a mug, the sparkle back in her eyes. "Sam assured me that hot cocoa cures all kinds of boo-boos, even bruised pride."

"Why don't you have a seat and see for yourself that she's okay," Sam said, nudging Niall toward the chair he'd just vacated. "Let me go wait on the Drummonds before Dad tries to give them half the store for free again, and then we can have our talk about finding you a jail." He shook his head with a grimace. "Either Dad's losing his touch or getting senile, because last week I caught him filling Jason Packard's pockets with shoelaces when he saw one of the kid's sneakers didn't have a lace and the other one was a mess of knots."

"What did he mean about his father losing his touch?" Hazel asked, watching Sam limp down the aisle.

"Ezra is apparently in the habit of giving half his store away," Niall said as he sat down beside her. "Only he usually isn't so blatant about it, instead preferring to simply forget to charge folks for some items. Mostly to those he feels could use a little help making their dollars go further."

"And they don't notice?" she asked in surprise.

"Some do. But Olivia or Peg usually takes them aside and explains it would hurt Ezra's feelings if they call attention to his little deception."

"The man can afford to just give away his merchandise?"

Niall nodded. "I've been told he's been doing it for over fifteen years and hasn't gone bankrupt yet. So, Hazel, are ye sure you're not hurt?" he asked, having noticed when he'd first met her that the woman had a subtly guarded stride, as if she suffered from arthritis or a stiff back.

"Only my pride. Mr. Waters happened to come outside just as I landed in the *only* puddle on the street, and . . . and he picked me up and carried me inside," she said, sounding a bit breathless as she glanced in the direction Sam had gone. She looked at

Niall, her cheeks turning a soft pink. "He may have a limp, but he's as quick as lightning and amazingly strong."

"I suppose ye might consider Sam quick and strong for a man his age."

Those cheeks went from pink to red. "*I'm* almost his age."

Niall gave her a wink. "But much prettier."

Hazel blinked at him, then burst into melodious laughter as she took another swat at his arm. "And you, sir, are a shameless flirt." But she just as quickly sobered and brushed at the drying mud on her jacket. "Could you do me a favor, Niall, and not tell Birch that I walked into town alone?"

"Your secret's safe with me, Hazel."

That got him a small smile. "And if Noreen tattles and Birch should ask if you ran into me, I would appreciate it if you didn't mention that I fell and *especially* that you saw me talking with Sam."

Niall shot her another wink. "Well now, should she find out — would Sam ambushing you with a cup of cocoa in hopes of getting his store a loyal new customer not be the truth?"

"Oh, yes, that's an excellent way to put it," Hazel said, her worry turning to excitement. "Although I'm not surprised you came up with the perfect story for me to tell Birch, since I know you highlanders are naturally protective."

Niall lost his smile. "What exactly am I protecting ye from? Why mustn't Birch know you were talking to Sam?"

"She might think I deliberately came into town to flirt with him."

"And that would upset her?"

Hazel nodded. "My daughter would probably jump to the conclusion that I'm already looking for my next husband, and feel compelled to remind me that the ink isn't even dry on my latest divorce papers."

"Your, ah . . . latest divorce papers?"

Hazel leaned closer. "You don't have to worry I'm going to break the law, Niall. Birch already told me people can only get married four times in America."

Niall ran a hand over his face to hide his frown. Hazel had been married four times, and Birch was afraid her mother was already hunting for husband number five? He lowered his hand once he'd wrestled his grin back into place. "You've been married and divorced four times?"

"Well, my first husband died. I only divorced the last three."

"So Birch's father is deceased?" he said gently.

Hazel shook her head. "I never married Claude. When I got pregnant with Birch, my father threatened to disown me if I compounded the problem by marrying him."

"He didn't want ye to be with the father of your child?" he said in disbelief. "But that shouldn't have stopped Claude from fulfilling his duty to you."

"Oh, Niall," she said with a soft laugh. "Your heritage is showing again. I wasn't about to go against my father for a boy I barely knew. I only went to the prom with Claude because he'd just transferred to my high school and hardly knew anyone. And even though he probably couldn't afford it, he hired a limousine and took me to a fancy restaurant, and was so handsome in his cadet uniform that I . . .." Her cheeks turned a soft pink again. "I guess I got wrapped up in the magic of the night. And even though he did offer to do the right thing when I went to his house and told him I was pregnant, he was already packed and leaving for the military academy." She shrugged. "Not marrying Claude was probably the only smart decision I've made concerning men. It was bad enough Birch had to go live with him and his family when she was six; I can't imagine she would have survived with her spirit intact if I hadn't managed to get her back four years later."

Niall scrubbed his face with both hands as he wondered how to respond, only to drop them when he felt Hazel touch his knee.

"My *mémère* Hynes always said, 'what doesn't kill us makes us stronger,' and I personally think Birch turned out wonderful."

"Aye" was all Niall could think to say.

"So now you know my dark little secret, and also why Birch worries about my coming to town all by myself."

"I'm sorry, Hazel, I don't. How does having a child when you were young turn into your daughter not wanting you going anywhere alone now?"

A distinct light came into her eyes. "Because it appears that every time I find myself single, I fall in love and get married."

"Excuse me?"

"While Birch was living with her father, I married Phillip. That marriage lasted almost eight years, until a woman claiming she was Phillip's mistress called to tell me he'd run into a tree and died while skiing in the Alps." She gave a heavy sigh. "It's just as well, I guess. Birch never did warm up to him."

Niall stifled an urge to rub his face again. Hazel Callahan, it seemed, either was very unlucky in love or had very poor taste in men.

"Then shortly after Birch left to attend university, I met Gerard at a fund-raiser," she continued. "But that marriage ended a little over a year later when Birch discovered Gerry was only pretending to be a deposed king of some obscure country in Europe." She leaned forward and lowered her voice. "He was really from Idaho."

Niall stiffened his jaw when he felt it slacken.

"I was on my best behavior for three years, until I met Ernie at a Valentine's Day ball and married him just before Birch got her master's degree. But we were divorced by Thanksgiving." Her eyes lit up again, Hazel obviously realizing she'd rendered him speechless. "I managed to stay single four whole years while Birch worked as a family counselor. But wanting to advance her career, she went back to school to get her doctorate." Hazel canted her head. "She appeared more resigned than upset when she came home at Christmas and discovered I'd married Leonard."

Niall mentally took count. "Er, would Leonard be the gentleman with the ink still drying on your divorce papers?"

"Yes," Hazel said, her shoulders hunching. "Birch stormed in the house three months ago and sent him packing. She brought me to our lawyer to start the divorce procedure, put our house on the market, then took me back to Ottawa so she could present her dissertation."

"What had changed her mind about Leonard?"

"Apparently the bank had called Birch saying they needed her signature because Leo was trying to take out a mortgage on our house, and her name was on the deed with mine. That's when she also discovered he'd already spent most of this year's installment of my trust fund."

Niall decided he wasn't letting Hazel go anywhere alone, either. "What do ye mean when you say Birch sent him packing?"

"Well, I don't know if you've noticed, but my daughter can be a bit . . . prickly when she gets her panties in a twist."

"Nay," he drawled, "I haven't noticed at all." But then he sobered. "Was there an altercation, Hazel, or did Leonard leave peacefully?"

The woman's expressive eyes turned troubled. "I can't imagine he was very happy when he returned from his fishing trip to find his key no longer fit the locks and saw the note on the door saying all his belongings were sitting in a storage locker." She dropped her gaze, her cheeks flushing a dull red. "I'm ashamed to say I never realized Leo had a dark side hiding behind all that charm. He followed us to Ottawa and waited for Birch in the underground garage at her apartment, and if it hadn't been for another tenant getting off the elevator and Birch screaming for help, I . . . I don't know what he would have done."

"Did she call the police?"

Hazel nodded, but just as quickly shook her head again. "She did, but apparently because she screamed and Leo ran off, they said no crime had been committed so they couldn't really do anything."

No wonder Birch had *her panties in a twist* over his refusal to arrest Logan Kent. "Did Leonard bother either of you again?"

"Once more," she whispered, her eyes turning pained as she fingered the jacket on her lap. "He must have been watching our building, because two days later he ran Birch off the road and . . . and he . . ."

"And he what?" Niall gently prodded, covering her knee with his hand.

"After forcing her car into the ditch, Leo got out and started beating on the driver's window when Birch locked the doors, shouting that she had no right to interfere in our marriage. But she managed to back out of the ditch and drive off even though the passenger window was blown out and the right front fender had crumpled in on the tire." Hazel crumpled like Niall assumed the fender had and hid her face in her trembling hands. "My *bébé* could have been badly hurt or even killed because of me."

"Hey there," Niall murmured, sliding to one knee in front of Hazel and pulling her hands into his. "We both know it's going to take a lot more than some cowardly man to bring down your daughter."

Hazel drew in a shuddering breath. "Well, I certainly don't need any stupid law to tell me I can't ever remarry, because when I saw the bruise on Birch's cheek and her swollen knee, I swore on my *mémère* Hynes's soul that I'm never even *smiling* at another man again."

She must have forgotten her vow today with Sam, Niall decided as he fought his own grin. "Ye best start practicing in the mirror then, because I believe your mouth is permanently lifted at its corners. Or better yet," he continued at her surprise, "maybe Birch could give ye lessons. She seems to have perfected a good scowl."

The corners of Hazel's mouth twitched higher. "Oh, Niall," she said, wiping her eyes with the backs of her hands. "You're incorrigible."

"Aye," he said on an exaggerated sigh as he stood up. "I've a fear my dear sainted mother would agree with ye."

"Oh, go on now," she said, waving him away. "Go see what Sam meant about finding you a jail so you can finally arrest someone."

Niall hesitated, until he saw Hazel wipe her eyes again and realized she wanted time alone to compose herself. "As soon as I'm done with Sam, I'll give you a ride home," he said, turning toward the back of the store.

"But you can't arrest Logan Kent," she added, making Niall stop. "I think that poor man should be given a medal for staying married to Noreen for forty-six years."

"If that's how ye feel, then I'm afraid you're in the minority of women in town."

"Only because none of them have lived with Noreen for the last two weeks."

"You'll stay put?" he thought to clarify, "and let me drive you home?"

"I'll stay put. Oh, there's Peg and Charlie. Peg," Hazel called out, not a tear in sight as she motioned for Duncan's wife and three-year-old son to come over.

"Mizry Hazel!" the boy shouted, hurling himself at her. "Eww, you is all wet."

"And look at you, Mr. Charlie, as dry as a duck in a desert."

"Ducks don't live in deserts; them live in seas. And I'm Mur the Magwificant."

"Not today you're not," Peg said, plopping down in the chair beside Hazel and resting her hands on her very pregnant belly. "Today you're Mr. Incorrigible."

Apparently forgetting she was through smiling at men, Hazel beamed Niall a brilliant smile as she pulled Murdoc — the kid's name was Murdoc Charles MacKeage, with Duncan calling him Mur and Peg calling him Charlie — up onto her lap and ruffled his curly blond hair. "That's okay, Mur the Magnificent, because it so happens I adore incorrigible rogues."

Which is why your daughter doesn't want you talking to them, Niall refrained from saying. He nodded at Peg, then headed down the aisle, thinking it was more like Hazel adored incorrigible bastards — remembering that one of her husbands had cheated on her, one had claimed to be a king, and the last one had already spent this year's trust fund installment.

Upon realizing he'd likely be living in twenty-first-century America for the rest of his natural life, Niall had made a point of educating himself on modern finance, U. S. and world history, and as much as he could fathom of the sciences. So he was fairly certain that trust funds involved monies bequeathed from a deceased family member, implying that whoever had set up Hazel's trust had obviously known her quite well.

"That lady needs a keeper," Sam said as he stepped out of a nearby aisle.

"You heard?"

Sam gave a shrug and continued toward the back of the store. "Eavesdropping is a hard habit to break."

"Especially when the subject is interesting," Niall said.

"Hey, I'd be a hundred times dead if I hadn't perfected that particular habit. So who in hell told Hazel four husbands is her limit? Never mind; from what I heard, your Miss Callahan did."

Niall lost his grin even as Sam's widened. "My Miss Callahan?"

"Hearing things I shouldn't isn't my only talent," the store owner said, grabbing a thick brown envelope off the counter on his way to the storage room. "Speaking of eavesdropping, the two guys I found you have it down to an art, which is something you won't see on any résumé from law academy graduates." Sam exited the side door and turned down the narrow dirt lane toward Bottomless, his limp barely noticeable — but then, it was still early in the day. "I doubt you'll find explosives expert, either, or scuba diver, parachutist, or sniper."

"I need police officers," Niall said dryly, "not men who can sneak into a foreign country and take down the government."

Sam stopped in front of the first of five cabins he and Ezra rented to tourists. "Hey, you never know when a new mythical god might show up and start rearranging these mountains again. Wait; you got any magic in you like Duncan?"

"Nay," Niall said, unable to stifle a shudder. "That would be my cousin's blessing to shoulder."

"Probably just as well," Sam went on as he mounted the porch stairs. "I don't know how Olivia puts up with all of Mac's hocus-pocus, because personally, that shit gives me the heebie-jeebies."

Sam was Olivia's father, which she'd discovered four years ago when he'd hired on at Inglenook posing as a camp horse wrangler in hopes of saving his daughter from her ex-in-laws, only to then end up trying to stop her from marrying a . . . man who had the audacity to move mountains.

Sam threw open the cabin door. "Well, here's your new police station and jail," he said, gesturing inside. "Or rather, your station and interrogation room, since the council said they didn't want the liability of a jail." He slapped the envelope he was holding against Niall's chest. "And if you're even half as smart as I think you are, these two men will be your first and second officers."

Niall grasped the envelope and stepped inside. "My first officer is right now out patrolling the town," he said as he looked around the small rental cabin, noticing that instead of a table and couch there were only two desks, a bookcase, and an ancient woodstove in the corner. There was still a kitchen area against the back wall of the front room, but the rugged-looking wooden door with bars set into a windowless opening leading into the bedroom was definitely new. To the right was a regular pine door that he could see opened into a bathroom.

"But unlike Shep," Sam said with a chuckle, "my guys have opposable thumbs and can use a cell phone, shoot a gun, and blow up stuff."

"But can they run a man to ground on a

moonless night, swim the length of Bottom-less without getting winded, and track scent through any weather?"

"With their eyes closed."

Niall tossed the envelope onto the larger of the desks and folded his arms over his chest as he faced Sam. "Why are two highly trained warriors wanting to come play policeman in the Maine woods?"

"Because they're tired of policing the world, where they just put one bad guy out of business only to have another one pop up someplace else. Cole and Shep have decided they'd rather touch people's lives in a more personal way."

"One of the men's names is Shep?"

Sam nodded. "Short for Jayme Sheppard. So you're probably going to want to change your dog's name."

"Or I can call the man Jayme."

"You could if you're real fast at ducking," Sam said, walking into the back room. "He's been known to answer to Jake, but as a heads-up, I heard the bastard once shoved a man off a bridge for calling him an ass-hole." Sam swept an arm around the small room when Niall stepped into the doorway and saw it held only a narrow cot. "So, what do you think?" Sam asked. "This would hold Logan Kent, wouldn't it?"

Niall also noticed that instead of pine paneling, the walls had been refinished with solid oak boards and that iron bars had been put on the two windows. "Jack Stone has a private office, *two* holding cells, a full-time secretary, and a town-issued snowmobile, ATV, and boat."

"I've seen Pine Creek's police station," Sam said, "although I haven't seen the cells up close and personal like I heard you have. This is the best we could come up with until the townspeople can vote on where to put the new safety building. Duncan's working on getting you a snowmobile and ATV, and Dad suggested you use one of our rental boats for now."

Niall moved aside when Sam headed back out to the front room.

"Titus offered to buy any equipment you needed," the storekeeper continued, "but Duncan and Mac agree that if the two towns want law enforcement, they need to have a vested interest." He picked up the envelope and handed it to Niall again. "Back in the twelfth century, did lairds have to wrestle town elders for a decent operating budget?"

Hell, he hated the idea of having to ask for money every time he wanted to purchase something for the department. "Nay. As long as my decisions benefited the clan, no one questioned them." Niall looked down at the envelope he was holding. "Does either Cole or Jake have any experience dealing with budgets and councilmen?"

Sam snorted and headed outside. "They're more inclined to hold a knife to someone's throat to get what they want." He stopped on the porch, his eyes turning as direct as his tone. "You need information on anything or anyone from *anywhere* in the world, I'm your man, but you're on your own when it comes to the town council. It took a year for them to let us put in gas pumps to service boaters, and then it only happened when one of the councilmen got tired of lugging cans of fuel to his new cabin cruiser."

Sam suddenly looked toward the Trading Post when someone called his name, and Niall stepped onto the porch to see Peg running down the lane. "What's wrong?" Niall asked when he saw her expression.

"Maybe nothing," Peg said in a winded rush, grabbing the handrail when she reached the steps. "But Hazel's worried because her daughter isn't answering her cell phone. Birch apparently went out to check on a young girl who might be in trouble, and now I'm worried, too, because

93

Hazel said the girl's name was Misty." She looked at Sam. "The only Misty I know who's in her teens is Ike Vaughn's daughter."

Sam nodded, the look in his eyes further alarming Niall. "Last time I saw Misty was about a month ago when she came in the store with her mother."

Niall stiffened. "What am I hearing in your tone, Waters?"

"What you're hearing is that Ike Vaughn is a self-righteous, fire-and-brimstone-spewing bastard."

"He's more fanatic than those people protesting the colony," Peg added. "In fact, I heard they asked Ike to leave when he suggested that instead of standing around holding signs, maybe it was time they took action against the devil-worshippers."

Niall felt the hairs stir on his neck. "And ye say Hazel believes Birch drove out to the Vaughns' house?"

Peg nodded. "She said a girl came to the shelter this morning and told Birch she was worried because Misty hadn't been at school in over a week and missed all her final exams." Peg hugged her belly protectively. "Apparently Misty confided to her friend that she's pregnant and was afraid of what her father would do when he found out."

Niall slapped the envelope against Sam's chest and headed down the steps, but stopped at the bottom. "Call your men and tell them to be here by the end of the week."

Sam shot him a grin. "Actually, they're arriving tonight."

Niall looked at him for several heartbeats before giving a nod, then took Peg's arm and started up the road, shortening his stride to match hers. "How far to the Vaughns' and how do I get there?"

"They live on the back side of Bent Mountain," she said, gesturing toward the mountain crowding the town up against the Bottomless Sea. "The Vaughn homestead is only about six miles away as the crow flies, but twenty by road. You head toward Turtleback and take a right just this side of the first bridge, then keep bearing right at every fork in the road after that. It's been forever since I've been out there, so Ike may have finally built a bridge over the brook about a mile from his house. If not, a four-wheel-drive can make it across."

Niall stopped when they reached the side door of the Trading Post. "Can ye give Hazel a ride home? And tell her not to worry," he added when Peg nodded. "I'll bring her daughter back safe and sound."

Peg grabbed his sleeve when he turned to

leave. "Um, you do know that if you shoot anyone, you're going to be filling out paperwork for weeks, don't you?"

Okay then; apparently Duncan had been voicing his doubts about giving his ancestor a badge and gun out loud to his wife. Niall reached inside his jacket and pulled his gun out of its holster, slipped out the magazine, grabbed Peg's wrist, and set the empty pistol and ammunition into her hand. "There's no bullet in the chamber. And do me a favor and tell my cousin that he's starting to piss me off."

Peg hugged the large-caliber weapon to her bosom. "The moment I see him," she promised, only to quickly sober. "Sally Vaughn does whatever her husband tells her, and I'm afraid for her, too, if you end up bringing their daughter back with you."

Niall nodded. "Are there any other children besides the girl? What does Vaughn do for a living?"

"No, they only had Misty. And like most everyone in these parts who's not catering to tourists, Ike's a woodsman. Think Logan Kent thirty years ago; compact, strong, nimble in the woods. But unlike Logan, Ike has a short fuse when he feels someone's questioning his authority. Wait," Peg said, catching his sleeve again when he turned away. "Let me call Duncan and have him meet you there." She went back to clutching the pistol with both hands, glancing around to make sure no one was nearby as she moved closer. "The magic might come in handy."

"Nay," Niall said as he finally strode off. "Jack Stone warned me that incident reports don't have a code for magical apprehension."

"Dammit, Niall, at least take your gun."

He waved without looking back. "I've managed to survive this long without it," he said, grinning when he heard Peg mutter a curse in good old understandable English just as he rounded the building.

Having developed the mysterious habit of suddenly appearing whenever Niall's mood turned dark, Shep came tearing down the road and jumped in the truck the moment Niall opened the door. "We're off to save our pretty neighbor," he said as he climbed in behind the wheel. "And if we can find a reason to arrest Ike Vaughn and throw him in the jail we now *have*," he continued as he checked for traffic and pulled a U-turn in the middle of the main road, "then maybe the lass will quit spitting at us long enough for me to ask her out to dinner and for you to finally give Mimi that bone I saw ye bury down on the beach."

Niall flipped on his sirens and lights when a group of tourists started into the crosswalk, then wove through traffic as cars pulled to the edges of the road and stopped. "Well, that's certainly handy when I'm in a hurry," he murmured, pressing on the accelerator once he passed the spot where the old railroad bed crossed at the end of the town proper. "Or we *may* finally win over the ladies," he told Shep, his mood darkening again, "if the only reason Birch isn't answering her phone is that she's out of range."

Because if Vaughn had caught her leaving with Misty and there'd been any sort of altercation beyond a verbal spewing of fire and brimstone, the bastard would be seeing the inside of a hospital instead of Spellbound Falls' new holding cell.

Aye, it would appear Birch was developing a bad habit of her own, in that she kept blindly rushing to women's rescue — armed with nothing more than a tiny canister of bear spray, no less — which had Niall thinking that Hazel wasn't the only Callahan who might be needing a keeper.

CHAPTER FIVE

Niall stopped his truck next to the familiar red compact car half-driven into the bushes, his hopes dashed that the absence of a bridge had been enough to deter Birch from her mission. But it was obvious the spitfire had simply waded across the fast-moving brook, which for her would be thigh-high in places. The only thing that kept him from roaring in frustration were the slip marks in the gravel on the opposite bank, indicating she hadn't fallen and been swept downstream. That the tracks were dry, however, said he was behind her by at least an hour.

A lot could happen in an hour.

Hell, a confrontation could turn deadly in the blink of an eye.

Niall engaged the four-wheel-drive and edged his truck into the water, ignoring Shep's whining as the dog stood on the passenger seat with his nose pressed against the windshield. They made it halfway across before the tires began fighting for purchase on the various-sized rocks, Shep giving a snarl when the truck lurched violently enough to send him tumbling over the console. "Will you relax," Niall muttered, shoving the dog away and gunning the motor to make it up the opposite bank. "I'm not letting ye out to run ahead. We'll go another half mile and make the rest of our way on foot," he added, also ignoring the fact he'd developed the habit of talking to his dog.

But hell, it had to beat talking to himself.

Niall eventually stopped and turned around by repeatedly driving the truck's nose and tailgate into the bushes until he was facing the way he'd come, then backed up the narrow road and stopped between two large trees to cut off Vaughn's escape route. He tossed the key on the floor as he got out ahead of Shep, deciding to leave *his* means of escape unlocked on the chance he'd have to tell Birch to make a run for it, then patted his leg to signal his first officer to stay beside him and broke into a ground-eating lope.

Spotting the unpainted two-story house a short while later, Niall veered into the woods and crouched on the edge of the clearing — Shep standing beside him on full alert, the dog's nostrils flaring like a blacksmith's bellows — and took note of the fairly new pickup and short-bodied logging truck parked next to a barn. But except for a large workhorse and two young cattle grazing in a small field and a dozen or so chickens milling about the yard, the place appeared deserted.

The only thing wrong with the peaceful scene was the heaviness he felt in the air, reminding Niall of the aftermath of hard and bloody battles when the deafening peal of clashing swords and screams of men would suddenly give way to an eerie silence. He stood up and reached under the back of his jacket and pulled out the compact pistol, jacked a shell into the chamber and checked the safety, then returned the weapon to the holster tucked inside his belt at the small of his back. He may have reached the advanced age of thirty-three without needing a gun, but then, he'd never really had to worry about anyone shooting at him nine hundred years ago, either.

"You go first," he said, nudging Shep with his knee. "Try to look pathetic and lost," he added, only to sigh when the dog bolted for the house.

Figuring Shep's nose had told him everything they needed to know, Niall sprinted across the clearing and followed the dog along the side of the house and up onto the porch. He opened the screen door but hesitated, looking around the yard as he slowly twisted the knob, fully aware he needed a warrant to enter a person's house uninvited. But if that person had left in a hurry without tightly closing the door, he decided when Shep gave an impatient growl, and the wind blew it open and a man's dog ran inside . . . well, going in to retrieve his dog was the neighborly thing to do. Especially since Shep appeared certain there wasn't anyone waiting inside with a gun.

Aye, Vaughn should be more mindful about locking up behind himself, because the door suddenly swung back on its hinges and his four-legged first officer charged inside. Giving up all pretense of being neighborly, Niall stepped into a sparse and obscenely neat kitchen all but humming with that same oppressive silence.

Well, it was silent but for the sound of Shep scratching at another door. Niall spotted the thick wooden bar being held in place by two metal brackets and grinned in relief, since he couldn't see any reason to lock a door unless whoever was on the other side was perfectly fine and likely spitting mad.

He lifted the bar and cracked open the door, half expecting Birch to come charging toward him armed with her bear spray, only to find nothing but dark, musty air on the other side. "Stay," he told Shep as he slowly opened the door to reveal a stairway leading down to a cellar.

But still no spitfire.

Forget driving him crazy; the woman was determined to kill him with worry.

Niall bit back a curse when Shep bolted past him and all but tripped down the stairs in his eagerness to get to the bottom. "We're going to have to work on that *stay* command," he muttered, following more slowly as the old steps bowed and creaked under his weight, stopping when he reached the bottom to let his eyes adjust to the stingy sunlight streaming through a small window in the fieldstone foundation.

Following the sound of claws scratching against wood again, Niall found Shep trying to tear his way through another door, this one apparently locked from the inside. Aye, Sam may have a point about policemen needing opposable thumbs, Niall decided as he gave the door a sharp tug — only to find himself scrambling to catch Birch when she exploded toward him.

"Sweet God, woman, it's me," he said,

folding her into a fierce hug as he closed his eyes in relief and merely weathered her ineffectual blows. "You're okay now, Birch. No one's going to hurt you."

Either he finally got through to her or she finally wore herself out, because she suddenly went as still as a stone. "Oh *mon Dieu,* I thought you were Ike Vaughn. Ah . . . you can let me down now."

Not that she felt ready to be let down, since she was hugging him back just as fiercely. "Would ye mind much if I held you a bit longer?" he said, slowly turning to look for something to sit on. "Just until *I* stop shaking?" Sweeping his arm under her knees when she leaned away, Niall sat on an old wooden trunk with her in his lap. "I'm serious," he said, cutting off her protest. "Ye gave me quite a scare."

Her face flushing, Birch looked down when Shep nudged her hand, and Niall couldn't help but notice she let the dog lick her fingers. "I'm sorry I attacked you," she whispered, darting him a quick glance before returning her attention to Shep. "I thought you were Misty's father coming back to . . . to . . . I'm sorry I hit you."

"I'm not," Niall said with a chuckle. "I was relieved ye came out swinging. What I'm referring to is the scare ye gave me when I saw your car at the brook but then got here and found the place empty." He nodded at Shep when Birch looked up in surprise. "Ye have the pooch to thank for sniffing you out."

She looked down again, this time giving Shep's ear a scratch. "I wouldn't really ever spray him," she said, finally relaxing into Niall.

"Speaking of your bear spray, where is it?"

"In my jacket on a peg upstairs. How did you know to come looking for me?"

"Your mum got worried when you didn't answer your cell phone, and she told Peg where you had gone this morning and why. May I ask where your phone is?"

"In my jacket with the spray." She finally looked up, and Niall felt the knot in his chest finish loosening when he saw a spark of fire return to her eyes. "Are you going to arrest Ike Vaughn for locking me down here?"

"Did he hurt you, Birch?"

The woman went from relaxed to deflated. "No. He certainly hollered a lot, but he never touched me. He just dragged Misty upstairs and locked the door."

"You were already down here, then?"

"Mrs. Vaughn — her name is Sally — was alone when I arrived. She invited me inside when she saw my pants and boots were wet, and took my jacket and hung it on a peg by the door and made me tea."

"So Misty wasn't home?"

Birch pointed at a small bed in the far corner. "I didn't know it at the time, but she's apparently been locked down here for the last week. When I asked Sally where Misty was, the woman went deathly pale and asked how I knew her. Figuring I wasn't disclosing anything she didn't already know, I told her what Misty's friend had told me this morning and explained that I could bring her daughter back to the shelter with me. I also told her that once Misty was settled, I could sit down with her and her husband and we could discuss their . . . options. Have you stopped shaking yet?"

"Almost. So Mrs. Vaughn brought you down here?"

Birch snapped her head up. "Don't you even think about arresting her. Sally was hoping I could *help* Misty." She took a calming breath and went back to fingering Shep's ear. "While we were having tea, I explained what the Crisis Center is all about, and Sally asked if it was only for young pregnant girls. And when I told her it's for any woman who feels threatened, I got the impression she wanted to come to the shelter, too. The three of us were down here when Ike came home. Sally had said he was working up back in the woods. You don't feel like you're shaking."

In truth, Niall was surprised she'd let him hold her this long, which had him believing that even though Vaughn hadn't actually touched her, the bastard sure as hell had scared her. "Aye, I'm feeling much better now," he said, pushing Shep out of the way and lifting Birch to her feet, only to realize that now his pants were damp, too. He stood up and walked to the corner, his gut tightening when he saw Sally Vaughn's attempts to make her daughter's prison comfortable, noting the colorful quilt and stuffed animals, the tiny radio on the nightstand, and the worn rug on the dirt floor beside the bed. "How long ago did the Vaughns leave?" he asked, remembering he hadn't met a vehicle on his way in or seen any sign that one had driven out the road this morning.

"About half an hour ago. They're probably all the way to Turtleback by now."

"Did you hear a vehicle leave? There's still a pickup in the yard."

Her eyes widened and she looked toward the stairs — even as she sidled closer to him, Niall couldn't help but notice. "He's coming back," she whispered, hugging herself. "He's stashing them in the woods and coming back to deal with me."

Aye, judging by her reaction, the altercation with Hazel's fourth husband wasn't the only time Birch had found herself dealing with an angry man. "He'd best be bringing a small army with him, then."

"You should let him see you're armed," she rushed on, pulling open his jacket. "Your holster's empty!"

Instead of responding, Niall pushed Birch behind his back when Shep gave an ominous growl seconds before loud footsteps stormed into the kitchen and the cellar doorway darkened with the silhouette of a male.

"What the — *Shep*?" the man said in surprise, slamming the door closed just as the dog reached the top of the stairs. "Niall, are you down there?" the now-muffled voice continued through the door.

"Is that you, Reggie?" Niall asked, heading up the rickety stairs to the sound of the heavy wooden bar sliding into place. "Dammit, boy, don't lock the door."

"Did you talk to Misty this morning?" the teenager said through the wood.

"Nay, she left with her father and mother nearly an hour ago." Niall crowded past Shep and pushed against the door. "What are ye doing here, son? Have you been seeing Vaughn's daughter?"

"He's going to kill her."

"Then unlock the door so I can help you go after her."

"I don't need your help. I only came to get the bag Misty packed so we can run away. We were supposed to leave tonight, but she texted me and said some lady showed up here this morning and that her father caught them."

"She has a cell phone?" Birch cried out as she raced up the stairs, making the old stairway groan and shudder under the added weight.

"Shep, go down," Niall said, freezing in place as the dog scrambled away.

"Reggie," Birch continued, apparently oblivious to the danger, "are you the baby's father?"

"I need to go," the boy said instead of answering. "Misty's old man is crazy and I don't know what he'll do to her. Her last text said she thought he was taking her and her mom to an old logging camp up at Spellbound Stream's headwaters. I'm sorry, Niall, but I can't let you stop me."

"I have no intention of stopping you; only helping."

"You'll get out of here eventually," Reggie

went on, "but I need to buy some time before you can tell Julia. I . . . I'm sorry."

"Wait!" Birch cried. "Reggie, I — *we* want to help you. Misty's mom is in danger, too. And Shep might be able to lead us to them. He can follow their scent."

"You that lady from the Crisis Center?"

"Yes. I'm Birch Callahan. Think about this, Reggie. What can you possibly do all by yourself when you catch up with them? We can —"

"You ruined everything! I gave Misty a cell phone a couple of months ago, but it won't work in the cellar, and she could only call me when they let her come up to take a shower. I was gonna help her escape tonight, but then you showed up. I know where she's going and can contact her when it's time to make a run for it."

"You'll never make it back to your truck being chased by a seasoned woodsman," Niall told him. "Let —"

"I came straight up the mountain on my four-wheeler just as soon as I got Misty's text," the boy said, cutting him off.

"Let us help ye, son," Niall continued calmly. "You're no match for Ike Vaughn." He suddenly stiffened. "Did ye bring a gun with you, Reggie?"

"What? No! Having Misty's old man after

110

us is bad enough; I don't need the sheriff looking for us, too." He hesitated. "Or you."

"What about your brother-in-law?" Niall drawled. "Because if you believe you can outrun Nicholas, I'm thinking Ike Vaughn may be the least of your worries. Unlock the door and let me go after them alone. I'll bring your girl back."

It turned silent for several heartbeats, and Niall was aware of Birch holding her breath and clutching his arm, her other hand pressed to her bosom.

"Even Nicholas won't find us," Reggie said, sounding like he was backing away just as a cell phone chimed, followed by another silence and then a curse. "The bastard is on one of his rants and Misty's scared," the boy hissed, the stairs they were standing on shuddering as he ran out of the house.

"Reggie!" Birch shouted, banging on the door. "Reggie, wait!"

"Sweet Christ, woman, don't —"

Niall's petition ended on a deafening snap, and all he could do was twist to take the brunt of the fall when the old stairway collapsed. But no sooner had they landed when Birch was shoving against him and scrambling to her feet, making Niall wonder if his ears were ringing from a blow to the head or from her screaming what he assumed were French curses.

Hell, even Shep was looking more stunned by her reaction than by the crash.

"You stupid little shit!" she shouted up at the door. "Don't you dare leave us down here!" She rounded on Niall as he shoved away a section of stairs, and actually tried hauling him to his feet. "Hurry up," she snapped when he apparently didn't move fast enough. "We need to stop that idiot. Reggie!" she shouted again as Niall stood up, his jaw going slack when she grabbed a broken piece of wood and hurled it up at the door. "You get your sorry ass back here!"

Okay then; it would appear Miss Callahan had more than just her bloomers in a twist at the moment. Niall pulled out his cell phone, but then shoved it back in his pocket when he couldn't find a signal. Seeing her reaching for a piece of broken handrail as she started in on her French litany again, he headed toward the small window on the far wall — partly to hide his grin but mostly worried she might find him an equally satisfying target. Shep also beat a hasty retreat, apparently deciding now wasn't the time for a game of tug-of-war. "Is cussing out whoever's cooperation you're trying to get," Niall asked conversationally, "something they taught you at university?"

112

Birch stormed over with the handrail clutched in her fist and glared up at him, the filtered sunlight exposing her flushed face. "I have little patience for macho idiots who think every problem can be solved with brute force. Who in hell is Reggie, anyway?"

"Reggie Campbell is Julia Salohcin's baby brother. By *macho idiots,* would you be referring to men?"

Her eyes narrowed as she apparently tried to read his expression. "What did you mean when you said that if Reggie thinks he can outrun Julia's husband, then Ike Vaughn will be the least of his worries?"

Niall stepped past her to study the window. "Olivia didn't hire Nicholas as head of her security because he's pretty." Realizing even a pint-sized spitfire wouldn't fit through the window, Niall turned his attention to the fieldstones around it. "So is it your contention that all men are macho idiots or just us hulking brutes?" he asked as he ran his fingers over the mortar holding the stones together.

"Are you going to get us out of here or not? Because it's obvious neither of us will fit through that window." She used the handrail to gesture at the empty stairwell. "We need to find something to stand on and break through the door."

Niall went back to studying the stones. "Near as I can tell, that door is the most solid thing in this house," he said, having to raise his voice when she stormed off in another heartfelt string of curses.

"What kind of cop runs around with an empty holster, anyway?" she muttered from somewhere behind him. "If you had your stupid gun, you could just shoot the door open. Well? You intend to look out that window until hell freezes over or are you going to help me find a way out of here?"

Niall turned in time to see her kick at the pile of broken stairs, and folded his arms over his chest as he faced her. "Since it appears we'll be working together in the future to protect your residents, there are two things ye might want to know about me."

She marched back over to him. "And they are?"

"The first is that contrary to my usual sunny nature, ye may notice that I slow down and grow quieter in direct proportion to the urgency of a situation. And if I go completely silent . . . well, ye might want to stop talking and start cooperating."

Up went that defensive chin. "Or what; you'll turn violent?"

Niall stifled a sigh, reminding himself the woman had a chip on her shoulder concerning males. "Nay. I'm saying that I find I'm more effective when I'm *quiet.*" He dropped his arms and stepped closer, this time stifling a grin when she held her ground. "And right now I could use your help getting us out of here sometime before Reggie catches up with Vaughn. And," he continued when she tried to say something, "the quickest way out is through the foundation."

"How is going through rock quicker than busting through wood?"

He turned and started pulling off some of the brittle mortar around the larger of the boulders below the window. "Ye may not have noticed, but I'm Scots, and finding a castle's weakness is in our blood. So with my knowledge of stonework" — he looked over his shoulder and grinned — "and a good deal of brute force, I can have us out of here in no time, providing I can *hear* the sound the stones make."

Flags of red darkened her cheeks even as her chin lifted again. "You said there are two things I should know about you, so what's the other one?"

Considering her mood, Niall plucked the broken rail out of her hand, then turned and used it to start chipping at the mortar. "I feel it's only fair to warn ye that whenever you get spitting mad — at me or anyone else, apparently — I find myself fighting a powerful desire to kiss you."

There, he'd said it. But Niall figured a man should probably warn a lass that he was interested, if only to save himself from getting his face slapped when he finally got around to taking action. The silence that ensued but for the sound of mortar hitting the floor, however, had him fighting a more immediate urge to glance over his shoulder to see her expression.

"Maybe there's a shovel or something down here," she muttered, her voice moving away.

Okay then; it would appear he in turn had learned a couple of things about Birch this morning. One, she wasn't so stubborn she couldn't be reasoned with, and two, the woman had one hell of a temper. No, he'd learned three things — the third being that his pretty little neighbor could out-cuss most men.

He was going to have to get a language translation app for his phone.

"I found this," she said, a rusty old pickax appearing beside him.

Niall took it without looking at her and drove the pick into the crack he'd managed to open up. "Can you explain something to me, Birch?"

"What?" she asked, sounding more defensive than cooperative.

"Well, I find myself wondering what would compel a young girl who's spent her entire life under the rule of a domineering father to trust a young man enough to run away with him. For that matter, if Misty is with child, how had she dared be intimate with Reggie in the first place? Would the lass not have worried she might be jumping out of the frying pan into the fire?"

"Not if she thought Reggie could *save* her from her father," Birch said, moving into his line of vision. "Teenagers turn to their peers for support, especially if the adults in their lives have proven untrustworthy."

Niall straightened. "Are ye saying Misty doesn't even trust her mother?"

"No. I believe she simply realizes that Sally is just as powerless."

Niall started digging again. "How can a woman allow her daughter to be locked in a cellar? For that matter, why would she even stay with an abusive husband?"

"Women stay for any number of reasons; anything from honestly believing they don't have a choice to feeling shame for being in such a position to begin with, or simply lacking the financial means to escape. It's been my experience that sometimes all it

117

takes is a complete stranger — someone like me, who has a fancy degree proclaiming I'm an expert — to tell them they can leave."

Niall saw her gesture at the house above them.

"Small-minded men like Ike Vaughn," she continued, "set themselves up as king of their little world by controlling everything. You probably didn't notice, but the first thing I saw when I sat down at the table was that the kitchen is immaculate; there's not one thing out of place, and every surface has been scrubbed so clean, the finish is worn off in places."

"Aye, I did happen to notice," he said, stepping out of the way when one of the smaller rocks tumbled free. "So you think that simply giving Mrs. Vaughn permission to leave is all it would take?"

"For Sally, I suspect that answer would be yes." Birch shrugged. "But for many women it would be no, especially if there's a history of violence. In the United States alone, nearly five hundred women between the ages of sixteen and twenty-four are killed every year by someone who professes to love them. And nearly seventy percent of those murders occur *after* the woman leaves the relationship."

Niall went back to work on the wall, his

blows more aggressive.

"Domestic abuse," Birch continued heatedly, "has always been considered a women's issue — a label likely coined by men to distance themselves from the problem. But there's been movement toward exposing the roots of abuse as being a *men's issue,* recognizing that *male* behavior is what needs to change."

Niall straightened again. "Ye make it sound as if all men are brutes, where I'll have you know that I've never raised a hand to a woman or child. Hell, I won't even hit a defenseless man, even if he deserves it."

"Abuse isn't only physical," she shot back. "It can be emotional, sexual, verbal, economic, or even neglect." She gestured toward the window. "And let's not forget isolation; Ike Vaughn has Sally and Misty living so far off the beaten path that only a four-wheel-drive can get here."

"All those things are considered abuse?" Niall asked, undecided which disturbed him more — that he hadn't realized or that he hadn't even *thought* about it.

"If a man destroys something a woman cherishes, embarrasses her in public, or controls what she does and who she sees," Birch explained, her words growing clipped, "he's being emotionally abusive. Constantly calling her ugly or stupid or clumsy is verbally abusive and insidiously effective. Not letting her work or taking her paychecks if she does have a job, and requiring she ask for money to buy even a pair of shoes is economic abuse." Her chin lifted. "But personally, I think getting punched in the face is actually the least destructive because it's openly hostile, rather than hidden behind a man claiming *he loves her so damn much that he wants to make sure she and the whole world know it.* Are you starting to get the picture, Chief MacKeage?"

Since he couldn't respond to save his soul, Niall mutely watched Birch suck in a calming breath and suddenly drop to her knees when Shep nudged her hand.

"I'm sorry if I've given you the impression that I hate men, because I don't," she continued softly, wrapping her arms around Shep and brushing her cheek on his head. "In fact, I've dealt with many abusive women. But domestic violence is still for the most part a men's issue. For centuries women the world over have tried to get laws passed to give them some semblance of protection, but only a man has the power to change another man's behavior."

"How?" Niall barely managed to whisper.

She lifted her head and smiled sadly.

120

"Have you ever sat at a table with a bunch of your buddies, playing cards or just drinking, and had one of them make a derogatory or sexist remark about a woman? And did you laugh it off, or agree with him, or maybe even add a remark of your own? Or did you speak up and say, 'Hey, cut it out. That could be my sister or mother or my daughter you're talking about.' " She went back to hugging Shep. "Laws making domestic abuse a crime don't work. But if one man is willing to speak up, then a dozen men, then a hundred, it will eventually become *socially* unacceptable."

She gave Shep a final squeeze and stood up, again smiling sadly as she lifted her hands in a helpless gesture. "But that's not going to happen until all men — *especially* the good guys — acknowledge that the problem begins and ends with them. It takes leadership to change society; strong male role models who can teach the next generation of young men how to treat their mothers and sisters and girlfriends."

Well, he'd asked. Niall went back to work on the wall, the ping of the axe echoing through the sudden silence as he sensed Birch hesitate before quietly walking away.

CHAPTER SIX

Birch unzipped Misty's runaway bag, which she'd found stashed under the bed, and pulled out the boots sitting inside, held them up to gauge their size, then tossed them down when she realized they were at least two sizes too small. Next she pulled out a pair of jeans and held them up by the waist, remembering the quiet, wide-eyed girl she'd met this morning was about her size, except maybe a little narrower in the hips.

Not for long, Birch thought with a sigh as she dug through the backpack for some socks. Maybe the Crisis Center should officially ask the Birthing Clinic to start handing out birth *control* — although there was a good chance her petition would be falling on deaf ears, seeing how three of their five mutual committee women were pregnant. Forget the legend about something being in the water around here; considering their husbands were freaking walking mountains of testosterone, the women had probably gotten pregnant just by holding their hands.

No, she might have better luck talking directly to Dr. Bentley, since he was acting as the town's general practitioner as well as the clinic's obstetrician. She might get the cold shoulder from Maude though, figuring not only was the scary-sweet midwife fairly tight with the famous five, but her livelihood more or less depended on it raining babies.

Birch glanced toward the window in time to see Niall step out of the way when several small rocks broke free of the wall. She picked up the jeans and rushed to the closet she'd hidden in, sat down on a wooden box and took off her wet boots, then stood up and stripped off her damp slacks. She was just slipping into Misty's jeans when another rock — this one sounding rather large — crashed to the floor, accompanied by what she assumed was a curse in a language she didn't recognize.

Birch sat down again and peeled off her wet socks, then took a moment to wrap her hands around her cold toes even as she felt her face flush with heat. Chief MacKeage hadn't really said he wanted to kiss her, had he? *Especially* when she got mad? Was he one of those weirdos who got turned on by a woman's anger, or just a typical horny toad making a run at the new girl in town after already working his way through all the local women? He'd probably left a trail of broken hearts in his wake, too, because what girl wouldn't want to be seen strolling down the street on the arm of a tall, handsome man with a shiny badge pinned to his chest?

Not that she thought this particular mountain of testosterone was handsome or anything. Birch felt her face heat up even more, remembering Niall calmly telling her that he grew slower and quieter the more urgent a situation became, while she'd been right in the middle of cussing out Reggie. And him. And the entire situation. Although, in truth, she'd mostly been angry for putting *herself* in danger this morning.

Mon Dieu, Ike Vaughn had scared her when he'd come home and found her talking to his wife and daughter. Apparently he had heard in town that she was running the new Crisis Center, so Birch had barely said her name when the man had gone off like a rocket. And although Ike Vaughn wasn't exactly a hulk, she wouldn't have stood a chance if he'd gotten physically violent.

She was going to have to keep her bear spray clipped to her belt. Oh, and her phone, too. *Merde;* at this rate she'd be running around looking like a cop. Shep poked his head in the closet, his body shaking enough that Birch could tell he was wagging his tail. "I'm coming," she said, quickly slipping on the thick socks, then wrestling her feet back into her wet boots. "I'm coming," she repeated more loudly when Niall called her name. "I'm changing into some of Misty's clothes."

Birch finished lacing her boots and ran out of the closet, but halted beside the broken stairs when she saw Niall had taken off his jacket and rolled up his sleeves. It wasn't so much the sweat-darkened shirt clinging to his broad shoulders that caught her off guard — she did watch the man go swimming regularly, after all — but rather the pistol tucked in the back of his belt. Not that she knew why the sight of it should surprise her, since her father never left the house without a backup weapon.

"I need ye to stand over here," he said, nodding to his right as he wedged a thick board under a boulder directly beneath the window. Holding the board in place, he pointed up at where the floor joists rested on the foundation. "Watch the foundation sill and tell me if it starts to bow or if any of the rocks along it start to loosen." He used

his sleeve to wipe his forehead. "The opera-
tive word would be *starts;* if too many rocks
around the window fall, this whole side of
the house could cave in."

"Do you really know what you're doing?"
Birch asked, walking over and frowning up
at the ancient beam. When she looked over
to see Niall was frowning at *her,* she
shrugged. "Your DNA or whatever's floating around in your Scottish blood hasn't
laid siege to a castle in at least what . . .
several hundred years?"

He stretched to grab the pickax, but not
quickly enough for her to miss his grin. "Ye
might be surprised how recently it's been
for my particular lineage," he said, placing
his shoulder under the board, then wiggling
to adjust his stance. He looked at her again,
completely sober. "Watch the sill. Wait," he
said, glancing around. "Shep, *falaich.*"

"What language is that and what did you
tell him?"

"It's Gaelic for *hide,*" he said, using his
shoulder to put pressure on the board, then
adjusting his position several more times.
"Watch the sill."

Birch turned her attention to the beam
above the window. That is, until she heard a
soft grunt and looked over to see Niall
slowly straightening, his eyes closed and

sweat breaking out on his forehead again as the board started bending from the strain.

"Well?" he said through gritted teeth.

Well what? Oh, she was supposed to be watching the *beam.* "It looks fine to me," she said, even as her gaze — of its own volition — slid to those amazing, straining muscles again. Yes, she might find men annoying, but she definitely didn't hate them.

"Here," he said tightly, holding out the pickax. "Pull more dirt away from under the right side of the stone. Keep checking that sill," he said when she started digging.

Birch alternated between digging and glancing up, being careful not to strike him with the other end of the pick as she widened and deepened the crack. "Oh, the rock just moved!" she said, stilling when the axe became wedged deep in the foundation.

"A few more strikes," he growled, straining upward on the board. "But be ready to run when I tell you."

She was trying to wrestle the pick back out of the crack when the board suddenly snapped with the force of a gunshot going off. Niall snagged Birch around the waist on his way by just as the huge boulder crashed to the floor, setting off a dust-billowing landslide when a large portion of the wall came down with it.

"Tabernacle!" Birch yelped. "You nearly brought the house down on us!"

She didn't know where the man found the strength, considering his entire body was quivering from the strain he'd just put it through, but he hugged her so tightly she actually squeaked — not that he heard it over his laughter. "Aye, but we're free," he said, just before he kissed her.

He honest to God was kissing her! And not just a peck, either, but taking advantage of the fact that she'd opened her mouth to give him hell. Birch was trying to decide how to respond when he just as suddenly stepped away, the kiss-stealing jerk apparently not feeling the situation was urgent enough to get all slow and quiet.

She was going to have to watch her cussing around him.

"Come on," he said, leading her over to the gaping hole. "Mind the broken glass," he added as he lifted her onto the pile of debris.

Propelled by a large hand on her backside — giving her a suspiciously lecherous *pat* more than a push — Birch scrambled up onto the lawn, his laughter drowning out her gasp. She'd barely made it to her feet when Shep came charging out behind her, and she was just wiping her hands on her borrowed jeans when Niall grabbed one of them and started toward the front of the house.

"I need ye to call Nicholas and explain what's happening and how to get here," he said, reaching in his pocket and pulling out his cell phone. "When he arrives, point him up the mountain." He stopped when they reached the porch and handed her the phone. "His number is programmed in, so after ye call Nicholas, call your mum and let her know you're okay," he added, sitting her down on the steps.

Birch popped back up the moment he stepped away. "I'm going with you," she said, shoving the phone at him. "You can call Nicholas on our way."

"You'll slow me down."

"I'll keep up."

"Your boots are soaked through and your feet will be blistered in minutes."

"If I fall behind, you can keep going and I'll catch up," she shot back, shoving his phone in her pocket when he didn't take it and bolting toward the woods. "I need to be there for Misty and Sally."

She was pulled to a halt within two strides, and he grasped her shoulders again, then simply stood staring at her. "Hell," he suddenly muttered, leading her back to the house. "Go inside and find some boots," he said over her heated protest — which she stopped when his words sank in. "And get your jacket."

Birch ran up two of the steps and turned to look him level in the eyes. "You're going to take off the moment I go inside."

He held out his hand. "I'm going to call Nicholas. Ye have two minutes."

She in turn eyed him for several seconds, then slapped the phone in his hand, ran across the porch, and slammed through the door. She found footwear lined up under the coatrack in the kitchen and grabbed what she assumed were Sally's garden boots — not that they had a speck of dirt on them.

Birch pulled a chair from the table and sat down, glanced out the open door to see Niall talking on the phone as he strode toward the barn, then unlaced her boots again. She kicked them off, squeezed her feet into the rubber pacs, and stomped them on as she went back to the pegs and grabbed her jacket. Glancing around the kitchen as she patted her pockets to make sure she had her phone and bear spray, Birch ran to the sink, found a glass in a nearby cupboard and filled it with water, then took a long drink. Then she refilled the glass, figuring Niall had probably lost a gallon of sweat digging them out of the cellar, and ran out to the porch.

Only when she got outside, the man was nowhere in sight. She ran to the barn and stopped just inside the huge open doors to listen for movement or talking, then ran back outside and around the building. "You lying jerk!" she shouted, scanning the edge of the woods for any sign of him or Shep, or even Reggie's ATV tracks.

"Are ye intending to roost there all day?"

Birch twirled to see Niall leading a giant horse out of the pasture. "I brought you water," she shouted, running to him.

"I drank from the hose in the barn," he said as he clipped a second rope onto the halter. He then vaulted onto the horse's back and held a hand down to her. "Swing up behind me and hold on."

She took a step back and glanced around, then used the water to gesture at the pickup beside the barn. "Maybe the keys are in the truck."

Niall plucked the glass out of her hand and tossed it away, then reached down to her again. "Do ye not think Vaughn would have taken it himself if he could reach the headwaters by truck?"

"There's no saddle."

"Scots learn to ride before we can walk."

He wiggled his fingers. "Don't chicken out on me now, lass. I can deal with Vaughn and Reggie, but the women need you."

"Merde," Birch muttered, reaching for his hand.

"Jump," he said on a chuckle, pulling her up behind him. "Hold on," he added just as the horse broke into a plodding gallop or lope or whatever it was called before she'd even gotten her balance.

Holding on to Niall as if her life depended on it — which she was pretty sure it did — Birch pressed her face into his jacket to keep from bursting into hysterical laughter as she tried to decide which one of them was crazier. Because honestly, who in their right mind chased after runaway teenagers on a *plow horse*?

Forget not having a saddle; even she knew Niall needed a bridle to steer. And what was up with all that "I'm Scots" business, anyway? Had the man been reading her mom's historical romance novels or something and gotten the idea that just because he was descended from Scottish highlanders that he could crumble castle walls, steal a kiss from the liberated damsel, and charge off on a mighty steed to rescue a family from a villainous ogre?

Well, okay; maybe he was two for three

this morning. No, two and a half, as they definitely were charging somewhere.

Still, if Chief MacKeage were the crazy one, what did that make her for galloping to the rescue right along with him?

CHAPTER SEVEN

Niall guided the surprisingly cooperative horse up the path in the direction Shep had disappeared, not at all surprised Birch was riding with him, considering the woman didn't seem to know the meaning of caution. Granted, he'd all but dared her to swing up behind him, but only because he didn't doubt she would strike out on her own if he left without her. And to his thinking, it was better to know exactly where Birch was rather than have her popping up in the middle of a potentially deadly situation.

He may not recall having met Ike Vaughn in town, but he'd certainly dealt with his kind — in a couple different centuries now, actually. Self-important bastards like Vaughn would willingly fight to the death defending their property or beliefs, and they didn't care who they took down with them.

When the narrow tote road he was following forked, Niall veered left without letting the horse break stride, as Reggie's ATV tires were leaving a trail a blind man could follow. He did have to reach back and catch Birch, however, when she veered right with a startled yelp.

"A warning would be nice," she muttered as he slid her upright. "Unlike you, I didn't learn to ride before I could walk. Ow!" she yelped, nearly falling off again as she jerked away. "Your stupid gun keeps poking me."

Niall gave a heavy sigh and reined the horse to a stop, then twisted to grab her. "Let go," he said, giving a tug when she clung to him like a cat on a screen.

"No, don't make me get off!" she cried, batting him away, then wrapping her arm tightly around him again. "I won't say another word. Misty and Sally need me."

"It'll be easier for you to ride in front."

"I don't know how to steer! Just go," she said, kicking the horse's sides — which merely caused the beast to switch its tail in agitation.

"Then pull the gun out of my belt and shove it in your pocket," he said, starting the horse off at a walk.

"I'm not touching your stupid gun. Where's the one you wear in your holster?"

"I gave it to Peg MacKeage to hold until I

get back."

"You can't just hand your service weapon to a civilian. She has a *toddler.*"

Since it didn't appear she was going to move his gun, Niall urged the horse into a lope. "Peg knows more about firearms than I do."

"Warn me!" Birch snapped as she became a clinging cat again.

"Hold on," he warned with a chuckle, pushing the horse into a gallop. "What was that?" he asked over his shoulder when she muttered something into his jacket, even as he politely didn't point out that she was still talking.

"I . . . I said *thank you.*"

Niall also politely refrained from calling her a liar. He continued following the ever-narrowing road that was now working its way between two mountains, giving Birch points for finally figuring out she needed to move *with* him and the horse. It was another fifteen minutes before he spotted Shep standing at what appeared to be a sharp turn in the path, the dog's tongue lolling out the side of his mouth and his tail giving a wag just before he bolted up a narrow game trail to the right.

The only problem was that Niall could see Reggie had gone left. He brought the horse to a stop when he reached the trail, then lifted his leg over its neck and slid to the ground. He immediately turned and caught Birch as she fell, then covered her mouth with his hand to stifle her yelp of surprise. "I think we're close," he whispered, pulling her against him when her legs buckled. "Listen."

She stilled inside his embrace as Niall caught the muted roar of rushing water and the sound of two males engaged in a heated argument. He grasped her shoulders and held her facing him. "Do ye have your bear spray? Vaughn doesn't know I'm here," he continued quietly when she patted her pocket and nodded, looking . . . hell, she looked *eager* to spray the bastard. "Are ye up to creating a distraction while I work my way behind them?"

"Oh yeah," she said, nodding vigorously this time. "What do you want me to do?"

They both stilled when the shouting came to an abrupt end with the unmistakable sound of a fist hitting flesh and a pained grunt immediately followed by a female scream. Niall gave Birch a squeeze to get her to look at him again. "Interrupt what's going on by showing yourself, but keep your distance, understand? Just catch Vaughn's attention and hold it." He grinned. "Swearing at him should work. But whatever ye do, don't be scanning the woods looking for me. Give me your word," he said roughly when she nodded again, "that you won't go anywhere near Vaughn."

"What if he has a gun?"

Niall shook his head. "We'd be hearing gunfire instead of shouting." He turned her to face the path Reggie had taken. "Ready?"

"How will I know what you're planning to do?" she asked, pulling her bear spray out of her pocket.

"You'll know when it's over," he said, giving her backside a pat that ended with a push, causing her to bolt as if he'd pinched her.

Niall waited, watching Birch run out of sight without so much as a glance back at him, only to mutter his own curse when he realized she hadn't promised him anything. He quickly tied the horse to a tree and high-tailed it up the trail toward Shep as he tried to imagine why Reggie hadn't waited until nightfall to steal Misty away — every scenario he came up with only further darkening his mood.

Niall left the trail and ran through the dense woods, the sound of the gushing stream drowning out any noise he might be making. He came to a halt at the edge of a large outcropping of ledge, catching hold of Shep's fur to stop him just as the young girl screamed again. Niall saw the lass being held back by a woman he assumed was Sally, then moved slightly to look at where they were staring to see Vaughn standing over Reggie lying on the ground, the boy apparently out cold.

"Get away from him, you cowardly little pissant!" Birch shouted as she marched into the clearing.

Well, there was no question the spitfire knew how to create a distraction.

Vaughn stepped back in surprise. "How did you get free?"

Birch continued advancing. "You're going to need to rebuild your foundation," she said as Vaughn, frowning at the small canister she was holding up threateningly, started retreating. "Assuming the house isn't completely caved in by the time you get out of prison," she added, dropping to one knee and, without taking her eyes off Vaughn, placing a hand on Reggie's neck. "Now aren't you just the big man, locking women in your cellar and beating up defenseless kids."

Niall signaled Shep to stay put, giving him a soft thump on the head to let the dog know he meant business, then started working his way around the clearing only to be stopped by a sheer vertical drop down to a stream gushing through a deep chasm. Well, sheer but for the hand- and toeholds conveniently jutting out of the craggy granite. With a sigh of resignation — because he really didn't want to shoot the idiot — and after a quick glance to make sure Birch was keeping her distance, Niall dropped over the side and began working his way behind Vaughn.

"Leave here!" he heard the bastard yell. "This isn't your business. And you can take that evil defiler of women with you!"

"Daddy, no!" Niall heard Misty scream.

"Let her go, you sick bastard!" Birch shouted.

Niall popped his head up to see Ike Vaughn dragging his struggling daughter toward the cliff and Birch rushing toward them. But he stopped from vaulting up over the side when a sharp crack of thunder suddenly split the air, making Vaughn halt and look up at the cloudless sky.

Birch also halted. "There you go!" she shouted. "Now you've pissed off God."

Nay, Niall thought with a grin; the bastard had pissed off *Nicholas.*

"You're the one making Him angry!" Vaughn retorted. "That was a sign your interference is unwanted as I rid the world of this fornicator and the devil's spawn she carries!" he shouted, giving his daughter's arm a shake.

Despite the sound of the rushing stream, Niall had no trouble hearing Birch's gasp as he finally realized why Reggie hadn't waited until nightfall. He reached to the back of his belt, pulled out his pistol, and rested his arms on the ledge and took aim — only to find Sally Vaughn had dropped to her knees and was blocking his line of sight.

"You really are a stupid son of a bitch," Birch shouted. "Everyone knows thunder is a *warning* that you're about to get *shot dead* if you take one step closer to that cliff."

Okay then; since Birch had obviously reached the same conclusion, Niall began inching his way to the right even as he wondered what was taking Nicholas so long. The moment he had a clear shot, he rested his arms on the ledge again and clicked off the safety — but had to jerk the muzzle away when Sally suddenly lunged forward.

With the feral growl of an enraged mother bear, the woman smashed the rock she was holding into her husband's head, the momentum of her charge pushing Vaughn closer to the edge of the cliff. Sally managed to tear her daughter free of his grip, then started pummeling the bastard, trying to free herself as Misty scrambled to her feet and frantically started tugging on her mother.

Niall dropped his pistol and stretched sideways, managing to snag Misty's jacket when Vaughn gave an angry shout and dragged both women over the cliff with him.

"Stop struggling," Niall snapped at the screaming girl as she flailed beneath him. "I have you, but ye need to stay still. Birch," he said when a shadow fell over them with a cry of relief accompanied by a canine whine. "Take off your jacket and lower the sleeve down to me. Misty, I need ye to calmly reach up and take hold of the sleeve, but don't tug on it or try climbing, understand? Say ye understand, lass."

"I — I understand. Where's Mama? Mama!"

"Concentrate on *us* right now." His position making it impossible for him to look up, Niall felt the shadow fall over them again a moment later. "Is there a sturdy bush you can use as an anchor?" he called up to Birch. "Something you can fold the other sleeve around to help offset some of Misty's weight?" he asked, knowing there wasn't enough material to tie it off. "I only need ye to hold her until I can reposition myself."

"I see something," Birch said loudly over the rushing water.

"Are ye braced?" he asked when the sleeve was lowered beside him.

"I am now," she called out after a moment.

Niall carefully lifted Misty closer to the dangling garment. "I won't let ye fall, lass," he said when she whimpered. "Okay, now slowly reach up and feel for the sleeve, but remember not to —"

"What's going on? Misty!"

"Reggie!" the girl cried, twisting to look up.

"Hold still!" Niall snapped. "Reggie, are you in any shape to help?"

"What do you want me to do?"

"Hold on to the jacket with Birch. Misty, reach up and grab the sleeve. Higher and behind your head. That's it. Now your other hand. Are you two ready up there?"

"She's not going anywhere," Birch said roughly.

"Misty," Niall said calmly. "Slowly turn until you're facing the ledge and feel for some toeholds. Easy now," he added when her shoulder bumped the wall and she cried out again. "Just feel with your feet and then make sure whatever ye stand on is solid before you put your full weight on it."

Niall gritted his teeth against the strain on his arm as the girl twisted and floundered to find her footing, her whimpers turning to sobs when she repeatedly slipped and banged against the sharp granite.

"I can't do it!" she cried. "Reggie, I don't want to die!"

"Calm down!" Reggie shouted. "Niall won't let you fall," he continued, his tone turning soothing. "He's stronger than Iron Man, Mist. If we have a boy, we're going to name it after him. You need to keep trying for our baby."

A small cascade of dirt fell at the same time Niall became aware of a shadow moving over him again. "Don't come down here!" he growled, afraid one of them was going to try climbing down to help her.

"I can see a small ledge just to the right of your knee, Misty," Reggie said. "It's wide enough for you to stand on with both feet. Raise your right foot."

Niall gave another growl when the lass started jerking again, then bit back a curse when a good deal of her weight lifted and the pain of a hundred stabbing daggers shot up his arm. "Don't move," he said tightly, not daring to release his hold on the trembling girl. "Just stand on the ledge and get your bearings."

"Niall," Reggie said. "I have a tow strap in my four-wheeler."

Finally able to look up, Niall saw Reggie hanging out over the edge, the side of the boy's face already swelling and his mouth oozing blood. "Birch, do ye have a firm hold on the jacket?"

"I do," she answered, although Niall couldn't see her. "And it's anchored."

"Even Shep has his teeth clamped on it," Reggie added, actually grinning.

"Then go get the strap," Niall said, looking at the wall between him and the girl as he surreptitiously rolled his right shoulder to relieve some of the sharp daggers — figuring the last thing he needed was for his arm to go numb.

Where in hell was Nicholas?

"He . . . he intended to kill me," Misty sobbed, glancing down into the chasm. "My dad was going to . . . He wanted to throw me away." She looked at Niall, her large, frightened eyes filling with tears. "M-my mom's dead."

"There's a chance she landed in a deep pool," Niall told her, wanting to deal with one situation at a time. He carefully adjusted his hold on her jacket to see if his hand would cooperate, and gave the girl an encouraging smile. "Your mama appears to be made of stern stuff, lass, and is probably clinging to a rock waiting for us to climb down and fish her out. Do ye feel steady enough for me to move over beside you?"

"No, don't let me go!"

"I need both of my hands to get to you. The ledge you're on is solid and the sleeve you're holding is anchored. Lean into the wall and see if you don't feel steady. I'll keep holding on while ye try."

"I have the strap," Reggie called out just as more dirt fell on them. "Do you want me to send it down with a large loop threaded through your end?"

"How long is it?" Niall asked.

"Twenty-five or thirty feet."

"Can ye tie it to something strong enough to hold our combined weight?"

"There's a pretty good-sized tree close by," Reggie said after a moment.

Even though the top of his head was only three or four feet below the lip of the cliff, Niall didn't dare risk using a slipknot for fear of snapping Misty's ribs if she lost her footing and fell. "Secure it to the tree, then lower the end without making a loop. I'll tie it around Misty and you and Birch can haul her up." He shot the lass a smile. "You ready to let me move beside you?"

Her eyes uncertain and her face as pale as new snow, Misty sucked in a shuddering breath and adjusted her grip until she was holding the sleeve with one hand, then grabbed a piece of protruding ledge with the other and nodded. "I . . . I'm ready."

Niall loosened his grip on her jacket, gritting his teeth against the pain shooting through his arm that now felt like lead. Transferring his weight to his left leg, he let go of the crag he'd been gripping, found a new handhold closer to her, then slowly placed his right foot onto the same ledge she was standing on. "You're okay," he said at her gasp when he pressed against her. "I'm just going to lean here beside you. Move your shoulders away from the wall, Misty," he instructed when the strap appeared. "I need to wrap it around you just under your arms and tie it off. That's my girl," he said when she leaned back ever so slightly.

Niall slipped the strap around her trembling body, tied it snugly, then slowly worked the knot around to just below her bosom. "There now, you're tied to a sturdy tree, so even if ye slip you won't fall. Let go of the jacket sleeve." He looked up to see Reggie watching them, the boy's face also pale except for the angry bruise and drying blood. "Birch, you can pull up the jacket now." He grinned when her head popped over the side. "Do ye have any strength left to help Reggie?"

"Oh yeah. I guess this means I have to take back every bad thing I've said about you," she said over-brightly before turning her smile on Misty. "Let me and your big hero boyfriend do all the work, Misty, and you just concentrate on the kiss you're going to give him." She looked back at Niall. "Are we ready, people?"

"When I say pull," he said with a nod. He checked the strap around Misty then lowered his hand to her backside. "I'm not getting fresh," he said when she gasped. "I'm going to steady you. See the crag we're both holding on to?" he asked, nodding at their hands. "Use it as a toehold on your way up. But keep your elbows as close to your sides as ye can, so you don't slip out of the strap." He gently brushed some hair off her face. "You're a brave young woman, Misty, and Reggie is a lucky young man."

"H-how can you say that? I've never been so scared in my life."

"I knew you were brave the moment ye said you didn't want to die." He gave her a wink, then looked up to see Birch smiling again and Reggie damn near close to tears.

"Pull," he said with a curt nod.

Their heads disappeared. "It's only a few feet, Mist," Reggie said through gritted teeth as the strap tightened. "And then I'm expecting that kiss."

Hell, Niall was tempted to hire the kid as his final officer. It was rare to find such competence and composure in someone Reggie's age, since seventeen-year-old boys were more known for chasing girls than risking their lives to save them.

"Up ye go," Niall said, steadying Misty as she slowly rose away from him, even as he wondered if Birch might feel inclined to give *him* a kiss.

Niall dropped his hand from Misty's backside to grab one of her flailing feet before she knocked him off the cliff, gave the girl one final push that sent her over the top, then leaned his forehead against the granite wall with a silent groan — not that anyone would have heard him over all the whooping and cheering.

A rain of dirt fell on him again. "We're sending the strap down just as soon as Reggie gets it untied," Birch said. "Chief MacKeage? Are you okay?"

Okay then; it didn't appear he was getting that kiss. "I'm fine, Miss Callahan," he said without lifting his head. "Don't bother with the rope; I'll just climb up."

"When?" she snapped when he still didn't move.

When I can feel my right arm again. "Soon," he said, not even having the strength to grin. When his single word was met with silence, and worried she might decide to climb down and drag him over the top herself, Niall took a deep breath and tensed against the pain he knew was coming. "Get out of my way," he growled so he wouldn't shout, reaching for another handhold and hoisting himself over the top — only to be grabbed by the belt as Birch attempted to drag him away from the edge.

"You idiot," she said, giving up and rolling him over, then shoving Shep away when the dog started licking his face. "Where are you hurt?"

"Not hurt. Just spent." He cracked open his eyes to find her giving him a visual inspection. "Even hulking brutes need to catch our breaths occasionally." When all that got him was a scowl, he lifted his head to see Reggie sitting on the ground cradling Misty, the two trembling teenagers hugging each other so tightly it was a wonder they could breathe. But knowing that if he didn't keep moving he'd be crippled with muscle spasms, Niall sat up with another silent groan and rolled to his hands and knees.

"Just lie still a minute," Birch said, stopping him from standing.

He lifted his head to look her directly in the eyes. "I need to go check the stream on the chance Sally Vaughn survived the fall," he said quietly so only she could hear.

Birch stood up with a gasp, then grabbed his sorely abused arm and tried hauling him to his feet. "I'll help you look," she said, giving another futile tug.

"What the — *Nicholas*?" Reggie said in surprise.

"Mama!" Misty cried, scrambling to her feet.

Niall looked in the direction the teenagers were running to see Nicholas walking out of the woods carrying Sally Vaughn, both the mythical warrior and definitely alive woman soaking wet. When Birch raced after them with a cry of relief — Shep following with an excited bark — Niall flopped back spread-eagle on the ground with a loud groan, guessing he'd have to forgive the tardy bastard.

CHAPTER EIGHT

Birch sat in the dark on the porch steps with Mimi on her lap, both of them looking down across the lawn at the campfire on the beach. But as she watched Chief Mac-Keage, with Mimi presumably watching Shep, Birch thought about how many times in the last eight years she'd considered walking away from her job, preferably before she became another casualty in a war that already had too many.

But then a day like today would inevitably come along.

Ike Vaughn was dead and, judging by the shredded fingers on the body the game wardens had pulled from the water nearly a mile downstream, the son of a bitch hadn't died instantly. And although that pleased her far more than it should, Birch was torn between being proud of and worrying over the fact that Sally had precipitated his demise. On the one hand there was nothing

152

more empowering for a woman than to free herself from years of oppression, but perversely, it could be even more victimizing if people saw her as a murderer. Or worse, if *she* did.

But there was a good chance Sally would make peace with her role in today's tragedy, most likely the very first time she found herself staring into the eyes of her grandchild. And thanks to one man's fearlessness, backed up by some pretty amazing muscles, that little miracle was going to happen five months from now.

Birch watched Niall awkwardly place another piece of wood on the fire and decided she really couldn't continue calling him Chief MacKeage, seeing how he'd saved her butt this morning — even if he had rewarded himself with a kiss. He'd also saved the girl, and had been on his way to go save the mother when Nicholas had suddenly appeared carrying Sally. Only there hadn't been any visible means of how the quiet, towering man had gotten there, Birch had realized as she'd followed Niall's truck back to town — with Nicholas driving the truck, Niall riding beside him and Shep in the backseat, and Sally and the two lovebirds riding with Birch in her car.

She lifted Mimi off her lap and held the

153

dog facing her. "I think it's time we start being neighborly, Mims, which means I have to stop growling at Niall and you have to stop snapping at Shep. But here's the thing; when we bring them our peace offering, try not to notice that Niall is hurt, okay? Because guys are funny about not wanting anyone to know they're in pain. You remember the two weekends you spent hiding in Dad's mudroom after he got shot and was so grumpy, don't you, until I gave in and just left you home with Mom?"

Niall had actually growled at *her* this afternoon when Birch had suggested — okay, insisted — that he let Dr. Bentley check him out when they'd taken Misty and Sally and Reggie to the clinic. But crumbling castle walls and saving young girls from falling to their deaths was apparently just an ordinary day for a *Scot,* and the one living next door could be a poster boy for stoicism.

Yeah, well, considering she had spent four freaking years being *brought down a peg* by her paternal grandfather, Birch guessed it would take more than a growling mountain of testosterone to scare her off. And so she set Mimi on the step, picked up the still-warm peace offering she'd filched the moment Noreen had gone to bed, and headed down the stairs with all the confidence of a woman whom a really handsome man had a powerful desire to kiss.

Mon Dieu, she couldn't believe he'd admitted that, and she sure as heck wished he hadn't *acted* on that admission not ten minutes later, because now all she could think about was when — or even if — he would kiss her again.

Because if he did, then by God she was kissing him back!

Well, not if they were anywhere near the park.

She didn't even care that the guy strapped on a gun before he left for work every morning, because really, what were the chances someone in this backwater town would be stupid enough to shoot a cop? She was pretty sure Spellbound Falls didn't even have any alleys, much less a couple of bad-ass street gangs fighting over them.

And anyway, it wasn't like she was husband-hunting or anything; cops didn't earn nearly enough money for her to consider ever marrying one. But that didn't mean she couldn't enjoy a bit of smooching or even crawl into bed with those amazing muscles, seeing how sex was on her list of reasons why she didn't hate men.

Yes, she'd actually made a damned list.

And she was pretty sure sex was right up there near the top.

So having a discreet affair with a man who had admitted he was attracted to her might actually be doable. Heck, it might even be fun to get up close and personal with all that muscle, since the guys she usually dated probably wouldn't even know which end of a pickax to *hold.* And as an added bonus, her having an affair with a real live highlander should also stop her mom from complaining about her nonexistent love life.

That he lived right next door might be tricky, though. It was bad enough they'd be within eyesight of the shelter, but earshot, too? On the plus side, since she didn't have her mom's propensity to fall in love with every guy who kissed her, Niall wouldn't have to worry about her getting all clinging and needy — something she should probably point out to him right after she kissed him back.

Realizing she was walking alone, Birch stopped and turned to see her *un*faithful canine companion standing by the door. She blew out a sigh and trudged back up the lawn. "So which is it; are you going to be Mighty Mimi tonight or Chicken Little?"

Birch couldn't help but smile when the dog's lips rolled back at the mere mention of the name Claude had given the tiny white puffball the first time she'd showed up at his house with her new puppy. Apparently taking it as a personal affront that she hadn't taken his suggestion to get a real dog, he'd started calling Mimi *Chicken Little* whenever they visited — which, now that she thought about it, was probably why her pet wasn't all that enamored with men, either.

But then, people couldn't pick their parents, could they? Although, to be fair, her father had had to live with *his* parents for *eighteen* freaking years. Well, plus the four that he'd moved back home when he'd taken custody of her, because really, what did a single guy know about caring for a little girl? It still confounded Birch as to how a bubbly, quirky teenager could have lost her virginity to such a serious, emotionally clueless young man — Hazel having shouted that latter attribute at the elder St. Germaines the day she'd swooped in and ripped her daughter from their coldhearted talons.

Hazel might be too trusting, but no one could ever accuse her of being a coward.

"Come on, Mighty Mimi," Birch urged, trying to sound excited. "Shep really is just an overgrown puppy." *With some pretty amazing muscles of his own,* she silently added, *and an equally fearless heart.* The dog had a darn good nose, too.

Mimi padded across the porch and down the stairs with all the enthusiasm of a canary going to a cat convention. "Just hop up on the log," Birch offered as they headed down the lawn, "and that way you'll be eye-level with Shep." She stopped at the edge of the beach when she saw Niall click off his cell phone screen and say something in what she assumed was Gaelic when Shep tried to sit up. "Can we share your campfire if we come bearing gifts?" she asked, holding out the towel-wrapped dish for him to see.

"Considering the day ye put in, I'd think you would long be in bed by now."

"I tried, but every time I close my eyes all I keep seeing is Ike Vaughn dragging his family over that cliff." She peeled back the towel and tilted the pie. "It's blueberry."

"Did Noreen make it?"

"It's nearly impossible to get food poisoning from a fruit pie. I brought forks."

He arched a brow. "Ye bring me a gift then expect me to share?"

"It's still warm from the oven."

He started to reach out with his right hand, but, without so much as a grimace, quickly changed to using his left hand to

158

pat the ground beside him. "I'll share on the condition you take the first bite."

"Noreen's being extra careful these days," Birch said dryly, walking around the log he was leaning against and handing him the pie, then sitting on the gravel beside him. She pulled a fistful of napkins out of her pocket and dug out the forks she'd wrapped inside them, handed one of each to Niall, then held her own fork poised over the dish and looked at him. "You really want me to take the first bite?"

"Did Noreen make this for you to give to me or for the shelter residents?"

"She made it and five more for the bake sale the grange is having tomorrow."

Up went that brow again. "Ye brought the police chief a stolen pie?"

Since the smell of cooking blueberries had been driving her crazy for the last two hours, Birch drove her fork down through the center of the crust and dug out a fork-ful, shoved it in her mouth with a hum of pleasure, then chewed and moaned and drove her fork into it again. "See, it not pwoisoned," she said around her second mouthful, using a finger to redirect an escaping blueberry when she caught Niall staring at her. "And it's weally good." Again she drove her fork into the dish that he was thoughtfully holding up to make the journey to her mouth shorter. Well, or else he was worried she might accidently stab his leg. "Noreen's pies always take blue ribbons at the local fairs, and the grange ladies charge double for them." She held the forkful of oozing, berry-laden crust level with his face, then shoved it in her mouth when he still didn't move. "Fine, be swubbon." She stopped chewing. "Wait, are you awergic to bwueberries? Or diabetic or sumfin?"

When all that got her was a scowl, she went back to chewing.

He set the pie down on his thighs and finally dug in. "Can I ask where Mrs. Vaughn and her daughter are?" he asked. "Once the state police finished questioning everyone, I assumed you would have brought them here." He shrugged — but only his left shoulder, she pretended not to notice. "Hell, I'm not even sure their house is habitable anymore."

Birch wiped her mouth with her napkin. "Sally has a sister living in the next town past Turtleback, and the woman probably broke the sound barrier coming to get them." She sighed, dropping her hands to her lap. "Reggie wasn't too happy about that, though. In fact, I was afraid he might try to run off with Misty after all."

"Nicholas is keeping an eye on the boy," he said after politely swallowing.

"Speaking of the giant, how did he get there so quickly? If he came directly up the mountain on an ATV like Reggie did, then why didn't he drive it to the Vaughns' house instead of leading the horse?" — which had been carrying Sally and Misty, while Birch had ridden on the back of Reggie's ATV with the teenager. Niall had also walked, with Shep leading the entire procession.

No one had mentioned going to look for Ike Vaughn.

"He likely ran," Niall said, just before filling his mouth with pie again.

"Up a mountain in under an hour from the time you called him?"

He shrugged while politely swallowing again. "Nicholas has really long legs."

"The guy doesn't talk much, does he? Dinner at the Salohcins' must be a real party." When all that comment got her was another scowl, Birch set her fork in the dish and wiped her mouth again as she looked around.

"She's right behind you, wedged between the log and the lip of the lawn," Niall said, obviously guessing she was looking for Mimi. He placed his own fork in the dish, then leaned across Birch — stoically pre-

161

tending it didn't nearly kill him — and set the massacred pie on a rock beside her. "Why don't ye try handing her to me."

Birch had to get to her knees to reach Mimi, then had to throw herself across the log when the dog un-wedged herself and tried to bolt for the house. "Chicken Little," she whispered, hoping to bolster her pet.

"Nay, she's no chicken," Niall said with a chuckle as he took Mimi and held her facing him. "She's wise enough to be *cautious.*"

Birch also pretended not to notice he'd said that while looking at *her.*

He lowered Mimi to his lap — the dog all but disappearing in his large hands — then spoke to Shep in Gaelic again, apparently releasing him. Shep simply raised his head and touched Mimi's nose, but immediately jerked back when his gentle greeting was met by rolled lips and a warning growl — just before Mimi tried to bite Niall's fingers.

Which, of course, only made Mr. Stoic chuckle again.

"How come you talk to Shep in Gaelic?" Birch asked instead of snatching up her trembling dog and running for the house before the poor thing peed herself.

"So a perpetrator we're trying to apprehend won't know what command I've given. And when it's given in Gaelic, Shep knows I mean business. Has Mimi not been handled by men very much?" he asked, his voice quiet and calm as he used his thumb to stroke Mimi's neck, completely ignoring her warning growls.

"Mostly just by my dad." Birch sighed. "Does it count if they spend time in the same room?"

Niall looked at her, his surprise obvious. "Ye see your father regularly?"

"Well, of course I do. He's my *father*. Before we moved here, I saw him at least every other weekend."

He dropped his gaze. "I'm sorry," he said, making Birch realize she had sounded defensive. "It's just that Hazel mentioned they had never married."

"No, but he was — is — an important part of my life." She sighed again. "Do you think I'm ever going to get Mimi to stop snapping at every man she meets?"

Niall looked up, the firelight revealing his amusement. "Not if she keeps taking her cues from you."

At least she hoped that was amusement. Maybe she should act on *her* powerful desire and kiss *him*.

"Birch."

Yeah, that would be a neighborly thing to

163

do. It certainly should let him know she was game for an affair if he was.

"Birch."

No, she better not, seeing how he was hurt. Because of course he'd want to pull her into his arms and kiss her back, and he'd hurt himself even more.

"Miss Callahan."

Well there he went growling at her again. Only not in a mean way, exactly, but rather . . . well, sort of carnal. "What?" she asked, lifting her gaze to his.

"Do I have blueberries on my chin?"

She squinted at him. "Ah, no. Why?"

"Because ye look ready to come at me the same way ye did the pie."

She snapped her gaze to his again, and yup, the laughter she'd heard in his voice was dancing in his eyes. But she also saw something else; sort of an underlying . . . awareness that sent prickles of heat shooting through her. Nope, she better not kiss him. "So, do you?" she asked instead.

"Do I what?" he asked back, staring at her mouth again.

Want to have an affair with me. "Do you think Mimi's too old to learn to trust dogs and men?"

She almost laughed out loud when those gorgeous eyes narrowed. Which reminded her that *easy to confound* was right up there on her list of reasons she didn't hate men, probably not far from *easily distracted*. Heck, most guys lost their train of thought if a girl simply smiled at them. And apparently Scots were no exception.

"How old is she?"

"Who?" Birch asked, trying to remember the conversation. "Ah, she just turned five," she said, hoping to God they'd been talking about Mimi.

Shep crawled forward on his belly, but this time instead of going for her nose, the dog touched Mimi's paw — which made the little brat attack Niall's stroking thumb.

"Have ye been up to Nova Mare yet?" Niall asked.

Birch stopped in mid-reach as she was just about to rescue him and dropped her hands. "No, actually, I haven't. My interview with Olivia was here at the shelter. I have been to Inglenook, though." She smiled. "Olivia let me raid the resort's stockroom, and I filled my car with household supplies and all sorts of fancy little toiletries for the residents." She started to reach for Mimi again, but stopped when Niall shook his head.

"She's fine, Birch. Five years of being afraid isn't going to disappear in two minutes — or ever, if you keep rescuing her."

"I was rescuing *you.*"

"I've had worse mosquito bites," he said with a chuckle. "So what would ye say to my taking you to dinner at Nova Mare this Friday evening? Though Aeolus's Whisper is known for its world-class dining, the view of Bottomless is even more spectacular."

The man was actually asking her out!

Wow; a kiss and a date on the same day. And not just any old date, but dinner at Nova Mare's super-exclusive restaurant. *Mon Dieu,* she'd heard the surf and turf there was — Birch suddenly stiffened. But then she just as suddenly deflated. "Oh, Niall, please don't take me to such a fancy restaurant." She gave him a warm smile when *he* stiffened. "I'd really be just as happy going to the Drunken Moose or the Bottoms Up, or even to a restaurant in Turtleback."

"But I want to take you to Aeolus's Whisper."

"But you can't," she shot back, losing her smile. "I've heard all about Aeolus's, and it's too expensive."

"*I'm* paying."

"You can't," she repeated, "because you're a *cop.*"

There were several heartbeats of silence.

166

"What," he asked really softly, the growl back in his voice, "is that supposed to mean?"

Birch got to her knees to look him level in the eyes. "It means you can't afford to blow an entire week's salary on *one date,*" she growled right back at him. "You want to impress me, then rent a boat and take me fishing. Or better yet, invite me to go hiking on one of the trails along the fiord. Or on a picnic. Or kayaking. Or anything," she said, waving at nothing, "that doesn't look like you're trying to buy your way into my panties."

Birch sat back on her heels when Mimi was suddenly shoved into her arms, and actually flinched when Niall got to his feet and silently walked away. Shep also stood, hesitated as he looked at her, then padded up the lawn after his master.

"Hey," she called after them. "You can't just leave the campfire burning."

Birch then called him a nasty name — not out loud — when he disappeared into the darkness without responding, only to flinch again when a plume of steam suddenly shot into the air with a boiling hiss. She looked over to see a wave lapping at the hot coals and realized he wasn't worried about the campfire because the tide was putting it out.

"So much for making peace with our neighbors, Mims." She cuddled Mimi to her chest and dropped her chin onto the dog's head with a heavy sigh. "So maybe I did get carried away thinking we could have an affair, but in my defense, I honestly felt Niall might be different."

Yeah, right; he was a guy, wasn't he? And weren't guys always looking for a way into a girl's panties that didn't involve having to reveal anything about themselves? Like how empty their bank accounts were, that they had a crazy ex-girlfriend stalking them, four children they somehow forgot to mention until *after* they got in her panties, or the fact that they'd moved back in with their parents for the *third* time because their *third* wife had gotten the house in the divorce.

Oh yeah, she'd dated some real winners.

And she'd still bet her trust fund none of them could use a pickax.

That's why his being a police officer had made Birch think she could have an affair with Niall. Who defined the saying "what you see is what you get" more than a cop? Usually blunt to a fault, with no pretense or hidden agendas — well, other than getting into her panties — and no "surprise, I'm broke," because she *knew that already.*

Mimi wiggled free and bolted for the

house when another plume of steam hissed toward them, and Birch stood up with another sigh. She picked up the pie dish, but went perfectly still when a large bird silently swooped out of the darkness and landed on the other end of the log. She eyed what she hoped to God was a seagull — what other birds were so bold when they smelled food? — eyeing her back.

Wait; seagulls liked blueberries, didn't they? Birch recalled visiting the Maine coast with her dad a few years ago and seeing purple bird poop splattered all over the granite shoreline in Acadia National Park. And when she'd asked the park ranger — who'd been trying to keep people from climbing on the railing and falling into Thunder Hole — why the poop was purple, he'd laughed and said it was blueberry season.

"Hey, bird, you hungry?" she asked, fishing the sticky forks out of the pie. She nearly dropped the dish when a virtual sauna of steam shot into the air just as the small wave responsible lapped at her sneakers. Birch looked back at the log, only to gasp in surprise when she found the bird now standing less than four feet away.

Definitely close enough for her to see it was holding something in its mouth.

There was just enough firelight left for her to also see it had sharply defined yellow eyes, but that its beak looked a little short and pointy for a seagull. It had some really impressive talons, too — putting her in mind of her paternal grandfather — although she'd always thought gulls had webbed feet. And this guy or gal was positively huge. But some species of seagulls were really tall, weren't they, and didn't some have motley brown and white feathers?

Then again, maybe it was a fledgling . . . something that thought a human holding a pie worked just as well as a mama bird holding a fish.

It padded even closer, now eyeing the dish in her hand instead of her. "Okay. Okay," Birch said with a laugh, glancing around for a place to scrape out what was left of the pie. "But I better not find my car decorated with purple splats tomorrow," she continued, deciding to just spoon it onto the end of the log, figuring the first rain would wash off any remaining juice. This was their campfire log, after all, and the residents preferred sitting on it instead of the cold gravel beach. "But feel free to use that big black pickup for target practice if you want."

The bird walked right up to Birch as she

tilted the heavy glass dish and scraped the pie onto the log, but instead of diving in, it pushed whatever it was holding against the sleeve of her jacket.

"Wow, aren't you tame," she said, straightening and setting the forks in the dish, then carefully reaching out. "Are you trying to give me this as a thank-you?" No sooner had the bird dropped the surprisingly heavy object into her outstretched hand than it started gobbling down chunks of crust as if it were starving. "You're welcome, Mr. Bird," she said, figuring it had to be male for having already learned how to get a girl to part with her . . . well, in this case, her food.

Birch bent toward the campfire to study what appeared to be a barrette, the clasp's weight and color making her think it was made of gold as she ran her thumb over what she suspected were genuine pearls covering what looked to be an ornately carved . . . seashell, maybe?

"Well, good-bye," she said, slipping the gift in her pocket as she watched the pie disappear down the bird's gullet. Feeling summarily dismissed, Birch walked the length of the log and up onto the lawn, but turned back to make sure the tide really was putting out the campfire before looking at the bird again. "Just remember it's the black pickup, not the little red crossover. Oh, and you get points for every time you nail his windshield, and I'll even steal you another pie if you manage to hit his driver-side door handle."

The man had no call to be acting all offended and storming off, Birch decided as she trudged up the lawn. Because really, how come it was okay for him to say he wanted to kiss her — when she was angry, of all things — but it wasn't okay for her to be up front about what she wanted? Which reminded her; *easily offended* was on her list of reasons why she *should* hate men, right up there with *easily confounded*.

Yes, she'd actually made two lists — the first one when she was seven and had been angry at *grand-père* St. Germaine, and the second one after reading the steamy romance novel she'd found hidden under the cushion of her mom's chair when she was fifteen — and *easily confounded* was on both, because sometimes it was an endearing trait and sometimes it was just plain annoying.

But was it her fault the men in her family — on *both* sides — had the personalities of amoebas? Well, that was a mean thing to say about amoebas, because she'd bet they were happy in their one-celled ignorance, whereas both of her grandfathers had been critical, opinionated, ornery men. Her three maternal uncles weren't exactly joys to be around, either, and she could only thank God that her father was an only child.

Hazel had been the odd duck of the Callahan family and likely wouldn't have survived her childhood if not for her grandmother Hynes. Birch had been six when *Grand-mémère* had died in a violent explosion, but she'd known the woman long enough to realize where her mom had inherited her quirkiness. They had both inherited Annette's fortune — although Birch had considered that substantial blessing more of a curse during the four years Fredrick St. Germaine had gone out of his way to make sure the little heiress living with him didn't feel superior.

She'd been *six;* what had she known about social classes? She'd been too busy missing her mother and mourning *Grand-mémère,* while trying with all her heart to get her parentally challenged father to love her. It had been during those four years that Birch had learned some battles were better fought in silence and some by simply not showing up armed — if at all.

But what really amazed her was how *she*

173

had turned out so normal.

Birch walked up the dark porch stairs, slowly opened the squeaky screen door, and quietly walked inside the silent house behind Mimi. "You might as well go up and crawl in bed with Mom," she whispered as she walked to the sink and filled the pie dish with water before looking around for someplace to hide it. "I'm going to read for a while," she told Mimi, opening a bottom cupboard door and setting the dish and two forks inside, then going back to the sink and washing her sticky hands. "Oh, and Mims," she continued in a whisper, making the dog stop in the hallway and look back. "You were definitely Mighty Mimi tonight. But I hope you noticed that Shep really is only trying to get to know you and not eat you. And I thought he took your rebuff like a gentleman." *Unlike his master, who stormed off in a huff,* she silently added as Mimi padded upstairs.

Birch turned on the light over the kitchen table, pulled the bird's gift out of her pocket, and sat down to study it. She couldn't find any maker's marks or hallmarks saying what the metal was, though. Heck, it didn't even say it was made in China.

It looked old; not *worn* old, just . . . well,

it appeared to be an antique.

She was fairly knowledgeable about jewelry, since she and her mom had inherited a king's ransom in jewelry from *Grandmémère* — almost all of which was in a bank deposit box in Montreal, because who wore fancy jewelry in the wilderness, anyway? And there were at least six barrettes that she knew of in the collection, but nothing as old-looking as this one. Heck, if she didn't know better, she might think it was more ancient than antique.

Then again, it just as well could be a reproduction.

Either way, it looked expensive; certainly not something a bird should be flying around with, much less exchanging for leftover pie. But lots of birds were notorious for snatching up shiny objects, weren't they? And Spellbound Falls drew ultrarich tourists from all over the world, so maybe her visitor tonight had filched it off a beach towel where some idiot had left it while she'd gone swimming.

Birch grabbed the grocery list pad from the center of the table, tore off one of the blank pages, picked up the pencil, and began her note with *Dear Chief MacKeage.* She explained that a really large bird — describing as best she could because it had been so dark and saying she initially thought it was a seagull — had given her the barrette tonight in exchange for some pie. Birch then went on to explain she hoped he had a lost-and-found drawer in his station's safe, unable to keep from smiling at her dig that he didn't *have* a station, much less a safe. Then she added she was certain it was an expensive — underlining *expensive* — barrette, on the chance the easily offended jerk thought about keeping it to give the next woman he had a powerful desire to kiss.

And finally, because she just couldn't resist, Birch added that she hoped he didn't find any purple splats decorating his monstrous, manly pickup in the morning.

Folding the note around the barrette as she walked to the counter and pulled a plastic sandwich bag out of a drawer, Birch slipped the barrette and note inside and headed back outdoors. She let her eyes adjust to the darkness, then made her way over to Niall's truck and, praying he didn't have it rigged with an alarm, tried the driver's door. Finding it locked, she climbed up on the running board, lifted the windshield wiper and tucked the barrette under it, then looked up at the star-studded sky.

"This truck, Mr. Bird," she said softly, holding on to the outside mirror with one hand and gesturing at the truck's windshield with the other. "Cover it in bright purple splats and I will be your friend for life."

Her moral obligation done, Birch returned to the house, kicked off her shoes and hung her jacket on the peg by the back door, then headed into the living room and pulled the familiar book off the bottom bookshelf. She flopped down on the couch and stretched out, propped the thick, heavy tome on her belly with a sigh, and opened it to the title page.

She smiled as she ran a finger over the handwritten *Happy Birthday, little cadet. Love, Dad,* then flipped to the bookmark and once again started reading how to break down and clean any of several caliber Smith & Wesson automatic pistols.

Oh yeah; they hadn't invented a pill that could put her to sleep any quicker than her seventh-year birthday gift — which was why its pages were worn ragged and all but falling out of the binding.

CHAPTER NINE

Fairly certain the symbol carved into the unsettling surprise he'd found on his windshield this morning had something to do with Atlantis, Niall had driven a mile farther down the camp road rather than into town. He was just glad Birch had thought to put the hairclip and note in a plastic bag, seeing how it had taken several buckets of hot water to wash off the large bird droppings that had hit his windshield dead center — having assumed the culprit had been a seagull until he'd read Birch's even more unsettling note. Now standing at the end of Titus's driveway as the magic-maker studied the hairclip, Niall stopped in the middle of surreptitiously rolling his shoulder when he spied Shep licking the plate Rana was holding as she sat on her porch steps, and hoped like hell she wasn't feeding the little beggar her husband's breakfast.

"I could heal that shoulder if you wish,"

Titus said without looking up.

"Thank you, but it's doing a fine job of healing itself."

Titus lifted his gaze. "For such intelligent men, you MacKeages are uncommonly suspicious of the magic."

"Likely because it's caused us more problems than it's solved."

"You can blame Pendaär for bumbling his spell and bringing your father and the others here along with Greylen. Also blame de Gairn," Titus added dryly, "for upsetting the Continuum to the point he nearly wiped out mankind. And if I'm not mistaken, it was Winter MacKeage who finally set things right." He arched a regal white brow. "Maybe it's the women who should be kidnapping you warriors."

"I'm not so sure Duncan and Alec would agree with ye, as they seem content with the way their courtships turned out."

"Speaking of intelligent women," Titus went on with a grin, lifting his other hand, which held the decidedly sarcastic note. "Some might consider your Miss Callahan as being more abrasive than spirited."

"Aye," Niall said on a sigh. "She does seem to get riled easily. Last night when I asked to take her to dinner at Aeolus's, Birch informed me that police officers can't afford to spend an entire week's salary on one date, after which she accused me of trying to buy my way into her bloomers."

"But is ending up in bed together not the very point of dating?"

Niall couldn't help but crack a grin. "Well, aye, eventually." He sobered. "I just don't care for being accused of having ulterior motives when all I wanted was a date."

"Have you considered that Miss Callahan might not be all that enamored with men in general and maybe police officers in particular?"

"When we were trapped in Vaughn's cellar yesterday, Birch made a point of saying she doesn't hate men. Although she did admit she doesn't care for macho idiots who think every problem can be solved with brute force."

Titus eyed him speculatively. "And yet you seem quite attracted to her."

Undecided where this was going, and thinking only a suicidal idiot would outright lie to Titus Oceanus, Niall merely nodded.

"But you find modern courtship difficult to fathom."

That made him chuckle. "Modern *science* is easier to fathom. Back in my old time, all that was required was for a man to declare his interest in a lass, prove he could protect her and the babes they would have, and do a bit of wooing." Knowing the powerful magic-maker had access to all the knowledge contained in the Trees of Life, the past as well as the present and future, Niall hesitated, but then decided he didn't have anything to lose by asking. "I would probably have a better chance of wooing Birch if I knew what had happened in her past to make her so short-tempered with men in general and police officers in particular."

Up went that regal brow again. "So you're willing to endure several days of pain rather than let me heal your shoulder, but you don't have a problem using the magic to help you get in a woman's bloomers?" Titus shook his head. "You must embrace the entire journey, Niall, to truly appreciate the destination."

"It was just a thought," he said with a shrug, only to immediately regret the action when sharp daggers shot across his shoulder blade. He hadn't wanted to feel beholden to the elder theurgist, anyway — not that bringing him to this century hadn't indebted him enough already. "So, do ye recognize the hairclip?"

Obviously not wanting to leave the subject of women in general or Birch in particular, Titus frowned down at the clip. "This barrette was in one of the satchels of provisions I manifested for Rana when we were hiking back from our shipwreck on Bottomless several weeks ago."

"And you think a seagull found the bags and took a liking to a shiny object?"

"No," Titus said quietly, slipping the hair-clip in his pocket. "A gull would have immediately recognized its origin and brought it directly to me."

Niall felt the fine hairs on his neck stir. "The new god," he said softly. "You told us ye saw him fighting the demons not far from where you were forced to abandon the satchels." He nodded at the note Titus was still holding. "But if the bird was the new god or his emissary, why give the hairclip to Birch?"

"Likely to let us know that he did indeed survive," Titus said, also slipping the note in his pocket. "And personally, I couldn't think of a better way to prove that I had gained command of the magic than to get within a mile of another deity's home." He went back to looking speculative, despite his grin. "As for giving the barrette to Miss Callahan, maybe the forest god is also attracted to pint-sized spitfires."

Niall didn't know which bothered him more: that they had a new and obviously powerful magic-maker to deal with or that the bastard had taken a shine to Birch.

"Forgive me for intruding, gentlemen," Rana said as she walked out the driveway — her smile implying she wasn't the least bit apologetic as Shep pranced beside her like the besotted beggar he was. "But I didn't want our hero to leave before I added my own admiration to what will surely be a throng of adoration in town today."

"Be mindful of his arm," Titus said when Rana clasped Niall's sleeve. "As I believe that's the one he injured saving young Miss Vaughn yesterday."

"Oh, I'm sorry." Only instead of letting go, Rana gently ran her hand up his bicep and patted his shoulder, her smile turning as lopsided as her unpainted and crooked little seaside cottage. "But then, I imagine you don't mind pulling a few muscles to save the life of a young girl, do you, Laird MacKeage?"

"Nay," he said, fighting an urge to roll his shoulder again when each gentle pat she gave him sent hot pinpricks pulsing down his arm.

"I happened to be at the clinic visiting Maude yesterday when you brought in Reggie and the Vaughn women," she went on, her eyes crinkling with mischief as she reached up with her other hand and used the sleeve of her fleece to polish the badge pinned to his jacket. "And your Miss Callahan told me that Misty wasn't the only damsel you rescued. You also apparently demolished a cellar foundation just like your *ancestors* used to crumble castle walls. Yes, I believe she specifically said *castle*."

Niall wondered if *his* Miss Callahan had been snickering as she'd related that part of their adventure. "Did Birch also happen to mention that she has the riding skills of a newborn, the temper of a termagant, and a vocabulary that I suspect would have *me* blushing if I knew French?"

"She did mention something about galloping to the rescue on a plow horse," Rana said, her eyes now sparkling with laughter as she gave his shoulder one final pat before dropping her hand. "And I wouldn't have thought anything could make a big strong highlander blush, much less a pint-sized spitfire."

Was there a reason his romantic pursuit of Birch had become a spectator sport?

"If you'll excuse me, ma'am," Niall said with a slight bow — proud of himself for finally learning not to use "her highness" but still not quite brave enough to call the regal woman by her first name. "But I'd best be getting into town to make sure the traffic is moving smoothly, as I heard the grange ladies are putting on a bake sale in front of the church again this morning."

"Yes, leave us to finish our business, wife," Titus said, making Niall wonder about the edge in his voice. "And please reheat my breakfast."

Niall couldn't tell if Rana was scowling or smiling as she glanced toward the licked-clean plate sitting on the porch. "Yes. Well. I believe I'll work off *my* breakfast by walking into town to see what baked goods might catch my eye. As for your breakfast," she added as she strode to the house, "I'm sure you remember how to work the cookstove, don't you, my love?"

Nay, definitely not smiling, Niall decided.

"I'm sorry, MacKeage," Titus said, the edge still in his voice as he watched his wife walk away. "But I swear three-year-old Ella has more restraint when it comes to using the magic."

"Excuse me?"

"That roof was only *half* as crooked before Rana decided to try straightening it herself," Titus went on, gesturing toward the house as he shook his head. "I have no idea what possessed me, after forty years of wedded bliss, to persuade my wife that she is just as capable of working the magic as I am." He looked at Niall, his grimace ruined by the gleam in his eyes. "I can put the pain back in your shoulder if you wish."

Niall snapped his gaze to the house in time to see Rana disappear inside, even as he flexed his perfectly healed shoulder. "Sweet Lord," he whispered, looking at Titus, "she has command of the magic?"

"A rudimentary command," the theurgist said dryly. "Couple that with a burning desire to fix *everything,* and I assure you I wasn't jesting when I said my granddaughter has more restraint. Don't worry, Mac-Keage," he added with a chuckle, "your arm isn't going to suddenly fall off."

Niall firmed his slackened jaw and wiped what he assumed was a look of horror off his face. "Are you and Mac truly not going to do anything about the new god?" he asked, deciding to get back to the original subject and save worrying about his arm falling off for later.

"What is it you think we should do?"

"Maybe find out if he is friend or foe? Despite only speaking with the colony's leader a couple of times," Niall went on when Titus merely looked at him, "I can't say that I trust Sebastian. It's my understanding the original group formed on the belief the earthquake four years ago was a magical event, and that they came here hoping to find a way to harness it to aid mankind. At least that was their intention until Sebastian showed up and persuaded them to call forth a new god to help control the energy."

"But you believe Sebastian has another agenda," Titus said quietly, "other than helping humanity?"

"I think the man is only interested in his own pursuit of power. Did Dante not say that more men of his ilk have been joining the colony these last few weeks?"

Titus nodded. "It appears Sebastian is moving his followers from a previous commune to this one. Dante feels the slow migration is deliberate so as not to call attention to themselves."

"And if Sebastian has the power of a god backing him?" Niall asked. "Ye said yourself that the new entity already has a strong command of the magic."

Up went that imperial brow. "So you've decided he will be Sebastian's puppet, rather than wonder why he hasn't let the colony know he's already here?"

"I assumed he was learning the extent of his power before showing himself." Niall blew out a sigh. "I'd just like to know what to expect, is all, before the people I've promised to serve and protect find themselves at the mercy of a madman who has the backing of a powerful new magic."

"We can't really help you with Sebastian, but you have my assurance, Niall," Titus said quietly, "that should your new *god* prove an adversary rather than an ally, mankind will have Maximilian's backing. And mine, should my son need assistance." He grinned. "You're on your own, though, if the entity has taken a liking to your Miss Callahan."

Not willing to return to that subject, Niall opened the door of his truck and motioned for Shep to jump in, then turned back to Titus. "Ye called him a forest god; are you saying his energy is rooted in the land?"

"From what I've seen of him so far, that would appear to be the case." Titus hesitated, then added, "The majority of the colonists who called him forth are original settlers, meaning it was *their* altruistic intentions that caused him to manifest. And because we have vowed not to interfere in man's free will, Maximilian and I must content ourselves with waiting to see how this plays out." He nodded. "While keeping Dante at the colony as our eyes and ears, of course."

Niall merely nodded back and got in the truck.

"Meanwhile," Titus continued before Niall could close the door, "I plan to take a stroll along the shoreline this morning. And if my timing is such that I happen upon Miss Callahan on the beach and thank her for helping return my wife's barrette, I could also mention that an anonymous citizen has provided you two free dinners at Aeolus's as a reward for your heroics yesterday."

"Thank you, but I'm going to give your suggestion to 'embrace the entire journey' a try first."

"Very well," the theurgist said, grasping the door to hold it open. "Oh, by the way; did I hear correctly that you've hired two new officers?"

Niall nodded. "Sam found them, actually. I believe they were in his old line of work and were supposed to have arrived last night."

"That leaves you with only one position to fill."

"Aye. And with luck, the right man will happen along before I'm forced to hire one of the women applicants."

"Times have changed, Niall, and keeping the peace requires more brain than brawn in this century."

"Firearms may be great equalizers, but there were still many instances when Jack Stone would have left a scene in an ambulance if not for his brawn."

"You can't fight progress, my friend."

Niall closed the door, started the truck, and rolled down the window. "I can damn well keep it out of my police force," he said with a grin. "And if ye happen upon *my* Miss Callahan on your stroll today, maybe you could point out to her the difference between a seagull and a large bird of prey that probably would have gone after her dog if she hadn't been holding that pie. You might also suggest that if it ever gets close to her again, she might want to give it a good douse of bear spray to keep it from returning."

"Why don't you tell her yourself?" Titus asked as Niall put his truck in gear.

That made him chuckle. "You read her note. Did you get the impression she'd be interested in anything I have to say right now?"

"No," Titus said as he stepped away from the truck. "In fact, I got the impression she wouldn't mind spraying *you*. Enjoy today's leg of your journey, MacKeage," he called out as Niall gave a nod and drove away.

Niall lost his smile as he twisted and flexed his right arm, undecided how he felt about Rana healing him, then gave Shep a not-so-gentle nudge. "Ye wolfed down a whole bowl of kibble before we left home, ye big beggar; are ye deliberately trying to piss off the one person who can send me back to my original time? Because I hope ye know that would mean you'd have to live with Matt and Winter and their growing tribe of heathens." He scowled when his obviously unconcerned passenger licked some errant egg off his snout. "Or do ye like wearing ribbons and doll bonnets and having little Fiona call ye Muffin Face?"

Niall turned his scowl to the road ahead and also tried to decide what he thought of the revelation that the new god had already grown powerful. Because even though Titus had assured him they would have Mac's protection, Niall also knew that neither theurgist would interfere in man's free will — which meant he was on his own should Sebastian gain control of even a small amount of the god's energy.

Well, maybe not completely on his own, Niall thought with a grin, as Duncan and Nicholas were not bound by the same oath. In fact, both his cousin and the mythical warrior would likely relish a bit of magical sport.

Then again, maybe he should simply send *his* Miss Callahan after Sebastian.

Niall lost his grin again as he brought the truck to a stop at the main road. Why in hell had the new god given the hairclip to Birch? A forest god, Titus had called him. Well, the bastard certainly had manifested in the right place, seeing how Bottomless was surrounded by thousands of square miles of forested wilderness in Maine alone, and more than a couple hundred thousand if he included Canada. Hell, maybe he should persuade Sebastian to move his colony and the new god twenty miles northwest and let them be Canada's problem.

Seeing the women were already setting up tables in front of the church, since their grange hall was too far off the beaten path to catch all those tourist dollars, Niall pulled across the road and parked in front of the post office.

"Oh no ye don't," he said, pushing Shep back over the console, then reaching into the backseat. "Today we're going to see what kind of response ye get wearing your vest. You know, the one that says *Working police officer; do not pat or feed* on it," he drawled, having to drag Shep up off the floor and onto the seat again. "Oh, quit your grumbling," he said with a chuckle as he slid the vest over Shep's head. "It makes ye look important, and little Fiona said the stitching brings out the yellow in your eyes." He cinched the straps under Shep's chest, making sure they were snug. "And not only will it get ye *inside* the stores and craft shops; it's also bulletproof in case someone doesn't particularly like being run to ground by a four-legged police officer."

Niall got out of the truck, opened the back door, then reached inside and started gathering up all his equipment and paperwork, only to sigh when he saw Shep still sitting in the passenger seat. "Do you think I *like* walking around with a badge pinned to my chest? It comes with the job, so either man up and get out of the truck or sit there staring out the window all day watching the world go by."

Shep crawled over the console with another grumbling growl, and Niall finished filling the box he'd brought along this morning, then set it on the ground beside his disgruntled partner. He closed both doors and crouched down, grabbed Shep's snout, and looked the dog in the eyes. "When we meet Cole and Jake today, I don't want ye taking it personal that they're going to be my first officers," he explained, figuring he'd probably better lump the two men together until he took their measure.

When all he got for answer was what he could only describe as a canine glare, Niall picked up the box and straightened with a chuckle. "At least give it a day to see if that vest doesn't get ye into places you couldn't go before," he said, heading across the road. "I'm willing to bet instead of chasing ye off, the lifeguards won't stop a K-9 officer in uniform from making the beach part of your daily patrol, and you'll miss little Fiona less if ye spend some time playing in the sand and swimming with the children."

Mentioning Matt and Winter's five-year-old sprite, who absolutely adored Shep, might have been playing dirty, but it obviously did the trick, and the dog shot off down the road in the direction of the beach. Niall entered the Drunken Moose and ordered a couple of the premade breakfast sandwiches, three cinnamon buns, and a large coffee to go. He then paid the waitress, carefully arranged the food and coffee in the box, and was just starting out the door when Vanetta called his name and rushed over.

"Logan Kent didn't come in again this morning," she said without preamble.

"Yesterday was the first day he's missed in the last couple of weeks, and I'm worried he might be sick again. Not from my cooking," she drawled. "More likely his own." But then she sobered. "I called his house twice yesterday and again this morning, but he never picked up, and the Kents apparently don't have an answering machine."

"I'm going to Turtleback this morning, so I'll stop and check on him."

"Oh, thank you." Vanetta glanced over her shoulder when a man setting plates of food on the kitchen pass-through called her name, then started backing away and shaking her head. "I don't know why Logan doesn't just buy Noreen a new stove. He knows they need one, so what's he waiting for?"

"Maybe he's waiting for Mur's sneaky little Special Delivery Fairy to drop one off one of these nights," Niall said, using his back to push through the door as Vanetta rushed off with a laugh. He turned onto the sidewalk to find Titus just about to enter the restaurant — the magic-maker apparently *not* knowing how to run a cookstove to make his own breakfast, as his wife had suggested he do to replace the one Shep had eaten.

"There was something I forgot to mention this morning," Titus said, stepping away from the door and starting down the sidewalk. "If you don't mind, I'll just walk with you and see your new police station. So, Chief," he went on when Niall fell into step beside him, "I hear you've managed to tame the mob of zealots protesting the colony."

"I read up on the state laws and explained they're free to protest all they want as long as they don't interfere with traffic, trespass on private property, or physically stop anyone from going in or out of the colony. I also told them that if I get complaints they're trying to stop vehicles to give people their message, I'll write them citations." He sighed as they turned down the lane. "They're all quick to point out their right of free speech allows them to protest, but they seem to forget the colonists have rights, too, including freedom to worship the devil himself if they wish."

"Narrow-mindedness is also a timeless and worldwide affliction, I'm afraid," Titus murmured. "Anyway, Niall, I hope we don't end up adding to the problem by giving your protesters another target when my Atlantean holdouts arrive in a couple of weeks."

"They're coming here?" Niall asked as

they walked up onto the station porch.

Titus turned to him and shrugged. "They claim they're simply not prepared to face the real world in any century, so Maximilian has agreed to let them set up their own colony of sorts here. Many islands were part of the large track of timberland my son purchased on the eastern side of Bottomless four years ago," he said, gesturing at the fairly large island sitting some five miles offshore, "and we felt that island in particular is both isolated enough for them to be comfortable yet close enough to interact with the townspeople and acclimate to modern society at their own pace. And who knows? Maybe they'll even start contributing." He grinned. "I think you might find that most modern problems would benefit from an ancient perspective, which oftentimes could make all the difference between success and failure."

Not really surprised that he wasn't exactly sure what point the magic-maker was trying to make, Niall merely grinned back and shook his head. "I don't think we need to worry about the protesters bothering your people, unless they start renting Ezra's boats."

"Or they set up a new staging ground right here in the middle of town," Titus said, opening the door and walking into the station.

Niall gave a sigh as he followed, hoping the theurgist was only speculating and not speaking from knowledge he'd gained on a recent visit to the Trees of Life.

Niall turned down Logan Kent's driveway and immediately noticed two things, the first being the new mailbox made of thin strips of wood and fashioned to look like the old beehives traditionally woven from sea grass sitting on a perfectly straight, sturdy post where the dented and rusty old metal mailbox had once stood — or rather, had leaned. The second thing was that all the potholes in the quarter-mile gravel driveway had been graded smooth and the overgrown branches that had scraped his truck on his last visit had been cut away. All of which were nothing compared to what Niall found when the house came into view and he saw the roof was in the process of being reshingled, the steps and porch decking had been repaired and painted, and the ugly plastic banking that had been wrapped around the foundation on his previous visit was gone.

There was no way Logan Kent could have done all of this all by himself in the two

weeks since Niall had been here. The flag-
pole had been painted and straightened.
The garden was tilled and already planted,
he noticed as he continued looking around.
There was a new clothesline in the side
yard, the light color of freshly peeled cedar
indicating it was only a few days old, and
last year's growth of dead grass and brush
in the two-acre clearing surrounding the
house had been mowed.

Hell, the Special Delivery Fairy must have
decided to gift Logan with a small army of
elves instead of a new cookstove, because
there was no way an arthritic, recently sick,
seventy-something man could have done all
this work.

Logan came walking out of a fairly large
shed brushing sawdust off his shirt, spotted
Niall still sitting slack-jawed in his truck,
and walked over sporting a huge smile.
"The saw was running so I didn't hear you
drive in," he said when Niall's wits returned
enough for him to finally get out of the
truck. "What brings you out this way today,
Chief MacKeage?"

"Actually, you, Mr. Kent. Vanetta was
worried that you had suddenly stopped eating, since you weren't in yesterday or this
morning."

"I got wrapped up in a project I'm work-

199

ing on and didn't want to take the time to drive into town. Come on, I'll show you," he said, gesturing for Niall to follow as he headed back to the shed. "I've been setting up a saw jig so I can mass-produce beehives."

"Like the one out at the road?" Niall asked, stepping into a well-tooled wood shop.

"Naw; that was just a fun little thing I made from scrap wood. These here," Logan said, lifting a large square of wood off a wooden frame, "are real working hives. After I make several for myself, I'm gonna start selling them on the Internet. Only I'll send them out as kits people will have to assemble so it'll save on shipping costs."

Niall looked around the shop in amazement. "How many hives are ye planning to keep for yourself?" he asked, seeing three fully assembled hives lined up against the back wall, each on a handmade wooden platform with legs, making their total height between four and five feet tall.

"Silas suggested I start out with just five my first year to see how things go."

Niall brought his attention back to Logan. "Silas?" he repeated.

Logan nodded. "Silas French. He's been helping me out around here the last couple of days." He lifted the hive frame he was still holding. "It was his idea I start a beekeeping business. He said that five hives will give me a good crop of honey that I can sell at a pretty good profit right off this first year. And there'll be even better profits the following years, since I should make more than enough to pay off my equipment investment in the first two years while still having money left over to spend."

"Is Mr. French a friend?"

"Naw, he's just traveling through. I was down in Turtleback visiting one of my old logging buddies a couple a days ago, and on my way home I come across this younger fella wearing a large backpack walking up the road just outside of town." Logan gave an arthritic shrug. "He didn't look like a tourist, so I figured he might be heading to that colony down the road from here, and thought I might as well give him a ride since I was going right by it. Turns out he's just a guy who enjoys traveling around looking to work for room and board. You know, like a hobo." He grinned. "He asked me if I had any stuff I needed done, and I thought, why not — figuring, how much can one man eat?"

"He couldn't have accomplished all the work I've seen here in only a couple of days," Niall said, undecided if he was amazed or frightened by Logan's trusting nature.

"Naw, I did most of it over the two weeks since you been here, because . . ." His cheeks darkened as he set the hive frame back on the workbench. "Since I didn't have nothing else to do." He turned to Niall and grinned again. "Silas said that if I got some shingles he'd redo my roof, which he just started yesterday. And he dug the posthole for the mailbox and rigged up a pretty neat box grader we filled with rocks that I can haul behind my pickup to grade the driveway. And the man cooks a mean steak on a barbecue grill, so I figure for what it was costing me to eat at the Moose, I can feed the both of us. That means I'm getting work done for practically free."

Niall walked out into the yard and looked around. "Where's Mr. French now?"

"I don't rightly know at the moment. He's got a habit of suddenly stopping what he's doing and going for a walk in the woods. He says it clears his mind and feeds his soul. Chief MacKeage," Logan said, moving around to face him, "I know you might think I'm crazy to take in a complete stranger, what with all the weirdos and serial killers running around these days, but

Silas ain't like that. Within ten minutes of talking to the man, I realized he's just a free spirit. He's educated, too, and knows all sorts of stuff about nature. And he's not only good with tools, he's good at building them — like the grader we made for my driveway. And he understands business, especially what he calls cottage industries, that one person or a family can do to earn their living."

He grinned again, waving at the shed. "Like the bees. I can earn money from beekeeping almost right up until the day I die, because Silas explained it's more about keeping a close eye on things than a lot of hard physical labor. He said when I taste that first spoonful of honey out of my *own* hive, I'm gonna think there ain't nothing sweeter on earth."

He stepped closer, his cheeks darkening again. "And Silas said selling honey and beeswax and building and shipping out hive kits was a perfect business for a husband and wife to do together, so I'm getting everything all set up so I can surprise Noreen. She uses honey in a lot of her baking."

Niall looked around at all the work Logan had been doing to his homestead in the last two weeks and realized that except for the roof, it was all mostly aesthetic — a lot of little things that would give a woman pleasure to look at and have pride in when family and neighbors came calling.

Things that would make a wife want to come home.

"Have you seen Noreen?" Logan asked, as if reading Niall's thoughts. "You live right next door to that shelter she's staying at, don't you?"

"Aye. And I do see her just about every day, but only in passing."

"How's she *seem,* then? I mean, does she look to you like she's eating good and getting plenty of sleep and all? Norrie gets to working so hard sometimes that she forgets to eat, even when she's up to her elbows in food. And then she gets herself overtired and has trouble falling asleep at night. Oh, Lord, where's my manners?" he said, suddenly stiffening. "Norrie would take a strip out of my hide for not inviting you in for a cup of coffee."

Niall started to say he needed to be going, but decided to stick around and see if Silas French didn't return from his walk soon, as he'd like to meet the man. He just hoped Logan could at least run a coffee-maker. "Thank ye, I'd love a cup," he said, going to his truck and grabbing the box of cinnamon buns. "And since ye didn't come in town this morning, I thought I might bring the Drunken Moose to you."

CHAPTER TEN

It was early afternoon before Niall made it back to Spellbound Falls, never having made it to Turtleback because he'd spent the morning at the Kent homestead waiting for Silas French to return — which he never did. Niall strode down the lane, deciding to check out the company Logan was going to buy his beekeeping equipment from. He now had a picture in his phone of the catalog's back cover Logan had brought out to show him the honey extractor and protective clothing he intended to order this week.

Alarmed to see his station door open when he reached the bottom of the lane, Niall scaled the stairs and strode inside to find two men holding one of the desks several feet off the floor. "Oh, Niall!" Hazel Callahan said in surprise, abandoning her project to rush over to him. "I thought you were spending the day in Turtleback Station."

Niall glanced briefly at the men still holding the desk, noting their expressions had gone from resigned to guarded upon hearing his name, then looked down at the excited woman in front of him. "What are ye doing here, Hazel?"

She also glanced at the men, then took hold of his arm and led him out onto the porch. "I talked Sam into unlocking the station so I could start . . . ah . . . well, I'm getting your office organized," she whispered to his chest, her cheeks flushing as she finally looked up with a sheepish smile. "When Birch and I ran into Peg at the bake sale this morning, she mentioned you needed a secretary, so I decided . . . I thought you might . . ." Hazel threw back her shoulders on a deep breath. "I want the job."

"I don't have a secretary's salary in my budget yet."

Her smile turned brilliant. "That's perfect, because I don't want to be paid."

"Excuse me?"

"I don't need a salary." She clasped the front of his jacket and leaned closer, actually standing on her tiptoes. "I already have more money than I know what to do with, Niall. Only you can't tell Birch I told you, okay?" She dropped to her heels and went back to smiling. "What I don't have is a reason to get out of bed every morning."

"Have you discussed this with Birch?"

Hazel nodded. "On our walk home from the bake sale."

"And she agreed?" Niall asked, putting just enough edge in his voice to let her know he was expecting a truthful answer.

Hazel nodded even more emphatically. "Birch understands how important it is for me to feel needed." A twinkle came into her eyes. "Especially after I pointed out that she can't just drag me off to the middle of nowhere, then expect me to sit at the shelter reading romance novels all day." She turned serious. "You don't have to worry that I don't know what I'm doing. I've helped establish several large charitable organizations, so I'm quite skilled at running an office, dealing with people, and managing budgets." The twinkle returned, making Niall realize he was gaping. "And if you don't mind my bragging, I was the most sought-after fund-raiser in Montreal, which means I'm also very good at getting people to part with their money." She took another deep breath and went back to staring at his chest. "Please let me be your secretary."

"Done," he whispered so he wouldn't shout. "On the condition you deal with the town councils," he added, taking hold of her arm and ushering her back inside before she changed her mind. "Assuming you're the gentlemen Sam sent me," he said to the men now leaning against the desk, their feet crossed at the ankles and their arms folded over their chests, "I'm Niall MacKeage, and I believe you've already met my secretary, Hazel Callahan."

Both men said nothing; the dark-skinned gentleman appearing slightly bored and the blond-haired gentleman studying him with emotionless blue eyes — that is, until Shep came racing through the open door and the blond straightened to his feet.

"What the — Sam never said anything about a K-9 on the force. I don't like dogs."

"You'll like Shep," Niall said quietly.

The other man also straightened. "The dog's name is Shep?"

Niall merely nodded.

"*My* name is Shep."

"Then I suggest you change it."

The man pointed at the K-9 in question, who was ignoring everyone in favor of letting Hazel admire his vest. "Why can't you change *his* name?"

"Because I hired him first. So you might want to pick another name if ye don't want me picking one for you."

209

Jayme Sheppard went back to leaning against the desk with his arms folded in front of him again, his sharp brown eyes no longer appearing bored as he cracked a small grin. "I'll answer to Jake."

Niall looked at Cole. "I thank ye for your interest in the job, Mr. Wyatt. Hazel will write you a check for a plane ticket home."

That put some emotion in those eyes. "You're *firing* me? Just because I don't like dogs?"

"Nay. I'm firing you because I don't like men who don't like dogs." Niall crossed his own arms over his chest. "You want the job, I'll give ye two days to decide if you can work with Shep — on the condition he's willing to work with you."

"You're leaving the decision up to a *dog*? His brain is the size of a baseball."

"Yet he appears smarter than you," Jake muttered. "Get with the program, you moron, or *I'm* going to fire you."

"Hazel," Niall said, stepping in front of her. "I know it's not part of your job and I promise not to make it a habit, but would ye mind going to the Drunken Moose and getting me a sandwich? I missed lunch."

He almost laughed, she looked so disappointed. But apparently also astute, she gave him a wink and headed for the door. "Do you like ham?"

"Wait, let me give you some money."

She waved away his offer without stopping. "Nonsense. I'll just have Vanetta start us a tab and pay it once a month."

"Shep, go with her," Niall said, turning to the men, only to bite back a chuckle when Jake Sheppard stopped himself in mid-step. "So gentlemen, do ye need more time to gauge the size of my pecker or are ye ready to hear my rule of employment?"

"Don't you mean rules, as in plural?" Cole asked.

Niall shook his head. "The rule is I'm the only one who may break the rules. You will do everything by the book, and if something isn't in the book then you may not do it."

Jake's eyes widened. "*Everything?* Hell, man, if we had followed even half the stupid rules written by a bunch of government pencil pushers, we'd both have been planted six feet under a hundred times by now."

"How about if we promise to play nice instead?" Cole offered. "Jake and I are intelligent men, seeing how we're both still *alive,* and we actually like ordinary citizens."

"It's just bad guys we don't like," Jake interjected.

"And since they never follow the rules," Cole added, "how in hell do you expect us to catch them if *we* have to? We swear we won't shoot any innocent people."

"Deal," Niall said with a nod, turning away to hide his grin.

"Well, shit," Cole muttered. "I think I just felt *my* pecker shrink."

"What are we supposed to call you?" Jake asked.

"Niall will do," he said, looking around the room. "Did either of ye happen to see what Hazel did with my box of paperwork and equipment?"

"She was setting an empty box on the porch when we showed up," Cole said.

"We're getting uniforms, right?" Jake asked.

Niall stopped opening drawers on the larger of the desks. "I like the casualness of jeans and a button-up shirt. We're Spellbound and Turtleback's first venture into having policemen, so I prefer we blend in so they'll see us as one of them."

"Maybe you didn't notice," Jake drawled, "but I don't exactly look like a local. Hell, I've hardly even seen any black tourists around here."

"All the more reason to dress like a local," Niall pointed out.

"But I thought we'd be wearing uniforms," Jake countered. "Crisp blues with a big leather belt loaded down with Mace and a Taser and handcuffs and extra bullets and stuff. Are you saying we aren't even going to be issued hats?" He straightened away from the desk to glare at Cole. "The only reason I let you talk me into this gig was for the uniform." He turned to Niall, his expression desperate. "I just spent eleven years *blending in* to every stinking hellhole on the planet, and now I want to *stand out* on the streets of good old America."

Cole straightened with a snort. "No, you want a uniform to help you score some good old American tail." He looked at Niall, his expression derisive. "Actually, I signed on for the same reason. And it's not uncommon in small-town forces for the officers to wear uniforms and the chief to wear only a badge."

Niall decided the interview was over. Based on what he'd spent half the night reading in the files Sam had given him — which he didn't doubt had disclosed very little of their actual . . . skills — Jake Sheppard and Cole Wyatt were men he wanted on his side in a fight. And now that he had met them in person, he could see the three of them would be a good fit. No; the four of them, since Shep was also a good judge of character and hadn't gone for either of their throats.

"Done," Niall said with a nod. "Tell Hazel what ye want for uniforms."

He went back to opening drawers but stopped when his cell phone rang, the tone telling him it was 911 dispatch. "Mac-Keage," he said by way of answering, only to stiffen as the woman related the details of an automobile accident. "Where again, exactly?" he asked as he opened several more drawers and grabbed a portable two-way radio out of the last one. "And ye say the driver called it in herself and claims she's not injured?" he continued, motioning for Jake and Cole to follow as he headed outside. "Is she still on the line with you? Tell her to sit tight, that help will be there in ten minutes. I'll call you back on my truck radio." He pocketed his cell phone on his way down the steps and handed the portable radio to Cole. "How did ye get here?"

"In my new pickup," Jake said as they strode up the narrow lane. "Cole's truck is being delivered tomorrow."

"Then the two of you follow me."

"What about Shep?" Cole asked. "You want me to go get him?"

"He's on his way," Niall said, reaching his

214

truck where it was parked on the main road just as Shep came racing down the sidewalk. "There's only one car involved, but it's apparently gone into the river and is wedged up against the bridge. Rescue has been dispatched, but the closest full-time fire station is another thirty miles south of Turtleback, so it may take a while for them to get there." He opened the door and let Shep jump up, then climbed in behind the wheel. "Since ye don't have sirens and lights yet, try to keep right behind me."

"I had the truck outfitted when I picked it up in Bangor," Jake said, heading across the road to a bright blue, four-door pickup covered with enough chrome and emergency lights to blind the sun.

"We'll keep up," Cole said as he sprinted after his friend.

Niall hit his own siren and lights, checked for traffic and pulled a U-turn in front of the men, then keyed the mike on his radio. "MacKeage here. Are ye still in contact with the woman? You say she claims the car isn't sinking?"

"She's still on the line," the dispatcher assured him. "She told me the car is tangled in a large tree that seems to be holding it up, and that the river's current has her

215

pinned against one of the bridge abutments."

"And she's all alone? No passengers?"

"Only her. She said her name is Birch Callahan. The car is a late-model red Lexus crossover with Quebec license plates, but she can't remember the tag numbers because she bought it only a couple of months ago," the dispatcher continued when Niall stopped asking questions in order to regulate his breathing.

Sweet Christ, it was Birch. "Can she climb onto the abutment?" he asked.

"Hang on," the dispatcher said, which was followed by a silence that seemed to stretch on forever. "She claims a man told her to stay in the vehicle."

"Someone's there?"

Another silence, then, "Birch said she didn't actually see anyone; she just heard a male voice tell her to stay in the car when she tried to crawl out."

"I'm only two miles away now. Tell her to stay put."

"Ten-four. Millinocket rescue and ambulance are en route, and Turtleback Station managed to gather together a crew of five and is sending their ladder truck."

"I'll be off the radio, but two new officers are with me; Cole Wyatt and Jake Sheppard.

216

They'll relay information to you. Stay on the line with Birch."

"Roger that, MacKeage. Good luck."

Niall dropped the mike on the console as he approached the bridge just as an empty logging truck crossed it coming toward him. Apparently unaware anything was amiss, the driver didn't slow down until he saw the two pickups racing toward him with lights flashing and sirens blaring. Not that Niall saw any sign of an accident, either, until he spotted the churned gravel just before this end of the bridge. Hell, there were hardly any rubber marks on the road, indicating Birch hadn't even slammed on the brakes until the last minute.

He hit his own brakes, stopping right in the middle of the lane, and jumped out. "Block off the other end of the bridge," he told the men as they pulled up beside him. "But leave room for rescue to get through."

Niall walked toward the churned gravel marks and saw where it looked like a large tree had been uprooted from the riverbank, then scanned down the side of the bridge until he saw Birch's red car, indeed tangled up in a large tree, caught against the middle granite pier. He returned to his truck and grabbed a bagged throw rope from the cargo bed and started running. Cole and

Jake met him in the center of the bridge and all three looked over the rail to see Birch crouched on the passenger door of her car as it rested on its side about twenty feet below them, her cell phone pressed to her ear.

"I heard sirens but they went right by me. Oh, they're here!" she cried through the open window — her pale face flushing as she dropped the phone and grabbed the steering wheel to stand. "Niall, help me. It's going to sink!"

"Don't move," he called down, straightening once he saw her freeze. He took off his jacket and unstrapped his holster. "Get out the rope," he told Jake, setting the gun on his jacket on the ground. He slipped his backup weapon out of his belt and tossed it down along with his cell phone, then reached for the end of the rope.

"Let me go," Jake said. "I have technical climbing experience."

"Nay, this is personal," Niall quietly countered, tying the rope around his chest. "And I have plenty of climbing experience, some as recently as yesterday."

"Yeah, we heard," Cole said, pulling the remaining rope out of the bag as he leaned over and looked down. "The tide must be going out and the current is really battering that tree. Maybe we should start by tying it off."

Niall climbed over the rail. "Nay, we could end up in more trouble if the tree breaks free." He stood on the edge and looked at both men. "If it does, you cut me free as well. I'll stay with the car and pull Birch out once we've cleared the bridge. There's another throw bag in my truck, so head downriver after us if that happens. Shep," he said to the dog standing with his head shoved through the rail looking down at Birch. "Go get the other rope bag. Show him the empty bag, Jake."

Despite his look of disbelief, Jake picked up the throw bag and held it out.

"Fetch," Niall said. "In the truck bed, Shep. Get the bag. *Thoir leat."*

"Son of a bitch," Cole muttered, watching Shep hightail it for the truck.

Niall waited until Jake had the rope slung around his back and his feet braced against the concrete curb of the bridge, then gave the men a nod and started climbing down the side of the old metal structure. "You're going to have to lower me the last four feet to the top of the abutment," he called up.

"We're ready when you are."

Niall transferred his weight to the rope and used his hand to steady his descent, then found his footing again on the top pyramiding block of the old granite pier. "Give me some slack," he called up, grabbing one of the tree branches and stepping down several more blocks before turning toward Birch. He then gave an exaggerated sigh through the open window. "I'm getting sorely tired of rescuing women off ledges," he said through his grin. "Are ye sure you're not hurt, Birch?" he continued when she didn't even crack a smile. "Your neck and back and ribs feel okay?"

She shook her head but quickly changed to nodding. "I'm sure," she said, reaching up to him — only to shoot to her feet when a large branch suddenly snapped, making the car drop a good foot as she banged against the steering wheel. "Don't let me fall, Niall! I can't swim!"

"If ye end up in the water," he said calmly, prying her fingers out of his shirtsleeves, "I'll be going in with you. Now reach up and wrap your hands around my neck, then slowly straighten. That's it, give me a tight hug," he said, stretching down to grasp the waist of her pants. "I need tension on the rope," he called over his shoulder, slowly straightening when he felt the rope tighten. "As soon as you're free of the car, wrap your legs around me," he instructed, cupping her backside and lifting her out, then leaning back against an upper block with a sigh of relief as he held her trembling body.

"Oh, *mon Dieu*," she repeatedly whispered against his neck as she clung to him, only to suddenly scream when several branches snapped in rapid succession.

"Look out!" one of the men shouted from above. "It's breaking free!"

Niall splayed a hand over Birch's head and twisted to avoid getting caught on a branch when the tree slowly rolled and then swung around the pier with a shrieking groan as wood and metal scraped against the granite. He stayed twisted, watching the current rip the car from the tree as both floated under the bridge toward Bottomless, the car bobbing and bumping on rocks just below the surface.

Niall turned his head and smiled into Birch's heather-blue eyes as he brushed a thumb over her cheek. "We definitely have to stop meeting like this, Miss Callahan."

Her whole body shuddered as she released the breath she'd been holding while watching her car float away, and buried her face in his shoulder as she began trembling again. "C-can you just hold me a minute."

"For as long as ye need, lass," he murmured, leaning back against the granite.

"Everyone okay?" Jake called down.

Niall tilted his head back. "We're good. Give us a minute."

"Who are they?" she whispered without moving.

"My two new officers, Jake Sheppard and Cole Wyatt. Can ye tell me how you ended up in the river, Birch? Did ye swerve for an animal?"

"No," she said, still not moving but for her trembling. "A car shoved me off the road." She finally looked up, the skin on her pale cheeks taut with tension and her eyes distant with lingering — or remembered — terror. "I saw it in my mirror and thought the driver was crazy to pass just before a bridge, but when it got beside me . . ." She looked toward the riverbank and shuddered again. "I was about to slow down and let it go by when the woman passenger gave me the finger just as the car rammed my front fender. I went airborne," she whispered, her eyes going distant again, "and saw I was headed for a huge tree. I hit it dead center, and it should have . . . but it didn't . . ."

"It didn't what?"

She looked toward the bank again, but Niall knew she was really looking out her windshield. "It felt like I hit a ball of cotton. My air bags didn't even go off. And I swear

I heard a loud grunt as branches wrapped around the car and the tree fell backward into the river. And then we just floated until we got caught against the bridge," she finished with another body-wracking shudder.

Niall closed his eyes on a silent growl, undecided as to what part of her story he had the most trouble believing — that someone had deliberately run her off the road or that the new forest god had saved her life. "Ye told the dispatcher that a man instructed you to stay in the car when you tried to climb out, but that you didn't see him. Is that right?"

She merely nodded against his chest again.

"You two gonna be much longer?" Jake called down, making Niall tilt his head back to see him leaning over the rail. "Because I can send out for pizza if you want," the grinning idiot offered. "You prefer pepperoni or vegetarian?"

"Ignore him," Niall said, cupping her head back to his chest when Birch tried to straighten. "We'll go up once you've calmed down enough to make the climb."

"I'm calm," she said into his shirt.

Aye, that was the problem; the Birch he was coming to know would have reared up and snapped at him for that remark. But it was her very lack of emotion in relating her tale of how she'd ended up in the river that truly scared him. Hell, she hadn't cussed once. "Did ye recognize the woman in the car?" he asked, wanting to keep her talking.

"No."

"Could you tell if it was a man or woman driving?"

"No."

"Did you recognize the car?"

She lifted her head and frowned. "I think I saw it parked beside the road not far from here when I was heading home."

"You were heading north when ye saw it parked there?" he thought to clarify, since she'd been traveling south when she left the road.

She dropped her frown to his shoulder. "I was maybe four or five miles from Spellbound when my cell phone rang. It was Noreen, and she said a man had called the shelter saying he'd just passed a young woman carrying a baby and dragging a rolling suitcase behind her, and that the guy was worried because he thought the girl was crying and she was miles from any house."

"But you hadn't seen this girl on your drive up from Turtleback?"

"No, but I thought she might have come from one of the camp roads."

"But ye did see the car that hit you parked on the side of the road?"

She nodded again.

"What color was it?"

"White. Large. An older model."

"Was anyone in it?"

"I didn't see anyone," she said, melting into him again, her sigh giving him hope she was beginning to relax.

He still wasn't moving until she stopped trembling, though.

"Can I tell you a secret?" she whispered into his shirt.

"Aye."

"The tree talked to me."

"You said he told ye to stay in the car."

She leaned back again, this time looking directly at him. "He also told me not to panic, that he'd hold me up until help arrived," she went on, her eyes searching his. "Only there wasn't anyone there, Niall. The voice wasn't shouting down from the bridge; it was soft and calm and . . . and as close as you and I are now." She hesitated, then rested her forehead against his chest. "He asked me what I thought of the name *Kci-skitap 'cey Kcihq* or something like that," she continued, her voice growing devoid of emotion again. "I asked him how it was spelled, and he rattled off some letters and said it was Maliseet for *Great Man of the Forest.* I told him that was too complicated, so he asked what I thought of the name *Telos,* and I said . . . I told him I like it." He felt the lass hold her breath for a heartbeat. "I'm not hysterical, Niall. I know trees can't talk." She straightened again. "Please don't tell anyone this one talked to me, or . . . or that I talked back to it."

He pulled her against him so she wouldn't see his scowl. "I won't. Now if you were to tell me the bird that gave you the hairclip last night had talked to you, then we might have a problem," he drawled when he realized she was holding her breath again. "So, do ye feel up to taking a little climb?"

"You should have sent one of your new officers down for me," she said without moving but to release another heavy sigh as she relaxed into him even more. "Whether you'll admit it or not, you hurt your shoulder yesterday."

He lifted his right arm and waved and flexed it when she straightened in surprise, then gently tapped her gaping chin. "Not even a twinge," he said, giving her a wink. "Scots are also quick healers."

"Here comes the cavalry," Jake called down just as Niall caught the distant sound of a siren. "So come on, man, let us haul

226

her up before those glory-sucking firefighters steal our thunder. Because I hope you know only guys wearing *uniforms* ever make the front page of the papers."

"He doesn't look like a local," Birch said, dropping her gaze back to Niall — the color finally returning to her face, he was glad to see.

"Aye. Jake's from away. You ready to climb?" he asked, standing her on the granite block beside him when she nodded, then untying the rope from his chest.

"Trees don't talk, Niall," she whispered as he secured the rope around her.

"Nevertheless, I think you were wise to listen to this one. The blocks on the pier are covered with damp moss and are slippery, and if ye can't swim, your chances were better with the tree to hold on to if you had ended up in the river before we got here." He grinned. "Cars don't float for long, but trees do."

"That's what he said," she muttered, her face flushing bright red as she took over the chore of sliding the knot under her bosom. She looked up at the two men and dog looking down at her as the siren grew louder, then back at Niall, her eyes narrowed in warning. "You tell anyone I talked to a tree, and there will be more purple splats on your windshield like the ones I saw there this morning."

"Scots keep their word." He turned her around and lifted her onto the next block, her growled threat finally letting him take his first full breath since the dispatcher had said her name. "And for the record," he continued as he lifted her to the next block, "*eagles* eat little white dogs for breakfast." He hopped up beside her, bent until their noses were nearly touching, and smiled at her gasp. "So if ye see your new feathered buddy again, I suggest you give him a blast of bear spray before ye find yourself having to rescue Mimi for real."

She scrambled up onto the next block on her own. "You guys waiting for an invitation?" she called out to the two grinning idiots. "Because you might want to pull me up before I shove your boss in the river!"

Aye, there was his pint-sized spitfire, Niall thought with a laugh, jumping to the next block and cupping her bottom to hold her steady as Jake and Cole pulled her up — her equally heated curse nearly lost in their laughter and the siren of the arriving ladder truck. *Tu maudit homme;* he'd have to find out how to spell that so he could punch it into his new language app.

CHAPTER ELEVEN

Knowing Birch's propensity to go looking for trouble — assuming it didn't find her first, apparently — Niall worried he may have made a mistake letting Hazel work at the station, since she would have firsthand knowledge of everything that was going on; a point that was driven home when they'd arrived to find the frantic woman standing at the top of the lane holding his second portable radio, which she'd shoved in her pocket in order to throw her arms around her daughter the moment Birch had gotten out of his truck.

"I don't need to go see Dr. Bentley," Birch told her mother yet again as they all stood in the sparsely furnished station. "The EMTs couldn't even find a scratch on me. And getting some color in my cheeks is nothing a couple glasses of wine at the Bottoms Up won't take care of," she continued, leading Hazel several feet closer to the door

— which, for the last ten minutes, had been an exercise in futility.

"Oh, your car," Hazel cried. "And your purse." She broke free and paced around the room with nervous energy, only to stop in front of Niall. "We have to call a tow truck or find a boat large enough to drag her car out of the river."

"It's being done as we speak, Hazel," Niall assured her. "Nova Mare has a crane helicopter, and Duncan and the crew will airlift the car out just as soon as the tide exposes the gravel bar it's stuck on." He leaned down next to her ear. "And I agree," he whispered, "that a good stiff drink will go a long way to calming your daughter." *And you,* he silently added as he straightened and led her over to Birch. "If I have any more questions, Miss Callahan, I know where ye live."

Birch may have returned his smile, but he couldn't miss the threat in her eyes — Niall presumed to remind him of the promise he'd made on their ride back that he not tell Hazel she'd been run off the road. "Thank you, Chief MacKeage. And Officers Wyatt and Sheppard," she added, ushering her mother outside.

"Well, so much for worrying this gig would be boring," Cole said, flopping down in one of the two chairs. "First day on the job and we already have a river rescue and attempted murd—" Having been in the backseat of Niall's truck with Shep for the ride home, Cole snapped his mouth shut when Hazel suddenly came running back inside.

"Niall," she said, grasping his sleeve. "I told Birch to go ahead and find us a table while I ran back to give you a message that came in while you were gone. Please don't tell her I said anything," she rushed on, "but you need to look into the possibility that another car may have been involved in the accident." She glanced over her shoulder toward the open door, then nodded at Jake and Cole to include them as well. "It wouldn't be the first time Leonard ran my daughter off the road. And while I was getting your sandwich, I called the shelter to ask if Birch had returned from her luncheon in Turtleback, and Noreen told me a man had called saying he saw a young woman walking down the road and that Birch had turned around to go find her. Did any of you see this girl?" she asked, looking at Cole and Jake again.

"Nay," Niall said.

The hand on his sleeve tightened. "Leonard knows the surest way to lure Birch into a trap would be to fabricate a woman in trouble."

"You think your ex-husband had something to do with the accident?" Niall asked in surprise. "It's one thing to act in anger after coming home to find himself locked out of the house and in the process of being divorced, but it's quite a different matter, Hazel, for a man to cross into another country to commit a crime."

"Leonard wouldn't let anything like a border stop him."

"But to what gain?" he asked gently. "You're legally divorced, so what good would harming Birch do him?"

Hazel looked up, her eyes swimming with worry. "It's possible he's still angry enough to want revenge." She put her back to the men and lowered her voice. "The bastard married me for my money," she whispered, "and he might think he could charm his way back into my life if Birch . . . if she were gone."

"Where are you from?" Jake asked.

"Montreal," Hazel said, turning to him.

Jake gave her a warm smile. "I thought I recognized the accent." He nodded toward Cole. "We have some connections in Canada, so if you give us Leonard's full name, we can find out if he's crossed the border recently. If he hasn't, there's no worry. But if there's a record of him coming into the States, then we'll take it from there."

"Oh, that would be a great help," she said, going over to them. "His full name is Leonard Calvin Struthers. He's forty-two years old, with dark brown hair and blue eyes, and I think he still has an Ontario driver's license."

Niall felt his jaw slacken at the realization Hazel had married a man much younger than herself, noting that both Cole and Jake were equally surprised.

"I have to go," she said, rushing to the door but stopping to look back. "Please don't mention my concern to Birch," she petitioned the three of them. "At least not until you can find out if Leonard really is in Maine. Then I guess we'll have to tell her, so she can be on guard."

"You have our word," Niall said, walking over and watching her run up the lane, then softly closing the door and turning to the men. "But while waiting to hear, we're going to presume Leonard was driving that car."

Both men nodded. "Any thoughts on the female passenger?" Cole asked.

Niall walked to his desk and sat down with

a heavy sigh. "A girlfriend, maybe."

"Do you know how long they were married?" Jake asked.

"I believe Hazel married Leonard shortly after Birch left for Ottawa to pursue her doctorate," he said, trying to recall their conversation in the Trading Post. "Hazel told me Birch had rushed home earlier this spring when she found out Leonard was trying to mortgage their home, then took her mother back to Ottawa while she finished her schooling." He shrugged. "They were married just over a year, I would say."

"Hazel's quite wealthy," Cole stated rather than asked.

Niall merely nodded.

"Then there's a good chance our boy Leonard — which is probably an alias," Cole said, "already had himself a *poor* wife or girlfriend when he hooked up with Hazel."

"There's also a good chance Hazel would have met with an unfortunate accident of her own," Jake added, "once the bastard had sweet-talked her into changing her will."

"You're implying this is a common practice," Niall growled.

"Because it is," Cole said. "Rich single women are a con man's favorite target." He gestured at the door. "And if they're as

234

pretty and sweet as Hazel . . . hell, she wouldn't have stood a chance against a pro."

"They usually cruise pricey fund-raisers looking for lonely widows or recent divorcées," Jake elaborated. "Even if they have to buy expensive clothes and drop a couple of grand on a ticket, they figure it's merely the cost of doing business."

Niall recalled Hazel mentioning that she'd met one husband at a Valentine's Day ball and, if he wasn't mistaken, that she'd met Leonard at a fund-raiser. He leaned back in his chair as several things suddenly clicked into place — not the least being Birch's little explosion last night when he'd offered to take her to an expensive restaurant.

No wonder she'd accused him of trying to buy his way into her bloomers; she'd probably been a target herself, if only as a roundabout way to Hazel's money.

Niall pushed his chair back and stood up. "Call your contacts."

"Ah . . . exactly how personal was your climb down that bridge this afternoon?" Jake asked, his gaze direct.

"Personal enough that you'll call your border people *tonight* and start hunting for that white car first thing tomorrow morning. Where are you staying?"

"With Sam and Ezra for now," Jake said,

also standing. "That little canister of bear spray I saw clipped to Birch's belt isn't going to do her much good, since Leonard's weapon of choice appears to be a vehicle. Maybe for your next date you should take the lady to a gravel pit and teach her how to shoot a gun. I have an untraceable nine millimeter that would fit her hand."

Nope, they definitely weren't going to do much if *anything* by the book — which suited Niall just fine at the moment. He grabbed his jacket off the back of his chair and headed for the porch. "Thank you. I'll pass on the gun but give your suggestion for the date some thought. Lock up when ye leave."

Shep stepped out of the shadows as Niall walked up the lane while seriously considering Jake's suggestion. On the one hand he'd feel better knowing Birch had a less up-close means of defending herself, but on the other hand he didn't think arming a quick-tempered spitfire would be all that wise. And if he remembered correctly, Birch hadn't even wanted to touch his "stupid gun" yesterday morning when it had been poking her on the horse.

Hell, had it only been yesterday? Because Niall was fairly certain he'd aged at least ten years in the last two days.

■ ■ ■ ■

Sitting in a crowded bar sipping a glass of wine (when she'd really wanted whiskey) and focusing on calming down her mother had had the added benefit of easing some of Birch's own terror of the accident. Performing the familiar tasks of soaking in a steaming bubble bath, shaving her legs, slathering every inch of her body with lotion, and even taking a curling iron to her hair had also gone a long way to putting some distance between her and that cold, dark, swirling river.

Yet despite leaving the bathroom feeling like a limp lavender noodle, everything had come rushing back the moment she'd crawled into bed and closed her eyes; the sound of that car ramming into hers, finding herself hurtling out of control toward a huge tree, then helplessly floating down that river toward Bottomless finally compelled Birch to leave her downstairs bedroom and go in search of her fail-proof sleeping aide.

But when the muzzle velocities of various-grained bullets blasting out of a .357 magnum couldn't quell the tremors still lingering deep inside her, Birch sat up with a sigh of defeat, slid the heavy tome under the couch, and simply sat in the quiet house listening to the thumping beat of her heart. Maybe instead of trying to block out the horrifying moment when she'd realized she was going to die, she should see each step that had eventually led her to the realization she would survive.

But where to begin?

Well, the first sign she knew she was in trouble was when that white car had slowed down beside her instead of passing. She hadn't actually seen the face of the woman passenger, only the gaudy, diamond-studded ruby ring and brassy red nail polish on the perfectly manicured finger flipping her off. Birch recalled that her first thought as she'd flown toward the huge, solid-looking tree had been that Leo the Leech had followed her to Maine — except the presence of a woman had made her quickly dismiss that idea.

Although *now* that she thought about it, maybe Leonard had already found a new lady to scam. Only he was supposed to be impotent because of some old horseback-riding injury — from playing polo, Birch remembered her mother saying. So how could he have a new girlfriend if he couldn't even get it up? Then again, a ruby-and-diamond ring — which the parasite had likely bought with Hazel's money to show his new lady that he wasn't after *her* money — might help a lonely woman overlook the lack of sex.

Heck, it had worked on her mom.

Leonard had found a younger victim this time, though, as that manicured finger had definitely belonged to a woman in her late thirties or early forties. Birch sighed, realizing she'd have to tell Niall about her violent encounter with Leonard in Ottawa, only this time not leave out the more disturbing details like she had with her mother.

Deciding she at least had a theory as to why she'd ended up in the river, Birch moved on to the next thought that had popped into her head during the accident, which had been that trees did *not* feel like big balls of cotton when you hit them.

She didn't think they grunted, either.

Next was the realization that she would have preferred dying instantly to drowning in a cold, dark river. But there she'd been, perched in a tree floating toward the bridge, hearing a deep-timbered voice telling her to stay calm. That she'd talked back to it had only further proved she was dead. But then the voice had suggested — drawled, actually — that she might want to find her cell phone and call her next-door neighbor to come save her . . . again. Not that she ever intended to tell Niall that part of her conversation with the tree. Because really, how had the tree *known*?

She also wasn't telling Niall that every time a branch had snapped, causing the tree to hiss a curse and settle closer to the cold swirling water, she had screamed like a six-year-old trapped in mangled steel beams and crushing concrete with her dead *grand-mémère* and unconscious mother. But unlike twenty-five years ago, this time she'd had a dispatcher assuring her help was on the way, which had kept Birch from outright panicking.

She took a mental step back to see if any of this was helping.

Nope; because if the fact her heart had gone from thumping to pounding was any indication, reliving both the accident *and* the explosion was only making things worse.

Damn, she really needed to get some sleep, because she was in for a really busy day tomorrow. The first thing she would have to do was explain to her insurance company why she'd totaled a second car in only two months, then start shopping for a new one. But she was buying a truck this time; something big and heavy enough to ram back anyone trying to run her off the road. Yeah, a four-wheel-drive like Niall's, only red.

She also had to replace her laptop and cell phone and all the important stuff in her purse. But maybe she could ask her mother to help with that, which should keep Hazel too busy to continue fussing and worrying over her.

Oh, she forgot; her mother already had a job. Birch didn't know if she should feel sorry for Niall and his two new officers, or if she should warn them what they were in for. Because despite this being the first legitimate job Hazel Callahan had ever had, the woman could be downright scary when she was on a mission.

Used to watching her mother trying to save the world one charitable project at a time, Birch had immediately recognized the growing spark in Hazel's eyes this morning as Peg had talked about Niall's lack of funding for a desperately needed secretary. Birch had said yes before her mother had even finished trying to guilt her into letting her volunteer for the job — partly because she *did* feel guilty for dragging the woman away from all that was familiar to her, but also because she thought Niall deserved Hazel Callahan on a mission.

But then the jerk had gone and saved her butt — and likely her life — again.

So he might be easily offended, but he apparently didn't hold grudges.

Birch really didn't know what to make of Niall, because he didn't seem to fit her notion of a cop. Not only was he big and strong and handsome, he definitely knew how to impress a girl by crumbling castle walls and galloping to the rescue on plow horses. He also didn't seem to mind dangling off high places to save someone — although that more or less was expected of anyone who wore a badge.

Realizing she was actually smiling, Birch decided that instead of reliving her accident she should focus on her growing attraction to Niall MacKeage. Because even though her heart was still racing, it had changed to a shivery thump of anticipation.

Yeah; she definitely preferred this train of thought.

But once again, where to begin?

Well, she could start by revisiting last night's plan to have an affair with him. Because really, what better way to work off lingering terror than to have mindless sex with all that amazing muscle? She *had* spent over an hour in the bathroom shaving her legs and doing her hair and making sure she smelled nice, so why not sneak across the yard, knock on Niall's door, and ask if he might have a powerful desire to do more than just kiss her?

Seriously — it couldn't be any crazier than talking to a tree.

It could be embarrassing if he turned her down, though, seeing how they saw each other every day. But when Titus Oceanus had come upon her walking Mimi on the beach before she'd left for Turtleback this morning, Birch had gotten the impression the man also thought Niall was attracted to her.

After thanking her for returning his wife's barrette, which Rana had apparently lost while horseback riding on the other side of Bottomless, Titus had then asked Birch to describe her feathered visitor. Birch had told him that even though she'd always assumed seagulls were the only birds bold enough to approach a human holding food, she had questioned this particular bird's sharp yellow eyes and pointy beak. But she knew some species of gulls were that large and had motley brown and white feathers.

Titus, obviously fighting a grin, had told Birch he suspected her visitor had been an immature bald eagle; likely a juvenile that considered a shiny object might be fair exchange for the pie she was holding.

Mon Dieu, had the man been hiding in the woods watching her talking to a bird? "Do eagles fly at night?" she'd asked to cover her embarrassment.

"Not usually," he'd said with a shrug. "But then, most juveniles — animal *and* human — often take crazy risks for the simple thrill of feeling alive. Especially," he'd added with a wink, "if a beautiful woman is involved."

Birch was afraid she'd actually given a derisive snort, since Titus had arched a brow at her from his towering height, even as she'd recalled the Oceanuses were rumored to be royalty — though hopefully not the King and Queen of *Nowhere.* Titus had then praised Birch for her role in rescuing the Vaughn women, smoothly segueing into how fortuitous it was that they had such a strong, intelligent Scotsman for a police chief.

Birch had smiled and nodded — adding little murmurs of agreement when appropriate — as Titus had gone on and on about Chief MacKeage's many fine qualities, even as she'd wondered what dirt Niall had on him. Because no man she'd ever met, especially not one reputed to be richer than God, talked up another man to a woman unless someone was holding a gun to his head.

Birch had never been so happy to hear her cell phone alarm go off, allowing her to slowly back away as she'd explained she didn't want to be late for her luncheon with the Turtleback high school teachers.

"If I might be so bold as to suggest," Titus had called out, halting her sprint up the lawn. "You might find that embracing the ups and downs of your journey, Miss Callahan, is far less annoying than trying to control them."

Having absolutely no idea how to respond, since she had no idea what he was talking about, she'd merely waved and headed off again to the sound of the man's soft laughter.

Blinking in surprise to find she was sitting on the couch instead of walking up from the beach, Birch decided having an affair with Niall might be an easy journey to embrace.

So what to do? she wondered, drumming her fingers on the couch.

What to do . . .

Well, she could head across the yard and see if she couldn't *do* the highlander.

Birch stood up and headed to her downstairs bedroom before she could change her mind or lose her nerve, pulling the ratty old T-shirt she'd stolen from her father off over her head and tossing it on her bed on her way by. She then ran a critical eye over her body as she stood in front of her bureau mirror and hoped to God towering mountains of testosterone liked short women with small, perky boobs, petite nipples, and . . . oh, who was she kidding, even her freckles were so small they were almost invisible.

Still, she considered her figure *proportionately* perfect.

Birch opened the bottom drawer of her bureau, pulled out the nightgown she'd bought for Mr. Four Freaking Children and slipped it on, only to frown at her reflection as the satin material slithered down her petite curves. Deciding the gown more or less said *seducer of dorks,* she pulled it off and dug in the drawer again, then held up a semitransparent little number she'd bought to shut up her mother about her nonexistent love life. She tossed it toward the bed with a snort. "Definitely don't want to knock on his door wearing something that screams *slut on the hunt.*" The flannel granny gown she pulled out next said *I'm having my period so leave me alone,* and the baggy bottoms and oversized top . . . well, they basically said *I don't freaking care.*

Birch finally came to the deep purple silk pajamas she usually saved for room-sharing at conferences or girls' nights watching a movie at home with her mom. She held them up to her nose and sighed when she caught the hint of buttered popcorn, then slipped them on with a soft hum of pleasure. She unbuttoned the top button and turned up the collar, ran her fingers through her hair to give the curls a fluff, then studied her reflection. Not dowdy or off-putting and not the slightest hint of slut; this sleepwear said *Hi, I came over here wearing pajamas because I want to sleep in your amazingly muscled arms until I stop shaking inside.*

Yeah, the pajamas were feminine and sophisticated and modest while still being easily removable, their color made her eyes appear sort of lavender-ish, and they didn't make her look like a woman who talked to trees and eagles.

In fact, she looked exactly like her perfectly *normal* self.

Heck, she would invite the woman in the mirror inside if she came knocking on her door at eleven o'clock at night, and if Niall MacKeage didn't, then . . . well, she was writing his name in big bold letters at the top of her list of reasons she *should* hate men.

CHAPTER TWELVE

Niall had been staring up at his bedroom ceiling for over an hour now, wondering how to deal with the fact that someone might actually be trying to kill Birch, when he heard a soft knock on his door. He sat up and snapped on the bedside lamp, grabbed the pajama bottoms off the foot of the bed and put them on, then followed Shep's wagging tail into the kitchen. He opened the door, not really surprised but definitely intrigued, to find Birch wearing a bathrobe and getting ready to knock again. In fact, it looked as if she'd been about to pound on it with her fist.

"Is there a problem at the shelter?"

Her eyes widened. "You sleep in pajama bottoms."

"As opposed to?"

"Um, I thought you . . . I just always pictured . . ." She gathered her robe closed at the throat and aimed her gaze at his naked chest. "Everyone at the shelter is asleep."

"Except you," he said gently, the taut skin of her flushed face making him suspect she kept reliving the accident every time she closed her eyes. "Would talking about what happened today help?"

"Probably not," she said on a sigh. "I just wanted to see if . . . I thought maybe you and I could . . ." She took a deep breath. "You didn't kiss me. Today," she clarified when he said nothing, "after you pulled me out of the car, you didn't kiss me like you did after you broke us out of the Vaughns' cellar."

Niall made sure not to react when he finally realized why she was here. "I'm sorry; I didn't think it would be appropriate, considering we had an audience."

She dropped her gaze to his chest again, her blush kicking up another notch. "Oh. Yes. That makes sense. I guess it wouldn't look good for the police chief to kiss a woman he'd just rescued in front of his new officers." She took a step back. "Well, that answers my question. Sorry to have bothered you."

Not only not suicidal but sure as hell not an idiot, either, Niall caught hold of her shoulders before she could turn away. "Are you sure about why you're here, Birch?" he quietly asked. "Because I'm needing to hear ye come out and say it."

He didn't think she was going to, she was silent so long. But then she reached up and pressed a hand to the spot on his chest she was staring at. "I'm sure." She looked up. "And just so you'll be sure, I don't want you to worry that I'm the clingy type. Our sleeping together doesn't mean I'm going to text you every few hours or expect you to call me three times a day, and I'm definitely not looking to get married. Or pregnant," she muttered, her gaze dropping back to his chest.

"Deal," he said, sliding a hand under her knees and sweeping her off her feet, then kicking the door closed and heading for the bedroom.

"Wait, Shep's outside," she squeaked.

He stopped in his bedroom doorway. "You want an audience?"

"Ah . . . no." She looked down at *her* chest. "You . . . you can wear a condom if you want, but you don't have to worry about . . . I'm on birth control," she whispered, her cheeks flushing again as she fingered the edge of her robe. "And I don't have any contagious . . ." She sucked in a deep breath and gave him a sheepish smile.

"I'm not very good at this, am I?"

"I have no way to judge, since you're the first woman I've had knock on my door wearing pajamas."

That got him a snort. "You intend to stand here holding me all night or are we — oh!" she gasped. "Your bedroom is nearly wall-to-wall bed."

"It's a small room and a big bed. Are ye *certain* you're sure, Birch?"

That got him another smile, this one showing a hint of spitfire. "I guess that would depend," she murmured, twining her arms around his neck. "Have you had all your shots?"

Assuming that was a rhetorical question, since she kissed him before he could respond, Niall decided it might be wise to let her be in charge. Miss Callahan not only appeared to know what she was doing, she also seemed to know exactly what she wanted — which, for tonight at least, appeared to be him.

She was attacking his mouth much the way she'd attacked the pie down on the beach. Hell, she even started making the same little noises as she deepened the kiss, and he didn't know if he should get up to speed or try to slow her down.

Deciding he'd figure it out as he went

along, Niall took a step forward and bent to set her on the bed, only to have her arms tighten so she wouldn't lose contact with his mouth as she pulled him down with her. He hadn't even finished landing when she rolled away with a husky laugh, then immediately moved to sit straddling him.

Okay then; apparently he wasn't *letting* her anything — she was *taking* charge.

"You don't have a problem with leaving the light on, do you?" she asked as she undid the belt on her robe. "I like . . . looking."

"Nay," he somehow managed *not* to growl when the movement of her shrugging out of the robe sent a couple liters of blood straight to his groin — specifically to where her womanhood was intimately rubbing against him.

Her hands stilled on the buttons of her pajama top, her eyes suddenly uncertain. "You . . . ah, you're not a breast man, are you?" she whispered.

Her vulnerability caught him by surprise, but not enough to throw him off stride. "Aye," he said quietly, sitting up and gently clasping her head. "I like breasts. And legs. Pretty little backsides shaped for a man's hand. Lips. Necks. The translucent skin covering the pulse on a woman's wrist. Big eyes that can be scolding one minute and filled with passion the next. But mostly," he whispered with his mouth nearly touching hers, "I like a brain that knows what it wants and isn't afraid to go after it." He looked directly into her no-longer-uncertain eyes. "But I especially like when it comes packaged in a body just like the one you happen to have."

And that put that worry to bed, apparently, because Niall found himself flat on his back again, *his* brain telling his heart to ramp up that blood flow when those lips he'd told her he liked slowly started working their way down his neck to his chest — stopping to visit each of his nipples — then continued over his ribs and stomach, not stopping until they reached the waist of his pajamas.

She sat up straddling his thighs instead of groin this time, and Niall knew he was in trouble when she smiled — not at him, at his body — and simply pulled her top off over her head. But the lass bent again before he could see anything interesting as she scooted even farther down his legs — taking his pajamas with her.

Niall's last coherent thought before her warm, sexy mouth closed over him was that Greylen, Jack Stone, Duncan, Matt Gregor

— *somebody* — could have warned him that twenty-first-century women definitely weren't shrinking violets in the bedroom.

Hell, he wouldn't be surprised if *he* learned a few things tonight.

CHAPTER THIRTEEN

Birch trudged across the yard just as the sun broke over the opposite shore of Bottomless, thinking that of all the crazy, impetuous things she could have done, having sex with Niall MacKeage might very well top the list. The wall-crumbling, cliff-dangling Scot had positively — and probably irrevocably — ruined her for ever enjoying sex with another man again. But even crazier, Birch decided as she climbed the porch steps, was that she couldn't stop thinking about when they could have sex again.

Well, damn, the stupid door was locked. And her key was on the ring in her car, which was . . . somewhere besides here. She moved along the porch and tried each of the kitchen windows, figuring the way her luck had been running lately, the stupid car had fallen off the helicopter winch and was sitting at the bottom of the sea. For crying out loud, who closed windows in the middle of June?

Granted, the sea breeze could get chilly at night, but Noreen was a freaking *Mainer;* nighttime temperatures in the forties should feel balmy to her. You'd think the woman was paying the utility bills the way she guarded the thermostat and ran around shutting off lights and closing windows. She'd also taken over the kitchen — although considering the meals they'd been eating the last two weeks, no one was complaining. And Noreen did vacuum and dust and do the laundry. Heck, she even did bathrooms.

Birch rounded the corner of the wraparound porch and started checking the parlor-turned-into-her-office windows, remembering that she *had* planned to divide up the housekeeping chores to give the residents a sense of pride in their temporary home and feel like valued, contributing members of their temporary family. But Noreen didn't like the way Cassandra packed the dishwasher; Macie apparently didn't know how to fold a fitted sheet; and Hazel did have a bad habit of vacuuming only the traffic areas. Again, not that anyone was complaining. In fact, there was a good chance Cassandra kept placing bowls and cups faceup in the dishwasher on purpose.

Heck, Birch had sabotaged some of her own chores to get out of them.

But then, who was she to squelch a confused woman's need to feel needed? And since only two of the five pies had sold at the bake sale — to tourists, apparently — Noreen had gone to bed early rather than hear the watered-down version of Birch's accident. After, that is, the humiliated woman had let everyone know it was her husband's fault the pies hadn't sold, claiming she wouldn't put it past Logan to have run around town warning everyone they would be spending the next five days staring out their bathroom windows.

Wait; *her* bathroom window was open, wasn't it? Hugging herself against the chill beginning to penetrate her robe, Birch headed back down the stairs with a muttered curse. She had to get inside before anyone discovered she hadn't slept in her bed, because the last thing she needed was for anyone — especially motormouth Noreen — to suspect she was having an affair with her neighbor.

Well, *maybe* they were having an affair, seeing how neither of them had talked about when they might get together again. Niall had merely kissed her on the forehead and given her ass a pat on her way out the door instead of walking her home like the gentleman he obviously wasn't. The sex machine was probably right now back in his big warm bed, completely oblivious to the fact she was out here freezing her *patted* backside off.

Birch stopped at the side of the house and looked up at her bathroom window to see it was open a few inches, only to sigh in defeat when she realized even a giant would have trouble reaching it. She scanned the yard for something to stand on, but didn't see a ladder, a handy tree like the one growing beside Cassandra's window, or even a freaking lawn chair. So she trudged back to the stairs, sat down on the bottom step and propped her elbows on her knees, and dropped her chin in her hands with another sigh. Man oh man, she was in trouble. Wanting to have an affair with Niall was one thing, but falling *in like* with him could be a problem.

Okay, it already was a problem, because last night she'd caught herself liking his *mind* even more than his amazing muscles. Who knew the towering mountain could be so tender? He was a cop. A trained killer. Men who made their livings running around with guns strapped to their chests were supposed to be emotionally aloof, not *playful.* They certainly weren't supposed to make a woman feel pretty and feminine and over-the-moon special by making love to her three — or had it been four? — freaking times in one night.

For crying out loud, she hadn't made love four times in the last *two years.*

Wait; hadn't she gone over there to *sleep* in his arms? Yes, she'd intended to have mindless sex and then go to sleep, not spend the night going at it like two horny teen-agers. Niall had actually laughed out loud every time he'd had to catch her before she landed on her ass on the floor. (Note to self: Do not slather every inch of your body with lotion just before engaging in hot, sweaty sex.) *Mon Dieu;* she'd laughed out loud, too, picturing him as one of those kids at local fairs trying to hold on to a greased pig!

And speaking of asses, what was so fasci-nating about hers, anyway? She'd better not look in the mirror this morning and see —

Birch straightened at the realization that instead of staring out at Bottomless, she'd just spent the last five minutes staring at three strange vehicles parked in the drive-way. Well, one huge vehicle and two of those little golf cart thingies like Rana Oceanus used for traveling the camp road on rainy days.

Birch shot to her feet and ran down the walkway, only to slip to a halt on the dew-covered grass when she saw the small lettering on the rear side window of the SUV that said *Spellbound Falls Crisis Center.* She turned to the carts, which looked to be brand-spanking-new, and saw the same discreet lettering on the side panels.

Oh God, all three were candy-apple red.

But where had they come from? When had they been delivered?

"Oh God," she repeated out loud, covering her mouth in horror. Had whoever delivered them knocked on the door last night only to *not* find the center director home because she'd been next door having sex with her neighbor?

So why hadn't Shep barked? Even if the vehicles had been delivered after she'd snuck the poor dog back inside at two in the morning, his canine ears should have heard *something.* "The shelter's first line of defense, my ass," Birch muttered, unable to resist running a finger along the beautiful red paint as she walked around the SUV. She opened the driver's door, stepped up on the running board to slide in behind the wheel, and sucked in the new vehicle smell

— stopping in mid-suck when she noticed the linen card sticking out of a cubbyhole on the dash.

Birch grabbed it and started reading. *It has come to my attention that both the Crisis Center and Birthing Clinic are in need of safe and reliable transportation.*

She knew Dr. Bentley drove a compact . . . rust-bucket, and remembered wondering how the tall, lanky man folded himself into it, even as she'd pictured him wading through five-foot snowdrifts next winter trying to find the poor thing.

So please accept this truck, Miss Callahan, she continued reading, *to help you serve the good citizens of Spellbound Falls and Turtleback Station. The carts should make it easier for your mother to get to her new job, as well as give your residents a sense of self-reliance. They are electric, so please remember to plug them in each night.* It was signed, *The Special Delivery Fairy.*

P.S. I hope you like the color.

As in little Charlie MacKeage's special delivery fairy? Birch wondered with a smile as she tucked the card back in the cubbyhole. The safe and reliable transportation had to be Peg's idea. It was just like her to worry about Hazel having to walk to work every day, too. All five committee women were thoughtful and generous, but Peg seemed particularly sensitive to the plight of struggling women, making Birch wonder about her life before she'd married Duncan.

Well, Vanetta Thurber was also especially fond of the Center, having confided to Birch that she'd been married to a violent — and thankfully now dead — bastard ten years ago when she'd lived in Alabama. In fact, Vanetta had donated her freaking *house* to be used as a shelter, even though she could have gotten a small fortune for shorefront property this close to town. And Peg had told Hazel it had been Vanetta's idea to have Niall live in the converted bunkhouse rent-free in exchange for keeping an eye on the shelter residents.

Birch wondered if keeping his *hands* on the shelter *director* had been part of the deal. She sucked in a final whiff of new-truck smell, then got out and softly closed the door. With one final scowl at the still-quiet house, she hugged herself against the penetrating chill and started back across the yard, an added spring in her step at the thought of dragging Niall out of his nice warm bed to rescue her again.

He opened the door before she'd even finished knocking, wearing jeans and boots but no shirt, his hair damp from the shower and an errant dab of shaving cream near his sideburn. "Back already?" His gorgeous green eyes ran over her like a molten caress as Birch tried to remember why she was there. "Well, if ye insist," he said on a heavy sigh, sweeping her off her feet. "But I can't promise I'll be at the top of my game."

Birch hoped to God he was teasing.

Or maybe not.

"Wait. I'm not here to — Niall, stop!" she said on a laugh. "I'm locked out of the house." He halted in the bedroom doorway, looking so disappointed that she kissed his clean-shaven cheek. "I just need help climbing in my bathroom window." She toyed with a lock of damp hair at the nape of his neck, liking how the length made him appear roguish. "Do you happen to know anyone who's good at rescuing damsels in distress?"

"Not particularly," he said, opening his arms and making her yelp of surprise end in a *whoosh* when she landed on the unmade bed. "Why don't ye ask your new best buddy to fly in the window and unlock the door for you?" he said, walking away.

Birch gaped at his retreating back; the guy was jealous of a *bird*? "Or I can ask my newest best buddy, the Special Delivery Fairy," she said, scrambling off the bed in pursuit, only to bump into him when he stopped and turned to her.

He caught hold of her shoulders when she bounced off him. "When did ye meet the Special Delivery Fairy?" He turned away again, grabbed a shirt thrown over one of the stools at the counter peninsula, and continued into the small living area that was all of three steps away from the kitchen.

"I didn't actually meet her in person."

"Obviously," he said, shaking his head as he buttoned his shirt. "Because everyone knows Special Delivery Fairies are *hims.* So what did he bring you?"

"*She* brought me a brand-new truck," Birch said, going to the open door and gesturing outside with a smug smile. "A candy-apple red SUV just like the ones most of the committee women drive, with enough cargo space to move a mom and several children to safety." Birch turned her smile sinister. "And it's big enough that if anyone tries running me off the road again, they'll be the one floating down a — what?" she asked when Niall's entire countenance suddenly changed.

"One," he said ever so softly, "either I or one of my officers will accompany you whenever you go check on a woman who

264

might need help."

"Now wait a minute."

"And two," he added more forcefully as he took a step closer, "you're not to leave the town proper until we find out who ran you off the road."

"You're actually telling me what I can and can't do?" She closed the distance between them. "Don't even *think* last night gave you any rights over me."

He bent until their noses were nearly touching. "You leave town, you'd best head straight for the border and hope I don't catch ye before you cross." He straightened, grabbing his jacket on his way outside, but stopped and turned to her. "And for the record, I'd made my decision *before* you knocked on my door last night. And Birch?"

"What?" she snapped.

"Something else ye might want to know about me is that I never bluff. You leave town alone, and I will come after you," he said, turning and striding to his truck just as Shep came racing inside. The dog grabbed his Kevlar vest off the floor, gave Birch what appeared to be an equally quelling look, then raced back outside.

Birch stood listening to Niall's pickup start up then slowly idle out the driveway, and tried to decide what had just happened.

How had the man gone from teasing lover to bossy brute in the blink of an eye?

She also tried to recall the last time anyone had dared to tell her that she couldn't do something. About a month after her seventh birthday, if she remembered correctly, when *Grand-père* St. Germaine had suddenly decided she couldn't go to her new best friend's house after school anymore. Something about the girl being too uppity, he'd said, or some similar nonsense.

Birch had calmly — since she'd stopped crying within a week of going to live with the St. Germaines — called her dad at work to tell him good-bye. She'd gone on to say she was using her birthday money to buy a bus ticket to Montreal, and promised to call him again from her *real* home to let him know she'd made it okay. And for him not to worry, because the penthouse had a really nice doorman, and there were plenty of nice neighbors to help her out until her mom came home from the hospital.

Still dressed in his uniform, Claude had pulled up behind Birch as she had been walking down the road hoping a bus would come along soon. She hadn't made it a mile because her backpack had been filled with her birthday present from her dad and what

266

few possessions he'd retrieved from her *real* home six months earlier. He'd lifted the heavy pack off her shoulders and led her back to his truck with the promise he would take her to see her mom.

After traveling for several mostly silent hours, Birch had been confused when they'd pulled onto the sprawling grounds of what had looked like a resort. Claude had asked her to wait at the front desk with the nice lady, then had returned half an hour later, taken her hand, and led her down the darkened hall past several closed doors.

Birch had to give him credit; the parentally challenged man had stopped outside one of the doors, dropped to his knees and clasped her shoulders, and at least tried to prepare her. "I know you don't remember anything about the explosion, Birch," he'd said softly, his large hands warm and heavy on her shoulders. "But you do know that the reason you came to live with me is because your *grand-mémère* didn't survive and your mom was hurt too badly to be able to take care of you."

Birch had remembered every last detail; she'd simply chosen to forget them.

"And," Claude had gone on, "your mom agreed it would be better if you didn't see how badly she was hurt, which is why you've only been able to talk to her on the phone, and then only in the last few months." The man had actually smiled, which had only served to make Birch stiffen. "But I just explained to Hazel how grown up you are now that you're seven, and she agreed talking to her in person might help you understand why you can't be with her right now." His hands on her shoulders had tightened. "And maybe not . . . well, not until you're much older."

"How much older?" Birch had asked, deciding *she* wouldn't survive if she had to live with the St. Germaines much longer. "When I'm eight? Nine?"

"I'm sorry, Birch, but there's a good chance it won't be until you're old enough to take care of yourself." He'd taken a deep breath, further alarming her. "So when we go inside, try not to panic when you see your mom. And don't start crying, okay?"

"I never cry," Birch remembered telling him.

That had briefly brought back his smile. "Sorry, little cadet, I forgot. Let's go with shocked, then. Try not to appear shocked when you see the brace she's wearing. Hazel is . . . well, her spirit is just as fragile as her body, Birch." He'd stood up and taken hold of her hand again. "Ready?"

Birch had nodded with all the conviction of a seven-year-old about to see her mother for the first time in six months, but nothing could have prepared her for what was on the other side of the door. She'd honestly thought they were in the wrong room, because the person lying in that bed trussed up in a full-body brace had in no way resembled her mother, even though the woman had sounded like her mom as she'd held out a frail, trembling hand and beckoned Birch closer.

Birch later learned that at the time, it was expected her mother would never walk again. They'd apparently forgotten to tell Hazel, though. The doctors needn't have bothered welding metal rods to her spine, because the determination to get back her daughter had given her mother a backbone of steel. Two years after the explosion Hazel had taken her first unaided step, and eighteen months later she had swooped down on the St. Germaines and ripped Birch out of their coldhearted talons.

Claude had . . . Well, he hadn't spoken much when he'd come to pick up Birch at the hospital four years earlier, and he hadn't seemed to have much to say when she'd left, either. He'd actually sounded surprised when she'd called him two weeks later and asked if he was coming to Montreal for the weekend to see her.

And to this day, she was still dropping him clues on being a dad.

"Birch? Birch, are you outside?"

Oh, *maudit,* how long had she been standing there? "I'm here, Mama," she shouted, rushing out of Niall's cottage. "Did you see what we got?" she said, realizing the carts were a perfect excuse for why she'd been locked out of the house. "The note said they're from the Special Delivery Fairy," she explained as her mother came down the stairs carrying Mimi. "And Dr. Bentley got a new truck, too."

"As in Charlie's fairy?" Hazel asked, setting Mimi down on the walkway.

"How many Special Delivery fairies can there be? I got so excited when I looked out the kitchen window this morning," Birch rushed on brightly, "that I ended up on the wrong side of a locked door when I ran out to see them." She waved toward Niall's cottage. "So I went over to see if Chief Mac-Keage might have a spare key. I think Peg's the fairy," she quickly added when her mother stopped looking at the empty spot where Niall's truck usually sat and turned suspicious eyes on Birch. Birch herded Hazel toward the closest cart and urged her

270

to sit behind the steering wheel. "The fairy said in her note that you should use one of the carts to go to and from work every day, and the other one will give the residents a sense of independence."

"One of these is for me?" Hazel asked, gripping the wheel as she scanned the interior. "But I can afford to buy my own cart," she whispered, shaking her head as she looked up at Birch, only to start nodding. "I should do that, and leave these for the residents to use."

"Why, so Noreen can commandeer both?" Birch said with a laugh, heading for the house. "She's only going to complain that now she has two more things to clean."

"My, my, *bébé,*" Hazel drawled, following behind her. "Did you have a fight with your pillow last night? Because from the looks of your hair, I would say you lost."

Birch ran up the stairs, refusing to reach up and touch what probably looked like a bird's nest — hopefully not an *eagle's.* Yes, Hazel might be naive when it came to her own dealings with men, but she'd always been maddeningly perceptive when it came to her daughter's love life — or lack thereof. Birch stopped at the door and watched her mom stiffly mount the stairs, which told her just how taxing her accident yesterday had been on Hazel, since her old injury usually only acted up when she was stressed. "You know how wild my hair gets when I shampoo it just before going to bed."

Hazel stopped beside her and glanced toward Niall's cottage. "Niall left without helping you?" she asked, her eyes suspicious again.

"He was already gone," Birch said, finally entering the kitchen. "But I thought I'd check if his door was unlocked on the chance he had a key to the main house hanging on his . . . Oh, *mon Dieu,* Mama," she said in exasperation, heading down the hallway. "You better hurry up and get dressed." She stopped at her bedroom door and shot her mother a smirk. "Chief Mac-Keage looks to me like the sort of boss who will dock your paycheck for being even five minutes late."

CHAPTER FOURTEEN

Driving back from introducing Cole to more of the business owners in Turtleback Station, Niall thought about how he was finally starting to get a handle on Birch; the only problem being that most of what he was learning about her was secondhand. In fact, if not for the scent of lavender still lingering on his pillows, he might suspect he'd only dreamt her knocking on his door five nights ago.

He didn't regret issuing his little edict that she not leave town alone, although he did wish he hadn't been so blunt. But he'd been counting on the fact that losing her only means of transportation had effectively solved that particular worry for him — or it had until the Special Delivery Fairy had made a late-night visit. He couldn't even blame Shep for not warning him in time to come up with another plan, since everyone knew fairies were silent, sneaky little bastards.

Roger Bentley certainly appeared happy with his new SUV, especially when it came to making backcountry house calls at two in the morning. Hell, the good doctor was so grateful to the benevolent fairy, apparently, that he'd finally let Carolina talk him into opening a second clinic a hundred crooked miles away in Pine Creek next fall. But where Bentley had seen the truck as a personal gain, Birch had only seen all the women she could lug back to the crisis center.

She'd actually headed out again three days ago, this time in search of a young girl the high school teachers had told her they were worried about. And near as Niall could tell, the only reason the shelter didn't have a new resident was because Birch had asked Cole to accompany her. Again proving that neither of his officers intended to follow the rules, Cole had apparently pulled the boyfriend aside for a little man-to-man talk, after which he'd told Birch not to worry, since his being assigned to Turtleback had effectively put the young couple on his watch.

Oh yeah, hiring Jake and Cole had definitely been one of his wiser decisions.

But other than that one trip to Turtleback,

Birch had surprisingly stayed close to home. Niall wasn't surprised, however, that she hadn't spoken to him since the morning he'd threatened to chase her down if she left town.

Hazel had been a veritable fount of information these last five days, regaling him with stories of Birch's teenage years, including her daughter's pet names for each of the nefarious husbands. And after asking how to spell a French word so he could try out his new translation app, Niall had found a long list of colorful curses Birch was fond of using sitting on his desk the next morning, complete with pronunciations — on the chance he wanted to use them himself, Hazel had written at the bottom.

Niall decided the woman was an organizational wonder. She was also a nester. Hoping she truly did have a gift for getting people to part with their money and not that she was using her own, Niall had noticed his police station filling up with furniture, electronic equipment, and . . . hell, this morning he'd found an area rug in the holding cell, curtains on the barred windows, and a handmade quilt on the narrow cot. He now had an even larger desk, since Hazel had commandeered his old desk and given the small one to Jake.

Niall had no idea how the woman had managed it so quickly, but Jake and Cole were strutting around in crisp blue uniforms, complete with leather belts loaded down with an impressive array of law-enforcement paraphernalia. As for their heads, Hazel had proclaimed that dark blue baseball caps embroidered with the new *Bottomless Sea Police Force* logo she was having professionally designed would make them appear far sexier than the deputy sheriffs and state police. Honest to God, the two men were worse than nine-year-olds, and had been asking Hazel every day for the last three days when the caps were coming in.

Cole's truck had been delivered, and although also blue and loaded with lights, it wasn't quite as flashy as Jake's. But it would look just as impressive, Hazel had assured him, once the new decals arrived for the doors.

They never did find the white car that had forced Birch off the road, and there was no record of a Leonard Calvin Struthers crossing the border. And just yesterday Sam had informed them — after using his own network of sources — that Hazel's fourth husband had likely assumed the identity of the real Leonard Struthers, who had conveniently died six years ago.

All of which left them with exactly zero to go on. And even though Birch wasn't talking to him, she had listened when Niall explained what they'd learned so far, which he'd followed up by once again reiterating — this time nicely — that it was important she not be traveling alone until they could discover who was out to get her and why.

Aye, Birch may have a quick temper and lion-sized attitude, but she obviously also had a strong desire to stay alive. His offer to take her to a gravel pit and teach her how to shoot, however, had been answered with a haughty glare before she'd silently turned and walked away.

He'd have to ask Hazel about her daughter's aversion to guns.

Niall eased his foot off the accelerator when he noticed a man exiting the road that led down to the Kents' home and decided from the description Logan had given him last week that it was Silas French.

How convenient, since he'd been looking to meet Mr. French. Niall checked his rearview mirror and ordered Shep into the backseat, then lowered the passenger window as he pulled up alongside the man. "Would ye care for a ride?"

The man stopped and looked at him, then

slipped off his small backpack and climbed in the truck. "Thanks," he said, setting the pack on the floor between his feet and closing the door. He reached a hand toward Niall. "Silas French."

"Niall MacKeage," Niall said, shaking his hand then starting off again. "Would you be the gentleman staying with Logan Kent?"

"I am," Silas said, glancing over his shoulder as he fastened his seatbelt. "Can I pat the dog or will I pull back a stump?"

"Your choice, Mr. French, as Shep only bites criminals."

That got him a chuckle as Silas twisted in his seat and held out his hand to Shep. "He's a Chessie, isn't he?"

"So I've been told," Niall said, watching in his mirror as Shep took a sniff of the offered hand, then gave a doggy sigh when Silas tickled his throat.

"I guess I'm not a criminal," his passenger said with another chuckle, facing forward again. "And just so you know, I intended to walk to town, not hitchhike."

"I don't have a problem with a grown man sticking out his thumb," Niall assured him. "Providing all he's wanting is a ride."

"As opposed to?" Silas said softly.

"As opposed to bumming free room and board off a lonely old man."

"I'm earning my keep doing repairs on the house," Silas said, bending to unzip the front pouch on his backpack. "Logan's too stiff to be climbing a ladder, and his roof was letting in more rain than it was repelling." He pulled out a classified ads magazine. "I'm heading in town to see about buying a motorcycle from someone named Titus Oceanus." Silas pointed to a circled ad on one of the pages. "When I called, he told me he lives on Whisper Cove Road. Do you know Mr. Oceanus, and can you tell me where Whisper Cove Road is?"

"Aye. Titus lives about two miles down the first camp road after the church. So he's selling his bike, is he?" Niall chuckled. "I imagine his wife put him up to it." *Now that her husband is mortal,* he refrained from adding. He looked over at Silas. "It's one of the more expensive models."

"That won't be a problem," his passenger said, shoving the book in his pack. "As a matter of fact, I came here hoping to buy a large tract of land right on Bottomless."

"Came here from where?"

"From all over, actually, but most recently from Newfoundland."

"Can I ask why ye chose Maine to settle down in, and this area in particular?"

"Despite all the wonders of this vast

world, I guess I'm American at heart. I chose Maine because your state allows charter schools and this area in particular because I can't imagine a better place to establish a school that focuses on ecology. Maine already has the College of the Atlantic and Unity College, but no *high schools* with curriculums aimed at students wanting to move straight into self-employment. And in my opinion, developing cottage industries that cater to environmentally concerned consumers is a good way to grow a sustainable economy."

"Like raising bees," Niall said. "Logan told me ye feel he can nicely supplement his income by selling honey."

Silas nodded. "And beeswax and even the bees themselves, all with only a nominal investment and no more physical effort than his aging joints can handle. And since Maine is teeming with pine trees and Logan seems to have an affinity for working with wood, I suggested he could also manufacture hive kits to sell on the Internet."

Niall remembered thinking he'd pulled up to the wrong house the last time he'd visited Logan, as the man showing him around his workshop had had a decided spring in his step, his eyes lit with excitement and purpose.

"Can you imagine," Silas continued, "what Logan and Noreen's marriage would be like today if they'd been raising bees for the last forty years alongside his logging business? Logan wouldn't have any money worries, and Noreen would feel more like his partner than his housekeeper. But even starting this late in their lives, they'll have something they can continue doing *together* well into old age."

"Aye," Niall murmured. "From what Logan told me, beekeeping seems to require more vigilance than hard labor."

Silas gestured out his window. "Selling honey is only one of any number of op- portunities around here. This entire area, from its unique inland sea to its vast timber- land, is overflowing with resources. That's why I want to open a school here. Tangible, hands-on experience is far more effective in firing a teenager's passion than sitting in a stagnant room all day and only studying the world from a distance."

"You're a teacher, then?" Niall asked, intrigued as well as surprised. Although the man was well-spoken and his clothes were clean and of high quality, he appeared to be nothing more than a carefree vagabond.

Silas gave a soft chuckle. "I didn't have the patience to get a formal education, preferring instead to let the world be my teacher." He gestured out his window again. "I want to give kids the same experience, and encourage them to work with Mother Nature rather than exploit her. The school I'm envisioning will be based here, but the students will travel the globe — first as explorers and then hopefully as teachers."

"A tract of land right on the shore of Bottomless, especially one large enough to build what would have to be a campus, won't come cheap."

"That won't be a problem," Silas softly repeated.

"Other than finding the land, how close are ye to making it happen?"

"I've already visited the Oceanographic and Geological Centers, and the lead scientists have agreed to let my students collaborate on their studies of Bottomless and the surrounding mountains." Niall heard his passenger sigh. "My only real worry is finding teachers willing to live this far out. Especially," Silas said dryly, "after they hear the campus will function completely off the grid."

"Off grid doesn't necessarily mean primitive living," Niall said. "Nova Mare is a world-class resort on top of Whisper Mountain that isn't lacking for luxury, as it makes its own wind and solar power and is heated using geothermal wells. In fact, the woman who designed those systems spends her summers here." He nodded at Silas's backpack. "If you're interested, ye might want to mention your project to Titus when ye see him about his bike, as Carolina MacKeage is his daughter."

"And your wife, Chief MacKeage?"

"Nay," Niall said with a chuckle. "Ye might say my cousin stole the lady right out from under my nose. Alec and Carolina are spending the summer camped out at the north end of the fiord, where they're building their summer home." A thought came to him. "Ye might also mention to Titus that you're looking for teachers, as I believe he knows several families that have suddenly found themselves needing to relocate."

"Teachers," Silas asked, his tone hopeful, "who would share my vision?"

"Aye, they would be keen on passing their substantial knowledge of Mother Nature on to future generations. Titus can tell ye more about them," Niall added, not knowing how the magic-maker intended to explain the Atlanteans arriving next week.

"Well," Silas said, rubbing his hands together, "I guess my heading to town just as you happened along has proven mutually beneficial for us both."

"You gained a ride and some contacts," Niall agreed, slowing down when he reached the old railroad bed. "And I benefited . . . how?"

Silas shot him a grin. "You no longer have to worry that a mysterious vagrant is taking advantage of Logan Kent."

Niall gave a quiet chuckle, deciding the man was as astute as he was candid. "Aye, ye appear to be just what Logan is needing right now." He pulled into the parking slot in front of the Trading Post marked with the *Reserved for Chief of Police* sign Hazel had put up, and shut off the engine. "Whisper Cove Road is right after the church," he said, nodding in that direction. "Titus lives just two miles down in a small, unpainted house that sits across from a large garage."

"I appreciate the ride. And with luck, I'll be leaving on a motorcycle rather than on foot." Silas unfastened his seat belt and reached for his pack — only to stop in mid-reach as he looked out the windshield. "Well now, that's another thing I've discovered this area has to offer — plenty of beautiful women."

Niall looked at where he was looking. "That particular beautiful woman is taken."

"I don't see a ring on her finger," his pas-

284

senger said, watching the woman under discussion get out of the little red cart and rush into the Bottoms Up.

"Nevertheless," Niall said quietly, "Birch is already spoken for."

Silas finished picking up his backpack and straightened. "Birch, as in the shelter director who suggested Noreen should leave Logan?" he asked, grinning when Niall nodded. "I'd like to meet the man who has the courage to date Warden Callahan."

"You just spent the last ten minutes talking to him," Niall said, opening his door and getting out. He waited for Shep to scramble over the console and jump down, then closed the door and looked across the hood of the truck as his passenger also got out. "As ye said, Mr. French, there are plenty of beautiful women in the area."

Silas studied him in silence for several heartbeats, then nodded. "Duly noted," he said, hefting his pack onto his shoulder and heading down the sidewalk in the direction of the church.

Birch had always considered her decisiveness to be her greatest strength; the one failsafe trait she could rely on to keep her moving in the right direction. So where had that wonderful quality been the last five mornings when she'd stood in front of her closet trying to decide what to wear? And three days ago, when Cassandra had asked if she could go live with a foster family that actually *liked* kids? Or two days ago, when Olivia had stopped in with some furniture brochures, asking which desk Birch preferred.

She seriously hadn't been able to choose a stupid desk? What — was she hoping the freaking Special Delivery Fairy would magically plop one down in her office?

And where had her reliable decisiveness been yesterday, when she'd spotted the perfect leather purse in one of the artisan shops in town? She *specifically* had been shopping for a purse and had found *exactly* what she wanted, and yet here she was still lugging around the leather tote she'd dug out of a box after her accident — not that anyone in Spellbound Falls had noticed it was six years out of fashion.

This was all Niall's fault. The man couldn't make passionate, playful love to her all night long and then turn into a Neanderthal the next morning, thus ending what could have been a really fun affair before it had barely gotten started. Yes, her wishy-washiness had started the morning Niall had threatened to hunt her down if she left town alone, because instead of letting loose a blistering tirade pointing out his incredible arrogance, she had stood there like some clueless damsel listening to him drive away and feeling . . . well . . . cherished.

Then again, that warm and fuzzy feeling could have been nothing more than the lingering glow of a night of passionate, playful sex.

Seriously; she had to have been insane to consider having an affair with a cop.

Which was why, while staring into her closet this morning and realizing she once again couldn't decide what to wear, Birch had *decisively* decided she had to get a grip. Who needed to sleep wrapped up in all those stupid amazing muscles, anyway? So she'd pulled out a pair of white linen slacks and a purple sleeveless top, gotten dressed while giving *herself* a blistering tirade on the foibles of lusting after mountains of testosterone, and gone in search of her beachcombing, sand-digging pet.

Mon Dieu, she hoped that had been a harbor seal or whale bone Mimi had proudly dragged up from the beach yesterday and not a human femur. Apparently reading her mistress's mood, Mighty Mimi had endured her bath with minimal grumbling, then curled up in a sunbeam with a doggy treat to dry off while Birch had marched into the once formal parlor she'd converted into an office. After ten minutes of sitting at the rickety old table and studying furniture brochures, she'd called Olivia and *decisively* ordered the walnut reproduction desk — even though she preferred the modern design — because it better matched the stately old house.

Birch had then softly knocked on Cassandra's door, entered once a sleepy voice had invited her in, and sat down on the bed. She'd then told the semi-orphaned teenager that if after one more meeting she truly didn't want to live with her aunt anymore, they would start searching for a local family who, instead of throwing her sketch pad and charcoals in the trash, would encourage her artistic talent.

And now, armed with a healthy dose of righteous indignation aimed solely at herself — even though it was all Niall's fault she'd been wishy-washy for five freaking days — Birch was zooming out the camp road in one of the red carts, heading to that pretty little artisan shop to buy that *perfect* leather purse. And the next damsel-rescuing idiot who said he had a powerful desire to kiss her was getting a mouthful of bear spray.

Birch darted into the newly vacated parking slot in front of the Bottoms Up, rushed inside and hopped up on the large pine bar's footrail, and stretched to give Macie the key. "I left one of the carts out front for you to drive home tonight."

"But then how will you get home?" Macie asked, also having to stretch past her growing belly. She shot Birch a smile. "I'm not afraid of walking home in the dark."

"Or of dodging raccoons and skunks?" Birch said with a laugh, hopping down. "Don't worry about it; I've got errands to run in town and will hitch a ride with Mom," she explained, weaving through tables filled with patrons as she backed away. "But if you're not home by ten-fifteen, I'm going to —" Birch spun around when she bumped into a warm, solid object. "Oh, sorry, Officer Sheppard."

"Miss Callahan," he drawled, rubbing his belly where she'd poked him with her tote. He cocked his head. "Should I hazard a guess as to which one of your residents has you hitting the bar in the middle of the afternoon? Because my money's on Noreen Kent, since I wrote her a warning this morning for nearly mowing down a family in the crosswalk when she left the bank."

"Yeah, she told me. But in her defense, Noreen had just found out her husband had made a sizable withdrawal from their savings account a few days ago." Birch started backing away again. "I told her she can't use the carts for a whole week. Thanks for just giving her a warning," she finished before turning and rushing outside — only to step into the path of a man on the sidewalk, her momentum forcing her to grab his arm to keep from falling.

Birch looked up, her apology catching in her throat when she found herself staring into arresting blue eyes set in a sun-bronzed face, the man's hair pulled back in a tail at the nape of his neck and the humor tugging at his mouth only amplifying his handsome features. Birch immediately let go before she made even more of a fool of herself, and crouched down and began shoving things back in her fallen bag.

The man also crouched and started handing her items. "Silas French," he said, passing Birch her wallet.

She stopped shoveling and looked at him in surprise, then took the wallet but stood up without shaking the hand he continued to extend. "Thank you, Mr. French. I'm sorry for bumping into you," she added tightly.

"Wait," he said, catching hold of her arm. "It's Miss Callahan, isn't it?"

She turned back in time to see him glance up the sidewalk. "Yes, I'm Birch Callahan. And you're the . . . gentleman who's staying with Logan Kent."

He lost his smile. "It sounds as if you don't approve of my helping Logan make repairs to his house in exchange for room and board." He winced. "Well, Logan may be providing the food, but I've taken over running the gas grill," he said, darting another quick glance up the sidewalk.

"I hear he's also providing you with money to purchase *bees*. Since when, Mr. French, does a hive cost three thousand dollars?"

"Excuse me?" His eyes widened. "No, he didn't give *me* the money; Logan wrote the check directly to the supply house." He ushered them out of the stream of foot traffic. "The hives themselves and protective clothing are relatively inexpensive, but honey extraction equipment can get costly. And I told Logan it's actually more frugal to buy a high-quality extractor, and that he would be better off getting an electric one."

"You don't think starting a beekeeping business is something he should have discussed with his wife before he raided their savings? *Which,*" she added when he tried to speak, "Logan refused to touch for a new cookstove."

"But the bees could double his investment by this fall," he countered, even as another grin tugged at his mouth. "*Which* Logan tried to explain to Noreen when she called this morning."

"You have no business interfering in their — why do you keep looking up the sidewalk?" she asked when he did it again.

"I've been hoping to meet you on one of my trips to town to see if together we couldn't find a way for Logan and Noreen to reconcile — or that was my plan before your boyfriend warned me off," he said dryly, grinning again when Birch felt her jaw slacken. "That is definitely one man I don't want to cross."

"What are you talking about? I don't have a boyfriend."

"Tall? Green eyes? Wears a badge?" His eyes lit with amusement. "Have you told Chief MacKeage you two aren't dating?"

"We're not — he actually warned you off?" Birch repeated as *she* glanced up the sidewalk. She took a calming breath. "Look, Mr. French."

"Please, call me Silas," he said . . . expectantly.

She didn't reciprocate the offer. "If you truly wish to see Noreen and Logan get back together, then I suggest you pack up and *move on.* Now if you will excuse me," she said, turning away — only to nearly walk into the young girl standing directly behind her. "Oh, hey there. Are you lost?" she asked when she realized the girl couldn't be more than eleven or twelve years old. She looked up and down the sidewalk then toward the park. "Did you get separated from your parents?"

"Are you Birch Callahan?"

"That would be me," Birch said, smiling into her frantic brown eyes. "What can I do for you, sweetie?" Realizing Mr. French hadn't taken her advice to *move on,* Birch slid her arm around the girl's shoulders and began walking toward the Trading Post. "How about we start with your name?"

"I'm not supposed to tell you my name." She stopped and began pulling Birch back toward the church. "I've been looking all over town for you, and Mom's probably worried sick that I've been gone so long."

"Where is she?" Birch asked, not fighting her.

The nameless girl stopped again and leaned closer. "She's hiding in a gravel pit outside of town," she said, nodding to the north.

"Who's she hiding from?" Birch asked softly.

"My dad." She started off again. "We gotta go get her so you can take us to that house you run, where we'll be safe. But Mom said she won't trust no one but you and that you gotta come alone."

"Is there a problem?" Silas French asked from right behind them.

Ignoring him, Birch redirected the girl toward the cart and urged her into the passenger seat. "It'll be quicker if we take the cart," she explained when the girl started to protest. "You wait here while I run inside and get the key. I'll just be a minute," she added as she turned and headed for the Bottoms Up.

Silas French stepped between her and the door. "Maybe I should go with you," he said quietly, obviously having overheard their conversation.

"Better yet, maybe you should start minding *your own* business."

He caught hold of her arm again when she tried to step around him. "What if the husband shows up while you're there? The only gravel pit I know of north of here is at least two miles away and rather isolated."

"Le maudit tannant," she snapped, jerking free — only to stumble back when he

released her in surprise.

"Did you just cuss at me?"

"You're lucky that's all I did," she growled, taking advantage of several patrons walking out of the Bottoms Up to dart around him and slip inside. She immediately ran to the window to make sure the girl was still sitting in the cart and saw Silas French jogging in the opposite direction he'd been going when she'd first bumped into him.

Or more precisely, in the direction of the police station.

"Nosy, annoying man," she muttered, making her way to the bar as she searched for a police uniform. She veered left when she spotted Officer Sheppard heading to a recently vacated table and caught hold of his sleeve. "I need you to follow me," she said as he cooperatively — unlike certain members of the police force — let her drag him along. "There's a mother in trouble hiding in a gravel pit two miles north of here, and she wants me to come alone because she doesn't trust anyone." She hopped up onto the bar's footrail. "Macie, I need that key back," she called down the bar. Birch looked at Officer Sheppard. "She sent her daughter to find me, and I'm taking the girl in the cart to go get her mother. Can you follow us without being seen?"

He grinned. "*You* won't even know I'm there," he said, turning away.

She caught hold of his sleeve again. "Wait. Call your boss and tell him to ignore whatever the man coming to the station says, and explain that you're with me."

He gave a nod and headed for the door that connected the Bottoms Up to the Drunken Moose — so the girl wouldn't see his uniform, Birch realized. Oh, she really liked these new police officers, since *they* seemed to take her concerns seriously.

Well, okay; Niall had taken her getting run off the road seriously, to the point he'd turned into a caveman and actually forbidden her to go anywhere alone.

Not that she wanted to go anywhere alone while someone was trying to kill her.

"Thanks, Macie," she said, taking the key and hopping down off the footrail. "If I don't get the cart back to you later today, someone will pick you up at nine," she added with a wave as she headed for the door.

This time Birch checked up and down the sidewalk to make sure the coast was clear, then walked over and got in the cart and shoved the key in the ignition. She patted the young girl's knee, giving her a brilliant smile. "You leave everything to me, sweetie.

I'll have you and your mom safely settled at the shelter before supper," she promised, glancing over her shoulder and backing into the road when a hole opened in the traffic. "And I hope you both brought your appetites, because I'm pretty sure I saw Noreen putting a huge turkey in the oven this afternoon."

CHAPTER FIFTEEN

Niall stopped at the bottom of his station stairs and tapped the notes icon on his phone, opened the list of vehicles he intended to ask Sam to check out, and added the Quebec plate number of the Lexus parked at the top of the lane. He was likely more optimistic than efficient for noting all the Canadian plates he came across, but the only way he knew to find a needle in a haystack was to roll up his sleeves and start looking. Quebec and New Brunswick were neighboring provinces, and Hazel had said Leonard had an Ontario driver's license, but he wasn't ruling out vehicles from any provinces.

Not that Birch's attacker couldn't have already ditched the white car and simply gotten a rental in Maine. Hell, half the vehicles in town belonged to overseas tourists who had flown into Bangor International Airport and rented cars to make the three-hour drive into the wilderness.

"Chief MacKeage," a man called out, making Niall look up to see Silas French loping down the lane. "I happened to run into Miss Callahan coming out of the Bottoms Up," Silas said when he reached him, "and thought you might like to know she's leaving town in that golf cart with a young girl. From what I overheard, the girl's mother is hiding in a gravel pit north of here." A terse grin lifted one side of his mouth. "My offer to accompany them was answered with a French cuss and the suggestion that I mind my own business." He sobered. "The reason I'm telling you is that I heard what happened with the Vaughns, and it occurred to me things could get ugly if this woman's husband suddenly showed up."

Well, so much for not going anywhere alone — although Niall wasn't surprised Birch had grown tired of behaving herself, considering five entire days had passed with no one trying to kill her. Nay, he wasn't surprised, but he definitely intended to go after her. "I thank you for your concern, Mr. French," he said as he slipped his phone in his pocket, figuring he could catch the cart within a mile. But even before he took a step, Niall felt his phone vibrate and pulled it out to find Jake's name on the screen. "MacKeage," he said, only to slowly relax as the man filled him in on what was going on. "I trust ye can keep an eye on them without being seen? Okay, call me if you need backup," he added when Jake promised even the squirrels wouldn't see him.

"I thank you for your concern, Mr. French," Niall repeated as he mounted the station steps. "One of my officers is with Birch."

"That's it?" Silas said, making Niall turn and look down at him. "Logan told me word in town is your two new officers aren't from around here and that no one knows anything about them. Are you really going to leave your girlfriend's welfare in the hands of a man you met less than a week ago?"

Niall found himself wondering if Mr. French simply had a bad habit of sticking his nose in other people's business or if the *overly* concerned idiot hadn't taken his warning about Birch seriously. "I didn't hire Jake and Cole for their looks. Good luck negotiating with Titus," he added over his shoulder as he strode into the station.

But Niall didn't make it two steps inside before he was brought to a halt by a silence thick enough to taste as Hazel pulled her purse from the bottom drawer of her desk and stood up. He didn't believe the possibility she'd overheard his conversation with French had anything to do with the decidedly awkward silence, but more likely the gentleman sitting in a chair across the room.

"Niall," Hazel said as the man also stood up and approached them. "This is Claude St. Germaine. Ah . . . Birch's father."

She needn't have bothered with the clarification, as the resemblance was undeniable. Other than his height and age, Claude St. Germaine could be a male version of Birch — right down to his eyes, hair color, and several defining facial features. Hell, there certainly wasn't any question which parent had given Birch her direct stare. "Mr. St. Germaine," Niall said as he shook his hand, pleased to note the man's firm grip.

"I respond well to Claude, Chief Mac-Keage."

"And Niall works for me," Niall offered, turning and walking behind his desk. He picked up the small pile of memos on his blotter and shuffled through them. "Would that be your red Lexus parked at the top of the lane?"

"Yes. It probably looks familiar because it

was purchased at the same time as my daughter's," Claude said, making Niall lift his gaze at the amusement in the man's voice. "Birch insisted mine also be red, and since she was buying, I didn't argue."

A soft snort sounded off to his right, and Niall looked over to see Hazel's nose all but buried in her purse as she industriously searched for something. "Don't feel ye have to stay glued to the office when I'm not here, Hazel. Just lock the door and go sit in the park or out on the docks to eat your lunch, if ye wish."

She lowered her purse with a quick glance at Claude before looking at Niall. "I wasn't waiting for you; I'm waiting for Sam. He's taking me to Turtleback this afternoon so I can check out station sites several business owners have generously offered."

Instead of being amazed that in five days Hazel had accomplished what he hadn't been able to in three months, Niall honed in on the fact Sam was taking her. "Does Birch know you're going?" he asked. *Just you and Sam,* he refrained from adding. *Alone. For an entire afternoon and likely most of the evening.*

After another glance at Claude, Hazel gave Niall an impressively militant look as her chin lifted. "No, she doesn't. I intend to call

Birch from Turtleback and let her know I'm away on business and won't be home for dinner."

Niall caught himself also glancing at Mr. St. Germaine, apparently hoping for some sort of help, only to see the man lower his head on what appeared to be a sigh — but not quickly enough for Niall to miss his grin.

"Yes. Well," Hazel said when an awkward silence filled the station again. "I guess I'll go see what's keeping Sam." She opened the door but stopped and looked back at Niall. "Are you comfortable letting me choose the station site?"

"Aye, if you promise to consider Sam's advice on the matter."

That militant look was replaced by a twinkle. "He will have my undivided attention," she said deadpan, striding outside and closing the door behind her.

"How well do you know Sam?" Claude asked as Hazel's steps faded away.

Niall sat down and gestured at the chair opposite his desk. "Well enough to assure you he's not interested in her money."

That got him a chuckle. "It's not me you need to assure, but my daughter," Claude said, also sitting down. "You might want to warn your friend that Hazel comes with a formidable watchdog."

"I believe Sam is aware of Hazel's . . . history with men." Niall leaned back in his chair. "Can I ask why ye came to see the chief of police upon arriving in town rather than your daughter?"

"Before I answer that, I have the same question as Mr. French, only instead of a concerned citizen, I'm asking as her father. Is Birch really in good hands right now?"

"I wouldn't be here if she wasn't. Jake is more than capable of getting everyone back to town safely."

His visitor's eyes narrowed. "I heard French call Birch your girlfriend, yet not once in our recent phone conversations did my daughter mention she was seeing anyone."

Niall decided he liked Claude St. Germaine. Not only did the man obviously love his daughter enough to travel from Montreal to see her; it was equally obvious he was Birch's formidable watchdog. Niall answered the unspoken challenge with a shrug. "I imagine she didn't say anything because she's still getting used to the notion." He tossed the memos down on the desk and folded his arms over his chest. "So if sizing up your daughter's new boyfriend isn't the reason you're here, what is?"

Claude also leaned back and propped an

ankle on one of his knees. "Actually, I am here to size you up," he admitted. "But as a cop. I wanted to meet you in person to decide if you have what it takes to protect my daughter and Hazel from the bastards who are after them, or if I'll have to break a few American laws and do it myself."

"There's more than one?" Niall asked, not knowing which alarmed him more — that the man had just confirmed someone truly had tried to kill Birch or the fact there were several people involved. "Are ye saying it's not Leonard Struthers?"

"Leonard Struthers is dead." Claude gave a soft snort. "For the *second* time. They fished his body out of the Saint Lawrence some thirty miles upriver of Quebec City the same day as Birch's accident. It was decided he'd been in the water over a week, which means it wasn't Hazel's fourth husband driving that white car."

"Birch told you about the accident?"

"She called me the next evening and told me what had happened and who she suspected. But then she told me not to worry, because there were three badass police officers protecting her." Claude's eyes filled with amusement. "And that one officer in particular had gotten really good at saving her butt."

Which told Niall that Birch had called her father *after* she'd spent the night in his bed. "Did she also mention that I threatened to hunt her down if she left town without one of us accompanying her?"

Claude nodded. "That was the reason I didn't tell her about the body in the river until I had a positive ID, and also why I didn't show up here the next morning." His grin finally broke free. "I figured any man brave enough to order Birch not to do something was more than capable of protecting her."

"Exactly what have I been protecting her from?" Niall asked.

His visitor's amusement vanished. "I don't know *exactly;* at this point I'm only speculating, based on what I've pieced together since Birch told me Leonard Struthers had tried to mortgage their house." Claude dropped his foot and leaned forward. "His real name was Jacques Rabideu, and he'd assumed six identities that I know of over the last twenty years — likely taken from recently deceased men in other provinces."

"So Hazel wasn't his first victim?"

"I can't actually prove it, but she appears to be one of at least six."

"So if Rabideu died nearly two weeks ago, then who are the bastards ye believe are after Hazel and Birch? Did he leave behind a family; maybe a wife or brothers that might want Birch out of the way so they can exploit Hazel themselves?"

Claude was shaking his head before Niall had finished. "My guess is whoever murdered Rabideu is after something other than money. His body was missing several fingers and toes, and the medical examiner concluded he'd endured several days of torture before someone finally carved out his heart and shoved it down his throat."

Sweet Christ. "Who in hell did the man piss off?" Niall growled. "And what makes ye think his murder involves his marriage to Hazel?"

"From the research I've been doing, con artists of Rabideu's caliber operating in Canada are almost exclusively from three, possibly four families. And I think Rabideu may have crossed one of them, and they tortured information out of him and then cut out his heart as a warning to others." Claude shrugged. "My guess is he'd stolen from them or had incriminating evidence that he intended to use for blackmail, and I'm worried that whatever they're after unwittingly ended up in Hazel's possession. Birch said they packed up all of Leonard's belongings, sent everything to a storage facility, and left the locker key taped to the door of their house along with a note saying divorce proceedings had already been started."

"And you believe the women may have missed something when they packed, and that's why Rabideu followed them to Ottawa?"

Claude blew out a heavy sigh. "That's my best guess."

Niall stood up and walked to the window, then shoved his hands in his pockets and stood staring out at Bottomless. "Is it possible you're mistaken," he asked without turning around, "and Birch's attacker could be a vengeful husband of an abused woman she'd recently helped?"

"Birch stopped seeing clients two years ago when she went back to school to get her doctorate. And the timing of Rabideu's death is too coincidental."

"Aye," Niall murmured, not liking that Claude was probably right. He turned around. "Have you shared any of this with Birch?"

"No."

"Is that why you're here, then; so you can tell her in person?"

Claude softly chuckled. "I'm here because I miss my daughter." He cocked his head, his perspective appearing to turn inward. "My life did a one-eighty the day I walked into a Montreal hospital room and a frail-looking, six-year-old waif lifted her bandaged arms for me to pick her up. Whatever Hazel had told Birch about my absence in her life, she must have been kind in the telling, because even though I was a complete stranger, Birch hugged my neck, said, 'Hello, Daddy,' and thanked me for coming to see her. And then *she* explained to *me* that we would be living together for a little while, because some funny-smelling lady with crooked teeth had told her *Grand-mémère* was dead and her mom was hurt too badly to take care of her right now." His expression still distant, he grinned. "Birch has been teaching me the finer points of being a father ever since."

"Was there a car accident?" Niall asked softly.

"No, an explosion," Claude said, his focus returning to the present. "It was decided a compressor ignited a gas leak that had filled a third-floor utility room of the downtown mall where they were shopping. Four people were killed — Hazel's grandmother, Annette Hynes, being one of them — and sixteen were injured." His eyes turned somber. "I was told Birch spent several hours trapped under concrete and steel, protectively co-cooned by her dead great-grandmother and unconscious mother. The social worker who called to ask if I would be willing to come get my daughter said that, miraculously, Birch only had a broken finger, a few cuts that had needed stitches, and some bruising. But Hazel was critical and not expected to live; her back and both legs were broken, one lung had been punctured, and several vital organs were threatening to shut down. I was told that if she did survive, she probably wouldn't ever walk again."

"She obviously did both," Niall said.

Claude's grin returned. "Although it took six operations and several years of physical therapy, apparently just the thought of her precious little girl living in my father's house was all the motivation Hazel needed to recover."

"So Birch went to live with your parents instead of with you?"

"No, *we* went to live with them. I was a single, twenty-five-year-old career soldier at the time; what did I know about little girls? I left the military, moved back home with Birch, and turned into my old man by becoming a cop."

"You're a police officer?"

"I was until I handed in my resignation

five days ago. I spent the last four days packing up my belongings and putting my house up for sale, then got in my car this morning and drove to Maine."

"You're moving here?" Niall said in surprise.

Claude turned away and sat down again. "Montreal has felt rather empty lately."

Niall walked to his desk and also sat down, wondering if the seed of a notion he was forming was wise — or if he might very well be courting disaster. "How are you intending to make your living here?"

"I haven't *needed* to make a living since the day Annette Hynes died. In the letter she'd apparently written within days of Birch's birth and left with her lawyer to give me, along with a rather outrageous sum of money, Annette explained that if I ever wanted to have a relationship with my daughter someday, it would be better if no one could say my interest in Birch had anything to do with her wealth."

"Yet you still let her buy you a Lexus."

Claude nodded. "That's because I've never told her about my inheritance from Annette. Birch was eight the first time she insisted on buying me a new car, claiming she was doing the environment a favor by putting my old truck out of its misery. So as her legal guardian and knowing it wouldn't even dent the *interest* on her trust fund, I drove her to the bank and signed for her to take out the money." His eyes lit with amusement again. "Mostly because I knew the real reason she wanted to buy me that car was to piss off her *grand-père* St. Germaine. Because," Claude went on when Niall raised a brow, "my father often went out of his way to make sure the little heiress living with him never made the mistake of thinking she was superior to anyone."

And that, Niall realized, explained Birch accusing him of trying to buy his way into her bloomers, as her own inheritance had obviously made her as much of a target as Hazel — only not just by scheming men, but by her own grandfather's insecurities. It was a problem Annette Hynes had foreseen, apparently, and dealt with by taking wealth out of the equation for father and daughter by simply giving Claude his own money.

Niall put his seed of a notion on the back burner for now. "Where are ye planning on staying until you find something permanent?" he asked, fairly certain Birch wouldn't let a man sleep at the shelter, not even her father.

"Figuring all the cabins and hotels are booked this time of year, I stopped at that campground just north of Turtleback Station on my way up and rented a campsite."

"Does Birch know you're intending to move here?"

Giving only a soft snort for answer, Claude cocked his head. "Just how well do you know my daughter?"

That made Niall chuckle. "Admittedly not as well as I'd like. Hazel's been telling me a few tales, though, mostly of Birch's teenage years. But she's never mentioned the explosion or it being the reason Birch went to live with you."

"It's my understanding Hazel rarely talks about that time in her life," Claude said. "And even though when I picked up my daughter at the hospital the social worker assured me Birch didn't remember anything about the explosion or being trapped, I've always suspected she remembers every terrifying detail. But it appears both women have decided to pretend those four years never happened; Hazel likely because of the pain she endured getting back on her feet, and Birch most likely because if she can't say something nice about her grandparents, she'd just as soon not say anything at all."

"She still doesn't get along with your father? What about your mother?"

"Birch *tolerates* them; for my sake, she

once told me. My mother's not exactly the nurturing type, and she didn't know what to do with a little girl any more than I did. As for my father . . ." Claude winced. "Well, among other things, Hazel called him an emotionless, coldhearted bastard right to his face the day she came after Birch."

"So your daughter gets her mouth from Hazel?" Niall said in surprise, since he hadn't heard Hazel utter a single curse or even show a hint of having a temper.

"No, that wonderful trait comes from her great-grandmother. I never had the privilege of meeting Annette Hynes, but apparently even though she topped out at five-foot-three, the woman's ability to cut a person off at the knees with one of her verbal outbursts was legendary. In fact, when her daughter, Evelyn, died of cancer when Hazel was seven months pregnant with Birch, Annette caused a scene after the funeral that's still talked about today. Even back then, Evelyn's husband, Avery Callahan, had a reputation as a domineering, take-no-prisoners businessman, and he made sure to pass that trait on to his three sons." Claude grinned. "His only daughter, Hazel, was considered the black sheep of the family for actually *liking* people."

"Was Hazel the youngest?" Niall asked.

"Yes. And apparently Evelyn Callahan hadn't been in the ground an hour when Annette helped her granddaughter fill a suitcase with a few precious possessions and hustled the girl out the back door to her limo. The story goes that Annette then walked back in the house and told her son-in-law that she had kept her opinion of him to herself for her daughter's sake, but that his toxic, oppressive nature is what had really killed Evelyn. She then announced she was taking Hazel to live with her so that her grand- and great-granddaughters didn't suffer the same fate, and if he tried to stop them, she would ruin him both socially and financially."

Niall once again found himself in awe of Hazel's history with men, which had obviously influenced Birch's opinion of them. "Would the Callahan men all happen to be hulking brutes, by any chance?" he asked dryly.

Claude nodded, his eyes filling with amusement again. "A colorful vocabulary isn't the only thing my daughter inherited from Annette Hynes. When she was little Birch often wondered aloud if whoever had been in charge of handing out height the day she was born hadn't been sleeping on the job." He shook his head. "I seem to be the only male relation she wants anything to do with. But then, in her words, 'she's put a lot of effort into making me at least tolerable.' "

Aye, with nothing more than the bandaged hug of a six-year-old delivering a sucker punch to her daddy's heart, Niall decided. Because although he didn't know Birch well enough to guess how she would take the news Claude was moving to Maine, he didn't doubt the woman more than just *tolerated* her father.

"Did ye put any files together on those three or four families you suspect may have murdered Rabideu? Because it so happens I know someone with contacts in several international . . . agencies who might be able to help us," Niall said, picking his words carefully. "Then would you be willing to let me show my friend what you have?" he asked when Claude nodded, a different kind of light coming into the man's eyes.

"I had just started with military intelligence myself when I got the call about the explosion," Claude said. "But that was so long ago that I don't know anyone I can bring my information to now. It's mostly the Royal Canadian Mounted Police who've helped me get this far. Your friend can have everything I've got if it will help us find out who these bastards are and what they're after. Give me tonight to dig out my files and organize them so they'll make sense, and I'll bring you everything tomorrow morning."

Niall nodded. "It may take him a few days, but —"

"Chief! Chief MacKeage!"

At the sound of pounding footsteps on the porch, Niall stood up just as the station door burst open and an older gentleman he recognized but couldn't immediately place charged inside. "Thank God you're here," the man said in a winded rush. "You gotta come to the Drunken Moose. Now, before things get out of hand."

"What's going on?" Niall asked, moving around his desk toward him.

"Noreen seen that fellow who's staying with Logan get off a motorcycle and go in the Moose, and she ran in after him looking madder than an old laying hen caught in a rainstorm, and started shouting to everyone that the guy had rooked Logan outta three thousand dollars of their savings." The man sucked in a wheezing breath and headed onto the porch, gesturing for Niall to follow. "There's a whole table of grange ladies and other women taking Noreen's side, and if you don't get there quick, this town's gonna see its first all-out riot and maybe even a lynching," he continued as he scurried down the stairs, glancing over his shoulder to make sure Niall was following before starting up the lane. "A bunch of men moved their chairs to surround the poor bastard when he tried to leave, claiming he's got every right as anyone to eat at the Moose," the man motored on, shouting his last words because Niall had sprinted ahead and was almost to the sidewalk.

He'd dawdled long enough, Niall decided with a heavy sigh, and it was time to bring this public little war to an end. He was just glad Birch was out of town at the moment, because he really couldn't see her getting on board with his solution. And if she did stick her nose in his business when she got back . . . well, the pint-sized spitfire just might find herself sleeping in his holding cell tonight.

CHAPTER SIXTEEN

Aware Claude was keeping pace behind him, Niall rounded the corner of the Trading Post only to mutter a curse when he caught sight of Shep running flat-out down the main road well ahead of a little red cart. He wasn't surprised the dog had followed Birch, but he did wish their rescue mission had kept them out of town a while longer.

Niall actually heard the shouting two stores shy of the restaurant, and slowed just enough to ease his way through the crowd gathered on the sidewalk trying to see in the windows. "Let me through, folks," he said, his tone opening up a path as people pulled each other out of his way. He then entered the Drunken Moose to find battle lines indeed had been drawn; an impenetrable circle of male diners — some appearing to be tourists — sat two rows deep surrounding an obviously uncomfortable Silas French as they tried to outshout an

319

equally impressive — and definitely angry — wall of women.

"I was just about to call 911," Vanetta said as she approached, having to raise her voice to be heard. She stopped in front of Niall and waved a dishcloth toward the battle. "I haven't seen people this riled up since some idiot suggested the grange ladies should have to pay taxes on the railroad land they simply claimed for their park." She looked to Niall's left when Claude moved up beside him, blinked and did a double take, then shot Niall a smile. "You want me to go ahead and dial 911 and ask them to send you some backup, or should I just call Nicholas?"

"Let's save both for when I'm actually outnumbered," Niall said, giving her a wink and striding into the chaos. "Okay, people, let's quiet down," he said loudly, only to be ignored. "Enough!" he bellowed, effectively bringing the shouting to an abrupt halt.

Well, except for Noreen Kent, who pivoted in surprise, quickly recovered, and turned her angry glare on *him* as she pointed at Silas French. "I want that man arrested. And you make him give Logan and me back our money."

"He doesn't have your money, Noreen," Niall said gently. "I spoke with Logan on the phone not half an hour ago, and your husband said he mailed the check directly to the beekeeping supply company yesterday."

Her face darkened. "That doesn't mean this man's not scamming us. For all we know that company's just as crooked as he is and they're in cahoots together."

"I saw this kind of thing on *20/20*," Christina Richie piped in, the octogenarian giving an authoritative nod. "Scammers create a fake company and even make TV commercials that look legitimate so you'll call and give them your credit card number. And you get charged but never receive the product because it's fake, too."

"Why do you think crooks like him travel all the way up here," a woman added, "and then move in on the first man they come across living alone? I'll tell you why," she rushed on with an equally assertive nod. "Scammers got us pegged as easy marks, figuring only ignorant hicks live in the wilderness because we don't know any better."

"Ladies," Niall said quietly. "I checked into that company and it's —"

"That shows what you know, Inez," a man called out from the inner circle of chairs, cutting Niall off. "This fella came here because he prefers the wilderness just like we do, and he knows all sorts of stuff about the forest and animals and growing things. And I ain't never met a crook yet who was quick to roll up his sleeves and break a sweat showing a person how to fox-proof his henhouse without spending a fortune."

"Silas showed me how to get my hydrangeas blooming again by tucking pine needles around them," another man said. "He explained they like acidy dirt."

"I told you that two years ago, you idiot," a female voice called out from the back. "And of course he pretends to like the wilderness — that's how he lures people into his scams." Janice Crupp, another of the older grange ladies, pushed her way forward and also glared at Niall as she pointed at Silas. "I want to file charges against him, too, for waltzing in our driveway like he owned the place when he saw my husband weeding around our fence posts." She turned to address the women. "The guy told Amos that if he got himself a dozen geese he wouldn't ever have to dig out his noisy weed-wacker again. Noreen, do you know the name of that company Logan sent your three thousand dollars to? I bet it's the same fake company he wanted Amos to buy those geese from. We'd be out a hundred and twenty bucks plus postage if I hadn't asked Amos why he was looking for our checkbook."

"For chrissakes, Janice," one of the men spat out, "you can't file charges against someone for *suggesting* you buy something."

"Yeah," another man added. "And walking in a driveway that hasn't got a *No Trespassing* sign posted out front isn't a crime."

"People," Niall said, taking a step forward. "Why don't we —"

"My grandchildren *play* in that yard," Janice snapped. "Do you have any idea how much slimy shit a dozen geese drop in a day?" She swung toward Niall. "Are you going to arrest the crook or not? Because I hope you know we've all noticed," she rushed on instead of letting him respond, "that you've been police chief over three months now and haven't so much as written a parking ticket."

"And let's not forget he refused to arrest Logan," Christina Richie added, "even after Noreen had to flee for her life when the fool blew her stove to smithereens."

"Are you all forgetting he saved Misty Vaughn's life?" a male voice countered.

"And Sally Vaughn's, too," another man added.

"Have any of you noticed he isn't hiring any female officers?" a young woman shouted over the raised voices of several men now trying to defend Logan and Niall. "And that the two guys he did hire aren't locals? They're not even *Mainers.*"

"They both seem capable enough," one of the men managed to interject.

"We didn't vote for a police force just to have a bunch of strangers move here and start telling us what to do," the lady named Inez shouted right back at him.

There was a loud male snort. "Wally Coots applied for one of those positions. You want that idiot mama's boy walking around with a loaded gun?"

"The new officer ticketed me this morning for reckless driving," Noreen said, shooting Niall another angry glare, "even though my cart didn't come anywhere near that family crossing the road."

"Hell, Noreen, you don't even have a driver's license," a man called out.

Ignoring him, Noreen went back to pointing at the wisely silent Silas French — or maybe that was abject terror rendering him speechless. "Are you going to arrest this crook and get our money back or not?"

"He *can't,* because there ain't been no *crime* committed."

"No, the reason he won't is because all you men stick together!"

"Only to keep you women from stealing our pants so *you* can wear them."

"Or else because our new police chief is just as crooked!"

"Yeah, we don't know anything about *him,* either."

"Except that he's not hiring any women officers!"

"That's because he doesn't want to hear a hen squawking in his ear all day!"

"Or let one of you walk around with a loaded gun!"

And just when had this become about *him*? Niall dropped his head on a sigh as the two sides continued firing salvos at one another in ever-increasing volume, even as he tried to estimate how many people he could fit in his holding cell. Well, how many *women,* as he sure as hell didn't dare put the men in with them.

The ladies just weren't backing down, instead appearing to grow even more aggressive. In fact, several men suddenly slid back their chairs and stood up when one idiot commented on Noreen's poisonous cooking, to which she responded by grabbing a plate of half-eaten food off a nearby table and hurling it at him.

Well, son of a bitch. "Enough!" Niall roared when he saw two more women reaching for dishes, the added edge in his voice freezing everyone in place.

Knowing he was putting *himself* in danger of being lynched — with a pint-sized spitfire likely volunteering to slip the noose over his neck when she found out — Niall pulled his handcuffs out of his pocket. "I'm sorry, Mrs. Kent, but I'm going to have to arrest you for inciting a riot, damaging property, and possibly even assault."

"Those cuffs so much as touch her skin," an impressively threatening voice said from the doorway, "and I'm calling the state police to come relieve you of your badge."

Niall turned to see Birch shoving her way past onlookers until she bumped into a man who didn't budge, her eyes widening as she silently mouthed the word *Daddy*. But she quickly stepped around him and continued elbowing her way right past Niall, not stopping until she reached Noreen. "Easy there, honey," she said gently, wrapping an arm around the now pale woman. "He's not really going to arrest you."

"I'm afraid I am," Niall said, his footsteps echoing through the silent room as he closed the distance between them. "And you as well, Miss Callahan, if ye interfere," he added, barely restraining himself from reaching out and closing her mouth when her chin dropped. "Ye needn't bother seeking help from your father," he went on when she rose on her toes and looked toward the door. "His authority stopped at the border." He then held up the handcuffs. "Your choice, Mrs. Kent; the handcuffs, or you can give me your word to come along peacefully."

"Don't do this, Niall," Birch hissed under her breath.

"It's done, lass," he said just as softly, gesturing for Noreen to precede him out.

When the obviously shocked woman couldn't seem to move, Birch drew herself up to her full height, tightened her hold on Noreen and, with an *I'll see you in hell* glare and mutinous lift of her chin, started them forward — Shep leading the way through the parting crowd of equally shocked onlookers.

It might not be wooden stocks in the town park, Niall decided with a sigh as he followed, but it definitely was public. And, he hoped, just outrageous enough for two scared people to remember why they'd gotten married in the first place — as well as why they'd *stayed* married for forty-three years.

Now if only he could get Birch to see the brilliance in his plan.

Feeling more like a hulking brute than a peacemaker, Niall sat at his desk trying to do paperwork while also trying to ignore the murmured assurances interspersed with wrenching sobs coming from his holding cell. He glanced at his watch to see it was ten minutes past the last time he'd checked, and wondered how the hell long it took a man who seemed to love sticking his nose in people's business to ride a powerful motorcycle four and a half miles.

Their silent little procession hadn't reached the Trading Post when Niall had heard Silas French's newly purchased bike start up, and they'd just turned onto the lane when it had shot down the main road heading south. Niall had decided to forgive the man for disregarding the speed limit, since it was serving his purpose, figuring it would take Silas no more than five minutes to reach the Kent homestead. It should then take Silas only a minute to tell Logan his wife had just been arrested, maybe five or six minutes for Logan to find his checkbook — or his shotgun — and another twenty minutes for them to race back to town in Logan's tired old pickup.

So where the hell were they? Because his brilliant plan might not work so . . . brilliantly if Birch succeeded in getting Noreen to stop crying before Logan arrived. Then again, maybe Silas was well south of Turtleback by now, having decided *not* to settle in this area.

Realizing the sobs were lessening in frequency and volume, Niall picked up the phone and dialed the Drunken Moose. "This is Chief MacKeage. Can I speak with Vanetta Thurber, please?" he asked when someone answered, making sure his voice carried through the bars of the holding cell, then grinning when both the murmuring and sobbing abruptly stopped. "Yes, Vanetta," he continued when the restaurant owner picked up with a cheery hello. "Just two quick questions, since I know this is your busy time. First, has everything settled down there?"

"We're back to our normal dinnertime chaos," Vanetta assured him. "Well, except for the main topic of conversation being Noreen's arrest instead of the beautiful weather we're having. But it's all in whispers," she drawled, "because everyone's afraid you'll come back and arrest *them.* Man, MacKeage, I swear I felt the building shake when you roared."

Niall closed his eyes on a silent groan. "It was either that or pull out my gun and fire at the ceiling," he said, deciding to move on and raising his voice again. "Can ye give me the cost of the dishes Mrs. Kent broke?"

He was answered by silence, then a very unladylike curse. "I'm not pressing charges for a few broken plates."

"Only sixteen dollars and fifty cents?" he said in surprise. "What about having to pay someone to clean up the mess? Would another . . . oh, thirty dollars cover it?"

This time several seconds ticked by, then, "What are you doing, MacKeage? And why are you talking so loudly?"

"That's good then," Niall said. "I'm sure Mrs. Kent will appreciate your not inflating the prices, as at those figures she'll only be charged with a misdemeanor."

An even longer silence, then a sudden laugh. "Sure, Chief, whatever you say. I'm just glad I'm standing in *my* shoes and not yours. Good luck," she ended cheerily before the line went dead.

Niall set down the phone and wrote forty-six dollars and fifty cents on a pad of paper. He added seven hundred fifty dollars directly beneath it, drew a line, then wrote the grand total of seven hundred ninety-six dollars and fifty cents in big bold numbers.

Ignoring the approaching footsteps and keeping his head bent to hide his grin, he then wrote the word *BAIL* at the top of the sheet.

"When we were trapped in Vaughn's cellar," Birch whispered as her shadow fell over his desk, "you said we would be working together for the *good* of my residents."

"Do ye also recall my saying that I care about them as much as you do?" he asked without looking up.

"Then let me pay the damages and take Noreen home."

Niall set down his pen, glanced over to see the holding cell door was closed and the curtain drawn, then leaned back in his chair and finally looked at Birch. "Her home is four and a half miles down the road," he said softly, "with the man she's been married to for more than forty-three years."

"I'm well aware —" Birch stopped in midsentence and cocked her head — much the way her father did, Niall realized. "What are you up to?"

"About six-foot-three the last time I checked," he said, not exactly sure why he was baiting her. Except . . . well, he didn't like that she didn't trust him; not just with this situation, but as a man. No, a *lover.* Dammit, *she* had seduced *him;* if the woman could trust him with her beautiful, delicate body, why in hell couldn't she trust him now?

"Who's looking after the woman and child you just rescued?" he asked, deciding to change the subject before he said something he truly would regret.

"Macie," she growled in a whisper. "I sent Cassandra into the Bottoms Up when I caught her standing in the crowd and she told me what was going on. I had her and Macie take the woman and daughter to the shelter and stay with them until I got back — which I promised would be *in a short while.*"

Niall disguised the fact he was checking his watch again by folding his arms over his chest, and stifled a scowl when he realized French had been gone nearly an hour. "I find myself wondering how a crisis center that didn't even exist a month ago is all but bursting at the seams all of a sudden. What did all these women do before?"

"They suffered in silence," she snapped. Birch took a deep breath in an apparent attempt to rein in her temper. "It can go either way when a new shelter opens," she said calmly, likely thinking to soften him up by answering his questions. "There can be a stampede of women hoping they'll finally

332

get help, or no one will show up because they don't trust something they've never seen before." She shrugged. "It seems to be fifty-fifty here; Noreen and Macie came on their own, but I've had to go after some — mostly younger girls like Misty and Cassandra — and explain what it is I do and point out that they'll be safer with me than they are right now."

"Are you expecting things to slow down, then? Ye have what — eight beds?"

She nodded, her voice losing more of its tightness while remaining low. "There will be times when we're full because of children coming with their mothers, but for the population of this area I expect to have four or five residents on any given night. Hopefully even less than that, once I start having counseling sessions and hosting one-day workshops with various state agencies to show women they have several options. Speaking of full beds, can you have Officer Sheppard patrol the camp road in case the woman's husband comes looking for her?" She glanced toward the holding cell. "And maybe have him patrol *all night*?" she added, some of her anger returning.

"It's already done, Birch. Both Jake and Shep are there now."

Apparently not wanting him to see her

surprise, Birch looked toward the closed station door. "Do you know where my father is?"

"Seeing how you were rather busy, I imagine he decided to stay and have dinner at the Drunken Moose."

"Since he never called to tell me he was coming, do *you* know why he's here?" Her eyes narrowed. "And since you obviously knew who he was earlier, can you tell me why he introduced himself to you before coming to see me?"

"I'm afraid that's something you're going to have to ask —"

They both looked toward the door at the sound of a vehicle speeding down the lane and skidding to a stop out front. Niall ripped the top page off his notepad and stood up, then walked over to stand in front of the holding cell as two truck doors opened and slammed shut. Uneven footsteps pounded up the stairs and Logan burst into the station looking . . . well, madder than a *rooster* caught in a rainstorm, Niall decided smugly.

"Where is she!" Logan shouted, causing one stunned spitfire to scurry out of the way when the man advanced on Niall without slowing down. "Where in hell is my wife!"

"Logan? Oh, Logan, I'm in here!" Noreen

cried as the bedsprings squeaked and the curtains parted, her blotchy, tear-swollen face appearing in the window as she gripped the bars. "I've been *arrested.*"

"The hell you are. You're coming home with me right now!"

"There's a small matter of damages that have to be paid first," Niall said quietly, moving to block the door when Logan tried to go around him.

The man shot him a glare even as he reached into his back pocket. "I'll pay for whatever goddamned dishes she broke. Just tell me how much."

"I'm afraid there's also a fine that has to be satisfied before she can leave."

Logan stilled with his wallet half open. "A fine for what?"

"Inciting a riot." Niall held up the piece of paper for Logan to see the total, which caused the man to pale to the roots of his gray hair on a strangled gasp.

Another gasp sounded off to the side. "You can't just arbitrarily make up a fine," Birch said. "Only a judge has that kind of authority."

"We do things differently here in America, Miss Callahan," Niall blatantly lied, giving her a pointed look and hoping to God she was perceptive enough to get with the program. "Chiefs of police in towns situated this far from their county courthouses are allowed to set our own fines to expedite matters."

Logan pointed at the piece of paper. "But that's highway robbery!" His eyes narrowed. "And what proof you got it was Noreen who started the riot, anyway?"

"I have at least thirty witnesses."

Logan shot an uncertain glance over his shoulder at the wisely quiet Silas French standing in the doorway, turned and scowled at Niall for several seconds, then leaned to the side to see Noreen — the man's chest deflating and his eyes suddenly softening. "Just look at you, Norrie," he said gruffly. "You been crying so hard you've gone and made yourself sick. You stop that now, you hear. I'm not gonna leave you in there a minute longer than it takes me to go to the bank and get the money."

"Th-the bank's already closed, Logan," Noreen said, tears streaming down her cheeks again. "And it's Friday. I'm gonna be here all *weekend,*" she ended in a wail.

"I can —" Birch started, only to snap her mouth shut when Niall shot her a glare.

"Then I'll run back and get our checkbook," Logan promised, his eyes hardening again as he looked up at Niall. "If I write you a goddamn check, will you let me take her home tonight?"

"Or, since I'd rather not get a reputation for being unreasonable," Niall said, "I'm willing to let you pay only the damages if you give me your word that you'll use the bail money to buy a new cookstove instead."

Two gasps sounded again — this time one from Birch and one from the holding cell — and Logan frowned so hard his face had to hurt.

"It just so happens," Niall continued, "that the appliance store in Millinocket had a flyer in this week's paper, and I noticed they sell several models of cookstoves that run anywhere from seven to eight hundred dollars." He shrugged. "Your choice," he said quietly. "Come back after the bank opens on Monday and bail out your wife, or take her home right now by giving me your word to buy a stove."

Logan looked down at the wallet in his hand for several heartbeats again, then stepped to the side and lifted his gaze to Noreen. "Ah . . . after I mailed the check for the beekeeping equipment, I drove down to Millinocket and went to that appliance store," he admitted gruffly. "And I saw a really fancy stove I thought you might like that's got a glass top so you don't have to

337

keep scrubbing those pans under the coil burners. It even has a second oven in the drawer on the bottom, and instead of knobs the whole back panel is smooth with little squares you just touch, so it's easy to clean, too."

"But a stove like that has to cost a fortune," Noreen whispered.

Logan's cheeks darkened as he shifted uncomfortably and dropped his gaze to his wallet again. "It's, ah, it was recently brought to my attention that having high-quality equipment can turn a daily chore into a . . . labor of love." He looked up, his faded hazel eyes filling with tenderness. "And remembering how you always insisted I buy the best and safest chainsaws back when I was logging, I got to thinking that a woman who loves cooking as much as you do deserves the best stove in that store."

Okay, Niall figured he'd have to concede that point to Silas French.

Logan pulled out two twenty-dollar bills and a ten, closed his wallet and slipped it in his back pocket, then held the money out to Niall. "This is for the damages. And you have my word the first purchase I make when I sell my honey this fall will be a stove."

Niall pulled his hand back without taking

the money and shook his head. "Your word to purchase it no later than Monday or the fine stands."

Logan's jaw momentarily slackened, but then his entire face turned as dark as a thundercloud. "God dammit, I can't! There's barely enough money left in our savings to buy a *cheap* stove. I'd have to cash in one of our certificates of deposit to buy that fancy one now, and the bank's gonna charge me an arm and a leg for early withdrawal."

"I'll wait," Noreen suddenly piped up. She rushed out of the holding cell — only a brute would have actually locked the door — and slid her arm through Logan's as she smiled up at Niall — making Niall wonder if he'd ever seen the woman smile before. "Really, I don't mind waiting until this fall if it means the difference between getting a regular stove or one with two ovens and a glass top and no knobs." She melted into Logan when he protectively slipped his arm around her. "I'll just get creative by making salads and sandwiches and using the gas grill." She leaned slightly away. "Do we still have that tin reflector oven you made after we saw that one at the lumber camp museum? Then I can still bake pies and biscuits," she said when Logan nodded. "That is, if you don't mind building me a camp-fire," she added in a . . . good Lord, the woman was all but *purring.*

She took the money out of her husband's hand when it seemed all Logan could do was nod again, and held it out to Niall. "And you have *my* word, Chief MacKeage, that I won't incite any more riots. I'll apologize to Vanetta, too," she added when Niall hesitated before finally taking the money. She then turned away, turning Logan with her, and started toward the door — which Silas French was no longer stand-ing in, apparently having realized he'd bet-ter start hunting for a new place to live.

"You remember when we used to make bean-hole beans?" Noreen continued to Logan as the couple walked away. "If you dig me a pit, I can cook other meals in the ground, too, including your favorite — pot roast and turnips."

"I'll dig you a pit," Logan said thickly as he slid his arm around her again and gave her a squeeze. "And I'll hang a tarp over the grill for when it rains. I can even give our old picnic table a paint job and set it up on the knoll under that big maple tree you love, and we can eat up there in the shade however often you want."

Noreen cuddled even closer to him with

what sounded like a sigh of contentment. "So when are the bees coming?" Niall heard her ask when they reached the porch. "How many hives did you order? Oh, Logan, who would have thought we'd be producing our very own honey. Does that company sell those cute little bottles shaped like bears? We're going to have to design a really nice label and come up with a catchy name for our new business."

Logan led her down the stairs to his rusty old truck and opened the passenger door, but stopped her from getting in. Even from where he stood, Niall could see the man's cheeks darken. "I, ah . . . I was thinking the labels we put on the honey jars could say *Norrie's Golden Nectar.*"

Niall felt his own jaw slacken as Noreen also gaped at her husband, before the woman suddenly threw her arms around him. "Oh, Logi, that's beautiful!" She leaned away just enough to finger his shaggy gray hair. "You look like a pirate, Mr. Kent."

"You could give me a haircut out on the porch tomorrow morning if you want. I fixed those two broken boards and painted the whole floor so everything matches."

"Mmmm, we'll see," she said, giving his unshaven cheek a kiss, then turning and climbing in the truck. She fastened her seat belt, folded her hands on her lap, and looked out the windshield with another sigh. "Take me home, husband."

Logan closed the door, did a stiff-jointed hustle around the front of the truck, and climbed in behind the wheel. The truck started with a loud rattling cough, made a six-point turn between the station and the shoreline, and disappeared up the lane.

"What . . ." Birch cleared her throat. "What just happened?"

Niall looked down at the two twenty- and one ten-dollar bills in his hand. "I believe we just witnessed a miracle."

"Um, how did you know Logan would come charging in here like an angry bear and pay Noreen's fine, when he wouldn't even buy her a cookstove before?"

Niall looked up and shrugged. "It's been my experience that no matter how out of sorts a man is with his wife, if he feels someone else is treating her badly, he will come out swinging — and not always just verbally."

"But you couldn't know how Noreen would react."

He shrugged again. "I've seen many cold-hearted women turn into giddy lasses when the husbands they were angry at not five minutes earlier came riding hell-bent for leather to their rescue."

Birch gestured at the money in his hand. "Can you really set fines?"

"No."

"Would you really have pressed charges?"

"No."

"What would you have done if Logan *hadn't* showed up?"

"I have no idea."

She took a step closer. "How long have you been hatching this little scheme?"

"Since I visited Logan three weeks ago and realized the man was simply scared he might outlive his savings, although I didn't come up with a way to knock some sense into him until I saw that flyer in the paper." He grinned. "I was just about to create a situation when Noreen created it for me."

Another step closer. "And it never occurred to you to let *me* in on your plan?"

Now there was a loaded question if he ever heard one. "So ye would have given me your blessing to arrest Noreen?"

Birch opened her mouth but closed it without saying anything, then cocked her head and studied him in silence.

Niall became so busy trying to hear the conversation going on in her beautiful head that he was a bit slow to notice the growing fire in her eyes, barely giving himself enough time to prepare for her pounce.

He was not, however, prepared for such a . . . passionate explosion.

"You drive me *crazy*," she growled, wrapping her arms around his neck and her legs around his waist when he caught her.

"Then we're —"

Niall didn't mind that she didn't let him finish, since she seemed more interested in attacking his mouth than hearing what he had to say. So he dropped a hand to her luscious bottom and kissed her back, even as he glanced at the door trying to figure out how to close and lock it without her realizing what he was doing.

"Five stupid days," she rasped in a winded hiss when she came up for air. "Don't *ever* make me mad at you again by turning into a caveman. That bed in the holding cell felt really sturdy," she added, once again kissing him before he could respond.

And why wasn't he surprised she was two steps ahead of him? Niall settled her higher against his chest and started for the door — figuring he'd figure out how to lock it without setting her down when he got there — only to jerk to a halt at the sight of Claude St. Germaine standing on the porch, the man's arms folded over his chest and his expression unreadable.

Birch leaned away, her expression *totally* readable. "Don't you dare go all slow and quiet on me now. It's been five freaking days and I'm —" Her eyes widened at the sound of a clearing throat, just before she dropped her forehead to Niall's with a muttered curse — Niall now knowing *merde* meant *shit* — followed by a whispered *Daddy.*

"Five days since what?" Claude asked.

Birch wiggled to be lowered to the floor, then ran the back of a hand over her mouth, tugged down the hem of her blouse on a deep breath, and finally turned around. "Thanks for letting me know you were coming to visit," she drawled, apparently deciding to go on the attack rather than answer.

Claude sighed rather loudly. "I thought you *wanted* me to be more spontaneous." He unfolded his arms, held them out from his sides, and grinned. "Surprise." When Birch didn't appear in any hurry to respond, Claude looked over the top of her head at Niall, his grin widening. "Am I going blind, or was that the woman you just arrested cuddled up to a man driving the beat-up old truck that nearly ran me down when I stepped around the corner?"

"What are you doing here, Daddy?" Birch asked at the same time Niall nodded.

"I found myself missing Mimi."

345

Niall was glad to see he wasn't the only one who enjoyed baiting Birch, although he did wonder at Claude's motivation. That is, unless the man was stalling because he didn't want an audience when he broke the news that he wasn't just visiting.

Then again, maybe the guy was tired of being *parented.*

Nay, that wasn't it, as Claude had spoken fondly of Birch's efforts to make him a tolerable father, beginning when she'd been six.

"Oh *maudit,* come on," Birch muttered, stepping onto the porch and slipping her arm through Claude's. "If you're going to insist on being annoying, you can do it while driving me home. Because unlike some people who take their vacations without telling anyone and just show up without calling first, I'm still on the clock." She stopped them both at the top of the stairs and turned back to Niall. "Speaking of which, where's Mom? Her cart's still here."

"She and Sam went to Turtleback to check out station sites for me," Niall said, stifling a grin at her gasp and Claude's *are you insane?* wince.

"Sam Waters from the Trading Post?" Birch squeaked. "You let her go to Turtleback with him? Just the two of them?

Alone?"

"I'm sorry," Niall murmured, brushing a hand down over his thin leather vest — the weather having forced him to trade in his jacket. "I didn't want to come across as a caveman by *ordering* Hazel not to go anywhere with Sam . . . alone."

"Oh, *tu l'homme tannant!*" she snapped, dragging her father down the stairs and heading up the lane. "I can only deal with one crisis at a time, and right now that would be the woman and her daughter waiting for me at the shelter. I just hope Macie and Cassandra thought to take the turkey out of the oven before it turned into a brick."

Thanks to Hazel's list — which he'd made sure to memorize — Niall also now knew Birch had just called him a *maddening man,* which he figured beat *hulking brute.*

Well hell, he seemed to be making progress.

Birch suddenly stopped walking again, also pulling her father to a stop. "Dammit to hell and back," she growled in good old English as she shot Niall a good old spitfire scowl. "I just lost my cook."

CHAPTER SEVENTEEN

Even though he'd enjoyed the ride down Bottomless in Nicholas's powerful fishing boat — winning the undeclared race with Duncan and Alec in Duncan's boat — Niall hadn't much cared for having to put ashore a good half mile from their destination, their subsequent hike through the woods providing swarms of mosquitoes plenty of fresh blood. Niall slapped his neck when his fine hairs stirred again, still not sure why a mythical warrior felt he needed to drag a modern magic-maker and two mere mortals along on his little spy mission. But rather than lying in his big comfortable bed hoping Birch's passionate pounce today portended a soft knock on his door tonight, he would instead be staring through binoculars while getting eaten alive watching *mostly* well-intentioned people dancing and chanting and tossing perfectly good food into a bonfire.

As Sebastian was apparently too focused on calling forth a new god to realize the bastard had manifested months ago, Dante had sent word that the colony's leader was having another go at it tonight, the ritual once again taking place on a secluded island two-thirds down the inland sea just off the uninhabited eastern shoreline. And when Niall had asked why they needed to attend if they already knew the guest of honor would be a no-show, Nicholas had explained that if the colonists had managed to successfully bring forth one god, there was an equally good chance they could call forth *another* one.

And wasn't that a goddamned wonderful notion.

"Well, this is new," Nicholas murmured, his ancient spyglass trained on the island and his tone making Niall, Duncan, and Alec grab their binoculars and scramble over to the fallen log. "It appears we're not the only ones interested in tonight's ceremony." He snorted. "Although I don't find it very sporting to *fly* in and perch right in plain sight."

"Where?" Duncan asked.

"He just landed in the taller pine slightly south of the center of the island, on the third branch down from the top." The warrior chuckled. "Is that dried blueberries I see in his head feathers?"

Niall finally found the tree and realized the *he* Nicholas was talking about was a fully-matured bald eagle. "The bird that gave Birch the hairclip was still immature."

"Over a week ago," Nicholas reminded him. "Our new resident god appears to be coming into his powers amazingly fast."

"Telos," Niall murmured when he zoomed in on the eagle watching the colonists below preparing tonight's bonfire.

There was a heartbeat of silence, and then Nicholas gave him a nudge. "Where did you hear that word?"

Niall lowered his binoculars to find Alec and Duncan also looking at him. He turned to sit leaning against the log and fingered the hilt of his sword as he wondered how to tell the men — without breaking his promise by actually *telling* them — that the forest god had given Birch his name. "When ye airlifted Birch's car off that gravel bar the day of her accident," Niall said to Duncan as he and Alec also turned to settle against the log, "did ye notice that the air bags hadn't deployed?"

Duncan eyed him curiously, even as he shrugged. "I assumed she didn't hit the

350

water at a steep enough angle to set them off."

"Nay, she didn't. That's because when she left the road, Birch hit a large oak tree on the bank of the river first, which was the same tree the car was tangled in when I found it pinned up against the bridge."

"But the front of the vehicle didn't have any damage," Duncan said, now eyeing him suspiciously. "Expect for being soaked through, the car appeared untouched. Hell, I don't remember even seeing any scratches."

Niall looked over at Nicholas. "Titus said he saw the new god change into an innocuous weed or bush to escape the demons the day it manifested, and we're fairly certain the bird who found Rana's hairclip was also the god." Niall looked down and fingered his sword again. "Could he not also have been the oak that saved Birch's life by gently breaking her fall, then holding her car against the bridge until help arrived?"

"That doesn't explain you just calling him Telos," Nicholas said.

"He actually spoke to her," Alec apparently decided when Niall didn't respond. "The forest god told Birch his name."

"What else did he tell her?" Duncan asked. He kicked Niall's foot when Niall remained silent. "Did he happen to mention what his intentions are?"

"I'm more interested," Nicholas drawled, "in hearing Miss Callahan's reaction to having a tree talk to her."

"Why aren't you answering?" Duncan asked.

Alec chuckled. "My guess is Birch made him promise not to tell anyone she had a conversation with a tree. The lass talked back to it, didn't she?"

Duncan kicked Niall's foot again when he still said nothing. "Dammit, man, we're not playing twenty questions here. Just tell us what the bastard told Birch."

"All I know," Niall snapped, standing up before Duncan could kick him again, "is that an *oak tree* broke Birch's fall, then kept her from sinking until I could get there." He glared down at the three grinning men. "The water rushing through the branches made a lot of noise, so maybe I only *thought* I heard her say Telos. Hell, maybe the bastard said it to *me,* so I'd know who I was indebted to for saving Birch's life."

"Okay, then," Duncan said dryly. "Did the tree tell *you* why he's here?"

Finally; it had taken them long enough. "Nay," Niall said on a sigh as he sat down again, this time leaning against a cedar out of foot-kicking reach. "But after thinking about his appearing to Birch as both an eagle and a tree, I believe Telos is deliberately showing us that unlike Titus and Mac, he intends to be more . . . personal when it comes to using the magic. More hands-on."

"Titus did mention he thought the new god had taken a *personal* interest in your Miss Callahan," Nicholas drawled.

"Aye," Alec said. "Giving jewelry to a woman is definitely personal."

"So is saving her life," Duncan added.

Not being able to read their expressions since he was facing into the setting sun, Niall had no problem hearing the amusement in their voices. "Birch may not be the only person whose life he saved," he said, deciding to turn the subject back to the matter at hand. "About a month ago I came upon a man walking along the road as I was driving up from Turtleback, and at first thought he might be drunk, since he was weaving more than walking. But as I drew near I could see he was hunched over holding his ribs, and what I thought was a red shirt turned out to be blood from a gash in his head."

"It was Foster Graves, and he is a drunk," Duncan said. "I heard ye wrapped his head in your T-shirt and drove him to the clinic."

"Aye," Niall said with a nod. "I was worried he'd bleed out before an ambulance could arrive. At the time, considering he smelled of whiskey as much as blood, I dismissed the story he told me about what had happened as nothing more than the ramblings of an inebriated man with a head injury." He shrugged. "But lately I've been thinking that what Foster kept calling 'divine intervention' was actually Telos."

"I heard he told anyone willing to listen," Alec said, "that a huge black bear just sauntered up to his car and lifted it off him. But like you, everyone thought the blow to his head had made him delusional."

"Aye, that's the tale he told me. So after leaving him in Bentley's care," Niall continued, "I went back and found the car. It took some doing, as it appeared Foster had been going quite fast when he missed a curve and ended up deep in the woods down a steep bank. If he hadn't made it back up to the road, the man probably would have bled out within the hour and his body not discovered for days."

"And did you see any sign of this divine bear?" Nicholas asked.

Niall gave a nod. "The tracks were unmistakable. And from the size and depth of the paw prints, I'd estimate the bruin went six or seven hundred pounds."

"That's damn big for a Maine black bear," Alec said.

"I'm just telling ye what I found. There was a pool of blood where Foster had lain for some time, along with the impression of where his car, which was up on its side, had been covering a good part of his body."

"Maybe the car did land on him," Duncan speculated, "but the momentum kept it rolling onto its side before finally stopping. And the paw prints could have been made while you were driving him to the clinic. Hell, there's nothing to say a curious bear hadn't shown up while Foster had been lying there, taken a few sniffs, and left the man to die in peace."

"Aye," Niall said evenly. "All acceptable explanations, except for the tracks also indicating the bear had dragged Foster up the steep bank to the road."

Everyone fell silent, apparently trying to decide for themselves what had really happened — that is, until Alec suddenly chuckled.

"What?" Nicholas asked.

"It seems I may have also had a *divine intervention.*" Alec looked at Duncan. "You remember my mentioning several weeks ago that I went looking for a pond I'd heard had trout the size of salmon about twenty miles north of town?"

Duncan grinned. "What I remember is that ye caught hell from your wife for getting all the way up the fiord before realizing you'd dropped her and your son off at your mother-in-law's that morning."

"I wasn't thinking straight," Alec muttered. "I just wanted to get home because I was chilled from being caught in a rainstorm and had forgotten to bring extra clothes."

"What does your fishing trip have to do with Telos?" Nicholas asked.

"The rainstorm — nay, it was more of a deluge — that came out of nowhere. I'd left my truck parked about a mile from the pond and hiked in, but when I started back after getting soaked, not a quarter mile from where I'd been fishing I came to a small burned section of woods that *hadn't* been burned on my way in."

"Are ye saying you believe the forest god put out the fire?" Duncan asked.

"You got a better explanation for a rainstorm appearing out of nowhere on a sunny afternoon and hitting only a small area? My truck never got touched."

"Well, gentlemen," Nicholas said quietly, "for as . . . altruistic as Telos sounds, he may actually become a problem."

"How?" Niall asked.

"Using the magic to interfere or intercede on behalf of people — or worse, *directly interact* with them, as he did with Birch and Foster Graves — is the very thing Titus has been protecting mankind from all these millennia. Titus cultivated the Trees of Life specifically to keep gods from using mortals as nothing more than pawns, and sometimes even currency, in their petty wars against one another. Why do you think he and Maximilian practice a hands-*off* approach when it comes to man-made disasters?"

Duncan snorted. "They both interfere all the time."

"Not *directly*," Nicholas countered. "Mac couldn't force fishermen all over the world to stop using traps and nets that continue ghost-fishing for years after being lost at sea. But he could draw attention to the problem and encourage change in fishing practices by washing the offending equipment filled with dead and dying sea mammals and birds up onto beaches in every coastal country." He grinned at Duncan. "And Mac couldn't make you and Peg fall in love even though he knew you were a match, but he could create a situation where the two of you would decide *of your own free will* that you couldn't live without each other. And if I remember correctly," the warrior growled, losing his grin as he looked at Alec, "you were counting on the fact that Titus and Mac couldn't retaliate for your keeping Carolina's whereabouts a secret from them."

Alec grinned back and Niall stifled a grin of his own as he remembered his cousin walking in and out of the magically secured Nova Mare right under Nicholas's nose, frustrating the warrior to no end.

"And you, Niall," Nicholas continued. "Titus could only *invite* you to come to this century to vie for Carolina's hand in marriage. That you accepted was *your* decision."

Niall lifted a brow. "You would expect me to refuse a personally delivered invitation from Titus Oceanus?"

The warrior's grin returned. "You didn't seem to let who he was get in your way of *staying* here."

"What about moving mountains and turning freshwater lakes into inland seas?" Alec asked before Niall could form a response. "Ye don't consider that to be interfering in people's lives?"

"Mac manipulated the planet, not mankind," Nicholas explained, "which are two distinctly different energies. The people his little stunt affected four years ago were free to react to the change in their landscape however they wished. As with all natural phenomena — storms, earthquakes, volcanic eruptions — men are free to view them either as disasters or as blessings in disguise."

"And Mac bringing Matt Gregor's sister, Fiona, back from the dead and dropping her in this century," Duncan said, "as well as William Killkenny's sister, Gabriella; how is that not *directly* interfering in *their* lives?"

Nicholas folded his arms over his chest. "Both women stubbornly held on to their identities after their deaths, so Mac was merely granting their deep desire to continue the lives so crudely taken from them *as themselves.*"

A thoughtful hush fell again, with Alec and Duncan rolling to their knees and training their binoculars on the island and Niall simply staring out at the water.

"Do you know what *Telos* means, Niall?" Nicholas softly asked into the silence.

"I did some research after Birch's accident," Niall admitted. "And near as I can tell, it's the root word for *teleologia,* which refers to the belief that all in nature has purpose, at the same time promoting the existence of a . . . Designer, or what we refer to as Providence." He shrugged. "Some streams of philosophy contend that everything — plants, animals, people, and even the planet — is here seeking self-realization."

"*Télos* is Greek for *goal* or *end cause*," Nicholas elaborated, "implying that even the universe itself is seeking its ultimate purpose." He gestured at where Telos was perched. "And despite that train of thought running parallel with Titus's and Maximilian's, it would appear Earth's newest god has decided *his* purpose is to nudge mankind along on its journey." Nicholas turned and lifted his scope to his eye with a soft snort. "One person, plant, and animal at a time, apparently."

"So does that mean Mac and Titus *will* get involved if Telos continues taking a direct and active role in people's lives?" Niall asked.

Alec and Duncan also looked at Nicholas when the warrior glanced over his shoulder. "I can't imagine them standing by with their hands in their pockets while a fellow deity tries to impose *his own* definition of purpose on mankind." A dangerous look came into his deep blue eyes. "Because should Telos overstep a line only the Oceanuses can see," he said quietly, turning away and lifting his ancient spyglass to the island again, "I'm afraid moving mountains and creating inland seas will definitely seem like a blessing compared to the havoc two clashing divinities could wreak on this area."

"Sweet Christ," Niall whispered. "Are ye saying we could find ourselves at the center of a mythological war?"

Nicholas shrugged as he continued looking through his glass. "That, gentlemen, is a question I'm afraid only time can answer."

CHAPTER EIGHTEEN

Birch pushed the curtain aside and looked out the kitchen door window for the third time in ten minutes, only to see that Niall still wasn't home. The man had driven in around six yesterday afternoon, handed Jake what had looked like a take-out dinner from the Drunken Moose, changed his clothes, then left carrying an unusually long rifle case without so much as a glance at the main house. And the bright blue pickup still parked in the driveway meant Jake had stayed at the cottage with Shep, and Niall had spent the night . . . somewhere else.

Birch couldn't decide if her foul mood this morning was from plain old fear, or from *her* having spent the night tossing and turning in bed instead of sleeping draped over a warm mountain of muscle. On the one hand she was afraid police work — of the dangerous kind — was the reason Niall hadn't come home, and on the other she was worried his absence didn't have anything to do with his job. She didn't consider herself the jealous type, but if the maddening man was going to go around telling people she was his girlfriend, he damn well better consider them *exclusive.*

She had actually been inches away from knocking on his door last night when Birch had realized the pickup she'd just walked past hadn't been Niall's. So she'd shoved her hands in her pockets and trudged home feeling more disappointed than she cared to admit, but had stopped halfway to the main house and considered marching back and asking Jake where in hell his boss was. But she'd continued home, realizing that showing up at Chief MacKeage's door at eleven o'clock in her pajamas — okay, she'd been wearing her *slut on the hunt* little number under her robe — might have given Officer Sheppard the impression she and Niall were a couple.

Which they obviously were *not,* seeing how the man couldn't be bothered to tell her he'd be away all night. He had a cell phone; how much effort did it take to send a stupid text? Granted, she hadn't exactly been nice to him lately, but even an idiot would have realized that kiss in his station meant she'd forgiven him for acting like a caveman.

She let the curtain fall back and walked to the counter, disgruntled that men were so annoying — and she was lumping Claude St. Germaine in with the lot of them this morning. What did her father think he was doing, moving here? For that matter, what kind of work did he expect to find in the wilderness?

The man didn't know the first thing about cutting timber or driving something the size of a logging truck, and wood harvesting seemed to be the only industry in the area, other than tourism. And she really couldn't see Claude pandering to tourists, since she was pretty sure that required a sense of humor. Her father didn't even have any hobbies he could turn into a business except for his little obsession with weaponry, but he couldn't even legally carry a gun in this country, much less bring his collection here without having a damn good reason for lugging a small arsenal across the border. And if he wanted to stay in law enforcement, he'd have to go to an American academy, which would mean he'd basically be starting his career all over again at fifty years old.

Oh. Wait. She forgot. He didn't *have* to work because he was freaking *wealthy*.

Was there a reason he hadn't shared that interesting little detail with her in the last twenty-five years? *Never found the right time,* her ass. As for his feeling it wasn't all that important . . . *Mon Dieu,* who in their right mind carried a mortgage when they had a small fortune sitting in the bank collecting more dust than interest?

And to think she'd offered to chip in when he had insisted on purchasing a house in the suburbs instead of an affordable condo in the city because he'd wanted Mimi to have a yard to run around in every other weekend. "Yeah, well, you're buying your own vehicles from now on," she muttered, glaring at the cold coffeemaker — the one Noreen had always set the timer on every night so they'd all wake up to the smell of brewing coffee. "And you're taking me to dinner at Aeolus's Whisper *and* picking up the check."

Birch blew out a sigh as she glanced around the semiclean kitchen, wondering when her life had gotten so out of control. Forget that someone had tried to kill her — and still hoped to, for all she knew; her father had quit his job and was moving to Maine, her mother had spent most of yesterday with an unmarried man only to return home with a distinctive twinkle in her eyes, her *boyfriend* hadn't come home last night, and she'd lost her cook just as she was becoming overrun with residents.

Oh, and she still hadn't made it back to that cute little artisan shop. *Merde,* the way things were going, that perfect purse would probably walk past her slung over the shoulder of a freaking tourist.

Hearing tires crunching on the gravel driveway — because no one had closed and locked the windows last night — Birch ran to the door and moved the curtain aside just in time to see her father pull in next to her SUV. It wasn't the fact he was here at six in the morning that alarmed her, but rather the smashed roof and broken rear side window on his beautiful Lexus. But her alarm turned to outright panic when Claude rounded the bumper looking worse than his car.

Birch scrambled out the door and ran down the steps. "Did someone try to run you off the road?" she cried, skidding to a halt when Claude stopped in the middle of the walkway and frowned at her.

"Huh? No," he said, looking back and gesturing at the Lexus. "A huge tree branch at the campground snapped off and broke the window."

"But you're *limping*. And you look like hell."

He touched the goose egg above his left eye, then rubbed a hand over the stubble on his jaw. "I'm limping because I had to sleep in the car last night, and I look like hell because the only dry clothes I have are what I wore yesterday — which I also slept in." He looked past her at the house. "You got any coffee brewed? I didn't want to stop at the Drunken Moose looking like this, and my camp stove is probably halfway to Canada by now."

"What happened?" Birch asked, walking over and slipping her arm through his, then starting toward the house. "You told me you bought a tent and all the gear you would need to camp out until you found a house."

"A storm hit sometime around midnight," he explained. "And considering the wind was strong enough to uproot several trees, my tent probably *beat* my stove across the border." He gingerly felt the lump on his forehead and winced. "I think the lid off someone's cooler hit me when I crawled out of my tent just before it filled with air and shot off like a balloon. The campground erupted in chaos with people scrambling to their vehicles as gear and awnings and chairs turned into projectiles."

He brought them to a halt halfway up the steps. "The storm raged for almost an hour before the rain and wind suddenly stopped and a weird silence settled over everything. Nothing moved for a good five minutes, not even people. But just as I was about to go check on everyone, an engine started up, then another one, and headlights came on and most of the campers left without even bothering to hunt down their gear. And when daylight came and I crawled out of my car, I thought I'd stepped into a war zone. Tents and awnings were plastered against trees, several pop-up campers were mangled nearly beyond recognition, and three fifth wheels were actually tipped over. What few people had stayed were just standing around in a daze like I was, staring in disbelief."

Birch looked over her shoulder at the yard. "We didn't get a storm last night. In fact, I had to get up and close my blinds because the full moon was shining in my face."

Claude slipped his arm free, walked up one more step, and grabbed the rail for support as he turned and sat down on the porch with a groan. "The campground's at least twenty miles south of here," he said, squinting against the sun as he looked up at her. "The storm blew in from the east off

Bottomless, and I noticed on my drive up that the destruction stopped about a couple of miles north of the campground."

"But storms usually come from the *west*."

He shrugged, only to groan again and carefully flex his shoulders as if working kinks out of his muscles, then clasped his hands and rested his forearms on his knees. "The next vehicle you buy me will have to be a truck like that one," he said, nodding at her SUV. "Something big enough to let me sleep in stretched out."

"You're dusting off your bankbook and buying your own vehicles from now on."

He started to shrug again but stopped, giving her a wounded look that Birch didn't believe for a minute. "Will you at least help me pick them out? And also come house shopping with me? Once I've narrowed it down to one or two," he rushed on before she could respond. "I realize you're busy, but I value your opinion. And if you're there, the real estate broker can't take advantage of — what do you call it? — *my blatant disregard for budgets* when it comes to making large purchases."

"You can afford to buy a mansion right on Bottomless if you want."

He sat up a little straighter. "Well heck, I suppose I can." But then he shook his head.

"Not a mansion, though, because I don't want to have to dust and vacuum a bunch of rooms I'll never use. But I wouldn't mind a nice little cottage right on the water. One with a beach," he added, looking down the lawn at the Center's beach. "And also a dock, because I think I'd like to get a boat and take up fishing." He squinted up at her again. "So will you help me look at cottages?"

"You truly are moving here?" Birch whispered.

His gaze lowered to his hands dangling between his knees. "Would you prefer I didn't?" he asked just as softly.

"No, Daddy, that's not it," she said quickly, kneeling on a step in front of him and taking hold of his hands. "Of course I want you here. I know it's only been two months, but I've *missed* you. It's just that I don't want . . . What are you . . . You're a *city* cop. And this," she said, waving behind her then clutching his hands again, "is the middle of nowhere. What are you going to do all day? I know you don't *have* to work, but everyone needs something to get them out of bed in the morning."

He chuckled, reversing their grip and giving her hands a squeeze. "Your city-girl mama seems to have found a job here in the middle of nowhere. I swear a feather could have knocked me over when I walked in that station yesterday and found Hazel on the phone trying to explain to some lady that police officers have more important things to do than to keep breaking into houses every time someone locks themselves out. Then Hazel asked the woman why she hadn't hidden a key like Officer Sheppard suggested two days ago, after he'd had to climb in through her bathroom window." He shook his head. "In my wildest dreams I never imagined Hazel Callahan punching a time clock — especially at a police station."

"It's not like there's hordes of large charities looking for fund-raisers around here," Birch drawled. But then she turned serious. "That's the point I'm trying to make, Dad; just like Mom couldn't sit around reading all day, you can't fish seven days a week. And you gave up one career for me already; I don't want you to have to start all over again."

"I don't regret one day of the last twenty-five years," he all but growled, "and would do it all again in a heartbeat." The sun reflected off a sudden gleam in his eyes as he cocked his head. "Maybe I'm the one who needs looking after this time."

Birch barely stifled a snort. "You're *fifty.*"

"And you were six when you started taking care of me. You can't just suddenly stop. Who's going to complain that I have too many take-out containers in my fridge? Or tell me vests went out of fashion three years ago, or that it's time to buy new sheets, or that I need a haircut?"

"You definitely don't need a haircut," she said, fighting a smile. "You need to arrest whoever gave you that scalp-job. You went to a barber, didn't you, instead of the salon I set you up with?"

He nodded. "There's one just down from the station that all the guys go to because he's convenient. So," he said gruffly, the gleam fading from his eyes as he looked directly into hers. "Can I stay?"

Birch slipped between his knees and wrapped her arms around him. "Of course you can," she said just as thickly, giving him a gentle squeeze. "But only because I need you here to remind me that *some* men are tolerable."

The chest she was hugging rumbled with his chuckle. "Surely there's at least one tolerable man around here; oh, like maybe a tall, broad-shouldered Scotsman who wears a badge?" He tightened his embrace when she tried to pull away. "That I hope is a patient man if he's waiting for his girlfriend to admit the two of you are dating."

Birch tilted her head back. "He told you we're dating?"

"No, I overheard some guy named French call you Niall's girlfriend. All Niall would say when I asked why you never mentioned you were seeing someone, was that you were probably still getting used to the idea." He ducked to look her directly in the eyes again. "Is it okay to say I like this one, Birch?"

"No, it's not, because you just met him," she said, wiggling free and standing up. "And because I haven't decided if *I* like him." She gestured at Niall's cottage. "Because in my book of how the world should work, boyfriends tell their girlfriends when they're spending the night somewhere else."

"He's a cop, honey. How many nights did I not come home when you were living with me? And after I moved to Montreal, how many weekends did you stay over, only to see me all of a few hours?"

Birch hugged herself on a sudden shiver. "I remember one weekend you didn't come home at all," she whispered, "and I got a phone call at three in the morning from your captain saying he was sending a squad car to take me to the hospital."

Her father stood up, pulled her up the last step to the porch, and folded her into his embrace. "I doubt they have street gangs here in Spellbound Falls, little cadet," he murmured, his lips brushing the top of her head. "And Niall MacKeage strikes me as a man who can take care of himself."

"He doesn't even wear a bulletproof vest. And he didn't bring his gun when he followed me to the Vaughns'."

"You told me he had a backup weapon. So," he went on brightly, obviously attempting to lighten the mood as he stepped away and looked at the door, "what's a person have to do to get a cup of coffee around here?"

"The kitchen was Noreen's department," Birch said, heading inside. "Just give me a minute to make a pot. Come on," she added, waving at him to follow when the screen door closed and he was still on the other side. "Come sit at the table and I'll make you some eggs and toast."

He looked toward the cottage, then back through the screen at her. "I don't want your residents to come downstairs and find me inside. I'll take the coffee down to the beach and drink it, then go see if Niall will let me use his shower."

Birch grabbed the carafe and filled it with

water. "I told you, he's not home. That's Officer Sheppard's truck." She poured the water into the coffeemaker then started opening cupboards, looking for the filters. "I think Niall had Jake spend the night in case my new resident's husband came around." She found the filters, then looked at her father. "He didn't even take Shep, and that dog goes everywhere with him."

Claude lifted his hands from his sides in resignation. "I'm sure he'll be home soon, honey. He's probably still dealing with the aftermath of that storm. Judging by the destruction at the campground, there's a good chance the man's up to his ears in accident and property damage calls."

"He left here at six last night," Birch said, stuffing a filter in the brewing cup thingy, then going in search of the coffee. "And you said the storm hit around midnight."

"Didn't you tell me Niall has another officer covering Turtleback Station?"

"Cole Wyatt," she clarified with a growl, having to jump to grab the coffee off the top shelf of a cupboard. "Jeez, Noreen was a freaking Amazon."

"Then maybe Cole asked Niall to come down to Turtleback," her father went on, even as he chuckled at her frustration, "and they both ended up dealing with the storm.

Things got pretty wild last night; I don't think I've ever seen red lightning, and I sure as heck never heard wind sound like that."

Birch stopped scooping coffee. "Red lightning?"

"It was the damnedest thing," he said, shaking his head. "The sky looked almost alive with constant blood-red flashes that appeared to be shooting *up* from the water. Thankfully most of the lightning stayed offshore, except for one strike hitting a huge pine down on the beach. And the wind sounded like something out of an old horror movie. Over the thunder and snapping trees and debris crashing into everything, I'd swear I heard vicious, bone-chilling screams coming from out on Bottomless."

"Screams?" Birch went back to scooping coffee. "It sounds to me more like you smuggled some of your cheap rum across the border and cracked open a bottle last night." She slid the coffee-laden filter into the machine, tapped the on button, then walked over and scrunched up her nose at him. "I told you that stuff will make you see flying elephants. Storms move *west* to *east*, lightning is *white*, and wind *howls*."

"All I smuggled across was that bottle of overpriced Scotch you bought me, and it's still full but for the few shots we had the night before you left Montreal."

"You . . . you don't like it?"

"No, I like it. I just prefer not to drink alone." He grinned. "I had it in the car last night and almost brought it down to the beach for our little talk."

"You hadn't made it to the main road when you left," she admitted with a crooked smile, "before I was taking a guzzle out of my own bottle."

"I'm sorry I shocked you yesterday, Birch, but I thought it would be easier on both of us if I simply showed up and told you in person."

"No, you thought to avoid an argument by not telling me until *after* you quit your job. Oh no," she suddenly groaned, palming her forehead. "Your moving here means we'll have to stay with your parents *overnight* at Christmas." She shot him a glare. "Since it was only a three-hour drive from your place, we could get in, politely smile and nod for six hours, and get out." But then Birch clutched her throat. "Oh God, what if they decide to come here instead? They'll stay an entire *week.*"

"Who's staying a week?" Hazel asked, walking into the kitchen carrying Mimi.

Mimi spotted Claude standing on the other side of the screen door and immediately started wiggling and whining to be put down; Birch's sigh was lost in her father's laughter when Chicken Little's feet touched the floor and the blur of white fluff raced back into the hall and up the stairs.

Even though her mother momentarily looked as though she also wanted to turn tail and run, Birch was proud and more than a little impressed when Hazel walked up beside her. "Good morning, Claude," she said in her polished, fund-raiser voice. "Have you —" Her words ended on a gasp. "*Maudit,* you look like hell!"

Birch felt her jaw slacken at her mother's so-unlike-her outburst, only to then feel her chin drop when she glanced over to see her father actually crack a smile.

Claude never smiled *at* Hazel; only when he talked *about* her.

He brushed down the front of his wrinkled shirt. "I guess I've become somewhat of a slob since my daughter left. Don't worry, *chére,*" he said, switching to French — which he was quite fluent in when he felt like it. "I'm sure I'll be back to my old uptight self in a day or two. Birch did tell you I'm moving here, didn't she?"

Birch blinked up at him. Her father couldn't actually be *teasing* her mother, could he?

No, of course not; he didn't know how.

"Was your trip to Turtleback a success?" he asked, returning to English when Hazel just mutely gaped at him, apparently just as dumbfounded. "I hope Sam took you to a nice restaurant for dinner. Or did the two of you go to that club the owner offered you space in when I was at the station yesterday? It's been awhile, but I seem to remember you were quite a vision on the dance floor."

What the — did he just *wink* at Hazel?

Birch was tempted to run down to the Lexus and see if this imposter had bound and gagged her *real* father and stuffed him in the backseat. Because really; Claude St. Germaine didn't know how to flirt any more than tease. Which was why, at the age of fifty, the man was still single. Oh, he dated, but none of the women ever seemed to . . . stick. Well, except for Miss Boss-a-Lot, who in her own words, "had wasted nearly two years of her life trying to pull that rigid broom handle out of Claude's ass."

It was obvious he'd never taken the woman home to meet his parents, because even idiots and six-year-olds knew that no amount of nagging could dislodge a genetic trait that had been nurtured along for eighteen freaking years.

Birch had often wondered how Fredrick St. Germaine had managed to find a wife. Well, except there was a good chance it had been love at first sight for Colleen, who was about as demonstrative as mashed potatoes. In fact, when her father had brought Birch home and introduced her to *Grand-mère* Colleen, the woman had stood deathly still when Birch had run up and hugged her.

Come to think of it, Colleen still acted scared of her.

As for *Grand-père* Fredrick, the man had actually scooted around the back of his chair when she'd gone over to him.

It had taken Birch months to teach her father to hug and nearly a year before he'd finally started doing it spontaneously. She had not, however, taught him to flirt. And that he appeared to be flirting with Hazel this morning made her feel . . . Well, it was just plain wrong.

Apparently still unable to form a coherent thought, much less a response, Hazel merely turned and walked away, her face as red as . . . Claude's freaky lightning, Birch decided as she glared up at him.

Wait; maybe instead of the lid off a cooler, a bolt of lightning had struck him in the head last night. It would certainly explain him acting like someone else's father.

Not that he saw her glare, since he was staring past her, which made Birch turn to see her mother walking down the hall and up the stairs with all the dignity of a bubbly, quirky teenager coming home from the prom . . . minus her virginity.

"Keep her away from Sam Waters, Birch," Claude said quietly.

She turned to him in surprise. "You've met Sam? No, you couldn't have, since Mom didn't come home until after you left last night." She went back to glaring at him. "Unless you went to the Bottoms Up hoping Sam would stop in after dropping Mom off."

Claude lowered his gaze to her. "It's amazing what you can find out for the cost of a few beers. I didn't have to meet Sam to learn some interesting things about him."

Birch glanced at the hall, then moved closer to the screen door. "Like what?"

"Mostly that he's a complete mystery. Sam Waters is half owner of the Trading Post with his father, but Ezra's last name is *Dodd.* And it seems even though Mr. Dodd has lived in Spellbound Falls for more than fifteen years, no one knew he even had a son until four years ago. Stranger still, Olivia Oceanus had no idea Ezra was her grandfather until Sam showed up at the family camp she ran for her ex-in-laws claiming to be a horse wrangler, but turning out to be her father. Olivia had thought he was dead, because she hadn't seen him since she was five."

Birch felt her jaw slacken again.

Claude shrugged. "The consensus seems to be that Sam is friendly enough and has even quietly helped out some folks with . . . unnamed personal problems, but the man is basically a loner. He dated the owner of the Drunken Moose for a while, but when the woman realized Sam wasn't the marrying kind, she broke it off and married Everest Thurber several months later."

"How does Sam not being the marrying kind pose a danger to Mom?" Birch asked, even more confused. "In my book, that makes him perfect. Mom can finally enjoy the company of a man without having to question his motives."

"It's not the social aspect of his life that concerns me, but what we don't know about him. It's as if Sam Waters didn't exist until four years ago. Look," he said on a sigh, "Hazel's welfare has always been your business, but *your* welfare is *mine.*" He pressed one of his hands to the screen. "And in *my book,*" he said thickly, "that means making sure you never have to deal with another

Leonard Struthers."

Birch started to lift her hand, but instead rested her forehead against his warm palm and smiled down at her slippers. "I did such a good job raising you, I should get a medal." She looked up when he pulled his hand away, and turned serious. "Thank you, Daddy, for loving me."

Two dark flags appeared on his unshaven cheeks as he shoved his hands in his pockets. "Right now I'd settle for a cup of coffee," he muttered.

Birch twirled away with a soft laugh. Oh yeah, twenty-five years and she still hadn't been able to eradicate that last stubborn St. Germaine gene keeping him from saying *I love you* to her. He could write the words — heck, he'd been able to do that by her seventh birthday — but he still couldn't say them out loud. Not that she minded, since everyone knew actions spoke louder than words, anyway.

Finding no clean mugs in the cupboard and discovering no one had started the dishwasher last night, Birch grabbed a dirty mug — which had been put in faceup — off the top rack, squirted some soap on a paper towel — because she didn't dare touch the wet dishrag in the sink — and washed the mug under the faucet. "You can probably buy a new tent and stove at the Trading Post," she said as she filled the mug three-quarters full of coffee, "and that way you can spy on Sam in person. Or if they don't have that kind of camping equipment, maybe a store in Turtleback does," she added over her shoulder on the way to the fridge, only to frown at the empty doorway. "Dad?" she said as she quickly finished filling the mug with milk and walked to the screen door. "Dad?" she repeated, stepping outside when she still didn't see him.

"I'm here," he said from the end of the porch facing the driveway.

Birch rushed over when she saw what had caught his attention, which was Niall getting out of his truck just as a man — yet another mountain of testosterone — she didn't recognize got out the passenger side. And if she thought her father looked like hell, Niall looked like death warmed over. Not only was he limping as he walked over to meet Jake coming out of his cottage, but he nearly fell over when he crouched down to greet Shep. Even more alarming — and downright weird — was how Shep's tail went from wagging ecstatically to being tucked between his legs as he halted several feet shy of Niall's extended hand. And even from the porch, Birch could see the dog roll his lips and hear his snarl as he backed away.

"Someone's going to have to go back to school," Claude said, taking the mug out of her hand. "K-9 officers really aren't supposed to growl at their handlers."

"I'm pretty sure Shep never had any formal training," Birch murmured, clutching one of the porch posts. "Niall supposedly rescued him from an abusive owner about a year ago. The dog must have smelled something on him. Oh, Daddy, he's hurt," she said when Niall set his hands on his knees and stiffly straightened.

Claude reached out and caught her arm when she pushed away from the post. "Leave him be, honey. He's still on the job. Is the other guy his officer from Turtle-back?" he asked as the three men began talking.

"No, I've never seen him before. Cole Wyatt is blond. The guy who just came out of the cottage is Jake Sheppard, and he covers Spellbound Falls. Mom said Niall is supposed to hire one more officer, so there will be two stationed in each —" Birch stopped talking when Niall suddenly looked at the main house, first glancing at the upstairs windows, then dropping his gaze to the porch. She saw him say something to Jake while still looking at her and Claude, and

Jake headed for his truck as Niall and the stranger started toward them — *both* men limping and looking like death warmed over.

"*Mon Dieu,* what were they doing all night?" she softly hissed.

"No questions, Birch," Claude said quietly, using his grip on her arm to lead her toward the stairs. "You let Niall do the talking. And from the look in both men's eyes, I suggest you smile and nod and agree with whatever either of them says."

CHAPTER NINETEEN

Niall was afraid he might pass out before he ever reached his bed, the Scotch-laced coffee he'd had at Duncan's house doing little to help his exhaustion. One more duty to perform and then he intended to sleep for twenty-four hours, more than willing to let the state police sort out the mess on the island and draw their own conclusions as to what had happened there last night.

They were, after all, better equipped to deal with multiple bodies.

As he and Dante headed to the main house, Niall noticed the broken window and mangled roof on Claude's vehicle, although he wasn't really surprised, considering all the reports of storm damage the sheriff's office had been receiving since midnight. But he'd learned only half an hour ago, when he'd finally made it back to his truck and checked his cell phone, that the destruction had reached the western shoreline.

After a fast, cold ride to Duncan's house to change into dry clothes, bandage a few gashes, and swallow several mugs of coffee, Duncan had shot Niall, Nicholas, and Dante across the fiord to the marina in his speedboat, since Nicholas's powerful fishing boat was now sitting some four hundred feet down on the floor of Bottomless.

As they turned up the walkway, Niall could tell Birch was dying to ask what was going on as she stood at the bottom of the stairs holding her bathrobe closed at the throat, but her father's hand on her arm appeared to be keeping her quiet. Then again, he'd learned early on that even though the lass had a bit of a temper, she also had the sense to know when to keep it in check.

Niall stopped in front of them, doing his damnedest *not* to notice Birch giving him a silent inspection, her eyes filled with worry. "Birch, Claude, I'd like you to meet Dante. And this is Birch Callahan," he told Dante, "the director of the Crisis Center, and her father, Claude. Dante's here because he's been living at the colony for a couple of months and is in fact the man who helped Macie escape."

Birch looked at Dante in surprise. "Macie said a man named Dan helped her."

Dante shrugged. "They know me as Dan

at the settlement."

"He's actually a security guard at Nova Mare," Niall said, the five men having decided at Duncan's house exactly what they would tell everyone, knowing half-truths were always better than whispered speculation. "But because of the mob protesting what they consider a cult, Mac Oceanus decided to have one of his men join the colony to see what was really going on." He glanced at the screen door. "Is Macie up yet?"

"I . . . I don't think so," Birch said, clutching her robe again. "Why?"

Niall shifted his stance when the gash in his thigh went from throbbing to burning. "You know that Macie told us the new leader was trying to create a . . . mythical god. Well, last night Sebastian held another ceremony out on an island that sits halfway down on the other side of Bottomless," Niall continued when Birch nodded. "All the colonists were there, including Dante, when a storm developed over the water and slammed into the island. I happen to know," he said dryly, "because Nicholas and I and Alec and Duncan were on the eastern mainland watching through binoculars."

"Why?" Birch whispered, her gaze darting to Dante then back to Niall. "Despite what the protesters think, everyone in town seems to feel the colonists are harmless."

"Macie obviously doesn't," Niall reminded her. "And last night we just wanted to make sure all they were sacrificing was *food.*"

"There was a lot of damage to the campground I was staying at," Claude said. "The wind uprooted trees, tore up tents, and even blew over large campers."

"Aye, so I've heard," Niall said with a nod. "The destruction appears to be a couple of miles wide along the western shoreline, but seems to have stopped at the main road." He looked at Birch. "The storm nearly leveled the island, and the reason I'm asking about Macie is because the father of her babe, Johnny, was hurt."

"Oh no," Birch said on a soft gasp. "How badly?"

"He was taken to the hospital in Millinocket and, last I heard, was in surgery to repair a broken leg. Johnny's a good man, Birch, and Macie has so much as admitted to me that she loves him. I'm sure she'd want to be with him now."

"Of course," Birch said without hesitation, stepping free of her father's hold. "I'll go wake her up and . . ." She frowned in thought. "I'll have Mom drive her to Millinocket. And I'll ask Cassandra to go with them; she must know where the hospital is, and I'm sure she'll also want to stay with Macie," she added as she ran up the stairs. She stopped at the top and looked down at them. "What about the other colonists? Macie lived there almost a year, and she'll want to know if any of her friends were hurt."

Niall shifted his stance again and nodded. "Five men are confirmed dead, although Dante said they'd all arrived at the settlement just recently. Several others were also taken to the hospital, and three men are still unaccounted for — lost at sea, we believe, when they tried to make it back to the mainland in a canoe. You can tell Macie all the women miraculously escaped unscathed but for some minor scratches and being scared half to death. And Birch?" he softly added. "Also tell her that Sebastian is one of the men who was killed, as I'm sure that's something Johnny will ask when she's finally able to see him."

Birch's beautiful and worried eyes darted to Dante, then back to Niall. "You got caught in the storm, too. The shirt you're wearing says *MacKeage Construction,* and you're limping."

He mustered the energy to give a negligent shrug. "It's nothing a few aspirin and twenty-four hours of sleep won't fix."

She stared at him for several heartbeats, nodded and grabbed the door handle, but then turned back. "Does Dante . . ." She shifted her gaze and spoke directly to him. "Do you want to go to the hospital to see Johnny?"

"Thank you, no," Dante said. "But I wouldn't mind getting a ride as far as the settlement entrance. I'd like to be there for the others."

Niall had to give the man credit; even though Nicholas had urged him to return to Nova Mare, Dante had insisted on helping the surviving colonists, even though he was one step away from falling into a coma himself.

But hell, fighting demons was damned exhausting.

And something Niall had decided he never, ever wanted to do again.

"I can give you a ride," Claude interjected. "And maybe I can be of some help to the colonists." He looked at Niall. "If you're going to be passed out in bed, will Officer Sheppard be running patrols by here today?" he asked. "In case a husband should come looking for his wife?"

"Jake will be staying right in town. And my four-legged officer will be here," Niall added as he gestured at Shep, who was still keeping his distance and looking thoroughly disgusted. Niall didn't know if the dog couldn't stand the smell of demon blood or was merely pissed at being left behind last night. Hell, they could have used Shep about the time they'd found themselves swimming to the island in the middle of a mythical battle. "Birch," he said as she opened the screen door. "Our deal stands. You'll be staying nearby, too, preferably right here at home."

She stared at him again, then suddenly shot him a smile that was far more spitfire than friendly. "Why of course, Chief Mac-Keage. I wouldn't dream of having you hauled out of bed to come rescue poor helpless me. *Again,*" she snapped, disappearing through the door.

Niall dropped his head with a heavy sigh, even as he heard Claude chuckle.

Claude walked up beside him and stood facing Bottomless. "She might be a little cranky this morning, but she's not stupid. And I'd bet my bankbook she spent a restless night worried about you, just like she used to worry about me." He looked at Niall and grinned. "It appears to me she's acting more like a girlfriend than a neighbor," he said dryly. He gestured at Dante to follow as he headed to his car. "Come on, Dante;

let's get going before you fall asleep on your feet. I hope you don't mind the sound of fresh air whistling through broken windows."

Thoroughly mesmerized by the nearly full moon reflecting off the gentle swells of Bottomless, Birch sat on the top step of the porch with her chin resting in her hands, too damn tired even to blink. She had intended to take a nap this afternoon to make up for the sleep she'd lost last night, but instead had spent the day settling her new residents in for what she was afraid might be a long stay.

Francine — she'd refused to tell Birch her last name or where she was from — had arrived with no identification, no money, nor any clothes other than what she and her daughter — the girl's name was Emily — had been wearing. They'd been on the road four days, Francine had said, the first three days aimlessly getting rides as well as food from kind-looking women they would approach at grocery stores in various towns. But after hearing from one Good Samaritan about the new Spellbound Falls Crisis Center, Francine had focused solely on getting here, certain it would be the last place on Earth her husband would look for them.

Birch had noted their dirty clothes not only were good quality and up to fashion, but metropolitan rather than rural — although they very well could have been purchased at a thrift shop in a large city. And from the way the two of them said certain words — though they had no obvious accent — Birch was fairly certain that large city was in Canada. Possibly Quebec City, since it was closest and there were dozens of backcountry logging roads crossing the border, or maybe Fredericton or even Saint John, New Brunswick, if they'd entered Maine from the east.

Birch figured a few days of rest and regular meals, as well as the camaraderie of the other residents, would go a long way to getting the hunted look out of their eyes. But once they realized they truly were safe, she would gently start pressing Francine to open up about what she was running from, and explain they needed a starting point from which to build her and Emily a new, independent life free of fear. And if they were indeed Canadian citizens, she'd figure out how to deal with that problem when it actually *became* a problem.

Once she'd gotten her mom and Cassandra and a very frantic Macie on their way to Millinocket, Birch had started calling around looking for clothes and personal items for her new residents. God bless Peg MacKeage, who had a daughter Emily's age, and Vanetta, who was very close to Francine's size, for digging through their own closets, as both women had shown up within an hour carrying huge boxes overflowing with entire wardrobes, right down to underwear and pajamas. Peg had also brought entertainment for Emily: age-appropriate DVDs and magazines, and even an electronic tablet already loaded with e-books and games. Vanetta had included makeup in her box, claiming a little primping on the outside went a long way toward making a woman feel beautiful and confident on the inside.

Rana Oceanus had arrived in her zippy little cart laden down with groceries, as well as a couple of pairs of shoes, a raincoat, and even a nice purse for Francine. Julia had shown up with enough grooming products to keep everyone smelling wonderful for a year, along with a box from Olivia containing laundry detergent, some of her daughter Sophie's clothes, and a pink backpack for Emily.

Oh yeah; the famous five were freaking fabulous.

But the next time residents arrived possessing only the clothes on their backs, Birch now knew she'd better *state* what she needed rather than just say . . . everything. *Mon Dieu,* even after Francine and Emily had taken armfuls upstairs it was still standing-room-only in the kitchen.

That would be the same kitchen Birch had spent four freaking hours cleaning up from last night's dinner and then reorganizing so she could *reach* everything.

Her dad had called in the late afternoon to say he was spending the night at the colony, which he'd discovered was quite a nice, self-sufficient facility. Far from being a cult, he'd told Birch, the colonists were really just a bunch of New Agers more interested in tapping into the kind of magic that turned freshwater lakes into seas than in creating a new god. Claude had then added in a whisper that the stories he was hearing from the survivors about what had happened on that island were even wilder than the storm, but that he'd save the details for another day because he'd had to go help . . . milk the goats.

And God bless her mom; Hazel had returned from Millinocket with news that Johnny would be just fine, but *without* Cassandra and Macie, having used her personal credit card so they could stay at a motel within walking distance of the hospital and given them all the money in her wallet for meals. The ladies were set for clothes, apparently, because while Birch had headed downstairs to dress after waking them up, Hazel had gone to their rooms and suggested they throw a few things in a backpack.

Oh yeah; her mom was also freaking fabulous.

No matter the crisis, Hazel always seemed to catch overlooked details or come up with a plan of action before anyone else did. And her newly acquired expertise appeared to rival Cassandra's when it came to sneaking off — in Hazel's case to go meet a full-grown, unmarried, and apparently mysterious man at the local watering hole. Her mom's little after-dinner walk this evening had lasted three hours, and the woman had returned home with an added spring in her step and a wine stain on her blouse.

Birch didn't know how Claude expected her to keep Hazel away from Sam, considering they were both adults. Besides, Niall hadn't seemed worried about them spending the day in Turtleback *alone* together, but in fact had been amused by her concern. And she was more inclined to trust the judgment of someone who knew Sam personally rather than secondhand information heard in a bar.

Mon Dieu, if she didn't know better she might think Claude simply didn't want any competition while he went after Hazel himself. And that had Birch changing her mind about him getting struck by lightning last night, deciding instead that something had to have happened in Montreal to make him throw away his career and move to Maine.

Then again, if she could talk to birds and trees — and the trees *talked back* — what was to say she and her father didn't share some freaky gene that made them do things others might see as out of character or downright strange? Birch had always thought she'd inherited her decisiveness from *Grand-mémère* Hynes, but maybe her deal-with-the-consequences-later approach was really Claude's fault.

Birch straightened when she caught the hint of a sound and looked over at Niall's cottage to see the door crack open and Shep come barreling outside. She held her watch up to the moonlight and saw it was half past eleven, which meant Niall had slept nearly sixteen hours straight.

"Well, big man," she said out loud, standing up and making sure her robe covered her *I don't freaking care* baggy pajama pants and oversized top, "I hope you still plan to sleep another eight, because I'm about to pass out draped over your amazing muscles."

Birch picked up the basket she'd packed with turkey sandwiches and a huge piece of the cake Rana had brought, then walked down the steps and started across the yard. "Don't worry, I brought something for you, too," she said with a laugh when Shep bounded over and started prancing beside her and nosing the basket. She stopped and pulled out the large beef bone she'd cut off the humungous roast Rana had also brought and held it just out of his reach. "But the deal is you have to eat it outside, so you don't make a greasy mess *inside.*"

Shep immediately sat down, licking his drooling lips as he stared at her — no, at the bone — in eager, puppy-dog anticipation.

"And when you're done and after you've washed the grease off *you* with a swim in the sea, just give a bark at the door and I'll let you back in. Deal?"

Figuring his impatient *woof* was as close to a yes as she'd get, Birch handed him the bone and then sighed when he bolted toward the beach without so much as a thank-you. She smoothed down her robe and continued across the yard, making sure the truck in the driveway was *Niall's* — only to go perfectly still on a silent gasp at the sight of the huge bald eagle perched on the rack of lights on the roof of the pickup.

Well, she was pretty sure it was a bald eagle, even though its signature solid white head appeared to be coated with dried mud or fish guts or . . . something. There was enough moonlight to see that its body feathers also looked tattered and that one of its wings was drooping slightly, making her wonder if the poor thing hadn't also gotten caught in last night's storm.

Were eagles' territories twenty miles long? Did they even have territories?

Birch guessed she was going to have to order a book about birds.

"Hello there," she whispered, although for the life of her she didn't know *why* she was talking to it, even as she hoped to God it didn't start talking back like the tree had. She glanced toward the cottage, then inched closer to the front of the truck. "Did your son or daughter tell you a gullible lady lives here and hands out food? Well, for the record, your kid paid for the pie with a barrette."

Birch scurried back with a startled squeak

when the eagle suddenly shifted and a small object dropped onto the windshield, then clattered down over the hood and fell to the gravel in front of her.

Seriously? Birch eyed the eagle silently eyeing her back, then bent to squint at the ground. She gave another quick glance at the roof of the truck, then stepped closer and picked up what appeared to be a ring. She held it up in the moonlight, only to go perfectly still again when she realized she had seen it — or one just like it — before. Seriously! It looked exactly like the freaking ring the woman in the white car had been wearing when the bitch had flipped her off.

But how was that possible? Even crazier, where had the eagle found it? Birch looked up with every intention of asking that exact question, only to see the bird now eyeing her basket — which she immediately hugged to her chest. "Don't even think about it. This is for Niall. I'm worried he hasn't eaten all day."

The eagle just stared at her, its steady yellow eyes appearing way too bright to be reflecting only moonlight. Birch looked down at the ring, glanced over at the cottage, then back up at the bird. *"Merde,"* she muttered, slipping the ring in her robe pocket. "Okay, you can have *one* of the sandwiches."

She walked along the length of the truck and, after looking toward the beach to make sure Shep wasn't around, set down the basket and took out one of the thick foil packages. She walked a bit farther up the driveway while unfolding the foil and started to lift out the overstuffed sandwich — but dropped the entire package and scurried away with another squeak when a dark blur silently glided past her.

The poor thing more or less crashed to the ground several feet beyond the fallen sandwich, and Birch grabbed her arm where the tip of its wing had touched her. "Now I know where your kid gets his boldness. Oh, you're limping," she rushed on as it made its way over to the food. At least she thought it was limping, unless that was just how birds with big sharp talons walked. "Well, Mr. Eagle," she said, deciding it was a boy, since every other male she'd seen today had been limping. "Thank you for the ring." She picked up the basket and started backing away. "I just wish you could tell me where you got it. No, no I don't," she quickly added in a whisper. "A talking tree was freaky enough; I don't need a bird talking to me, too."

Not that this particular bird was even

listening, having dismissed her in favor of gobbling up the sandwich it had quite handsomely paid for. Birch pulled the ring out of her pocket and studied it as she walked the length of the truck and turned toward the cottage, trying to decide whether or not to tell Niall what had just happened.

But then she remembered he hadn't seemed especially fond of the bird that had given her the barrette, even suggesting she douse it with bear spray if it came around again. So she slid the ring back in her pocket, worried he'd run out and start throwing rocks at the poor thing when he saw the foil wrapper on the ground and realized she'd given it one of his sandwiches. Yeah, she'd wait and tell him tomorrow morning after the eagle was long gone. She just hoped Niall would believe she recognized something she'd seen for all of two seconds while being forcibly run off the road.

She might not wear jewelry all that often, especially here in the wilderness, but she certainly knew a thing or two about it. In fact, whenever her father had escaped to his sanctuary in the St. Germaine basement to reload bullets, she would sit at the little desk he'd set up for her in the corner and study the jewelry sections of auction house catalogs. She'd give him credit; Claude hadn't even raised an eyebrow as his six-year-old daughter had added the catalogs to her dictated list of things she wanted from the penthouse when he went to get her clothes. But after *Grand-père* Fredrick's reaction the first time he saw them — his eyes bulging as he'd read the estimated values — Birch had started keeping the catalogs in her dad's gun safe.

She'd known her father actually *got* her when, after the sadly awkward birthday celebration at dinner the day she'd turned seven, he'd led her downstairs carrying her big heavy book on guns, opened his safe, and handed her several brand new catalogs. Twenty-five-year-old street cop Claude St. Germaine stopping into fancy auction houses asking for catalogs; now that truly had been an act of love. It was also when Birch had known everything would be okay.

Realizing she was standing in front of Niall's door, she took a deep breath, plastered a warm smile on her face, and knocked. She ran a hand through her loose curls when she heard a rasped "Just a minute" and had just lifted the basket in front of her when the door opened to reveal the pajama-clad — bottoms *and* top — gorgeous mountain of testosterone she intended to use as a mattress for the next eight hours.

"I brought you food," she said brightly, walking past him before he could realize her neighborly offering came with strings attached. It was, after all, his fault she was so exhausted. She set the basket on the counter, plastered her smile back in place, and turned to see him still holding on to the open door. "Shep's gnawing on a juicy beef bone down at the beach, because I told him bones are outside treats and to just bark when he's done and I'll let him in," she said, hoping he'd catch the hint that she was planning to still be here when Shep barked. "Well," she continued when Niall remained silent, politely covering a yawn with one hand while using the other to loosen the belt on her robe as she slowly inched toward the bedroom. "If you're hungry you can go ahead and eat now, but if you still need to catch up on your — Oh, *maudit,*" she growled when she saw him arch a brow. "I'm only here looking for a nice warm body to drape over so I can finally get some sleep."

She marched into the bedroom while shedding her robe, dropped it on the floor, and climbed up onto the mattress. "You might have spent last night dodging lightning and falling trees," she muttered as she rearranged the pillows on the unmade bed that was . . . oh, God, it was still warm with his body heat. "But I'd take that over tossing and turning all night worrying about getting a call at freaking three in the morning, and then spending all day dealing with a mother and daughter who show up with only the clothes on their backs and who won't tell me their freaking last name."

Looking over her shoulder to see him silently standing in the bedroom doorway holding the remaining foil-wrapped sandwich, Birch turned to sit in the middle of the mattress, took a calming breath, and gave him a sheepish smile. "I really am really tired, Niall. And I'm pretty sure I could finally fall asleep if I had a nice strong heartbeat to listen to instead of the crazy chatter going on in my brain. If I promise not to attack you, can . . . can I stay?"

She dropped her head on a silent shudder when he turned and walked away without saying anything, so damned tired she was dangerously close to bursting into tears — even though she *never* cried. Yeah, well, she didn't need to sleep draped over some dumb old man anyway, any more than she needed a stupid boyfriend. She crawled to the edge of the mattress looking for where she'd thrown her robe, spotted it beside the door, then turned and climbed off the monstrously tall bed — only to yelp a nasty curse when the light in the hallway went out half a second before she was swept up against a big solid chest.

Birch started to say that a little warning would be nice, but snapped her mouth shut when she realized he was climbing into bed *and taking her with him.* So she started to sigh in relief, but sucked it back in when she realized he still hadn't said one single word since . . . Oh, God, what if *he* wanted to have sex?

She really didn't think she could muster the energy to wrap her arms around all his amazing muscle, much less kiss him. Surely he'd noticed she was wearing *un*sexy pajamas; how much more blatant did she have to be? Damn; she knew she should have worn her *I'm having my period so leave me alone* granny gown.

"I . . . ah, I really don't think I have the energy to —" she began as he stretched out with her on top of him, his soft *shush* cutting her off.

"Go to sleep, lass," he whispered as he held her head against his chest. "I prefer my women awake when I make love to them."

Birch thought she should probably thank

him for letting her stay, but she was so tired and he was so warm and solid and *here*. And he probably wouldn't have heard her, anyway, over the sound of his strongly beating heart. Yeah, she'd thank him tomorrow, right before she told him about the eagle giving her the ring.

But she'd probably leave out the part about her giving it one of his . . .

The woman was passed out as limp as a rag doll before Niall even finished positioning her away from the gash in his thigh. Not that he minded being used as a mattress now that he understood why she preferred sleeping draped over him rather than wrapped securely in his arms. Aye, he supposed being trapped under the crushing weight of concrete and steel as a child might haunt a person all the way to their grave. Hell, he wouldn't be surprised if Birch intended to be cremated instead of buried.

Niall grinned up at the ceiling, deciding her coming over *only to sleep* with him was a good sign the lass was getting used to the notion they were a couple.

But then he scowled, thinking that true couples were honest and open with each other. But how, exactly, did he tell a woman he was coming to care deeply for that he was living proof the magic was real? He knew the MacKeage, MacBain, and Gregor men had all wrestled with the same dilemma since the first wave of them had arrived in this century nearly forty years ago; on the one hand feeling honor-bound to reveal they were time-travelers or magic-makers, and on the other fearing the truth might be more than a woman raised in an age of science could handle.

Niall also knew that upon deciding to propose marriage to Mary Sutter, Michael MacBain had confessed to being born in the year 1171, and that a magical storm had brought him here. Not only had Mary fled in confusion to her sister in Virginia — Michael unaware she was pregnant with his child — but she'd gotten in a car accident several months later trying to return to him, and died mere hours after giving birth to their son, Robbie.

The men born in *this* century had also had to deal with introducing their women to the magic — men such as Robbie Mac-Bain, Duncan, young Ian, and Hamish MacKeage. Even Greylen's daughters had been compelled to reveal their family secret to their husbands. The only first-generation highlander who *hadn't* wrestled with the problem was Alec; but then, he'd had the questionable good sense to fall in love with the daughter of the biggest magic-maker of them all. But the true magic, as far as Niall was concerned, was that their modern wives loved them *despite* their fantastical origins and ancient-mindedness.

Niall went back to grinning at the ceiling, thinking Birch had dealt rather well with a talking tree, although the fact it had just saved her life may have helped. And now that he thought about it, her two interactions with Telos appearing as a tree and an immature eagle might actually work in his favor when it came time to explain the magic.

Hell, just thinking the bastard's name made him scowl again. Almost as if to prove Nicholas's dire prediction of the havoc clashing deities could wreak, last night Telos had — without compunction, apparently, and with ruthless precision — not only made short work of the new god trying to manifest, but had also made damn sure Sebastian and his equally power-hungry cohorts could never call forth another one.

Dawn had revealed eight dead men — five ruthlessly crushed by giant oaks and three lost at sea — a few others with broken bones, and a good number sporting gashes inflicted by . . . claws. The precision component of the attack was that none of the women were hurt, other than a few minor scratches. And even those likely had been self-inflicted when the women had fled to the southern end of the island and hidden in the crags of huge boulders on the shoreline — almost as though Telos had herded them to safety before unleashing the full brunt of his power.

A *demonic god* Nicholas had called the newly manifested entity just before charging into the maelstrom; the mythical warrior's own ruthless precision with a sword being something Niall had never witnessed before and never cared to again. Hell, half the time he hadn't been able to tell if Nicholas was fighting *against* Telos or *with him* against the small army of demons the new entity had brought with it, since Niall, alongside of Duncan and Alec, was himself rather busy trying to protect the confused and terrified colonists.

Niall had felt rather unsettled, however, to see the five of them — Dante having joined the fight — using swords while Telos had slaughtered more than his share of demons using two large-caliber, semiautomatic pistols with a seemingly endless supply of bullets. And when Niall had asked Nicholas about it later, the warrior had in turn asked why he was surprised a *modern* god preferred a modern weapon. He and Dante and Niall, as well as Titus and Mac, were more comfortable using swords simply because that had been the weapon of choice at the time of *their* births. Nicholas had also gone on to say that Telos would likely continue using modern technology to his advantage and eventually not even bother with guns.

And wasn't that just a goddamned wonderful notion.

Well, Niall thought on a stifled snort as he threaded his fingers through Birch's hair — if the original colonists had come here wanting to be close to the kind of magic that created inland seas, they'd certainly gotten their wish last night. He only hoped they now understood that just as every coin had two sides, so did the energies that powered the world. And after personally seeing the flip side of Telos, just the idea of the bastard being interested in Birch sent cold chills down Niall's spine.

He touched his lips to the top of her head when he felt a wet spot he suspected was drool begin to form on his pajamas — which he'd put on to cover several *demon*-inflicted scratches — and closed his eyes on a sigh of contentment. Aye, he did admire a woman willing to go after what she wanted.

413

And that tonight Birch had wanted to fall asleep listening to his heartbeat was enough for him . . . for now.

CHAPTER TWENTY

Birch woke up lying facedown on a plain old regular mattress, and shot to her hands and knees when she realized the light was angled downward coming through the window instead of sideways — which meant the sun had been up over an hour!

"*Merde.* Why didn't you wake me?" she growled when she heard Niall moving in the kitchen. She scrambled off the bed, grabbed her bathrobe off the floor on her way by, and marched down the hall. "Everyone at home is probably up by now."

"I did wake you," the fully dressed man said as he poured coffee into a pair of mugs. "Three times, in fact. The first time all I got out of you was a grunt, and when I tried again a few minutes later you called me a nasty name." He stopped pouring and grinned over his shoulder. "I quit trying after you took a swing at me."

"I did not," she said on a gasp. "I've never

taken a swing at anyone in my life. I am not a violent person."

He shrugged and went back to pouring the coffee.

Birch walked to the window and looked toward the main house as she un-balled her robe and tried to find a sleeve hole. "The back door's still closed and I don't see Mimi, so maybe Mom's not up yet."

Niall walked over beside her and took a sip from his mug as he also looked out the window. "Do you usually sleep with your bedroom door closed? I could give ye a boost through your bathroom window, so if anyone's in the kitchen they won't —"

Something clattered onto the hardwood floor and Birch looked down to see the ring the eagle had given her roll to a stop against one of Niall's socked feet.

He picked it up before she could, held it up between them and frowned, then arched a brow when she snatched it out of his hand. "Oh, I'm sorry," he said, setting his coffee on the windowsill. He ran his fingers through his hair, straightened the collar of his shirt, then clasped his hands behind his back on a deep breath. "Okay, I'm ready. No, wait; are ye not going to get down on one knee at least?"

"Huh?"

"Although knowing you're not much of a traditional woman, I do admit to being surprised you brought your own ring. But I suppose ye might be particular about what you'll be wearing every day, and probably wanted to make sure it fit properly."

"What *are* you talking about?"

Up went that brow again. "Are ye saying you didn't slip the ring in your pocket before coming here last night with the intention of asking for my hand in marriage?"

Birch felt her chin drop nearly to her chest, even as she tried to decide if the man was serious or not. He certainly looked serious. No, wait. There; that had to be laughter turning his gorgeous eyes an even deeper shade of green.

"Nay, what am I thinking," he said on a groan as he picked up his coffee and headed back to the kitchen area. "You told me the first night ye knocked on my door that you weren't looking to get married. Or pregnant."

"Will you get serious," she said, rushing after him. "This is the ring the woman in the white car was wearing when she flipped me off while I was being forced off the road. Or if it's not the exact ring, it's an identical twin."

He frowned down at the ring, then at her.

417

"How can ye possibly know that? I was under the impression you were rather busy at the time trying not to be killed. You don't recall what the woman looked like, yet ye recognize a ring you must have seen for all of two or three seconds?"

"Look, I have a thing for jewelry, okay? Being a cop, you know that if you ask ten people to describe the same event, they'll each mention different details based on their particular lifestyles and interests. And since I've always been interested in jewelry, this ring is the one detail that stood out to me," she said, holding it up between them again. "And I can't recall what she looked like because her hand was blocking my view of her face. But I can tell you that hand belonged to a woman in her thirties or early forties, that she was wearing a ring exactly like this one, and that the nail polish on her middle finger was a very ugly passion red."

"Okay," he said slowly, "if we assume this is the ring she was wearing, can I ask how you got hold of it?"

She gestured toward the door. "A bald eagle gave it to me last night when I was on my way over here. It was perched on the light rack on the roof of your truck."

She saw him stiffen, his gaze darting to the door, then back to her. "A fully mature bald eagle, or the younger one ye fed the pie to?"

Birch grew a little concerned when she realized he had the same really focused look in his eyes the eagle had had last night. "This one had a white head and tail feathers," she said softly. "Only it was covered in dried mud or something. It looked sort of beaten up, and one wing drooped a little, so I figured it got caught in the same storm you did." She gave him a tentative smile when he didn't say anything, because she really, really didn't want him to think she was crazy. "Do you suppose eagles can communicate with one another; like when they find a food source they can go back and tell their buddies where it is? I saw a Discovery Channel special that showed how bees come back to the hive and do a little dance to . . . Anyway," she went on when his eyes narrowed. "This one could have been the mom or dad of the bird that was here last week . . . couldn't it?"

"Did ye get close enough to touch it?"

"No," she assured him, shaking her head. "It was perched on the roof of your truck. It shifted its stance and the ring hit the windshield, rolled down the hood, and fell on the ground in front of me."

"Did the eagle say anything to you?"

Still unable to read his expression, Birch dropped her gaze to his socked feet. "I'm not crazy, Niall. I know I told you at the river that the tree talked to me, but that was . . . it was just my way of coping with my fear of drowning." She looked up. "My dad tried to teach me to swim when I lived with him, but every time my head went under I felt like the water was crushing me to death. So thinking about it later, I decided that while I was stuck against the bridge, I talked to the only thing keeping me from falling in that cold, dark river. And I imagined the tree talked back because it . . ." She looked at his socks again and hugged herself on a shudder. "Because it was better than screaming and screaming and not having anyone hear me," she ended on a whisper.

"Ah, lass," he murmured, pulling her into his arms and pressing her head to his chest. "Hush now, don't cry."

"I never cry," she mumbled into his shirt.

He released her just enough to sweep her off her feet, then walked to the living room area, sat down on the couch with her in his lap, and slid his fingers in her hair when she hid her face in his shirt. "Aye," he said thickly, "the sun reflecting off your beautiful eyes must have tricked me into seeing a tear." He gently tilted her head to look at him, his own eyes softened with concern. "So ye found a mature eagle perched on my truck, and it gave you the ring and then . . . what?"

"I, um, I walked up the driveway a short distance and gave it one of your sandwiches." She leaned against him with a heavy sigh. "I reinforced its belief that the gullible lady who lives here gives out food in exchange for trinkets, didn't I?"

Niall took the ring out of her hand and also sighed. "I'm afraid so. But in this instance, I would say it was a fair trade. I only wish we could find out how the eagle got hold of it." He held the ring up in front of her. "If ye know about jewelry, can you tell me anything about this piece? It appears old."

Happy to be off the subject of eagles, Birch turned the stone toward him by turning his hand. "I'm ninety percent sure the ruby and diamonds are real, and that the setting is quite old. The insignia on this side," she went on, turning his hand again, "appears to be some sort of family crest, and the one on this other side could be the family motto, but I don't recognize the language. My best guess is the ring is from an eastern European country, or might even be Russian."

"Would ye mind if I held on to it awhile?" he asked. "I know someone who might be able to trace the ring's origin, which could help lead us to whoever's after you."

"You can keep it for all I care." She tilted her head back. "Daddy told me about Leonard Struthers — or rather, Jacques Rabideu — being found dead on the same day I was run off the road," she admitted softly, not hating the man enough to want him murdered. "And that he may have crossed a family of professional con artists. Dad said there are actually several families operating in Canada."

"Aye, he told me the same thing when he came to the station the day he arrived. And since ye feel certain this is the ring the woman in the white car was wearing," he said, holding it up to see again, "it may tell us which one of the families Rabideu was involved with. So," he went on, lifting his hips just enough to slide the ring in his jeans pocket, then capturing her chin to look at him. "Will I hear another knock on my door tonight, and maybe this time have the pleasure of making love to an *awake* woman?" he asked, his grin lighting up his eyes.

Birch went perfectly still. "What are you

talking about? You and I . . . we didn't make love last night."

"No? Are ye saying you usually wear your pajamas inside out, then?"

Birch pulled her oversized top away from her chest, only to gasp when she saw the label in *front* instead of the back as well as on the *outside.* She lifted a leg to look at her pants, but seeing they were on correctly she went back to staring at the label on the shirt, trying to remember if she might have had an erotic dream. People sleepwalked, but could a person actually have sleep-sex?

Finally realizing the mountain she was sitting on was shaking with silent laughter, Birch scrambled off his lap and rounded on him. "We did not have sex last night. I want you to admit right now that you're just teasing."

"Aye," he said, pushing himself to his feet and pulling her into his arms again. "But only because I can't resist seeing your eyes fill with fire," he murmured as he bent and kissed her gaping mouth.

Birch couldn't stop herself from melting into the maddening man and kissing him back, even as she tried to remember the last time anyone had teased her. Imagine pretending to think she'd brought a ring over here to ask for his hand in marriage. And then implying they'd had sex but that she'd slept through the whole thing.

Like she could ever sleep through his love-making.

She leaned slightly away. "I . . . ah, I'm wide awake now."

He touched his forehead to hers with a groan. "And so is your mother. I believe I just heard her calling to you."

Birch pushed away from him with a gasp and swiped her robe off the floor. "Dammit, I forgot." She stopped trying to find a sleeve hole and glared at him. "This is all your fault. What in hell am I going to tell her?"

He walked to the counter and picked up the basket, walked back, and held it out. "Tell her you were worried I might be hungry after sleeping twenty-four hours and thought you'd be a good neighbor by bringing me breakfast."

"Yeah. Okay. That'll work," she said, finally getting her robe on. She neatly tied the belt, combed her fingers through her hair to smooth out the tangles, then took the basket from him just as she heard her mother call her name. "So how do I look?"

"I'm sorry to say a lot less tousled than the last time ye left here in pajamas," he said dryly. He opened the door only to have

Shep come barreling inside, then followed her out. "She's over here, Hazel," he said, actually waving at the woman and then lowering his hand and holding it out to Birch.

And like an idiot, she automatically reached out and shook it.

"Thank ye, Miss Callahan," he said a bit loudly, continuing to pump her hand as her mom came across the yard toward them. "After sleeping all day and night, your sandwiches were just what I needed to finish feeling like myself again. Good morning Hazel. Can I ask if ye have any news on Johnny?"

Birch watched her mother's eyes, slightly narrowed in suspicion, dart between the two of them before finally settling on Niall. "I stayed at the hospital until Johnny was out of surgery. The doctor told Macie everything went well, and that he should be able to go home tomorrow. So I booked Macie and Cassandra into a motel until then."

Birch slipped the basket over one arm, slid her other arm through her mother's, and started toward the house. "Come on, Mom; let's let Chief MacKeage eat his breakfast in peace." But she stopped in front of Niall's truck when she spotted dried bird droppings splattered all over the roof and running down the windshield. "Looks like you're going to need another bucket of hot, soapy water," she said, stifling a snicker when she saw Niall also looking at his truck and having no problem reading his eyes this time, since they perfectly matched his scowl. She could not, however, stifle a laugh when he muttered a nasty curse in French — completely slaughtering the word with his Scottish brogue.

Wanting to head off any questions about why she'd taken breakfast to her neighbor wearing pajamas, Birch decided to ask one of her own. "So, Mom," she went on as she started across the yard again, "what are your plans for today? Because I thought we could go to this nice little artisan shop in town and you could give me your opinion on a purse I'm thinking of buying."

"Oh, sorry, but I'm afraid I already have plans."

Birch stopped as they reached the walkway and slid her arm free. "What plans?"

"Just plans. So tell me, when did you start making your bed first thing in the morning before you even get dressed?"

Damn, she should have messed up her blankets and pillow last night. Heck, maybe she better ask Cassandra for pointers on sneaking around. No, wait; she just had to

426

ask her *mom.* "Now that Noreen's no longer here, I'm trying to stay ahead of the mess. Speaking of which," Birch rushed on, deciding to redirect the conversation, "I'm going to call a house meeting to discuss dividing up the chores. And just so you know, I'm including Emily so she'll feel like a valued member of the household. She can vacuum and dust and even help with the meals by setting the table."

Birch realized her plan had worked almost too well when she saw her mom's eyes darken with sadness. "That poor child; she didn't say two words at dinner last night. I really don't understand why some men feel they have to prove their manhood by terrorizing women and children."

"Now, Mom," Birch said gently, touching her arm. "We had this discussion when we agreed I'd take this job even though it was a live-in position. Remember my saying you have to be careful about letting the women's circumstances break your heart? Children are far more resilient than most people realize. What's really important is that Emily will learn right along with her mother that not only do they have choices, but that there are plenty of people willing to help them."

"But I'm not sure how to act around Emily," Hazel whispered. "I don't want to appear as though I pity her. Or Francine, for that matter; I'm afraid I might say the wrong thing."

"Just be your happy self, Mom. Emily's only a few years younger than Cassandra, and you two have become good friends. Do the same with Emily; find out what her interests are and encourage her to pursue them."

"Cassandra's an amazing artist," Hazel said, her smile returning. "She showed me some of her pastels, and I told her to take them around to the artisan shops and see if they might be interested in selling them on consignment. I'm glad you weren't upset that I left her in Millinocket with Macie; Cassandra can be quite a mature young woman when given the chance to feel needed."

"I think it was a wonderful idea to have her stay with Macie, and I agree there's a lot more to Cassandra than first impressions," Birch said as she started up the walkway.

Hazel caught her sleeve to stop her, glanced toward the house, then stepped closer and lowered her voice. "Can I ask what your first impression of Francine and Emily was?"

"A very scared mother and daughter.

Why? What's your impression of them?"

"That's exactly what I thought, too — at first," Hazel said softly. "But when I came back from Millinocket and went up to my room, I . . . well, I realized someone had been snooping around. Did you go in my bedroom yesterday looking for something?"

"No. I spent the morning cleaning the kitchen and dealing with all the stuff the committee women brought over. What makes you think someone was in your room?"

Hazel shook her head. "Everything in my bureau drawers was right where it should be, but . . . messy, like clothes and items had been pushed back and forth as if someone were looking for something. I don't want to accuse anyone," her mother rushed on, "and it never occurred to me that we should lock our bedroom doors. But when you think about it, Birch, we take in complete strangers we know nothing about."

"Well, shit," Birch muttered. "Being my first live-in position, I never considered that could be a problem. If we keep our bedroom doors locked, it's going to create an atmosphere of mistrust. But I also want everyone to feel secure." She cocked her head. "Did you notice if anything was missing?"

"No, not that I could see. I checked my

jewelry box and it didn't look like it had even been gone through. It was mostly my bureau, and it seemed that every drawer was touched. It also looked like some of the boxes on the floor of my closet had been pulled out and gone through, then shoved back in."

"But your jewelry box was completely ignored?"

Hazel nodded, then shook her head. "I'm not saying Francine or Emily was in my room, but if you weren't looking for something . . . well, I don't know what to think."

"Neither do I, at the moment," Birch said, giving her a quick hug, then stepping back with a smile. "Let me kick this around in my head for a while and see if I can't come up with a solution."

Her mother's smile returned. "It might be as simple as providing each resident with a small lockbox for their more precious possessions. I think you were wise to have us leave our more expensive jewelry at the bank, although I do wish I had my emerald necklace and earrings."

"You only wear those emeralds with your beige gown," Birch said in surprise. "And both are a little dressy for Spellbound Falls, don't you think?"

"They're not too dressy for Aeolus's Whisper."

"You're going up to Nova Mare? Who with?"

"I didn't say I *am* going," Hazel said quickly, heading for the house. "I merely wish I had my emeralds in case I want to dine there. And if I might suggest, *chére,*" she continued as she walked up the stairs, "the next time you feel compelled to call on your neighbor before you've dressed, you might want to wear something other than those ratty old pajamas under your robe." She opened the screen door to let Mimi in the house, then looked back and gave Birch a wink. "And try to remember the tag goes in the back on the *inside,*" she drawled, disappearing into the kitchen.

CHAPTER TWENTY-ONE

Birch sat in her new executive office chair that had been delivered yesterday, a warm cup of coffee resting on her belly and her socked feet propped up on her beautiful new desk, and stared at the matching floor-to-ceiling bookcases on the opposite wall as she tried to decide whether or not to tell Niall what she suspected about her newest residents. Based on Hazel's certainty that her room had been searched, Birch had been keeping a closer eye on Francine and Emily No-Last-Names for the last two days and had started wondering if, rather than running for their lives, they might actually somehow be connected to both the white car and Jacques Rabideu's murder.

Three or four families of con artists operating in Canada, Claude had said. And weren't children indoctrinated into most family businesses starting in the cradle, such as ranching and farming and fishing and even the circus? Heck, Birch figured she had known more about guns by age eight than most adults ever would.

But what kind of parent made a thirteen-year-old play the daughter of an abused woman? Because if that truly were the case, the really scary — or very sad — part was that Emily was one hell of an actress. But who better to get inside a women's shelter than a mother and child? And of course it had to be *two* people fleeing for their lives, so one could be a lookout or a distraction while the other one searched.

But searched for what? Because someone was definitely searching for something; the deciding factor for Birch occurring this morning after sneaking home from Niall's just before sunrise. Intending to grab clean undies on her way to the shower, she'd stopped in mid-reach and started opening all the drawers of her bureau. She'd checked her jewelry box next, rushed over and opened her closet, then slowly backed away at the realization her room had been me-thodically searched sometime during the night.

And they'd ignored her jewelry, just like they had her mother's, which implied that whatever they were looking for didn't fit in a jewelry box. Birch scanned her office, only able to assume it had also been searched, since it was still a mess of unpacked boxes, making it impossible to know if anything had been disturbed. But surprisingly, at this point she honestly didn't care, figuring she'd much rather have strangers pawing through her stuff than be run off the road. *Merde,* if they would just tell her what they were after, she'd *help* them look.

No, the only thing stopping her from confronting them or even telling Niall what was going on — which on the surface would seem the wiser thing to do — was the possibility she might be wrong. She was running a safe house for women, meaning she was in the business of *trust.* And if word got out she'd asked the police to investigate one of her residents for merely suspecting something . . . well, the new Spellbound Falls' Crisis Center would be dead in the water less than six weeks after opening its doors.

She needed solid evidence to take to Niall, or at least something more tangible than a few rearranged drawers and closets.

Despite the fact she'd only been sleeping with the man for three nights now — if she didn't count the night he'd made wonderful, playful love to her and then turned into a caveman the next morning — Birch felt she was getting to know Niall quite well. And not just how his amazing body worked, either, but his actual *mind.* He was probably the most innately protective, old-fashioned, noble guy she'd ever met. He was also quite understanding for not writing her off as crazy for admitting she talked to trees and had apparently become the new Bottomless Bird Lady.

So she was pretty sure if she mentioned what she suspected about Francine but asked him not to do anything until they were certain, Niall would likely turn into Chief Caveman right before her eyes again.

Birch dropped her feet to the floor when she heard her mother moving around upstairs, and realized there would be no more sneaking off at night in the foreseeable future, since she couldn't very well leave Hazel alone in the house with two possible criminals now that Noreen and Macie and Cassandra were gone.

Macie had moved back to the colony yesterday to be with Johnny, since the only reason she'd left was because of Sebastian, who was . . . no longer a problem. And having befriended a kind, middle-aged nurse — who just happened to be an amateur artist — at the hospital, Cassandra was spending the next few days with Nurse Beverly and her husband to see if they might be a good fit. All thanks to a really sharp social worker who happened to be sitting in the hospital cafeteria doing paperwork and had overheard Cassandra telling Macie she would gladly move into a foster home if the couple were upbeat and encouraging like Beverly.

Seriously; what were the chances? Some might call it serendipity or perfect timing or all the planets moving into alignment, but Birch was putting it up there in the good old *miracle* category, since Beverly and John Hallstead had done the paperwork nearly a month ago to be foster parents and were actively looking for a downtrodden and discouraged girl like Cassandra.

Birch was still breathless from how fast the social worker had made it happen — which is why she now had the engaging and obviously bold woman on speed dial. And although she was over-the-moon happy to see Noreen and Macie and Cassandra getting on with their lives, she was finding the house felt eerily . . . silent.

"Birch? Are you here?" Hazel called from the kitchen.

"I'm in my office, Mom."

Birch heard the screen door open and Mimi's claws tapping on the porch, her mother appearing in her office doorway shortly after.

"They're gone," Hazel said, sounding as perplexed as she looked. "They must have left sometime in the night. Their beds were never slept in."

"Well, shit," Birch growled, not having to ask *who* was gone as she rushed out of the office and ran up the stairs, her mother following at a slower but just as urgent pace. Birch went into Francine and Emily's room, stopped between the two beds, and looked around for . . . *merde,* she didn't know what she was looking for. She went to the bureau and started opening drawers just as her mom came in.

"Everything's still here," Hazel said as she opened the closet. She frowned, and took down the purse hanging on the inside of the door. "Francine even left the purse Rana gave her. I don't recognize the designer, but it's definitely expensive."

"They searched my bedroom last night," Birch admitted.

Hazel arched a delicate brow. "While you were in it?"

"No, Mom. You know damn well I've been sneaking over to Niall's the last three nights." She dropped her head. "I'm sorry. I never should have left you alone in the house with them."

"Oh, *bébé,*" Hazel said, tossing the purse on one of the beds, then walking over and pulling Birch into a hug. "I didn't survive four years in hell to be taken out by a scrap of a woman and a thirteen-year-old child. You're not the only one who owns bear spray." She leaned away slightly and smiled. "And I wasn't alone. Mimi might be infatuated with Emily, but she would have given them the business if they bothered me."

"Mimi didn't hear anything?"

Hazel stepped away and shook her head. "If she did, she never woke me. But then, she's likely getting used to people coming and going all hours of the day and night around here," she said dryly. She turned serious as she glanced around the room. "Do you suppose they finally found what they were searching for?" She turned to Birch, her expression hopeful. "If Claude is correct in assuming we were still in possession of something that belonged to Leo — to Jacques Rabideu, and Francine found it, that would mean this whole ordeal is over. There's no more reason for anyone to want you out of the way, and Sam can stop playing the bodyguard under the pretense of being romantically interested in me."

"What?" Birch said on an indrawn breath.

"You think Sam's been escorting you around to protect you?" She'd told her mom everything Claude and Niall had told *her* about Jacques Rabideu, but neither man had mentioned Sam's role in this whole stupid mess.

"Really, Birch," Hazel said, rolling her eyes as she walked out of the room and started down the hall. "Even I know a confirmed bachelor doesn't suddenly become interested in a woman who swaps husbands as often as most people swap vehicles." She stopped at the top of the stairs and shot Birch a smile. "Make that *two* confirmed bachelors, since Claude's sudden interest is even more suspect."

"But how come I didn't realize what they were doing?"

"Probably because you've been rather occupied getting laid," Hazel drawled, her muttered "and it's about damn time" trailing behind her as she walked down the stairs with all the poise of a Shakespearean actress exiting the stage.

Niall sat at his desk with his fingers laced together behind his head as he rocked back in his chair and grinned like the village idiot, feeling quite pleased with how his courtship was coming along — even though

Miss Callahan likely wasn't even aware she was being courted. Hell, for all he knew the lass thought *she* was courting *him* — only as a longtime lover, not a husband. But he really didn't see Birch changing her views on marriage anytime soon, considering the less than stellar examples she'd had since . . . well, since birth, apparently.

But unlike his modern clansmen, several of whom had given their women only *days* to get used to the notion of becoming wives, Niall was glad he was a patient man. That he happened to be living in the twenty-first century certainly helped, seeing how it was no longer frowned upon — much less considered a crime — for a man and woman to live together outside of marriage. But even though he would openly live with Birch if that was the only way he could have her, Niall knew he still had the mind-set of a twelfth-century highlander, which made him guilty of wanting her complete surrender.

Hearing stilted footsteps accompanied by prancing claws on the station stairs, Niall sat forward with a snort, thinking that besides requiring patience waiting for Birch to embrace a vow-and-ring commitment, he was also going to need nerves of steel.

"Don't you ever feed your dog, Mac-

Keage?" Sam asked as he walked in carrying a box sporting the Drunken Moose logo. Niall sighed when he heard a loud grumbling as Sam quickly closed the door, leaving Shep on the *wrong* side of it. "You do know we sell dog food at the store, don't you?"

"Despite how fast he goes through fifty-pound bags, he's still the cheapest officer on my payroll," Niall said with a chuckle, only to sober when he noticed the large envelope tucked under Sam's arm. "You've heard back from your contact."

"In spades," the man said, setting the box on the desk and opening the cover to reveal what had once been half a dozen warm cinnamon buns but were now only four — one of which was likely in Sam's belly and the other in the belly of the greedy beggar still grumbling out on the porch. "You eat, I'll talk," Sam continued as he pulled a chair up to the desk and sat down. He dropped the reading glasses perched on his head to his nose, took the envelope from under his arm, and pulled out a handful of papers.

"Edward Leopold," he began reading, making Niall stop reaching for a bun and lean back in his chair, "is the recently ordained patriarch of the Leopold dynasty, which at last count consisted of one hundred seventy-three adults and fifty-eight children spanning four generations. The respectable side of the family business is overland shipping, both truck and railroad, as well as controlling interests in a couple of hydropower companies and a corporate-sized cattle ranch in Saskatchewan."

"Ye got all that from a ring?" Niall asked when Sam looked up.

Sam grinned and shuffled through the papers, then set one of them on the desk facing Niall — a photo of the ring accompanied by a description. "Seems Birch does know a thing or two about jewelry," Sam continued, "because what she told you was pretty much spot on. The ring in the photo is definitely old and eastern European, and that's definitely the family crest. But the man in Canada to whom I sent pictures of the ring you gave me said ours is a high-quality, *exclusive* reproduction of the original ring Ivan Leopold was wearing when he stepped off a boat in Nova Scotia ninety-three years ago. There are two versions of it still being reproduced today in very limited quantities; one sized for a male and the other for a female. Every Leopold gets his or her ring after completing a rite of passage and, according to my contact, it's always worn on the . . . ah, right middle finger." Sam grinned again. "So I guess what Birch saw the day of her accident holds with tradition."

"And the non-respectable side of their family business?" Niall asked, undecided which amazed him more: that Sam had gotten all this information from a ring or that he'd gotten it in two days.

Hell, he felt his debt to Telos growing with every word Sam spoke.

"Another Leopold tradition that apparently crossed the Atlantic with Ivan," Sam went on, "is adding to the family wealth by swindling unsuspecting chumps out of *their* wealth. That rite of passage I mentioned? It's when a family member succeeds in pulling off his or her first million-dollar scam."

Niall felt his jaw slacken. "What sort of scams bring in a million dollars?"

Sam shuffled papers again, stopped at one, then shrugged. "Fake businesses and charities mostly, marriages like Hazel had with Rabideu — except it seems to be the younger Leopold women targeting rich, lonely old men — and one notable investment scheme that damn near wiped out a large oil company's retirement fund."

"And the entire family has managed to stay in the *business* of cheating people out of their money for ninety-three years without being caught?" Niall asked.

"For the most part," Sam said with a nod. "But then, there are several Leopolds in Canada's federal government; some elected officials and some department heads appointed by those officials. And if the news media starts connecting the Leopold name to corruption or bad business practices, an older member will take the fall and even do time in jail — handsomely compensated, of course — for the good of the family." Sam snorted. "Apparently you Scots don't have a monopoly on the definition of *clan*."

Niall leaned forward and rested his arms on the desk. "Is there some way we can find out if any of them crossed the border into Maine recently?"

"Well, now," Sam said as he shuffled papers again, going stone sober when he pulled out a page. "Beginning three days before Birch's encounter with the white car, Leopold men, women, and teenagers started entering the United States. Over the span of a week they crossed the border in Houlton and Jackman, Maine, a couple of cars came through upstate New York, and two parties rode the ferry to Portland from Nova Scotia. And those are just the ones carrying Leopold passports." He shrugged. "I'd need more time to research the married names of the women."

"Sweet Christ," Niall whispered, slumping back in his chair. "You're talking about a small army."

Sam nodded. "It appears to be a deliberate and well-thought-out operation, and I'd bet my half of the store that not only is Spellbound Falls their destination, but that everyone is already here."

"What about the vehicles they crossed in? Can we get that information?"

Sam shook his head. "These people haven't survived for nearly a century by being stupid. They would have quickly rented cars and trucks with U.S. plates."

"What in hell could Rabideu have had of theirs to warrant such an invasion?"

"Something damaging enough to the family to get the idiot tortured and killed. My contact said there are rumors Edward Leopold is planning to run for parliament next election, with his sights set on eventually being prime minister of Canada. It's possible Rabideu was holding information that could kill Edward's chances of even being elected town dogcatcher."

Niall stood up and walked to the window, then stared out at Bottomless in silence for several minutes before turning back to Sam. "How in hell am I supposed to fight an enemy I wouldn't even recognize if he passed me on the sidewalk? Short of locking them up with a twenty-four-hour armed guard," he growled, gesturing at the holding cell, "there's no way I can protect Birch and Hazel from a determined army of Leopolds."

"That's not as farfetched as it sounds," Sam said, relaxing back in his chair and folding his arms over his chest with a grin. "Only instead of your holding cell, why not book them a stay at the securest place on the planet?"

"Nova Mare?" Niall said in surprise. But then he also grinned. "Works for me."

"Well, except for two possible problems; the first being that I can't see you ever getting Birch to leave her residents or Hazel ever agreeing to leave Birch."

"That one's easy," Niall countered. "They're both so protective of each other, I just have to persuade Birch she needs to go for her mother's sake, and then tell Hazel it's the only way to keep her daughter safe. What's the second problem?"

"Time," Sam said. "As in how long you might have to keep them tucked away in their gilded cage. If whatever Rabideu had is powerful enough to bring this many Leopolds across the border, they're not about to give up until they get hold of it, even if that takes months."

Niall scrubbed his face, so damn frustrated he wanted to roar. He suddenly dropped his hands to look at Sam. "Then *we* find whatever they're after. It's agreed Rabideu must have hidden something in Hazel's house, so all we have to do is find the accursed thing and turn it over to the Canadian authorities."

"Whatever it is moved with Hazel and Birch, because the Leopolds wouldn't be bothering with them now unless their house — which is sitting empty with a *For Sale* sign out front — was searched with a fine-toothed comb."

"Then we have Birch and Hazel look through everything they moved here."

Sam took a moment to think about that, then shook his head. "They obviously didn't bring their entire household, so there's a good chance a lot of their belongings are sitting in a storage facility in Montreal."

Niall slid his hands in his pockets and turned to stare out at Bottomless again.

"Up until a year ago when his father handed over the reins," Sam went on softly, "Edward Leopold was the family's . . . enforcer. But old habits die hard, and I wouldn't be surprised to learn he personally cut out Rabideu's heart and stuffed it down the idiot's throat. And even though my contact sent me a picture of Edward, it's likely useless to us. Men planning to run for public office won't risk getting caught in another country committing a crime, so Edward would have sent his hand-chosen successor to deal with the problem. But my contact couldn't find out who took over that notable position. And Niall?"

Niall turned to look at him.

"You're not without a small army of your own; it so happens you know a warrior with *centuries* of fighting experience, several modern highlanders who don't particularly care to be on a losing side in a fight, a couple of wizards with a bunch of magical tricks up their sleeves, and two — no, three — highly effective government weapons who used to specialize in toppling small dynasties. And don't forget Birch's father; an ex-cop determined to keep his daughter safe is nothing to sneeze at, either."

Niall shook his head. "I went to Titus yesterday and asked for his help finding out what was going on, but he explained it's not his place to interfere. He also asked me to understand that having to merely watch mankind's struggles is a lot harder on him than it is on the ones who are struggling."

"Then ask Mac for help."

"I did," Niall said quietly, "and received the same answer. Like it was for Titus, Mac's duty is to protect man's right to deal with each other *without* divine interference." He shrugged. "I have no doubt he'd open Nova Mare to Birch and Hazel, but the Leopold invasion is my responsibility."

"Duncan has magical powers."

Niall gave a small grin. "He has a limited command of nature, but even that's useless against an enemy we can't recognize."

"And Nicholas?" Sam growled.

Niall nodded. "He will certainly lend us his sword-arm, once we have something tangible to fight."

Sam propped his elbows on his knees and rested his head in his hands. "What in hell good is all this hocus-pocus shit," he muttered to the floor, "if it's only used to move around mountains that were perfectly fine right where they were?"

Niall walked over to his desk, grabbed a cinnamon bun out of the box, and sat down. "I'm willing to bet my own sword-arm that not all of our resident magic-makers are going to stand back and merely watch — especially not if he's taken a shine to *my* Miss Callahan."

Sam straightened. "The new god." His

eyes narrowed. "Olivia told Dad some oak tree told you his name is Telos. You think he'll help?"

Niall gestured at the photo on his desk. "Who do you think gave Birch the ring?"

"I asked you that," Sam snapped. "And you said a *bird* did."

"Aye," Niall agreed with a chuckle. "Telos."

"Then where did *he* get it?"

"My best guess is he slipped it off the right-hand middle finger of a tourist with very poor taste in nail polish," Niall said just before biting into the bun.

CHAPTER TWENTY-TWO

"Okay, so here's the plan," Birch said, sliding into the passenger side of her mother's cart. "We tell Niall about Francine and Emily leaving and what we suspect they were doing here in the first place, then you'll earn your outrageous paycheck and I'll finally go buy my perfect purse. How's that for . . . Mom?" Birch said softly when she realized Hazel was clutching the wheel and staring straight ahead, her complexion as pale as snow. "It's over, Mom. You have nothing to worry about anymore."

"Can you ever forgive me?" Hazel whispered.

"For what?" Birch said on a gasp.

"For getting us in this mess in the first place by marrying a man I obviously knew nothing about." She looked over, her eyes swimming with unshed tears. "Four times, Birch; I've let four men charm their way into our lives, each one of them as duplicitous as the previous. You're the expert on women continuing to repeat harmful patterns; why do I keep marrying bastards? Why do I marry at all?"

"Oh, Mom," Birch said on a sigh, wrapping her in a fierce hug. "You keep getting married because you're an unwavering optimist." She leaned away just enough for Hazel to see her smile. "And because when you look at a person — *every* person — you always see the goodness in them."

"My optimism nearly got you killed," Hazel said thickly.

"Only because Rabideu was a master con artist. Your first three husbands might have been two-faced, but there wasn't any malice in them. They were just looking for a well-funded free ride." Birch used her thumb to brush a tear that had managed to escape and smiled again. "In fact, if I remember correctly, you took some wonderful trips with His Highness the King of Nowhere."

"But instead of learning from my mistakes, I keep getting worse. You said yourself I'm a good judge of character, so how did I let Leonard fool me so completely?"

"Because men who make their living taking advantage of women spend *years* practicing being debonair and charming until even *they* forget they're acting. The bastards cruise fund-raisers specifically looking for warm, loving, softhearted women like you." Birch sighed dramatically, determined to lighten her mother's mood. "I'm sorry, but I'm afraid the only way you'll stop being a target is if you turn yourself into a cold, hard-hearted bitch. I know," she said with an excited gasp. "You can take lessons from your stepmother. Madame Holier Than Thou has her nose stuck so high in the air it's a wonder she doesn't trip over her own importance. You spend a couple of weeks with Phoebe, and men will run for their lives the first time you open your mouth. Well, unless they're like Grampy Avery and shrill, snobbish women turn them on."

That got rid of those tears, Hazel's expression horrified as her mouth opened then mutely closed.

"No?" Birch quickly went on, deciding to add a bit of insurance. "Then how about your oldest brother's latest bride? You could call up Ms. Can't Hold Her Liquor and ask if she can give you some insider info on spotting the difference between a pro and an ordinary lazy bum looking for a free ride." She snorted. "Talk about role reversal; I'm pretty sure *Charlene* targeted *Alvin*. In fact, I wouldn't be surprised to find out she's from one of those families of con artists Claude mentioned. Or Uncle Aaron's wife; you could ask her how to —"

"Birch Callahan, you stop right now," Hazel said sternly. Birch saw the corner of her mom's mouth twitch upward as Hazel gripped the steering wheel again, her complexion definitely not pale anymore. "Phoebe is not snobbish, she's . . . guarded. And you'd buy gin by the case, too, if you lived with Alvin."

"Your stepmother sent you freaking *sneakers* for Christmas last year, along with a gift certificate to a local *gym.*"

Hazel's mouth twitched again as she reached down and put the cart in reverse, backed out past the SUV with only a glance over her shoulder, then all but shot out the driveway. "That's because three months prior, I sent Phoebe a beautiful arrangement of goldenrod and milkweed for her Thanksgiving table." She looked over with a full-blown smile, albeit diabolical. "Do you have any idea how many florists I had to call before I found one willing to send their poor clerk around to vacant city lots looking for goldenrod?" She pulled onto the camp road. "I paid three hundred dollars for *weeds,* and two hundred dollars to have them hand-delivered to Papa's country home."

"Oh, Mama," Birch said on a laugh as she leaned her head on her mother's shoulder. "*Grand-mémère* would be so proud."

"Where do you think I got the idea? Annette sent the exact same arrangement to my father the first Thanksgiving after she took me to live with her."

Birch straightened at the sound of a racing engine coming from behind and gave a startled shriek when a large silver SUV pulled around them on the narrow camp road. Hazel slammed on the brakes and jerked the wheel to the right with a shriek of her own when the truck suddenly cut in front of them and skidded to a stop mere inches from their bumper. Doors shot open before Birch had even finished righting herself, and Hazel cried out when a man grabbed hold of her arm and tried dragging her out of the cart as she frantically clung to the steering wheel.

"No! Get away from her!" Birch screamed as she reached under the hem of her shirt and grabbed the bear spray clipped to her waistband. "Mama, lean back!" she shouted, shoving the canister past Hazel and pulling the trigger.

The man immediately let go and covered his face, his strangled shout turning to retching gasps just as Birch's head suddenly exploded in pain when she was yanked out of the cart by the hair and slammed to the gravel road. Her hand holding the spray was grabbed in a crushing grip. *"Drop it,"* her assailant growled, his knee pressing into her back and making it impossible for her to catch her breath.

Birch opened her fingers to release the canister at the same time she heard her mother's pain-laced scream end abruptly. The bruising knee lifted and Birch's arm was nearly wrenched out of its socket when she was jerked to her feet. But before she could even suck air into her lungs and call out to her mother, a large hand covered her mouth and yanked her head back at the same time an arm of steel pinned her own arms to her sides, completely immobilizing her.

"You make a sound," a deep and menacing voice snarled beside her head, "and one of your mother's fingers gets snapped off. Understand?"

Birch couldn't even move her head to nod as she helplessly watched Hazel kicking at the man carrying her toward the open door on the passenger side of the truck.

"Yvonne, get that damned cart back to the house," her captor snapped to the woman — who Birch recognized as Francine — rounding the truck. Yvonne/Francine scooted behind the wheel of the cart, backed it away from the SUV while turning to point down the road, then serenely drove toward the shelter. "For chrissakes, Phillip, shrug it off and help your idiot brother," he went on when Birch saw Hazel change from kicking the man to bracing her feet against the SUV's door. "And get the hell out of here before someone comes —"

The rest of his command was lost in his grunt when Birch screeched into his hand at the top of her lungs and frantically began twisting and kicking at the realization they were taking her mother but not her! She struggled through the pain of his arm tightening until she thought her ribs might crack, only managing to bite the fleshy pad of his palm. But instead of pulling away the bastard merely ground his hand into her face while also covering her nose, completely blocking off her air.

Birch tasted blood from her teeth slicing the inside of her mouth when she tried twisting her head to breathe, then screamed into his hand again when she saw Hazel suddenly go limp after getting punched in the head and then roughly stuffed into the backseat. But try as she might, Birch couldn't escape the bastard's suffocating grip; her last hysterical thought as her vision started dimming was that the SUV carrying her mother away was idling down the camp road with no more urgency than tourists out sightseeing.

Birch woke to the sharp pain of having her face slapped, and she kicked at the guy kneeling over her even as she rolled away, only to have her scream cut off when he shoved her face into the moist forest floor and held her down with his knee on her back.

"It's going to be damn hard to save your mother from a hospital bed," he said with utter calm. "So, Miss Callahan; are you ready to listen to my instructions, or do you need a few more bruises to prove I'm not fucking around?"

Birch stilled, and the pressure on her back lessened briefly, then lifted away. She slowly turned into a sitting position and looked around as she reached up a trembling hand and wiped dirt from her face. Realizing he'd carried her into the woods out of sight of the road, she glared straight into the expressionless black eyes of the man crouched in front of her. "What do you want me to do?"

"For starters, you don't speak. You agree with me, you nod. You disagree . . . Trust me, you don't want to disagree with me. Yes?"

Birch very slowly nodded.

"Then I suggest you listen carefully," he said, holding up her cell phone, which he must have taken off her waistband when she'd been unconscious. "You call anyone and Hazel immediately dies." He smashed her phone against a rock with enough force to fold it in half and tossed it into the woods, then reached to a rear pocket of his pants and pulled out another cell phone. "I also suggest you keep this phone very close, as it's your lifeline to your mother. My number is programmed into it, and I'm the *only* person you call. I can track your movements, and if you call anyone else, I can monitor how long you talk, who you talk to, and where *they* are located. Nod if you understand."

Birch slowly nodded again and started to reach out, but dropped her hand when he turned the phone toward himself, tapped the screen several times, then turned it to show her a timer running down from eight hours. "Seeing those seconds speeding into minutes gives a person a sense of urgency, don't you think," he drawled, his sudden grin as cold as his eyes. He tossed the phone at her lap. "When that timer goes off, if I'm not holding what I came here for, Hazel loses a finger. You'll have to reset the timer yourself, and if you still haven't given me what I want eight hours later, Hazel loses a second finger. One finger every eight hours until I either leave here a happy man or Hazel bleeds to death."

Birch picked up the phone and clutched it to her chest so she'd stop seeing the seconds speeding into minutes. "Wh-what do you —"

He moved so fast she had no time to react, her head snapping to the side with the force of his backhanded slap, which he followed by slamming into her and pinning her to the ground. "Let's hope you get better at following instructions, Miss Callahan. Now, Jacques Rabideu, whom you knew as Leonard Struthers," he continued calmly, "happened to come into possession of something of mine. And just before I cut out his heart, he kindly mentioned that his ex-wife was holding it for him. You're going to find it, then call me on the phone I gave you so I can instruct you on how to get it to me. Nod if you understand."

Understanding only too well, Birch nodded again, and was rewarded by his weight lifting off her. She slowly sat up, once more having to wipe her face, this time her hand coming away bloody from where his slap had cut her cheek.

"I imagine you're wondering what that something is, no?" He hesitated, waiting for her nod. "You'll be searching for two privately burned DVDs. One is yellow, the other blue. No labels, but each has a barely perceptible *L* etched along the center hole. When they left my possession, they were in a case which once held the movie" — his ugly grin returned — *"Dances with Wolves."*

Birch flinched when he suddenly stood up, making him softly chuckle as he brushed dirt off his pants. But then his eyes hardened again as he stared down at her. "You call me the moment you find the DVDs, and I will return your mother intact — assuming I hear from you within eight hours. And a word of warning; besides being able to track you by the phone, there are no fewer than two dozen of my family members here with me, also enjoying the beauty of this unique area. You talk to anyone, I'll know it. You leave the phone at home and go anywhere, I'll know it. You do anything to even make me uncomfortable, and your mother is going to die a very slow and painful death. Nod if you believe me."

Birch tilted the phone and looked at the seconds speeding down, then clasped it back to her chest and also stood up. But instead of nodding, she tensed in anticipation of another slap. "There's a good chance the DVDs are in a storage locker in Montreal. Or even in our house," she softly rushed on when he didn't move. "Leo— Rabideu could have hidden them in a wall or something."

This time the bastard's grin was almost civil. "Trust me, they're in neither place. So that means there's an even better chance you can complete your task before Hazel has to learn how to hold a pencil again." Birch flinched when he stepped forward, but instead of a slap, he reached for her hand holding the phone and pulled it away from her body at an angle that allowed them both to see the screen. "Which she will have to do if I don't receive your call within seven hours and fifty-six minutes. The road is two hundred meters that way," he added, gesturing to his right, then turning away and walking in the opposite direction. "Good luck, Miss Callahan."

Birch stood staring after him while clutching her lifeline to Hazel against her pounding heart, waiting until he was out of sight before collapsing to her knees.

Sweet mother of God, this couldn't be happening.

Who in hell *was* this bastard, anyway?

Not that it mattered; the important question being, what was she going to do?

Well, she should probably not kneel here like an idiot who had all the time in the world. Deciding she could walk and think at the same time, Birch staggered to her feet, then had to grab a nearby tree to keep from falling and took several deep breaths in an attempt to slow her trembling before finally forcing her rubbery legs to move in the direction he'd pointed.

And as she walked, she thought.

Her dad had said there were whole families of con artists operating in Canada, so it was possible this guy did have dozens of family members watching her every move while pretending to be tourists. And that meant there was no way she could risk going to town or be seen talking to anyone — especially Niall. Or her father, or even a neighbor, or . . . *Merde, no one* could help her, because hell yes she believed the bastard would kill her mom.

But she didn't believe he'd give Hazel back in exchange for the DVDs. No, the moment she handed them over, both she and her mom were as good as dead.

Birch reached the camp road only a short distance from where they'd been caught, which she realized was a perfect place for an ambush, since it was a heavily wooded section that didn't have any houses nearby. But she stopped at the edge of the woods and looked in both directions while listening for approaching vehicles, figuring the last thing she needed was for a Whisper Cove resident to stop and ask why she looked like someone had just used her for a punching bag. She took another steadying breath and finally stepped into the road, knowing she was only a few hundred yards from home and could duck into the bushes if she heard an engine approaching.

Realizing she was still clutching the phone to her chest, Birch shoved it in her pocket and started running as fast as her rubbery legs would carry her, even more glad Noreen and Macie and Cassandra were gone. She turned off the road the moment she reached the edge of the shelter property and wove down through the trees of the deep lot, then along the side of the house. She stopped when she reached the porch, peeked around the corner to make sure Niall hadn't come home or her dad hadn't decided to visit, then sprinted to the walkway. She grabbed the key she'd hidden behind a planter at the bottom of the steps for her residents, ran up the stairs, unlocked the door and ran inside — then immediately turned and closed the door and locked it.

She staggered to the sink, turned on the faucet, and started splashing water on her face and drinking out of her hands, spitting out blood with a pained hiss that turned into shudders. Birch shut off the water when her shudders turned into gut-wrenching sobs, until she started crying so hard her legs gave out and she turned and slid down the cupboard doors to the floor.

She hugged her knees to her chest and hid her face in her thighs, unable to do more than simply ride out the storm. That is, until she became aware that something was digging into her hip and realized it was the bastard's phone — the one with all those racing seconds eating up her precious time. Birch stretched out her legs, but left the phone in her pocket as she took several calming breaths until her crying returned to sobs and eventually just the occasional shudder.

"Okay, get a grip," she scolded herself, her voice seeming overloud in the eerily silent house. Birch sucked in her breath on the realization it *shouldn't* be silent. "Mimi," she rasped, scrambling to her feet and running to the hall. "Mighty Mimi!"

Nothing; no yip, no whining, just . . . silence.

She ran to the door and looked out to see her mother's cart parked between the other cart and her SUV, and slowly backed away, remembering The Bastard — it was his official name now — had had Francine/Yvonne drive it back to the house, knowing no one would be suspicious of a strange woman driving a shelter cart.

And considering Emily had spent the last few days playing with Mimi like any normal thirteen-year-old, Birch could only surmise that Francine — now officially The Bitch — had used the key to let herself in the house and stolen the dog — who knew Francine as just another resident, not The Bitch — for her daughter.

"Who in hell *are* you people?" Birch whispered, feeling behind her for the table and plopping down in a chair. "Do any of you have even a sliver of conscience?"

She dropped her head into her hands on the table. "It'll be okay. Emily will take care of Mimi. The poor dog might be confused when she doesn't come home tonight, but no one's going to cut off her toes." She straightened and looked around. "Mom's the one in real danger, so *focus*. Before you find those DVDs, you have to find a way to

466

—" Birch snapped her mouth shut before finishing that sentence.

The Bastard obviously knew how to use technology; what if he'd had Francine hide electronic bugs throughout the house during her stay, and he could hear if she talked to anyone on some other phone? Birch got up and went to the counter and grabbed the house phone, hit the talk button and held it to her ear, but didn't hear a dial tone. Of course Francine and Emily would have cut the line when they'd left last night, because they were freaking *professionals.*

Wait; she had *eight* other cell phones. Birch rushed to her office and started pushing boxes around until she found the one Olivia had brought with her the day the shelter had opened, containing everything on the list Birch had e-mailed her from Montreal after agreeing to take the job. Five cell phones had been on that list, and Olivia had given her freaking *ten,* all of them already activated.

Birch had given one to Macie and one to Cassandra — which they still had — but after an hour of lessons, Noreen had decided not to waste her time learning how to operate something she was certain was just a passing fad.

Birch pulled out one of the phones and

turned it on, sighing in relief to see it was still fully charged. She walked over to her desk, took The Bastard's phone out of her pocket, but stopped in the act of setting it down, her thumb lightly resting on the button that would wake it up. She took a slow, deliberate breath, pushed the button, then slid her thumb across the screen to unlock it.

Seven hours and twenty-three minutes.

She took an even slower breath to keep from screaming, set The Bastard's phone on the desk and then ran out of the office — only to stop in the hall, not knowing where to run *to.* In the movies people who thought their houses were bugged usually went into the bathroom and turned on the shower to block out their voices. But if The Bastard was listening, wouldn't he find it odd that she'd take a shower *now*?

She ran up the stairs and down the up-stairs hall, shoved her shelter phone in her pocket, and lifted the large picture off the wall. She leaned it against the railing, pushed the small chest of drawers out of the way, and opened the well-disguised attic door. Quietly closing the door behind her, Birch carefully crept up the steep, creaky old stairs, but stopped when she reached the top and studied the floor. She stepped onto one of the old boards, stepped back, and saw her footprint in the dust. But there was only that one print, which meant The Bitch hadn't searched the attic — likely only because she hadn't spotted the door.

Birch pulled the phone out of her pocket as she walked toward the small round window, silently thanking her mom for suggesting they preprogram in several numbers for the residents; Hazel also volunteering to make the list and input the numbers for the shelter, as well as the Trading Post, Drunken Moose, and a few other places. Hazel had even asked Niall if she could add his personal cell number on the chance a resident was in *immediate* danger, and told Birch the man hadn't even hesitated to give it to her.

Oh yeah; her mom was freaking fantastic when it came to details.

Birch sat down on the floor near the window but not close enough to be visible from outside, found Niall in the contacts, and tapped his number — nearly bursting into tears again when he answered with a strong, solid, "Chief MacKeage."

"Niall, it's me, Birch," she said in a rasped whisper.

There was a heartbeat of silence. "What's wrong?"

"Th-they took Mom. They ambushed us

469

on the camp road on our way into town in the cart. A large silver SUV cut us off and three men jumped out and I sprayed one with my bear spray when he grabbed Mom but another one yanked me out of the cart and made me drop the spray and Mom was screaming and I couldn't —"

"Birch," Niall snapped, cutting her off. "Take a breath, lass," he said quietly. "Where are ye now?"

"A-at the shelter."

"Keep talking. I'm on my way."

"No!" she cried. "No, you can't come here," she rushed on in a whisper. "They're watching. Dozens of them, pretending to be tourists. And The Bastard said he'd know if I called or talked to anyone or went any-place, and if I did that he . . . he'd kill Mom. And he's going to cut off one of her fingers in eight hours, and another one every eight hours after that, until I find two DVDs Jacques Rabideu hid in our stuff."

"How can he know if you call anyone?" Niall asked softly.

"He smashed my phone and gave me one of his so I can call him when I find the DVDs. He said he can even tell who I talk to and where they are. And Francine cut the house lines. She's one of them. Mom and I were on our way to tell you that Francine and Emily left sometime in the night, and that they'd been searching the house since they came here."

"Then how are ye talking to me now?"

"I have a bunch of cell phones to give out to the residents. Oh, God, I was going to give one to Francine today! She would have told The Bastard I have them."

"Easy, lass. Ye didn't give her one, so he doesn't know."

"I'm up in the attic because I'm afraid Francine might have put listening devices in the house." She stopped and took a deep breath. "I don't know what to do, Niall. If I find the DVDs and give them to him, he's going to kill Mom anyway . . . and me."

"Nay, I'm not going to let that happen, Birch."

"He . . . he told me he cut out Jacques Rabideu's heart. I only have about seven hours now. I need to start looking for those discs."

"Did ye leave some of your belongings in Montreal? In storage?"

"He said they're not there. Or in our house. He must have already searched them. What . . . what do I do? He's got Mom."

"You're going to stay put and look for those discs," Niall said calmly. "Let me think on this a bit, and then I'll call and let ye know what's going to happen. Keep this phone with you, but put it on vibrate on the chance they are listening to the house." He hesitated, apparently thinking right *now*. "I'm going to send ye Shep. They've been in town for days checking us out, so they won't think anything of seeing the dog hanging out in the yard. But don't bring him inside; have him lay on the porch. Give him the command *earalaich*. Say, 'Shep, guard,' and then say, '*Err*-al-ech.' Repeat it to me."

"Err . . . *err*-al-ech. Oh, Niall, they took Mimi."

"She was in the cart with you?"

"No. Francine drove the cart back here so no one would see it abandoned on the road. And she used the spare key I hid for the residents and let herself in and took Mimi. I . . . I think for Emily."

"I'm sorry, Birch. When we catch them, there's a good chance we'll get Mimi back as well. I've changed my mind, then; bring Shep in the house with you. When he comes to the door, step out on the porch and make a big show of being excited to see him, then act as if you're relieved not to be alone anymore and take him inside."

Birch snorted. "I won't be acting.

Th-thank you."

Niall went silent again, then said, "If Shep's wearing his vest, leave it on him. The vest has a couple of small pockets, but don't check them until after ye bring him inside. I need to think a bit first, but Shep might be a good way for me to get something to you."

"O-okay. Um, Niall? When we were in the Vaughns' basement, you said you grow quieter and slower in direct proportion to the urgency of the situation."

"Aye," he said, softly.

"Well, seeing how this is a really, really urgent situation, you won't grow . . . ah, too slow thinking about what to do, will you?"

Birch held her breath when Niall went pretty damn quiet right now, and didn't start breathing again until she heard a heavy sigh come over the phone. "I'll try to hurry my thinking along."

"Th-thank you. Oh, another thing; I think you should call my dad instead of me, because I might get . . . Well, I need to start looking for those discs. But he needs to know what's going on, because if he keeps trying my phone and I don't answer, he might come here to find out why. And you can't call your officers or Sam or anyone else and have them suddenly come to the station, because The Bastard said he'll kill Mom if he sees anything that even makes him *feel* uncomfortable. Wait; you said they've been checking us out for days. You *knew* these people were here?"

"I just found out this morning and have been trying to decide what to do before I said anything to you. Don't worry, the Leopolds won't see anything unusual happening. Did ye get the name of the man in charge of the ambush? Did any of the others call him by name?"

"No. So I'm just calling him The Bastard."

There was a short silence. "Did he hurt ye, Birch?"

"N-not really. I got a small cut on my cheek when he . . . knocked me down."

There was a slightly longer silence; Birch assumed he was trying to decide if he believed her or not. "I'm going to hang up and think about this," he said quietly, "but I want ye to call me the moment ye find those DVDs. Oh, and, lass?" he added, his voice dropping a couple of notches.

"Y-yes?"

"There's two more things ye should probably know about Scots; the first being we don't like losing, so we don't. I'll get Hazel back within the next seven hours."

Birch closed her eyes and dropped her

head on a silent sigh, actually believing him. "And the other thing I should know?"

"Scots protect what's ours. And ye may not have noticed, but almost from the day ye moved in next door, I've considered you mine."

CHAPTER TWENTY-THREE

Niall set the phone on his desk and lowered his head into his hands as he fought back an old and familiar anguish before it immobilized him, and once again found himself wondering why Titus had brought him here. Considering the elder theurgist had access to all knowledge throughout time, had he known this day would come? And was it possible that because he couldn't interfere, Titus had decided two years ago to *invite* Niall to this century then *suggested* to Duncan he would make a good chief of police, simply so he would be here in Spellbound Falls on this particular day?

But sweet Christ, why *him*? There were any number of men living in this century who were unquestionably better prepared to deal with the Leopolds. A strong sword-arm was next to useless against technology. Hell, his sword had barely been effective against a bunch of brainless demons.

476

Many modern problems would benefit from an ancient perspective, Titus had said, which could make all the difference between success and failure.

And Niall had just told Birch he really didn't care to be on the losing side, and promised he'd get Hazel back — within seven hours and possessing all her fingers. That was one hell of a boast from a man who couldn't even keep a seventeen-year-old lass from sneaking off to a high mountain gleann to pick her wedding bouquet, and then fail to find her before she'd bled to death.

Niall remembered Nicholas saying Mac couldn't make Duncan and Peg fall in love, but there hadn't been anything stopping the wizard from devising a way to put two people he knew were destined to be together in each other's path.

And Titus did seem unusually interested in Niall's attraction to Miss Callahan.

Could Birch be his destiny? Would a powerful magic-maker manipulate time itself just to give an unimpressive mortal a second chance? Or could this be about Birch needing a second chance?

Did it really matter? Because for whatever reason, he was here.

And so were the Leopolds.

But unlike nine hundred years ago when he hadn't even known Simone was in a life-and-death battle with a wild boar, modern technology not only made it possible for Birch to tell him she was in danger, it was also allowing them to stay in communication as they fought the enemy *together.*

And he now had weapons far more effective than swords.

Niall lifted his head and stared down at his phone, thinking of one precise and ruthless weapon in particular. Aye, maybe he should take advantage of that right of free will Titus and Mac were so determined to protect, and *feel free* to ask a *modern* god — who didn't seem to have a problem getting personally involved — for help.

Well, provided he could find a way to contact the bastard.

Because even though, as Nicholas had pointed out, Telos would embrace the technology of *his* era, the forest god had yet to give anyone his phone number. And just like the Oceanuses, mankind's newest magic-maker was likely walking around in human form, which meant Niall could have passed Telos on the sidewalk for all he knew. Hell, he may have even spoken to him.

For over a week now, he'd wondered how it was Telos happened to be on the bank of the river at the exact moment Birch was being forced off the road. Or how he'd known Foster Graves lay dying under his car, or that a forest fire had ignited twenty miles away. Hell, the bastard had even known a new entity intended to manifest that night on the island.

So why hadn't Telos interceded when the Leopolds had taken Hazel? Did he only help when he was in a benevolent mood? Or only when it served *his* agenda?

Niall picked up the envelope Sam had brought this morning, opened the flap and tipped it on end, and dropped the ring the eagle had given Birch into the palm of his hand. He sighed, hoping Telos wasn't going to be like the Oceanuses in one other regard, which was the habit of only giving obscure clues and talking around a subject instead of coming right out and saying what they meant.

Surely a powerful, modern god knew how to write; the bastard could at least have included a note with the ring instead of making them waste two days trying to —

Niall's cell phone gave a chime indicating a text, and he set down the ring and picked up the phone, frowning when he didn't see an ID displayed. He unlocked the screen, thinking it might be Birch, only to stiffen as he read the text.

Though technically correct, I don't care for being referred to as a bastard.

Son of a bitch. The bas—Telos was *texting* him.

And as much as it pains me to admit, I find myself agreeing with the great Titus Oceanus . . . on this occasion. So having heard it said everyone needs a reason to get out of bed in the morning, I didn't include a note because I felt you might as well earn the air you breathe by saving your Miss Callahan and Hazel yourself. And since protecting what's yours appears to be a matter of personal pride, I also didn't want to steal your thunder. But I wouldn't mind tagging along for the ride, and maybe you'll even be generous enough to let me lend a . . . human hand?

Son of a bitch! Niall tapped letters. You can goddamn read my thoughts?

Not exactly or completely. But just like your faithful first officer, I can choose to tune in to your energy — which at the moment is blasting off you like an erupting volcano. I'm sure you've noticed Shep's mysterious habit of showing up whenever your mood darkens? Well, for reasons only he knows, the beast has chosen to link his energy to yours. Don't worry, MacKeage; with only a little effort you can control when you want me to know your thoughts. Then again, this is the twenty-first century; you could always just shoot me a text. I don't have an actual number, but you — and only you — will find me in your list of contacts.

Niall typed again. Where's Hazel?

You're really willing to risk angering Titus by ignoring the very thing he's spent his entire existence protecting by asking me to directly intercede in this matter?

Niall typed, Whatever it takes to get Hazel back.

Your heritage is showing, my friend. I'm sorry, but it appears I'm not willing to risk starting a mythical war — yet.

Niall glared at the screen, undecided if Telos merely got his jollies toying with mortals, or if something — or powerful some*one* — was making him keep his distance.

Not really caring since neither way was any help to him, Niall stood up and typed, Fuck off, you bastard, hit the send button, and shoved the phone in his pocket.

He walked onto the porch to wait for Shep, and stared out at Bottomless as he thought about the problem at hand — calmly, so he wouldn't be broadcasting like an erupting volcano. Finally deciding on as much of a plan as he could without fully knowing his enemy, Niall took out his phone, opened the timer he'd set right after Birch's call, and saw they were down to six hours and fifty-three minutes.

He closed the timer and called Sam. "Did ye once tell me there's such a thing as an electronic tracking device," he said without preamble when Sam answered, "that's small enough to hide on a person . . . or a dog?"

"I must have," Sam said, his voice alert. "Why?"

"Do ye happen to own one?"

"As a matter of fact, I do. Why?"

"Can ye get it to me in the next . . . Fifteen minutes is all the time I can give ye."

"Why?"

"The Leopolds have Hazel, and she's going to start losing fingers in less than seven hours if Birch doesn't find and turn over two DVDs to them. I'll bring ye up to speed when you bring me the tracking device."

"I'll have it to you in five minutes."

Niall lowered the phone, found Jake's number, and called him. "Exactly how good are ye at blending in," he asked when Jake answered, "in a town where you've been standing out for over a week now?"

Niall heard a heavy sigh in his ear. "I could fool my mother if I had to. Why?"

"How long before you can turn yourself

into a tourist?"

"That depends. Caucasian — three hours. An old black guy — one. Why?"

"Ye have thirty minutes to be blending in enough to fool *me.* Text Sam when ye get to the Trading Post as a tourist, and he'll go up and fill you in on what's happening. And Jake? Make sure there's room in your disguise for a couple of weapons and enough ammunition to deal with an army of two dozen."

There was a heartbeat of silence, then, "I'll come loaded for bear."

Niall called Cole and made the same request, but gave him forty-five minutes to drive up from Turtleback. He lowered the phone again just as Shep came racing down the lane, took a moment to quiet his mind, and called Claude. Their conversation not nearly as succinct, Niall explained what Sam had discovered as well as Hazel's and Birch's situations. And as he'd expected, Claude was halfway out the colony road by the time they finished their talk, having agreed to keep his eyes and ears open sitting in the Bottoms Up until he got the signal they were moving.

Niall called Duncan and Alec, explained what was going on and what he'd like from them, and had just gotten off the phone with Nicholas when Sam — his demeanor rather aggressive and his limp barely noticeable — came striding down the lane.

"I brought along a little something else," Sam said as he walked past Niall and into the station. He set a small Drunken Moose box on the desk and opened it, pulled out a compact pistol, and held it up. "Since you asked if the tracking device was small enough to hide on a dog, I assumed Shep will be wearing it. How about we also secure this under his vest on the chance he can get close enough to Birch or Hazel for them to get it? Do you suppose either of them know how to handle a gun?"

"Shep's going to carry the transmitter to Birch at the shelter, where she's searching for two DVDs Rabideu hid in their belongings. My plan is to have *her* wearing the tracking device when she trades the discs for Hazel," Niall explained. "And to the best of my knowledge, Birch has an aversion to guns."

Sam grinned tightly. "I bet she'll warm up to this one real quick when she realizes it could save her mother's life."

Niall looked down into the box and shrugged. "I don't see any reason not to include the pistol. That's the transmitter?" he asked, pointing at the tiny black device no larger than a disposable cigarette lighter.

"This is it," Sam said, pulling out the transmitter and holding it up. He snorted. "You can take the spook out of the game, but apparently you can't take the game out of the spook. I like to keep up on all the latest toys. This one allows anyone with the code to track it right on their smartphones, so we can all see where Birch is in real time. And the best part is the little bugger's range is unlimited because it works off satellites."

"Hop up, Shep," Niall said, tapping the top of his desk. The dog jumped up, sniffed the Drunken Moose box, then stood quietly as Niall removed his vest. "There's a pocket on either side of the vest," Niall went on, signaling Shep to get down, then laying out the vest on the desk. He unzipped one of the pockets, slipped the pistol inside, then zipped it closed. "Aye, we'll send Birch the gun, seeing how the pocket doesn't bulge enough to be noticeable, especially from a distance."

He took out the pistol, dropped out the magazine, checked to make sure the chamber was empty, then reseated the magazine and put the gun back in the pocket — all the time aware of Sam fiddling with the transmitter. Niall then picked up the Leopold ring, unzipped the other pocket, and slipped it inside.

Sam stopped fiddling and arched a brow. "Mighty generous of you to return their ring while you're at it."

"Birch is going to use it to buy us time to get into position." Niall looked at the transmitter Sam was holding. "Is it on?"

"Up and running." Sam set it on the desk and held out his hand. "Give me your phone so I can link it to the transmitter." He then took his own phone out of his pocket and exchanged it for Niall's. "Go ahead and look at mine while I program yours. There should be a pinging dot coming from this location on the map."

Niall looked down at the map of the northwestern half of Bottomless and saw a small blue dot pulsing in the center of Spellbound Falls.

"You can zoom in and out with your fingers," Sam went on as he worked on Niall's phone. "And change back and forth from map to satellite photos. Cole and Jake already have the app on their phones, so I just have to give them the code."

"Duncan and Alec are on their way, as well as Claude St. Germaine," Niall said. "And Nicholas is bringing Rowan, Micah, and Dante. I want everyone to be able to track Birch, since we'll likely all be closing in on her from different directions."

Sam stopped tapping the screen and looked up. "MacKeages and Atlantean warriors against the Leopolds; bet you find it hard to believe," he said dryly, "that nine hundred years after you were born, we're still having clan wars."

Niall snorted and set Sam's phone on the desk. "From what I've read, I can't believe mankind hasn't blown itself out of existence by now." He picked up the transmitter and studied it briefly, then slipped it in the same pocket as the ring and closed the zipper. He patted the desk again. "Shep, up."

"So let me get this straight," Sam said. "You're going to tell Shep to go see Birch, and he'll head straight to her without getting distracted by some tourist eating a hot dog or a cute poodle wagging its tail at him? And he's never had *any* training?"

Niall settled the vest onto Shep's back and cinched the straps. "He seems to know when a situation is serious." Satisfied the vest was secure, he moved to look over Sam's shoulder. "Can I send him to Birch now, or do ye still need access to the transmitter?"

"No, I'm good. There, see, it's also pinging away on your phone."

"Is the transmitter waterproof?"

"To a point," Sam said, frowning at Shep standing with his nose pressed to the door. "But I don't know if it would survive salt water if you're thinking of having him approach the shelter from the beach."

"Nay. Any Leopolds watching the house won't find it odd for the dog to show up at home in the middle of the day."

"You're not including a note with the transmitter, explaining what Birch needs to do?" Sam asked, handing Niall his phone.

"The man in charge of the ambush smashed her phone and gave her one of his to use, which he claims he can monitor," Niall said, going to the door and opening it. "She called me on a phone she keeps for residents, but she's been going up to the attic to talk because she's afraid he may have put listening devices in the house. I'll call her on the shelter cell phone and explain everything."

"Have her tape the transmitter someplace on her body instead of just putting it in her pocket," Sam said, following him out onto the porch. "But just sticking it in her bra isn't secure enough; she has to tape it."

Niall dropped to one knee and pulled Shep up against his side. "Go to Birch," he said close to the dog's ear. "And stay with her. Go to Birch and stay," he repeated in

Gaelic, opening his arms and then standing up when Shep leaped off the porch without even bothering with the stairs.

"I've seen a lot of K-9 soldiers and operatives in my day," Sam said as they both watched the dog hightail it up the lane. "But it seems as if Shep intuitively knows what you want from him." He squinted over at Niall. "He didn't bubble up from a magical spring or anything, did he?"

Niall had often wondered the same thing. "Nay, he came slinking out from behind the tree he was chained to at the house of a man I'd heard was selling a boat."

"Let me guess; you bought the dog instead."

Niall looked down at his cell phone. "Aye, something like that," he murmured, watching the pulsing dot on the map race past the church and turn onto Whisper Cove Road.

Birch finished inspecting the backside and bottom of the bureau drawer, tossed it away with a curse, then sat back on her heels in the middle of the mess she'd made of her mother's room in a thirty-minute frenzy. Dammit to hell, she was going about this all wrong. Instead of acting like a panicked maniac, she needed to think like a stupid-ass criminal. So if she were Jacques Rabideu, where would she hide two thin discs?

Well, to begin with, she wouldn't stash them where her wife might run across them in the course of everyday life, which meant they wouldn't be in drawers or closets or any box she and Hazel had packed. No, she'd hide them in the structure of the house — except the stupid-ass idiot hadn't, apparently.

"No, I wouldn't," Birch decided out loud. "Houses can burn, so I'd want the DVDs to be easy to grab in the middle of the night if there was a house fire. Well, unless I could find a way to sneak them into my wife's safety deposit box."

But Hazel never visited the bank unless Birch was with her, and then usually only to swap out pieces of jewelry. Heck, her mom hadn't even wanted a key to their bank box, so Rabideu couldn't have talked Hazel into taking him. And now that she thought about it, he probably wouldn't have gotten his own box, either, because he would have wanted quick access to the discs if he needed them for . . . whatever.

And that brought Birch back to her grab-and-go theory.

The DVDs were in something mobile, or something sitting in plain sight that could easily be reached in a crisis. But it had to be something Hazel didn't handle very often, if at all. So what had they brought with them from Montreal?

Clothes, mostly. Several boxes of academic books and novels. Their bedroom furniture, thinking to free up the beds and bureaus already here for the residents. They'd donated their living room set to the shelter, along with two televisions, a bookcase, and a modern-style grandfather clock that didn't at all fit with the theme of the house.

Grab and go . . .

Birch jumped to her feet and ran downstairs and into the living room, where she stopped and looked around for something mobile. Had Rabideu lived with Hazel long enough to realize the woman rotated furniture the way people rotated the tires on their cars? Because if not, he could have hidden them in something that was now sitting in someone else's freaking house. Because every time one of her mom's charities held an auction, Birch would come home to find a new couch or chair replacing the one Hazel had donated. And if a group home happened to open nearby, she ate off paper plates with plastic forks until Hazel could replace their silverware and bone china — which unwed mothers or foster teens were likely tossing in the dishwasher.

"Please don't have hidden the discs in the furniture," Birch whispered, going to one of the end tables beside the couch. She picked up the lamp that had a round base the size of a DVD, turned it upside down, and used her thumbnail to peel back the felt bottom to expose . . . nothing but a wire. She lifted the table to see if anything was taped under the top, did the same to the other lamp and table, then checked the coffee table — again finding nothing. She pulled all the cushions off the couch, tipped it onto its back, and studied the underside.

"Merde," she growled, going to the clock. She opened both little side doors to look around the mechanism, checked the outside and inside of the tall case, then carefully tilted the freaking thing and crouched to run her hand under the base — despite realizing it wasn't exactly a grab-and-go hiding place.

But dammit, she wasn't leaving anything to chance, even if it meant she had to open every last book they owned and tear apart every damn piece of furniture. She went to the bookcase Hazel thought should go in the living room and had already filled with nonacademic books, and sat down on the end of the coffee table and pulled out a book, turned it upside down and fanned the pages, then tossed it on the floor so she wouldn't end up looking through the same one twice.

She was just reaching for the next book when she jerked in surprise, barely stifling a gasp as she slapped her vibrating left boob. She pulled the shelter phone out of her bra, accepted the call, and held it up to her ear. "Hmm," she hummed in a whisper, covering her mouth with her free hand. "Let me run up to the attic to —"

"Nay, ye only have to listen. Or, since I imagine you've been cursing out loud for the last half hour, how about ye just say *merde* for yes and *maudit* for no?"

"Merde," Birch growled rather loudly, earning her a little chuckle — which earned Niall huge points for being so strong and solid and in her ear.

"Shep's almost there. Set the phone on the kitchen table but leave the line open, then go out on the porch and make a show of being pleased to see him and bring him inside. Then I'll tell ye what he brought you and what to do with everything."

Birch grabbed a book off the floor and dropped it with a bang on the coffee table behind her. *"Merde,"* she growled as she stood up and headed for the kitchen.

She hadn't even made it to the door when she heard a sharp bark — Niall's sigh indicating he had also heard. She set the phone on the table, unlocked and opened the door, and stepped outside — leaving the inside door open. "Well, hello, big boy. You're home early today," she said, kneeling down to hug him, then hugging him tighter when he started trying to lick her face. "Oh, Shep, your timing couldn't be more perfect. You know the lady who was staying here with her daughter? Well, that bitch stole Mimi!" she cried loudly, burying her face in his neck. Birch then stood up, briefly glanced around the yard, and opened the screen door. "Come on, Shep. Come inside and keep me company while I tear apart this house," she added, walking in behind the dog.

She closed and locked the inside door, then ran over and picked up the phone. "Oh, yes, you're such a good boy," Birch said into the phone so Niall would know she was back. "You want a cookie? You . . . you can have one of Mimi's," she said thickly.

"There's a pocket on either side of his vest," Niall said, getting right down to business. "One is holding a small tracking device that I need ye to carry on your body in an inconspicuous place. Inside your bra, maybe," he added, sounding a bit gruff himself. "But Sam says tape it in, so it can't slip out if you bend over. Understand?"

"*Merde,* Shep, you swallowed that cookie without even tasting it."

"In the same pocket is the ring the eagle gave you. I want ye to take it with you. Here's why," he rushed on, apparently a mind reader. "When you meet with the bastard and after ye give him the discs, I want you to show him the ring and tell him you found it in a small cloth bag in your mother's jewelry box. Then mention the bag also held a photo of Leonard Struthers kissing a woman who was wearing the ring, and ask if he might be interested, since ye noticed he wore a ring just like it. Are ye following me?"

"Yes, Shep, you can have another cookie," Birch said.

"In the other pocket is a small pistol," Niall said quietly. "Do ye know anything about guns, Birch? Have ye ever watched your father handle his?"

"*Merde,* Shep, that's enough. Come on, I'm working in the living room," she said, going to the living room. She sat down and started pulling out books again, grabbing them by one cover with her free hand and giving them a shake.

"If you can have the pistol on you when you meet Leopold, I would feel . . . well, I'd like for you to have some means of protecting yourself and Hazel if things go to hell in a handbasket. You don't have to worry about shooting yourself; there's no bullet in the chamber. But just before your meeting, pull back the top of the barrel to load the gun. Study the weapon before you leave the house, so you'll know where the safety is. Red means it's ready to shoot; not red, ye won't be able to pull the trigger."

"Yes, big boy, you might as well lie down, because this could take a while," Birch said, continuing to pull out books and shake them.

"Okay, let's get back to the ring," Niall went on. "I'm only guessing here, but making Leopold believe he has a traitor in the family might stall him long enough for us to get in place. Can ye do that, Birch? We'll be able to track you to the exchange site, but . . ." he hesitated, then quietly said, "but I can't guarantee he'll have Hazel with him or that he won't insist on taking you to her."

Birch kept pulling books, refusing to let the fact she was shaking uncontrollably stop her. "Yes, Shep, I-I know you're disappointed Mimi's not here."

"That's why I'm thinking," Niall continued just as softly, "you should tell Leopold ye destroyed the photo because you didn't trust he'd let Hazel go once you gave him the discs. And say that if he wants to find out who the woman is, he's going to have to drop Hazel off in a public place. Tell him once ye see your mother is safe, you'll sit in the town park together and he can show you photos of his family off his phone and you'll point out the woman. Can ye do that, lass?" he repeated.

Birch couldn't answer because her jaw was nearly touching the floor as she stared at her outstretched hand holding the cover of her birthday book, the weight of the well-worn tome having caused the inner cloth liner to rip away from the binding and expose the edge of a disc.

"Birch," Niall growled. "What's wrong?"

She'd found them. She'd found the freaking DVDs!

"God dammit, woman, *say something.*"

"Come on, Shep," she finally said, having to set the heavy book on the floor to close it, then scooping it up one-handed and cradling it to her chest. "I just remembered the movers put some boxes up in the attic. Let's go see what's in them."

It was Niall's turn to go silent as Birch

ran upstairs, Shep beating her to the top.

"Ye found the DVDs," Niall whispered.

"*Merde,* Shep, the door's stuck," she said calmly even though she was screaming *ohmigods* over and over in her head.

The stupid idiot had hidden them in her freaking birthday book!

Birch pulled the phone away from her ear long enough to close the attic door behind her and Shep, then quietly raced up the stairs, turned to sit on the top step, and rested the book on her lap. "I found them, Niall," she whispered. "Rabideu hid them in the liner of a huge book my dad gave me for my seventh birthday. The idiot must have chosen this particular book because he knew it would never be donated," she explained as she opened the cover and slowly peeled back the liner to expose more of the DVD. "Oh no. It-it's red."

"What's red? The disc?"

"Yes. But The Bastard said they were privately burned DVDs with a small *L* etched next to the center hole of each one, and that one disc was blue and the other one yellow. But this one is *red.* It's not one of them."

"It is, lass," Niall said gently. "Leopold was making sure ye didn't try to give him fakes. If you showed up with blue and yellow discs, he'd know you hadn't found them."

"The sneaky rat bastard."

That got her a soft chuckle.

"So . . . um, do I call him now?"

"Are both discs in the book?"

"Yeah, they're both here," she said, giving up and just ripping the liner all the way off. "*Dieu,* Rabideu must have panicked when I took this book back to Ottawa with me on one of my trips home."

"Unless he was glad to have them out of the house," Niall said. "If he knew it was a birthday gift from your father, he wouldn't have worried about you losing it. Ye said it's heavy; is it a large children's picture dictionary or book of nursery rhymes?"

Birch turned the page and ran her finger over Claude's inscription. "No," she said on a sigh. "It's a six-pound encyclopedia on guns."

At a complete loss as to why a man would give his seven-year-old daughter a book on guns, Niall checked his watch because he didn't want to lower the phone, and saw they were down to slightly less than five hours. "I know you're anxious to have your mother back," he said, "but I need more time to get everyone in position. Can ye handle waiting another half hour to call Leopold?"

"What . . . what if he's already killed her?" an unsteady voice whispered in his ear.

"He hasn't, lass. Hazel's only good to him alive. Take this time to ready yourself," he went on, wanting to redirect her focus. "Hide the transmitter on you where it can't be seen, get comfortable handling the gun, and practice your story about the ring. But on the chance they are listening, keep making sounds as if you're still searching and keep talking to Shep."

"Don't hang up," she cried in a whisper, making Niall's gut tighten at the fear in her voice. "I . . . I'm supposed to call you in a half hour, right, before I call him?"

"Aye. But you can call me before then, too. Ye don't have to run up to the attic or even talk, if all you're needing is a reminder that you're not alone." Niall walked to the end of the porch away from Sam and lowered his voice. "We're in this together, sweetheart, and we'll come out of it together — along with Hazel. There's more than just me, Birch; there's a small army of highly capable men eager to get their hands on every last Leopold who dared invade our home."

"And . . . and Daddy?"

500

"Claude's coming for you, too, just like he did twenty-five years ago."

Hearing what he suspected was a sob, Niall didn't want to let the conversation end on a low note. "Don't cry, lass."

There was a heartbeat of silence. "I never cry," she snapped thickly.

"Sorry, I forgot," he drawled, then added, "Get to work, woman," just to piss her off — the first half of a very unladylike curse in good old English being the last thing he heard before his pint-sized spitfire ended the call.

"She's doing remarkably well," Sam said, moving up beside him. He shook his head. "I can't believe she actually found the DVDs, especially this quickly. Damn, I'd like to know what's on them." He gave Niall a speculative look. "It would only take a couple of minutes for her to shove them in a computer and make copies."

"I don't care if they contain goddamn launch codes for nuclear missiles."

"Naw," Sam said with a chuckle, shaking his head again. "I'm thinking more along the line of access codes to overseas bank accounts holding millions of swindled dollars. Or maybe to the accounts of people Edward Leopold *intends* to swindle."

Niall grinned tightly. "Let's see if we can't

get you the *originals.*"

"What the hell?" Sam muttered, looking up the lane.

Niall broadened his grin at the sight of Nicholas atop his huge gray warhorse prancing toward them, Micah and Dante and Rowan — dressed as tourists — following on deceptively gentler-looking mounts. "Just bringing some ancient perspective to a modern problem," Niall told Sam as they walked down the steps. "Horses are still the fastest and easiest way of maneuvering through the woods."

"Duncan should be airborne shortly," Nicholas said, stopping his horse in front of them. He glanced around then bent over to hand Sam his cell phone. "He said he'd make it appear as though the helicopter is doing some work at Inglenook. But he's afraid spotting a silver SUV in all the vehicles coming and going might be —"

"Hey, Mister Trail Boss," Rowan suddenly drawled loudly, causing Nicholas to turn in his saddle and for Niall to look around. "We're paying to *ride,* not sit here on lazy old nags while you swap recipes with the local lawman," Nicholas's second-in-command continued, just as Niall spotted a man and woman strolling hand-in-hand up the boardwalk that ran along the shoreline behind the stores. The couple stopped and sat on a bench in front of the docks not fifty feet from them.

"I'm sorry, Mr. Spade," Nicholas drawled back. "I was just making sure Chief Mac-Keage doesn't have a problem with us taking the horses on the park trails."

"Not as long as ye clean up after them," Niall said, glancing over to see how Sam was coming along programming the tracking app into Nicholas's phone.

"Just don't think any of us are cleaning up horse shit," Micah interjected. "At the price we're paying, you can hire someone to follow us around with a broom and shovel."

"You're all set," Sam said softly, moving so the horse blocked his line of sight to the couple and handing Nicholas his phone.

"The trail's that way, gentlemen," Nicholas said to his men, nodding toward the lane behind them.

"Birch found the discs and is calling Leopold in twenty minutes," Niall told him as Nicholas slowly turned his horse away. "Since he'll want privacy, my guess is the exchange will take place somewhere north of the Nova Mare entrance. If that's the case, the old railroad bed will give you a straight run up as far as the abandoned sawmill."

Nicholas turned in his saddle. "Is there a chance he'll simply go to the shelter to get them?"

"Alec is fishing out front and Cole is in the woods across the road just in case," Niall said. "But I doubt Leopold will risk coming that close to town again."

Nicholas gave a nod, then urged his horse into a trot to catch up with his men.

"Well, I guess it's time I wander over to the Bottoms Up for a beer and introduce myself to Mr. St. Germaine," Sam said. "A description of the man would help."

Niall walked up the steps just as he heard the deep, rhythmic thump of a helicopter in the distance. "He's a taller, older, male version of Birch."

Aye, he hadn't been boasting when he'd told Birch a small army of capable men were backing her up; every one of them mere mortals — with the possible exception of Nicholas — exercising their *free will* to get personally involved.

CHAPTER TWENTY-FOUR

Birch slowed almost to a crawl as she approached the spot where they'd been ambushed, and checked her rearview mirror to see Shep standing in the road at the end of the driveway, staring after her. The poor dog wasn't happy at being left behind, and had even growled and blocked the door when she'd tried to leave the house. So she'd had to hold the phone up to his ear and have *Niall* tell him in Gaelic he couldn't go.

Not that she expected Shep to listen to either one of them.

Birch flinched when the rear hatch opened, but quickly composed herself when the SUV rocked slightly as Niall slipped into the cargo area, her sigh of relief lost in the sound of the hatch mechanically closing.

"Hello, sweetheart," he said thickly. "I've been thinking," he went on before she could respond, "how I wouldn't mind ye wearing that tracking device permanently."

Her second sigh at hearing his wonderful, *in-person* voice came out as a snort. "Do you think Mom's at the abandoned saw-mill?" Birch asked as she resumed a respectable speed for the camp road. "Or that they're keeping her someplace else?"

"It makes sense she's at the mill," that steady voice replied. "Ye better not talk once we reach town, since there's no one in the truck for you to be talking to. But if ye do need to say something, hold a hand up near your mouth."

"Shep's not going to stay," she said, since she wasn't at the main road yet, although she did rub her nose to cover her mouth.

"Aye," Niall replied on a sigh. But then she heard a soft chuckle. "I sometimes wonder if the sneaky bugger hasn't planted a tracking device on *me*."

"Where did you get this one?"

"From a friend who likes playing with electronics. I don't suppose ye happened to see your eagle buddy hanging around the yard when you came out to the truck?"

If Niall's intention was to keep her calm with small talk, he was succeeding, and Birch relaxed her death grip on the steering wheel. "Nope, no eagle. And none of the trees in the yard talked to me, either. Okay, I'm just reaching the main road, so I'll shut up. But . . . but you can keep talking."

"I was thinking," Niall said as she halted at the stop sign and tried not to look suspicious as she eyed the two men crossing in front of her, "that maybe you and I and Hazel and Claude could have dinner at Aeolus's Whisper tomorrow evening. We could let your father pick up the check," he added dryly.

"Mmmm," she hummed, turning right onto the main road.

"Drive faster than the speed limit as soon as ye get out of the town proper," he instructed, his voice serious again. "So you'll appear frantic."

She *was* frantic. And scared. And angry at The Bastard for stealing her mom, at Francine for stealing Mimi, and at that stupid idiot Rabideu for causing this whole mess.

"Keep an eye on your mirror and tell me if any vehicles are following."

Birch checked the mirror, then pressed down on the accelerator to bring the truck up to a frantic speed. "Nothing," she answered after the car coming toward her had passed by.

"You're doing fine, lass. Ye slid a bullet into the chamber of the gun?"

"Yup," she said calmly instead of pointing out he'd asked her that *twice* over the phone before she'd left the house.

"And ye memorized how to click off the safety without having to look?"

"Umm-hmm," she hummed on a positive note when she met a Nova Mare limo. But then she silently scolded herself, realizing it must be killing Niall to see her involved in this stupid mess, what with his being a protective Scots and everything. *Dieu,* it was killing *her* to have *him* involved, knowing he'd be the main target if bullets started flying.

"We just passed the turnoff to Inglenook," he said, apparently able to see the sign from the floor of the cargo area. "The marina's another three miles, the entrance to Nova Mare a bit farther, and the mill about four miles after that," he explained — again for the third time, obviously worried she was unfamiliar with the area north of town. "Is there anyone behind us?"

Birch rubbed her nose as if it were itchy again, even though there was nothing but freaking trees to see her talking. "One vehicle," she said through her hand. "But it's too far back to tell if it's a car or truck or even what color."

"Go ahead and speed up even more. If it doesn't turn off at the marina or Nova Mare, let me know. When we get to the sawmill road, there's a sharp curve about a quarter mile in, and I want ye to slow down and get close to the trees so I can slide out."

"Mmm-hmm."

"If your gut tells ye something's not right when you meet Leopold, try to buy us time by distracting him with the ring. Your father and Sam headed out as soon as Leopold told ye to meet him at the old abandoned sawmill, and they're posing as two beer-drinking buddies out fishing the stream just north of the mill."

Birch didn't like that her father was involved in this mess, either, feeling strongly that his having been shot once was already one time too many. She scratched her nose again. "We just passed the Nova Mare entrance and the vehicle didn't turn in. It's close enough now that I can see it's a black pickup with at least two men inside. What about your officers; are they following us at a distance?" she asked, realizing Niall had been so busy telling her what to do before she'd left the house that he hadn't told her any of *his* plan.

"We'll have to come up with another way for me to get out if the pickup turns down the mill road behind us. Jake and Cole are hanging back in town," he continued, "watching if any *tourists* suddenly head north. Duncan's in the resort helicopter pretending to be working at Inglenook, and Nicholas and three of his security guards are racing up the old railroad bed to the mill on horseback."

Birch stopped in mid-scratch. Some of the men were *galloping* to the rescue? "But Nicholas isn't a Scots," she blurted without thinking.

There was a moment of silence. "No, he's not. But he somehow manages to stay in the saddle despite the shortcoming."

Birch decided to get back to *her* plan. "What am I supposed to do if they search me and find the gun?"

There was an even longer hesitation. "Ye give it up without a fight. That could also be a good time to distract Leopold by showing him the ring. Ye can explain away the gun as something you had in the house, but the game's up if they catch you wearing a tracking device. Where did ye hide the transmit—"

"Shit!" Birch cried, slamming on the brakes when a four-door pickup shot out of a dirt road on her left and stopped in the main road right in front of her. "They —"

"Don't talk," Niall snapped at the same time the phone Leopold had given her started ringing.

She snatched it off the console. "You idiot," she said *before* hitting the answer button as she glared at the ugly grinning bastard holding his phone in front of his mouth instead of up to his ear.

"Put your phone on speaker," he said calmly, "then pull down the tote road on your right and keep driving until I tell you to stop."

"Just as soon as you prove my mother's okay," Birch shot back — ignoring the soft growl coming from the cargo area.

"Every time you speak without being asked a direct question, Miss Callahan, *Hazel* will be the one getting slapped. Understand?"

Birch held up her phone for him to see and hit the speaker button, set it on the console, then nodded at him through the windshield.

He gestured toward the tote road. "Drive."

Birch briefly glanced in her rearview mirror to see the pickup that had been following her was stopped several yards back, and she took her foot off the brake and turned onto the overgrown tote road. Dammit, Niall wasn't supposed to still be in the truck when she met The Bastard. If they checked her SUV, he'd be a sitting duck!

"Keep going," Leopold said when she

tapped her brake because the road was narrowing. She looked in her side mirror to see the pickup he was a passenger in right on her bumper, and caught a glimpse of the second pickup turning in behind them. But instead of following, the second truck stopped at the beginning of the tote road, the daytime running lights went off, and two men got out wearing fishing vests and holding rod cases. Lookouts, she decided, so their little meeting wouldn't be disturbed by real fishermen. She drove for what seemed like a mile on the overgrown tote road, which rose and fell with the terrain as it skirted a steep ridge to her left.

"Did you say something?" The Bastard asked.

Merde, had she? Was she supposed to answer him? "I . . . um, I might have mumbled a curse."

He chuckled. "That does seem to be a habit of yours."

Francine *had* put listening devices in the house!

"Stop in the center of the clearing," he instructed when the road suddenly opened into what appeared to be an old logging yard.

Birch heard another man's voice in the background, only he spoke too low for her to make out what he was saying except for maybe the word *helicopter.* "I've changed my mind," The Bastard said. "Drive to the stand of tall pines on your right at the edge of the clearing and stop under the branches."

Birch shouted a litany of thankful *ohmigods* in her head. Being close to the trees, she could create some sort of distraction if they started to check the interior of her truck, and Niall could slip out of the back and into the woods.

"Shut off the engine and open your door," The Bastard said as the pickup he was in made a wide circle and stopped several yards away, facing her. "Then get out while holding up your hands. And please make sure, Miss Callahan, that one of those hands is holding my DVDs. Excuse me, did you say something?"

"I . . . I might have wondered out loud if you watch a lot of cop shows," she said, figuring she better say something. She shut off the engine, grabbed the DVDs — which she'd put in a *Harry Potter* movie case — off the passenger seat, and opened her door. She stuck her hand holding the case out of the truck, unfastened her seat belt, then stuck out her other hand and slid her feet to the ground.

All four doors on the pickup opened and four men got out, the driver and two rear passengers carrying pistols under the jackets they were wearing on a freaking eighty-degree day, with The Bastard wearing a short-sleeved polo shirt and his signature ugly grin. Wanting to get away from the SUV and Niall, Birch walked toward them, even as she semi-hysterically wanted to ask how they'd gotten those guns across the border so she could tell her dad how he could sneak his over.

"I neglected to ask when we spoke earlier. The DVDs are yellow and blue, no?"

"No, they're both red."

Birch saw his even uglier beady eyes flair with triumph. "Jean, get the DVDs. Trevor, search her."

Two men walked up to her; one snatching the case out of her raised hand and taking it back to The Bastard like a well-trained puppy as the other man, giving her a puke-inducing grin, began *rubbing* instead of patting her down. Birch endured the slow groping by watching Leopold open the case to make sure she hadn't been lying.

Birch snapped her attention back to The Lecher when his hands stilled on her waist and his grin disappeared.

He lifted her shirt, pulled on the waistband of her linen pants, then pushed his hand inside all *three* pairs of panties she'd put on to stop the gun from falling down her leg. His hand reemerged holding the pistol, and Birch saw his jaw drop as he held it up for The Bastard to see. "There's no clip," he said in French. He pulled back the slide and a bullet flew into the air, pinged off the hood of her SUV, and fell to the ground, making the guy's jaw snap taut as he looked at her. "Where's the clip?" he growled.

"Clip?" she repeated in English, frowning at the gun. Still holding her hands in the air, she pointed down with several waggling fingers as she jutted out her left hip. "Is that what you call the thing full of bullets?"

He reached in her pants pocket without even copping a feel and pulled out the pistol's magazine, his jaw going slack again as he held both items up to show The Bastard — who Birch noticed also looked confounded.

Oh yeah, she'd done more than just work on a story about the ring hoping to buy time, having remembered that *easily confounded* was on both her lists of men's traits.

Birch sighed heavily — partly for effect and partly because she was pretty sure Niall would like to be wringing her neck right about now. "Okay, look; apparently someone thought the women's shelter needed a gun for protection in case an irate husband came looking for his wife, and I didn't have the heart to tell the committee women that being a city girl, I don't know anything about them except which end the bullet comes out. And even though the clip thingy kept falling out every time I shoved it in the damn handle, I decided to bring the gun anyway, in case you . . ." She gave The Bastard an apologetic smile. "Well, I thought I could use it to scare you into letting my mother go if you tried to renege on our deal."

The problem with confounding men she didn't know very well, Birch suddenly realized, was that she couldn't guess how they'd react once they started thinking again. But she'd been expecting a thorough and even crude pat-down, which is why she hadn't tried too hard to hide the gun.

Birch steeled herself for the coming slap when she saw The Bastard's beady eyes harden again, but wasn't at all prepared for what came out of his ugly mouth instead. "You have two choices, Miss Callahan. You can undress yourself, or I will give the honor to Trevor."

■ ■ ■ ■

Niall stopped in the middle of his text to Duncan when Leopold's words — coming in the door Birch had left open — caught his attention. And figuring no one sure as hell was looking at the truck right now, he slowly peeked over the rear seat to see Birch standing as still as a statue several yards away, her hands in the air.

Dammit to hell. Knowing she wasn't exactly a shrinking violet, he imagined the lass was more worried about the transmitter being discovered than she was about four lowlifes seeing her naked. And even though it burned to the very core of his being to do nothing, he had to concede that no one had ever died of humiliation, whereas being caught in the middle of a gun battle was almost always lethal.

Niall saw Birch lower her hands to the front of her blouse, and he rolled to his side and finished his text to Duncan — capitalizing the word Now — only to grit his teeth to keep from roaring when Duncan immediately replied: ETA six minutes

Christ, in six minutes Birch could be running through the woods *naked.*

Ten mins me an Ro, Nicholas texted. Dan

517

Realizing it was hard to text from the saddle of a flat-out galloping horse, Niall concluded Nicholas had read the group message he'd sent out when Birch had been forced to turn off the main road, and that Dante and Micah were continuing on to the sawmill in hopes of finding Hazel. Nicholas and Rowan had obviously left the railroad bed and cut through the woods to the main road, taken care of the lookouts posted at the beginning of the tote road that Niall had warned them about, and were now riding hell-bent for leather toward him. Niall glanced out the windshield again in time to see Birch's blouse slide down her back to the ground, her hands stilling on the way to the waist of her pants when Leopold said, "The bra, too, Miss Callahan."

Niall slowly rolled to his knees and pulled his gun out of his holster, gritting his teeth at the sight of Birch staring straight ahead as she reached back and undid the clasp, shrugged the straps off her shoulders, then threw the bra toward Leopold just as Niall aimed at the bastard's forehead.

"See anything interesting?" she growled.

"Now the slacks."

Niall moved his finger away from the trigger at the realization Birch hadn't taped the

518

transmitter under her bra. Okay then, it was in her pants. *Show him the goddamned ring.* Hell, she should have used it *before* taking off the blouse.

Niall saw her pants slide down her legs and pool at her feet.

"The panties, too."

He watched Birch hook the waistband of her purple bloomers and push them down — exposing a red pair underneath them. She then slid the red pair down to expose *another*, bright pink, pair under them, but hesitated with her thumbs in the waistband.

Not really sure why she was wearing multiple bloomers, Niall ducked to aim at Leopold's forehead again, but changed his mind and trained the front sight on the head of the man beside Birch staring slack-jawed at her, and could only hope the windshield wouldn't deflect his bullet.

"Have you twelve-year-olds seen enough to realize," she said, pushing the pink — and last pair — of panties down to her knees and then straightening, "that I don't have any knives or hand grenades or ballistic missiles on me?"

Christ, the woman was ballsy.

Wait; where in hell was the transmitter? He'd told her to wear it, not just bring it in the truck. And she was naked but for her . . .

well, her shoes. She must have hidden it into the sole of her sneakers. Or maybe she'd sewn it into the hem of her pants.

Aye, his spitfire was as smart as she was ballsy.

Niall lowered the barrel of his pistol but held it resting on the back of the seat as he wiped the sweat off his forehead before it reached his eyes, and watched Birch bend down and grab her blouse. She slipped it on without bothering with her bra or buttoning it, then began pulling up her bloomers one by one.

"Why are you wearing three underpants?" Leopold apparently couldn't help but ask as he watched her get dressed.

Birch finally pulled up her slacks, then started buttoning her blouse. "Because the gun was heavy, and I was afraid it would fall down my pant leg."

Leopold stared at Birch as if he couldn't quite decide what to make of her, and Niall stiffened when he saw the bastard's expression turn almost sad. "Well, Miss Callahan," he said, lifting the case holding the DVDs, "it was nice doing business with you. Give my regards to your mother when you see her," he added as he turned and headed to the passenger side of the pickup.

"Wait," Birch called after him. "Where *is* she?"

He stopped at the open passenger door. "I've given Trevor the honor of taking you to her," he said, sliding his gaze to the man beside Birch and nodding — making Niall look down the barrel of his pistol and set the sight on Trevor's head again.

Where in hell was Duncan?

Again proving she wasn't just a pretty face in a pintsized body, Niall saw the moment Birch realized what that *honor* was. "Wait!" she shouted, reaching into her pocket and *finally* pulling out the ring. "I found something else of Rabideu's I think you might want."

That got the bastard's attention, and he came back around the door. "What?"

Birch jerked her arm out of Trevor's grip and took several steps forward. "In the woods this morning you said Rabideu had come into possession of something of yours, only you didn't say how. But while I was searching for the DVDs, I found this," she said, holding up the ring. "And I remembered you were wearing a ring exactly like it," she added as Leopold closed the distance between them.

He took the ring from her and held it up, turning slightly to examine it in the sunlight, then looked at Birch. "Where did you get this?"

"It was in a small jewelry bag hidden in a secret compartment built into the headboard of my mother's bed."

Okay, then; apparently the lass preferred making up her own story rather than going with his. And why wasn't he surprised?

"It's a cleverly designed hiding spot, so don't be too mad at Yvonne/Francine for not finding it," Birch continued. "Speaking of which, my mother better be holding my dog when I see her. And they *both* better have all their fingers and toes or our deal's off."

Leopold looked momentarily startled. "What deal?"

"You listen, I'll talk," she snapped as she raised a hand to her cheek — which Niall only just noticed appeared slightly red, making him break into a sweat again when he saw Leopold's eyes narrow. "Before you cut out his heart," Birch went on, "did Jacques Rabideu tell you how he got your DVDs?"

"He somehow managed to get invited to a large party at my house."

Well now; it would appear the Leopold patriarch was *personally* retrieving his belongings, suddenly making Niall as curious as Sam as to what was on those discs.

"Then maybe the question you should have asked the idiot before you killed him," Birch drawled, "was how he knew the DVDs even existed."

Sweet Christ; she was scary. And just as soon as he got her alone, they were having a little heart-to-heart talk about her recklessness.

Birch gestured at the ring Leopold was still holding up between them. "There was also a photo in the bag; it looked like one of those pictures you get from a carnival photo booth. And in it, the man I knew as Leonard Struthers was kissing a woman I didn't recognize." She canted her head. "Two things immediately struck me: Leonard was wearing the wedding band my mother had given him, which meant he was cheating on her, and the woman with her tongue stuck down his throat was wearing that ring."

Leopold was back to looking startled.

"And I know enough about jewelry to recognize a family heirloom when I see it," Birch pressed on. "So while I kept searching for your DVDs, I kept thinking about how Rabideu had managed to steal them from you."

"Where's the picture?" Leopold asked.

"I destroyed it," Birch said far too smugly for Niall's peace of mind. "Because I don't trust you any farther than I can spit. So if you want to know who in your family is a traitor, you're going to let me drive out of here. I'll go sit in the town park, and after I see you drop off my mother *and* my dog in front of the Trading Post, you can come to the park and show me the pictures of your family I'm sure you keep on your phone, and I'll point out the woman." Niall saw Birch shrug. "Then you can take your army of tourists back to Canada, and I can forget you even exist."

Edward Leopold closed the ring in his fist and stared down at her for several seconds. "Why should I trust you to point out the correct woman?"

"Because I don't give a rat's ass," Birch snapped, "about you, your DVDs, or your freaking family. As far as I'm concerned, that woman is as much to blame for this whole mess as Rabideu, and she can go kiss him in hell for all I care."

Leopold fell silent again, and Niall could see the man definitely wanted his traitor identified. But then Niall stiffened when he also realized *why* the bastard was stalling. "Well, Miss Callahan, there may be a problem with my giving back your —"

Because he'd been listening for the rhythmic thump of rotors, Niall was five seconds ahead of everyone else to react when the huge crane helicopter suddenly shot up from behind the mountain ridge to the east. Taking advantage of the noise, he was out the back hatch with both guns drawn and crouching beside the front fender as the helicopter swooped toward the clearing like a hawk diving at prey.

Both Edward and Trevor lunged for Birch but came up empty-handed, as she was halfway to the woods before they'd even righted themselves from falling into one another. And because none of the men knew he was here, Niall moved back behind the rear bumper to keep it that way, certain they wouldn't shoot at Birch, since the identity of the traitor was running into the woods with her.

Aye, he could love a woman who was as quick in her thinking as she was fast on her feet. Niall backed toward the woods as the four men — three of whom had drawn their weapons — scrambled for cover behind several large pine trees, then holstered one of his guns and pulled out his cell phone. Hover clearng Birch me south in woods don't shoot us, he told Duncan, although he sent the text as a group message to bring everyone up to speed. Do u see Nich—

He stopped tapping letters when it came

to him that Edward Leopold had been one of the men holding a gun and Trevor *had not.* Niall hit the send button, then opened the tracking app as he moved deeper into the woods. Birch must have grabbed the pistol out of Trevor's holster as she'd pushed away from him, making Niall break into a cold sweat as he wondered if she knew different models had different safety mechanisms.

Best case — she shoots herself in the foot; worst case — she decides to circle back and shoot Leopold for killing her mother but the bastard shoots her first because she can't click off the safety. Niall zoomed in the satellite photo of the surrounding area and started running toward the pulsing blue dot moving away from the clearing — as relieved as he was surprised that Birch was doing exactly what he'd told her to do if things went to hell in a handbasket.

Except he noticed the dot was actually making a wide swing to the right, which would bring her out on the tote road just short of the clearing. He stopped when he saw the dot stop at the sudden burst of gunfire — aimed at a helicopter hovering an inch out of pistol range, Niall assumed — and it was all he could do not to roar when the blue dot started moving back *toward* the clearing.

Seeing his little heart-to-heart with Birch growing longer by the minute, Niall headed at an angle to intercept her. But he stopped again when the dot stopped again, this time at the sound of returning gunfire that was all but lost in the nearly deafening thump of the rotors. Could Birch tell the difference between handgun and rifle shots?

Estimating they were a good couple hundred yards apart, Niall saw the dot moving again, now in an easterly direction instead of south like he'd goddamned told her to, and wished he knew what she was thinking. He was fairly confident Birch wouldn't risk her life going after Leopold simply to avenge her mother's death, partly because despite having a temper she really wasn't a violent person, but mostly because she would realize he in turn would risk *his* life charging to her rescue.

How the hell much ammunition did the Leopolds have? Better yet, did they honestly think they could bring down a chopper with handguns?

The shooting finally lessened to intermittent salvos, though mostly rifle shots, which Niall assumed was Duncan keeping the men from reaching their truck. He looked down at the pulsing blue dot to see it had stopped again, even though he'd specifically told her to run as fast and as far as she could until she collapsed from sheer exhaustion.

Christ, maybe she *had* shot herself in the foot.

Hearing a twig snap to his left, Niall dropped the phone and drew his second gun as he crouched down, knowing it had to have been damn close for him to hear over the helicopter. But he holstered his gun when he caught sight of a dark gray horse moving through the trees at a brisk walk, picked up his phone and straightened, then let out a single sharp whistle.

He heard another whistle — he assumed from Nicholas to Rowan — then saw Nicholas veer toward him. Niall noticed both warhorse and warrior were soaked with sweat, and although Phantom was also sporting a fair amount of lather, the mythical beast appeared ready to flat-out gallop another ten miles.

Nicholas, however, just looked hot and bothered and royally pissed off.

"Those idiots out at the main road are damn lucky," he said as he dismounted, "that Rowan and I speak French, or they'd both be polluting the stream they were pretending to be fishing instead of becoming intimately acquainted with the trees they're tied to." He looked toward the clearing when another round of gunfire cracked over the thump of helicopter blades, then down at the phone in Niall's hand. "Is there a reason you're here and your woman's there?" he asked, tapping the pulsing dot on the screen that still hadn't moved.

"She stole one of the men's pistols just before she ran into the woods, and I'm concerned she might shoot first and *then* realize it's me."

"Take Rowan's mount," Nicholas said as Rowan wove through the trees toward them. "Unless the Leopolds had a horse in the back of their truck, she'll know it's you."

Niall shoved his other gun in its holster, took the reins from Rowan when the man dismounted, and vaulted into the saddle.

"And Niall," Nicholas said when he started to turn the horse away. "Once you get her, keep riding. We'll clean up what's left of this mess."

Niall dropped his head on a heavy breath. "I'm fairly certain Hazel's —"

"Alive and well and crowing like a proud hen," Nicholas said.

Niall snapped his head up in surprise.

"According to Micah, she has a few dislocated knuckles and he believes one of her toes is broken," the warrior drawled, "from punching and kicking her guard when Waters and St. Germaine burst into a room at the sawmill from opposite directions, apparently both so determined to be the hero that Hazel ended up rescuing herself."

Even though he wanted to crow like a *rooster,* Niall simply gave a nod, looked down at his cell phone, and turned the horse toward where the pulsing dot said Birch was. He waited until he was out of sight before running a hand over his sweating face, then finally let go a long, deep, shuddering sigh.

But his relief was short-lived when a few minutes later he caught movement out of the corner of his left eye and immediately reined to a stop. He slowly drew his gun, at the same time turning the equally alert warhorse to conceal their profile behind a large tree, then stole a quick glance at his phone.

Seeing Birch was now only about a hundred yards away and still hadn't moved, Niall turned his attention back to the woods; his patience rewarded not two minutes later when Edward Leopold emerged from behind a dense growth of bushes, *his* attention focused on the ground as he slowly followed Birch's foot tracks.

Niall figured he had two choices; he could end this here and now by shooting the bastard — which from an ancient perspective was the smart thing to do — or he could be a twenty-first-century lawman and *arrest* the bastard.

With more regret than he cared to admit, Niall started to dismount, only to freeze when he glanced down at his phone and saw that not only had the blue dot moved — it was racing straight toward them.

CHAPTER TWENTY-FIVE

Birch didn't know which emotion was in charge of her right now — heart-numbing sorrow or mind-numbing dread — only that she needed arms of amazing muscle holding her so she could finally have a good cry. And she was done listening to stupid trees that kept telling her what to do, because if she'd stayed curled up in a ball of sweat in those boulders any longer, she would have gone insane from not freaking *knowing*.

The shooting had stopped two full minutes ago and she'd heard the helicopter land in the clearing and its engine shut off, and she really, really needed to know that none of those hundred flying bullets had hit Niall.

If things go to hell in a handbasket, promise me you'll run as fast and as far as ye can until ye collapse, and I'll come find you when it's over, Niall had told her three times before she'd left the house. Yeah, well, he couldn't come find her if he was dead, now could he?

Dead just like her mom was. Maybe. Probably.

No, she was going with *maybe,* because maybe those four men galloping up the railroad bed had reached the sawmill in time to save her. Or her dad and Sam had rescued her. Or maybe Hazel had escaped all on her own, since she'd been getting really good at being really sneaky.

Birch stumbled to a halt when a giant galloping horse suddenly crested a knoll on the small tote road she was crossing, and felt her jaw drop when she realized it was carrying Niall, then tried to scramble out of the way when she also realized he wasn't slowing down. She didn't even have time to scream before she was swept off her feet, plopped sideways across his lap and plastered up against the *two* holsters strapped to his chest, and squeezed so tight she could barely breathe.

Birch wrapped her arms around him and squeezed back, so freaking glad none of the bullets had hit him that she was in danger of bursting into tears. In fact, a tiny sob did escape but turned into a scream when five sharp gunshots suddenly split the air in rapid succession. She screamed again when

Niall jerked — twice! — and the full weight of his body fell against her, his groan coming out in a whoosh as they slowly slid off the galloping horse.

There was a bit of a wrestling match on the way down, but neither of them managed to break the other's fall and they hit the ground together — making the air whoosh out of Birch as well. Niall immediately started trying to push her to her feet while rasping at her to run, but when she realized he couldn't follow because he couldn't breathe, she slapped his hands away and hauled one of his pistols out of its holster. She checked to make sure the safety was on and set the gun pointed up the road on his stomach, then gave him a quick inspection.

"Oh, thank God you're wearing a bulletproof vest," she softly cried when she popped a button on his shirt and saw Kevlar. "You're not dying, Niall," she went on as she looked for the source of the blood soaking his entire right shirtsleeve. "It only feels that way because the force of the bullet knocked the wind out of you. You'll be able to breathe enough to move in a few minutes, but you're going to have one hell of a bruise for the next week."

"Put . . . gun . . . my . . . left hand," he

choked out as his chest rose and fell and twitched with each obviously painful word.

Birch pulled the gun out of the second holster and placed it in his left hand while continuing to keep an eye on the road. "Is it The Bastard or Trevor or both?" she asked as she quickly glanced around taking stock of their situation. "How many?"

"Jus . . . bas . . . tard."

"I need to get you farther off the road."

"Run," he groaned more than growled.

"Not going to happen, big man," she muttered, walking sideways on her knees to get a better look at his arm. But she couldn't see anything for the blood and tried but couldn't rip the material.

"Knife . . . belt."

Birch looked down to see a multi-tool on his belt, opened the pouch and took it out by feel as she watched up the road again, then stilled to listen. Niall realized what she was doing and stopped fighting for the breath he desperately needed, and Birch slowly picked up the gun off his stomach, only to have the hand on his wounded right arm grab hers.

"Could . . . be . . . Nicholas," he mouthed more than whispered. "Heard . . . shots."

"I won't shoot him," she whispered back just before pulling away. She rose into a half-kneeling position and aimed the gun at the edge of the road halfway up the knoll.

"Get in . . . woods."

"You roll toward them and I'll cover you," she said, sliding off the safety with her thumb and firing five shots in two-second intervals, each one hitting a large pine at head-height and sending chunks of bark and wood in all directions.

It took two shots for Niall to realize she was serious, and all of the last three to make it as far as the shallow ditch. She knee-walked over to him. "Maybe now that he thinks you're still alive and kicking he'll just give up and go."

"G-go where?" Niall rasped. "No . . . truck."

Birch snorted, keeping her eyes trained up the road. "If I found myself all alone having to face down the men in Spellbound Falls, I'd freaking *walk* to Canada."

"Or you could ride there holding a gun to a hostage's head," a familiar, ugly voice said, making Birch look up to see The Bastard standing next to a tree fifty feet away with his gun pointed at Niall's head. "Toss the gun into the trees across the road, Miss Callahan. And now his," he added the moment she threw hers across the road.

She leaned over Niall, but just as she was

reaching for the gun she glanced up toward the knoll behind Leopold and widened her eyes in surprise before quickly looking away, which made the idiot immediately jerk around in a crouch to see what she'd spotted. But before Birch could snatch the gun out of Niall's hand, he sat up and shoved her behind him in a single lightning-fast motion, and lifted his arm. Leopold was just spinning back around to them when a tiny hole suddenly appeared on his forehead half a second before the crack of a high-powered rifle shattered the air.

He stood motionless, his beady dark eyes wide open and his expression blank, but instead of crumbling to the ground, The Bastard slowly tipped forward like a tree uprooted by a strong wind.

Niall twisted to look past Birch as she also twisted to look behind them to see a man standing in the middle of the road on the crest of a hill at least a quarter mile away — too far to make out his features. All Birch could see was that his feet were planted in a wide stance and the rifle he was holding at his side had an oversized scope. He appeared to nod — she was pretty sure at Niall — then turned and simply walked away.

"Um . . . he's not one of your guys, is he?" Birch whispered as the man's easy, languid gait made him slowly disappear down the other side of the hill.

"Nay."

"Wh-who do you think he is?"

"I have no idea."

She looked at Niall. "If I tell you a secret, will you promise not to tell anyone?"

"Aye," he said with a slight nod, sliding his eyes from the hill to her.

"A . . . another tree talked to me today. When I stopped running away and started running back to the clearing, I tripped and fell," she softly rushed on. "But before I could get up, a male voice that seemed to come out of nowhere told me I was going the wrong way. And then it said to follow a . . ." She dropped her gaze to one of the holsters on Niall's chest. "A bird," she whispered. She looked up. "A Canada jay. The voice said it would lead me to a good hiding place."

"And did ye follow the jay?" he quietly asked.

She nodded. "It led me to the bottom of a short cliff not too far away, where huge boulders had created bunches of caves and crannies. The bird landed on a . . . an oak tree branch hanging out over one of the crannies that looked just large enough for me to hide in."

She briefly glanced toward Leopold's lifeless body, then looked at Niall's chest again and took a deep breath. "I crawled inside and stayed scrunched up in a ball listening to the helicopter and gunfire, but when I started to crawl out after the shooting stopped and the helicopter landed, the same voice — it was coming from the tree this time — told me to stay put, and that you would be able to find me by the transmitter."

"Okay, then," Niall said softly. "If ye took a tree's advice to stay in your car that day at the river, can I ask why you didn't take *this* tree's advice to stay put today?"

"Because trees don't talk," she growled, scrambling to her knees to look him level in the eyes. "And even if they could, what makes them think they know what's best for a person more than the person does? I wasn't going to *stay put* because some stupid tree told me to when there was a chance my mother was still alive and we could reach her in time. And I sure as heck wasn't going to sit there thinking you could have been hit by any one of a hundred flying bullets and were bleeding to death."

"Ye mean like I am now?"

"Oh. Oh, *merde*!"

Niall captured her hand reaching for his

bloody arm and held it against the side of his face. "Your mom's fine, Birch." He grinned. "Or as Micah told Nicholas, 'She was alive and well and crowing like a proud hen for saving herself.' " His grin lessened but didn't go completely away. "She's got a couple of dislocated knuckles and a broken toe, apparently from punching and kicking the man guarding her up at the abandoned sawmill." He sobered, slid her hand to his lips, and kissed her palm. "I'm sorry, sweetheart; there was no sign of Mimi. But we're intending to round up as many Leopolds as we can before they leave town, and we'll send word to Border Patrol to watch for a woman crossing with a small white poodle. We'll find your pet."

"Oh, Niall," she said on a stifled sob as she leaned over and picked up the multitool, then reached up to his bloody sleeve, "I'm so sorry for putting everyone through all this and getting you shot. I was so sure moving to the middle of nowhere would stop the craziness and instead we brought it with us."

"I prefer to see it as the craziness brought *you* to *me,*" he said gruffly as she cut away his sleeve, "because I'd resigned myself years ago to the fact I'd never know what being in love felt like."

Birch stilled with the knife halfway down the sleeve, and looked over to see him grinning at her. *Merde,* how much blood had he lost? "I . . . ah . . . I . . ."

He touched a finger to her lips. "I'll settle for ye admitting I'm your boyfriend," he whispered, only to wink as he added, "for now."

He had to be light-headed or drunk or something from blood loss, because he really couldn't have just said he loved her . . . could he?

His grin broadened. "See, we're already rubbing off on each other like an old married couple."

"H-how?"

"You've started going all slow and quiet just like I do when ye feel something important is happening."

"You said it was when something was *urgent.*"

"And I've been finding myself cursing in French as much as in Gaelic now."

Birch went back to cutting his sleeve, but stopped again when Niall suddenly perked up, and she also looked up the tote road in the direction the mystery man had been standing to see four men on horses cresting the hill at a lope, followed by her beautiful bright red SUV, followed by the Leopold's four-door pickup.

Within ten minutes of taking charge, Nicholas had some man named Rowan bandaging Niall's arm, Duncan collecting guns, Dante and a man named Micah covering The Bastard's body with fir boughs to keep away the varmints and vultures until the state police arrived, and Sam keeping an eye on the horses — one of them being the horse she and Niall had fallen off of, which Niall's men must have found wandering the road.

And while Sam loosened the horses' belts or whatever they were called, he gave Birch a blow-by-blow account of *his* version of what had happened at the sawmill. She'd have to wait to hear her dad's version, though, because Claude had won the coin toss and was driving Hazel to see Dr. Bentley about her swollen knuckles and toe. His harrowing tale told, Sam then asked for his transmitter back.

"I'll bring it to the Trading Post tomorrow, okay?" Birch said, giving herself the job of carefully folding Niall's two shoulder holsters inside his Kevlar vest.

"Why can't you just give it to me now?" Sam asked, which for some reason made all the men stop doing their jobs and look at her.

Merde, what was she supposed to tell them?

"That's right," Niall piped up, saving her from having to answer, only to dig her embarrassing hole deeper. "I meant to ask where ye hid it."

"Has anyone seen Shep?" she asked, glancing around at all the still-staring men. "How long would it take a dog to run . . . what, maybe nine or ten miles?"

Niall reached out and caught her hand picking at the thread on his Kevlar vest, then slowly pulled Birch toward him and tucked her under his good arm so she was leaning against the tree with him. He then moved his gaze — a glaring gaze, actually — to all the men, and they all suddenly went back to work.

"Tell me where it is, lass," he said softly, his face only inches from hers.

Birch began picking at a loose button on his shirt. "You said to make sure I hid it where no one could see it," she whispered, "and . . . and so I . . ."

He sighed hard enough to move her hair. "And so ye what?"

She wiggled free to kneel beside him, clasped his head, and leaned in to press her mouth up to his ear. "Let's just go with my realizing the transmitter was the size of . . . of a tampon, okay? And since it was your repeated warnings to hide it someplace secure that made me get creative, let's have *you* tell Sam he'll get it back *tomorrow.*"

But hey, at least she'd wrapped it in plastic wrap first.

Niall looked up at Sam. "The tape came loose because she was sweating, and she thinks it fell in a brook she was crossing. Check and see if they haven't come out with an improved model, and I'll replace your old one."

"But it's still pinging," Sam said, holding up his cell phone for Niall to see. "And it says it's right here," he added, gesturing at the group of them.

Niall shot him a tight grin. "Then I guess it is waterproof. Didn't ye tell me that its error of accuracy could be off several yards in any direction, and that sometimes mountains," he added, waving to the one behind Sam, "can throw it off even more?"

"But that transmitter used WAAS technology, which is the newest and best."

Birch saw Niall drop his head on a sigh for several seconds, then finally look over at her. "You said ye needed to . . . use Mother Nature's powder room, so now would be the time, lass, before we leave." He pulled her close and kissed her cheek. "Take it out and turn it off and bury it," he whispered in her ear, continuing to hold her when she tried to nod and pull away. "And if ye can't find an off switch, smash the damn thing on a rock. Just make it stop transmitting," he added, his whisper somewhat strangled as though he was holding in a laugh as he kissed her cheek again and released her.

Birch jumped to her feet and ran past the vehicles, only to skid to a stop beside the black pickup when she spotted the three men tied up and gagged in the cargo bed — two of whom appeared to be napping and the third glaring out of his one unswollen eye at her. "Bet you wish you'd signed up to go whale watching today instead, don't you?" she told him in French, just before bolting up the road again. Birch made it halfway up the hill before she turned into the woods, dropped to her knees while hugging her belly, and burst into simultaneous sobs and laughter.

EPILOGUE

Niall sat at his desk trying to ignore the pinching and burning stitches in his shoulder muscle as he filled out yet another form documenting the events leading up to yesterday's . . . event. But it wasn't until he noticed the sun had set that he realized why he was having a hard time seeing what he was writing. He leaned back in his chair and started to stretch his arms over his head, only to remember too late he couldn't even lift his right hand high enough to scratch his nose.

But discovering nothing protested when he folded his arms over his chest, he did just that and rocked back in his chair, grinning at the memory of seeing a little white ball of fluff trotting up the road beside Shep yesterday, when he and Birch had been on their way home. Niall had been driving — the bullet had barely scratched his shoulder — and Birch had started bouncing in her seat and shouting *ohmigods* at the sight of her precious pet.

The dogs had made it all the way past the entrance to Nova Mare, and Niall doubted they'd ever know how Shep had rescued Mimi from the clutches of yet another nefarious Leopold. All he had to go on was Jake's report of seeing Shep, looking like a K-9 officer on a mission, racing south down the main road through town not five minutes after Birch had turned north on her mission to save her mother.

Niall knew dogs could be trained to follow a scent even if that scent was traveling in a vehicle and hours, if not days, old, but what really baffled him was Shep deciding to go after Mimi rather than follow Birch. Unless the scary-intuitive bugger really had bubbled up from a magical spring and somehow known Mimi was a loose end they couldn't deal with until Birch and Hazel were safe.

And speaking of magical things, Niall dropped down the front legs of his chair when the station door opened and Birch came strutting in wearing a daringly low-cut blouse and tight little skirt, her hair bobbing in loose curls and her eyes made up to look twice their size; all of which indicated she was a woman on a much more interesting mission this evening.

Well, except for the scowl on her face.

"They sold it. I *knew* some stupid tourist would buy that purse right out from under me. *Merde,* it's probably on a plane to freaking Germany right now." She stopped in front of his desk, also folded her arms over — well, under — her jacked-up breasts, and shot him a very unspitfire-like pout. "It was *the* perfect purse."

"When did ye decide it was perfect?"

Her scowl-turned-pout turned into a frown. "Sometime after the river swallowed my old perfect purse." She canted her head. "I can't remember . . . How many days ago was that?"

"By my calculation," Niall said as he stood up, "nine days and twenty years ago." He bent and grabbed the large paper bag he'd stashed under his desk this afternoon and plopped it down on *top* of the desk. "What did this perfect purse look like?" he asked, although he doubted she heard the question, what with her screaming and clapping her hands and jumping up and down the moment she spotted the artisan shop logo on the bag.

She snatched it off the desk, pulled out the purse and let the bag float to the floor, only to stop jumping and screaming, and lifted those oversized eyes to his and tried really hard to smile. "Th-thank you, Niall. It's beautiful. Yeah, it's a really beautiful purse."

"Aye, the *perfect* purse for Hazel, wouldn't ye say? She'll like it, too, won't she?"

Birch's cheeks turned three shades brighter than her lipstick. "She'll love it," she whispered, walking over and picking up the paper bag. She slipped the purse inside it and walked back, but stopped in the act of setting it down when she spotted a *second* large bag had magically appeared on the desk.

Niall waited one heartbeat . . . two . . . three . . .

And then she pounced — on the bag, not him — but waited until she pulled out *this* perfect purse before screaming and jumping up and down again, adding *ohmigods* as she held the purse against her jacked-up bosom as though it were a long-lost lover.

Okay then; score one for Hazel — which is why she was also getting a purse.

Because it was Hazel who had explained to Niall just this morning that for all of her take-charge, get-out-of-my-way, don't-be-so-annoying attitude, and despite her ability to break down, reassemble, and shoot any firearm ever made, Birch was a dedicated girly-girl at heart and would go bonkers (Hazel's term) over anything even remotely feminine that caught her eye.

And that particular combination is what had Niall going bonkers over Birch.

Hazel had also enlightened him on her daughter's love-hate relationship with guns, in that it seemed every weekend for the four years she'd lived with her father, then one weekend a month for the last twenty-one years, Claude had taken Birch to a firing range to shoot every make and model of gun he could get his hands on. Hazel had shrugged, saying she supposed a twenty-five-year-old military man hadn't known how else to bond with a precocious six-year-old. And then she'd added that on alternate visiting weekends, Birch had dragged her father to high-end estate auctions, resulting in Claude's little suburban home being decorated with some pretty pricey furnishings.

And then his astute secretary — who couldn't fill out police forms with two *re*located and bandaged knuckles — just happened to mention a particular purse sitting in a certain artisan shop that had caught her daughter's attention. The woman had neglected, however, to mention it cost over a week's chief of police salary — times *two,* because he couldn't very well buy Hazel a less expensive thank-you gift.

Niall was so busy patting himself on the back that he nearly missed the sudden silence, and was barely prepared when Birch pounced again — this time on *him*. Well, she hopped up on the desk — Lord, that skirt was short — and carefully threw her arms around his left shoulder and head, and kissed him like a woman on a *carnal* mission.

"How many bloomers are ye wearing under that skirt?" he asked when she let him come up for air, wanting to know how long it would take to get inside them.

"None," she whispered into his mouth just before she kissed him again.

Okay then; since he still had one working arm, Niall used it to scoop her off the desk and started toward the holding cell, only to turn and head for the door to lock it, only to stop when Birch pulled her tongue out of his mouth and said to stop.

"Not yet," she rasped. "Not . . . here." She wiggled to be put down, and the moment he reluctantly complied, she put her perfect purse back in its bag, grabbed Hazel's, and tucked them both back under his desk. "I'll come back and get it . . . later," she said, walking over to him — while running her sexy little tongue over her sexy wet lips, Niall couldn't help but notice — then slipping her hand in his and heading out the door. "It's a beautiful evening. Let's go for a walk."

Niall used his free hand to tug on a pant leg, sure as hell glad it was dark out.

"I thought Sam was going to start crying," Birch said as she led him up the lane, "when he discovered The Bastard had destroyed the DVDs."

"Aye. Aye," Niall repeated less thickly as he stopped dragging his feet to watch her cute little ass and moved up beside her. "Sam hoped they'd have information that could bring down the Leopold dynasty."

"Do you suppose giving him the copies I made would make up for losing his transmitter?"

Niall brought them to a stop and simply stared down at her, wondering if she hadn't bubbled up from a *witch's cauldron.* "Christ, you scare me," he muttered, starting them walking again.

"Hey, I was going to use them for leverage if the ring didn't work. No, this way," she said, pulling him toward the road when he'd started down the sidewalk. "Let's take a walk in the park," she added, her voice sounding a bit gruff to him. "Shep is teaching Mimi to swim," she rushed on as they crossed the road. She snorted. "Which only shows what crazy things a girl will do to impress a guy, because Mimi *hates* getting wet. Speaking of impressing," she continued as they started down the path leading into the park, "it looks like a florist shop exploded in our house. Dad and Sam each sent Mom huge floral arrangements, and they both showed up this evening to see how she was doing." Another snort. "Talk about awkward. Well, for Dad and Sam; Mom just kept hobbling into my bedroom while I was getting all doll— dressed, and rolling her eyes trying to pretend she wasn't flattered by all the attention."

She brought them to a halt at the bottom of the path and looked around at the few tourists also taking advantage of the beautiful evening to enjoy the park.

"There's a free bench over there," Niall said, pointing to the right. "It's far enough from the roar of the falls that we can talk."

She turned left onto the loop path. "I think there are a couple of benches near the base of the falls," she said, again sounding — nay, not gruff, exactly. More like preoccupied. Aye, she appeared a bit preoccupied about . . . something.

It must be something really troubling,

because she'd neglected to give him hell for trying to buy his way into her bloomers with a very expensive purse.

She suddenly veered off the path, the cool mist slowly enveloping them until it was so thick they lost nearly all the light from the park's streetlamps. "I thought there was a bench back here," she said, letting go of his hand. She hopped up to stand on the soaking wet bench, which put her eye-level with him — which made it easy to wrap her arms around his neck without putting any strain on his shoulder.

But instead of the kiss he was expecting when he pulled her into his arms, she leaned her forehead against his. "Do you remember yesterday when you said you thought you'd never know what being in love felt like?" she whispered just loud enough for him to hear over the sound of the falls.

"I remember."

"Was that . . . were you saying that now you know what it feels like because . . . you love me?"

"Aye," he said, sounding a bit gruff to himself.

"But why?" she half whispered, half cried. "I'm bossy and opinionated and get very annoyed when people don't agree with me. I always want things to happen my way, I have a temper and swear a lot, and . . . and . . . How can such an old-fashioned guy like you love someone like me?"

Niall threaded his fingers through her hair when she tried to drop her forehead to his again. "I may have noticed your gorgeous eyes and sexy little backside at first, but it's your confidence, your tenacity, your refusal to back down when ye know you're right that enchanted me. I like that ye never try to hide your feelings, so I always know exactly where I stand. I like your honesty and your loyalty — to your mom, to Claude, to your residents. To *me.* All with the added bonus of coming packaged in a beautiful body." He rested his forehead against hers with a sigh. "I fell in love with a spitfire."

Niall felt her take a deep breath a heartbeat before she lifted her head. "Well, Chief MacKeage," she said thickly, "I don't know if you've noticed, but we're two people who happen to be standing in the mist of Spellbound Falls."

"As a matter of fact, I did notice."

"And it's my understanding that if we were to kiss right now, we would *both* fall in love."

"Aye, that's what the legend claims. But," he added when she started to kiss him, "I'm fairly certain both people must believe in the magic for the legend to work. Do ye believe, lass, that there's a magic powerful enough to help two people destined to be together, no matter if they're separated by distance or even time itself, to find each other?"

"I didn't before I moved to a little town in the middle of nowhere and found myself living next door to this really amazing Scotsman. As a matter of fact, I'm going to kiss him right now, right here in the mist, and I guess we'll see just how powerful this magic is, won't we?"

And kiss him she did, and Niall would swear he heard the whisper of a chuckle in the roar of the falls — sounding suspiciously like an old magic-maker he knew — as the mist surrounding them sparkled with the light of a thousand fireflies.

But when he lowered a hand to pull Birch more intimately against him, the lass leaned back just enough to lock her eyes on his again, and Niall couldn't help but notice that hers were shining with mischief.

"You know," she said, quickly scanning the area around them before canting her head and flashing him a spitfire smile. "I wonder if there's a legend about what happens if two people *make love* in the mist of Spellbound Falls."

Niall also quickly looked around, then lifted Birch so she could wrap her legs around his waist, and walked deeper into the woods to find someplace less wet, not about to tell the lass that those really brave — or very foolish — couples likely found themselves changing diapers nine months later.

LETTER FROM LAKEWATCH

Dear Readers,

Every so often a character will quietly tiptoe into one of my stories and firmly establish himself (it's almost always a *him*) before I even realize he's there. Maximilian Oceanus did exactly that by sneaking into *Dragon Warrior* as a seemingly innocuous tiger; but it wasn't until he literally came storming back in *Mystical Warrior* that I realized the guy wasn't going to leave me alone until I gave him his own story.

I really hadn't intended to expand the magic beyond my Gaelic drùidhs, but here was this mysterious, larger-than-life . . . man messing with my highlanders and causing me many sleepless nights trying to figure out what, exactly, he wanted.

Because don't they always want something?

It's a bit embarrassing to admit that Mac

remains somewhat of a mystery to me even after eight books. And let's not forget his father, the great Titus Oceanus, who continues to surprise me seven books after first meeting him. As for Nicholas, from *The Heart of a Hero,* I honestly still don't know if the mythical warrior is an actual god or not.

Well, guess what? Another mysterious character — this one definitely a god — is right now slowly and methodically entrenching himself in Spellbound Falls. Heck, it's taken me two books just to learn his name is Telos — which, at this point, is about the only thing I know about him. So if you've just finished reading *The Highlander Next Door,* I imagine you have as many questions about him as I do.

Then again, maybe all you're asking is, who in their right mind creates a new god?

And I say, well, why not? How much fun could I have, I asked myself, if I created a new mythology to exemplify — and exaggerate — mankind's strengths and weaknesses? We've had fun with Mac and Titus, haven't we? But they're so ancient-minded. And that had me wondering what sort of excitement a *modern* god might bring to the series — especially if he didn't always see eye-to-eye with the mighty Oceanuses.

There's just one little problem; I don't exactly know a whole lot about Telos. He simply up and manifested in *For the Love of Magic* and has only given me glimpses of himself in *The Highlander Next Door.* And as I've admitted to you before, I write books pretty much the way you read them — which is to watch the story unfold one page at a time. I do have a sense of the overall theme before I begin, but I rarely know what's going to happen as near as the next scene.

For me, writing is an act of faith. If I sit down at my computer with nothing more than a general understanding of my two main characters — who they are, what it is they want, and how they're planning to get it — I start typing on the belief *they* will tell the story. And if a mysterious person happens to show up . . . well, I have to assume he's there for a reason.

So I guess reading is an act of faith for you, too, in that you believe I won't lead you down a dead-end path. Oh, that path might get rather crooked and sometimes even appear impassable, but I seem to recall Titus telling Niall that he "must embrace the entire journey to truly appreciate the destination."

So I give you my heartfelt thanks for joining me on this particular journey, and only ask that you share my hope the destination will be . . . magical.

Until later from LakeWatch, you keep reading and I'll keep writing.

Janet

The employees of Thorndike Press hope you have enjoyed this Large Print book. All our Thorndike, Wheeler, and Kennebec Large Print titles are designed for easy reading, and all our books are made to last. Other Thorndike Press Large Print books are available at your library, through selected bookstores, or directly from us.

For information about titles, please call:
  (800) 223-1244

or visit our Web site at:
  http://gale.cengage.com/thorndike

To share your comments, please write:
Publisher
Thorndike Press
10 Water St., Suite 310
Waterville, ME 04901